FRAMED

FRAMED

S.L. McINNIS

GRAND CENTRAL
PUBLISHING

NEW YORK   BOSTON

Copyright © 2020 by S. L. McInnis

Cover design by Brian Lemus. Cover illustration by David Wu. Cover copyright © 2020

Grand Central Publishing
Hachette Book Group
1290 Avenue of the Americas, New York, NY 10104
grandcentralpublishing.com
twitter.com/grandcentralpub

First Edition: February 2020

Grand Central Publishing is a division of Hachette Book Group, Inc. The Grand Central Publishing name and logo is a trademark of Hachette Book Group, Inc.

The publisher is not responsible for websites (or their content) that are not owned by the publisher.

The Hachette Speakers Bureau provides a wide range of authors for speaking events. To find out more, go to www.hachettespeakersbureau.com or call (866) 376-6591.

Library of Congress Cataloging-in-Publication Data

Names: McInnis, Sheri, author.
Title: Framed / S.L. McInnis.
Description: First edition. | New York : Grand Central Publishing, 2020. |
Identifiers: LCCN 2019036068 | ISBN 978-1-5387-3209-0 (hardcover) |
    ISBN 978-1-5387-5117-6 (ebook)
Subjects: GSAFD: Mystery fiction.
Classification: LCC PS3613.C536 F73 2020 | DDC 813/.6--dc23
LC record available at https://lccn.loc.gov/2019036068

ISBNs: 978-1-5387-3209-0 (Hardcover); 978-1-5387-5117-6 (ebook)

Printed in the United States of America

LSC-C

10 9 8 7 6 5 4 3 2 1

For Todd

"Each friend represents a world in us, a world possibly not born until they arrive, and it is only by this meeting that a new world is born."

—Anaïs Nin, *The Diary of Anaïs Nin*

"There is nothing like puking with somebody to make you into old friends."

—Sylvia Plath, *The Bell Jar*

1

BETH

Beth grips the steering wheel so tight, her knuckles push white through her skin. She has a Prokofiev symphony blasting on the stereo, trying to drown out her thoughts and forget the evening. She can still smell his cologne on her clothes. He wore so much of it, she almost couldn't breathe. Trying to impress Emily, of course. She grits her teeth, remembering the humiliation of watching her husband trip over himself to be sweet, to be funny, to be attentive to anyone but his own wife.

"*I can't believe it! You look amazing!*"

"*Are you kidding? I haven't been out of the house in months. I've been so busy with the baby, I had to cut off all my hair.*"

"*I love it! It suits you! You look great!*"

Beth wants to scream. Or cry. Maybe both.

She glances in the rearview mirror. Her eyes are swollen from pushing back tears, her frown lines caked with makeup. But did she look so horrible tonight? The black dress was a little plain, she admits that, especially next to Emily's tight red dress with her bust hanging out. Em was just oozing sexuality, like a fertility goddess. No wonder Jay couldn't take his eyes off her all night.

He picked up the tab again, too, even though Peter suggested they split it. He knows the trouble they're in. Does he want to lose the house? The cars? Jay never worries about things like that, of course. His parents always spoiled him, protected him from the realities of life. But it all added up.

1

Stop it!

She hates the sound of her own thoughts. The endless complaints are like music scales in her head, the same notes played over and over again, nothing ever changing. It's monotonous.

At a red light, she finds herself toying with her necklace, a double strand of Tiffany pearls; they're her prized possession; but they make her want to cry, too, because they're a reminder of everything in life she wishes she had but could never seem to get. She remembers hearing a story, a long time ago, about how pearls were made. They were mistakes of nature really. Accidents.

The light turns green and she hits the gas. Suddenly, the world is a clash of sirens and flashing lights, a cacophony compared with the music inside the car. She has to slam on the brakes as a police cruiser whizzes through the intersection, then another, barely missing her. She hadn't seen them coming. She'd been too preoccupied, the music too loud. Her heart hammers as the cars disappear into the night. She's embarrassed, trapped in the middle of the intersection, as other drivers honk at her trying to get by. She turns down the music and drives on more slowly.

She's in no hurry to get home.

2

CASSIE

Monday Night

Cassie stumbles along the sidewalk, dragging a small blue suitcase on wheels and hefting a red duffel bag over her shoulder. Her lungs ache as she pants for air. The night seems like a living thing, all energy and light, as sirens rise and fall in the distance. Janis Joplin's version of "Summertime" runs through her mind. She was listening to it earlier; that angry, desperate craving for comfort still hums in her ears.

Summertime.

She hobbles along, her blond wig swinging, making her scalp tingle and sweat. She looks around the dark street, seeing closed businesses, faded signs, windows boarded up or barred for the night. Where the hell is she? She doesn't know L.A. well. It makes her even more nervous.

God, the bodies. In a nauseating flash, she remembers the sound of gunshots, like hammers banging steel drums. Everything broken. Blood everywhere. Were they all dead? She didn't check. There wasn't time. She had to get out of the house. But where is she is going to go? Will the police be searching for her? Could she check into a hotel somewhere?

Maybe she should call Beth?

Beth still occupies such a special place in Cassie's memory, regal and pale, like the white queen on a chessboard. Beth owed her. She'd always said that. And she lives in L.A. now. Is it stupid to think her old friend would help after all these years?

She hears barking in the distance and flinches with panic. If the cops have dogs, they could track her anywhere. She has to get into a car so they lose her scent. A cab? But she can't flag a cab in L.A. She knows that. And she doesn't have her phone.

She's on a busier street now, headlights passing, more shops barricaded for the night. A bus wheezes toward her in the distance. She digs in her purse for change. She doesn't know how much the fare is, but she has to get off the street. She can't risk walking around like this.

The bus pulls up, stops in front of her. The door opens and an aging woman gets off, looking tired. But the bus is packed, blank faces staring at her from the windows. With the wig, it would probably be okay—who'd be able to make the connection, a blonde carrying suitcases on a bus this time of night? But she can't take any chances. The driver stares at her, waiting. She lowers her head and keeps walking. The door closes and the bus wheezes away.

There's a 7-Eleven sign glowing in the darkness, a few figures in the parking lot—young guys, she can tell. She hears their laughter. She takes off her leather jacket and drapes it through the straps of the duffel bag, adjusting her skimpy tank top so the edge of her black lace bra shows. She grabs a cigarette and heads toward them.

"Got a light?" she asks in her friendliest lilt. All three turn to look at her. Hispanic kids. Early twenties. She sees them all check her out.

"Sure thing, beautiful," the tall one says. She knows in an instant he's the leader of the pack. He's the one who takes a step toward her. The others are staring, but fall in behind him. Without saying another word—a real Prince Charming—he pulls out a lighter, sheltering the flame with his hands. She comes over to light the smoke, averting her face from the others, letting the wig fall against her cheek.

"Can I talk to you?" She nudges him around the side of the store, away from the bright lights. "Do you have a car?"

"Yeah."

"Can you take me somewhere?"

"Where?" He's getting suspicious.

"Just out of here. I'll do whatever you want if you just get me out of here."

The guy laughs. He doesn't believe her.

"I'm serious."

He reaches in his pocket, pulls out his keys. "After you," he says, grinning. He glances at his friends, who huddle together, laughing. "You need a hand with that?" He motions to her luggage.

"I'm good, thanks."

He leads her to a beat-up tan Ford in the corner of the parking lot. He goes to unlock the trunk, but she says, "I'll just put everything back here."

She opens the door, throwing the suitcase into the backseat, but she keeps the red duffel with her when she climbs in the front. The bag is heavy, twenty pounds at least, so she lets half of it spill off her lap onto the seat. But she grips the strap like the rope on a life raft. The kid walks around the car, throwing his friends another wave. She thinks she hears one of them yell something that sounds like a schoolyard taunt. He gets in behind the wheel, the vinyl seat squeaking.

"Where'd you like to go?" he asks, putting the car into gear and pulling out of the lot.

Cassie shoves the snout of her Glock 9mm against his ribs. "Just drive."

3

GOODE

Monday Night

The first responders are already on the scene when Detective Francis Goode pulls his brown sedan to the curb in Lawrence Heights. His mind is all input now. Calm and quiet. The front door's knocked down, the faded stucco chipped, a tiny yard with no grass. A broken front window, the curtain pushed through. No, not a curtain, a blanket, and there's glass on the ground in front. The window's been blown out from the inside. He gets out of the car as more units pull up, brakes screeching. So many flashing lights out here, it reminds him of Christmas Eve.

Goode is somewhere in his fifties and looks every day of it. Six-one, African American, two-ten. He can get around at a crime scene like a man half his age, taking the stairs to the front door two at a time.

He steps into a dimly lit, run-down living room. There's the sound of crunching glass. Flashlight beams circling like tiny klieg lights at a movie premiere. A broken lamp on the floor casts eerie shadows. It takes a moment before it all registers. The bodies, the blood. It's a small room, with a cheap brown couch on the left. A dining table near the front. A linebacker type in a white track suit sits at the table, but his head is down and there's blood oozing from a hole the size of a shot glass in his forehead. A skinny white guy is down by the door. Goode has to step over his body to get inside. But where's Butler? Where's—

Another big guy crumpled on the floor by the wall. It's him.

6

Curtis Butler. Six months he'd been working undercover on this case. He had a wife and kids, too.

A silhouette steps into sight from the back of the house. "All clear, sir. But we got another one down here."

Goode nods, following a heavy trail of blood into the hallway, where there's another body on the floor, the back of his white T-shirt blooming red from a single gunshot. Goode steps around the corpse into a small, shabby bedroom. The mattress is bare, except for a fitted striped sheet, and the blood trail is gone. He notices a bullet hole in the plywood door before heading back into the hallway.

In the kitchen, the counter is scattered with crushed beer cans and a pizza box, a bottle of Windex, and rubber gloves. The whole place smells of gun smoke, as if there's been a fire. A screen door is ajar, squeaking in the breeze. He pushes it open, stepping into the night, scouring his flashlight across the backyard. He sees trash cans and plastic lawn chairs, but no movement. Whoever was here is gone now. As he turns back into the house, toward the voices and the crackling radios, he catches a glimpse of the lights spread across the Hollywood Hills. He wonders what the view must be like from up there.

4

BETH

Beth sits in her car in the driveway. The music has ended, leaving a throbbing silence in her head. Jay's red vintage Mustang gleams in the darkness beside her. She left the restaurant first, so he must've raced all the way home to get here before her. He'd been drinking and she probably shouldn't have let him drive, but she didn't want to cause a scene at the restaurant. That's what she tells herself anyway, because the alternative is too perverse: maybe she doesn't even care.

The beautiful bungalow is perfectly landscaped, up-lights glowing. It's not a big house, only two bedrooms, two baths, but it's the kind of house any young couple coveted in L.A.—Jay especially. He always wanted a house in the hills, as if he were already Steven Spielberg or something.

Beth thought it would be the perfect place to start a family. She remembers seeing the extra bedroom for the first time, envisioning it full of Pottery Barn pink or blue, with matching curtains and shelves of stuffed animals. Not that they could have afforded to decorate a nursery the way she wanted to right now, but just thinking about it made her happy. At least, it used to. Looking at Emily's baby pictures over dinner was so hard. Trying to smile—when all she wanted to do was cry.

"I can't believe you picked up the tab again," she says, walking into the kitchen and locking the door behind her. Jay doesn't even

8

look up at her, scrolling on his phone. "It was our turn. They paid last time."

"No—*we* did."

She heads through the living room—a shrine of midcentury antiques—past the elegant wedding pictures in the hall. They mock her with their happiness. She in her off-white gown. Jay in his gray tux. The country club in the background. She'd been happy that day, hadn't she? She looks happy anyway. It's so hard to remember now.

Three years went by fast.

In the bedroom, she slips off the black dress and hangs it in the closet. She opens a blue Tiffany's box. Unclasps her double strand of pearls—a family heirloom—handling them like rosary beads, before curling them into the case.

Jay walks into the room without saying a word, heading to the adjoining bathroom. He seems to drag resentment behind him. So defensive all the time. She sees him in the reflection behind her, bending over the sink, brushing his teeth. She feels as if she's aged ten years in the last few months, and Jay, five years older, still seems so young. Clean-shaven, clipped hair. She shudders to think how much he spends on haircuts, when she's been trimming and dyeing her hair for a year now.

Fake it till you make it, he always says. *Gotta look the part.*

He's in such great shape, too, still a handsome man. And he knows it. That's the problem. But she doesn't want to go down this path again. It'll just make her more depressed. She tries to bring brightness to her voice.

"Emily looked good tonight, don't you think?"

"Hmmm?"

She walks to the bathroom door and leans against the frame. Even in her bra and slip, she doesn't feel exposed. She doesn't feel like a sexual thing right now. Maybe she never will again.

"Emily. She looked good."

He wipes his mouth. "She looked okay, I guess." He doesn't meet her eyes in the mirror as he opens the medicine cabinet, grabs his prescription bottle, and takes a pill.

9

She tries a different tack. "Can you believe all that baby talk, though? God, how can they sit there and talk about that stuff all night?"

"Because that's what new parents do, Beth." This time he glances at her, irritation in his hazel eyes.

She feels the gentle sting of the comment. "Still. She knows we're trying to get pregnant. You think she'd try to be a little more—" The house phone rings, cutting her off.

"Bet that's her. Calling to brag about the joy of breastfeeding again."

She walks over to see it's an *Unknown Caller*. "Hello?" There's a moment of silence, and a dial tone is next. Jay gives her a questioning look as she hangs up. She just shrugs. *Wrong number.*

There's a full-length mirror next to the bed, and she catches her reflection in it. She runs her hand over her flat stomach, sees her small breasts in the bra, her slim legs. Yet there's nothing sexy about her, is there? There never was. Not like Emily. So full of life. Compared with her, Beth feels like one of those expensive collectible dolls she used to have when she was a little girl, standing inside their boxes in her pink bedroom in Bryn Mawr. Like those dolls, Beth always looked perfect. She even seemed real sometimes; but it was an illusion, because she feels cold, hard—and untouchable.

She senses the tug of her melancholy and tries to shake it off again. "You think I should get my hair cut short like that? Just for a change. I thought it really suited Em."

Jay comes over, his shirt unbuttoned. She sees him loom up in the mirror, and it makes her suck in a breath of fear.

"Don't even think about it. I like your hair just the way it is." He wraps his arms around her waist and kisses the side of her neck. The look in his eye. The gleam. There's a sudden softness to his mood as he rocks her slightly in his arms. She can smell the stale cologne, mixed with toothpaste and liquor. "What's wrong with you tonight, anyway? Why are you so self-conscious?"

"Are you really asking me this?"

They still aren't facing each other, talking only to reflections, but he gives her an innocent shrug.

"You were ogling her all night, Jay. The flirting? It was embarrassing. For both of us."

"Beth, come on, I wasn't—"

But she twists out of his arms and walks into the bathroom, locking the door.

She opens the medicine cabinet and sees his Ambien. Every time she notices that bottle, she wonders what would happen if she swallowed them all.

Two hours later, the house phone next to her side of the bed starts ringing. She sees the time, after three, and gets a chill. It's an emergency. Has to be. Someone is dead. Or in the hospital. One of Jay's parents? He doesn't even stir in bed beside her; God, how she envies him those pills. But as she reaches for the phone, she hesitates. The screen registers another *Unknown Caller*.

"Hello?"

Silence. A moment later, a man asks, "Is this Beth?"

"Yes," she answers uncertainly. She doesn't recognize the voice, deep and raspy. "Who is this?"

"Is Cassie there?"

She feels a trill of uncertainty. *"Who?"*

But the man hangs up. She holds the phone for a moment, staring into the darkness. Did he say *Cassie*? Couldn't be. It must've been *Cathy*. That makes more sense, a common name, a wrong number.

She glances at the framed photo on the nightstand, barely visible in the dim light. The shot was taken that last day in the Hamptons, the sun bright, the pool off to one side, the big white mansion in the background, the horizon of the pounding Atlantic beyond. She finally lays her head back down on her pillow, but she knows she won't be able to sleep for hours.

Cassie?

Is it possible?

A single phrase comes back to her, one she tries not to think of anymore. *You know what you are, Beth? You're a lotus flower. That's just what you are.*

A lotus flower.

She remembers that summer after freshman year, sharing the big yellow bedroom with Cass. How the air was heavy with the scent of brine. The canopy bed brimmed with yellow pillow shams, and the bookshelves were full of old stuffed animals, eyes gleaming like an audience in a darkened theater. They talked about everything that summer. Music and men and mischief. Their plans for life—and for the weekend.

With her husband sleeping beside her, Beth is transported away from this room. This life. She remembers wandering the corridors of the Residence Hall years ago, finding her new dorm room, with its view of Boston Harbor, empty. Two beds, two desks, two dressers, a small fridge. She can almost smell the woody scent of the recital rooms downstairs and the fresh paint on the walls.

She'd been assigned the bed on the left, piling her bags on the bare mattress. In her freshman orientation package, she'd been given a questionnaire to help new roommates get acquainted. *What is your major? Composition? Performance? Theory? Voice?* There were silly questions, too, like what's your favorite band, movie, or book. But the last question was different. It read "I hope my new roommate is—" and in the blank, Beth had written "nice."

After she unpacked, the other girls on the floor had met their new roommates, but hers still hadn't appeared. She kept busy studying campus maps, putting her books away, deciding what to wear for her first day.

As the sun set, there was commotion in the hall. A moment later, Cassie Ogilvy stood framed in the doorway. Wild dark hair, faded jeans, she was laden with knapsacks and gym bags, which she dropped with various thumps.

"Hey," she said, out of breath. She smelled like cigarettes. "I'm Cass."

"I'm Beth."

As they shook hands, the girl's wrists, layered with bangles and beads, clattered like pencils in a cup. The first thing she did was crouch next to her knapsack and fill the little fridge with a six-pack of beer, moving Beth's milk and orange juice out of the way, everything clunking and clanging.

"Want one?" she asked, holding out a can.

Beth shook her head. There was a strict no-drinking policy in the dorm, but she decided not to mention it. That was no way to make friends with a new roommate. Over the course of the next hour, she watched Cassie pile rumpled clothes into the dresser and stack jazz CDs on her shelf. She had lots of makeup and hair products—but no alarm clock. She lined up half a dozen prescription pill bottles on her desk, and Beth wondered what they could be for. The girl almost never stopped talking, a stream of confessions and jokes. Beth felt stilted in comparison.

"So? What about you?" she finally asked. "What's your story?"

Beth handed her the questionnaire. "I think I should just give you this."

"Oh yeah. I didn't fill mine out yet." She glanced at the page, skimming. She looked up, arching an eyebrow. "Nice?"

Beth shrugged.

"I would've put *cool*," she said with a grin.

Later that night, they were in their single beds, trying to fall asleep for the first time in a new city. A new life. Crosshairs of shadow from the harvest moon shone through the window.

Cassie's voice was quiet in the darkness. "Beth? Can I ask you a huge favor?"

"Okay..."

"Is it all right if we don't close the door?"

"At night?" Beth was confused. Was she afraid of the dark?

"No, I mean, ever. We can partly close it, just not all the way. None of the girls would be able to see in. It would just be a crack, so it's not completely closed. Would that be okay with you?"

"Um...do you mind if I ask why?"

"I don't want to dump on you so soon," she said. "You'll think I'm nuts."

"No, I won't," Beth insisted. "Cassie? What is it?"

She was quiet another moment longer. "You might not think it's a big deal, but I used to get locked in my bedroom," she finally said. "Not just at night. All the time. Whenever I acted up, anyway. I hated it. I felt so—trapped. So helpless. So now I just don't like closing doors all the way, that's all. I can't sleep."

"Oh." Beth shuddered. She preferred doors that not only closed, but locked.

"Would you mind?"

"Um…" She was flooded with remorse for this girl who burst in smelling of cigarettes, full of confessions and laughter. Yet beneath it all was this strange vulnerability. "How awful for you, Cass. I'm so sorry. Of course you can leave the door open a bit."

"Thanks," she said, sounding relieved. She got out of bed and tiptoed across the room. She opened the door not more than an inch. The lights in the hall were dimmed for the night, so it wasn't overly bright, but Beth still saw a thin, vertical strand glowing in the darkness. Highlights of Cassie's Gap T-shirt. The profile of her face. The sheen of her legs.

Cassie tiptoed back to her bed and climbed under the covers. "Thanks," she said again. "G'night."

5

GOODE

Tuesday Morning

On Ventura Boulevard, Goode drives his beat-up brown Chevy through morning rush hour. His gun and a manila file are on the seat beside him. The radio crackles: *"Unit nine in pursuit north on Washington, request backup. Standby for description..."*

He drives past McDonald's, considering. Egg McMuffin maybe? They say breakfast is the most important meal of the day, so who's he to argue? But the drive-through line is long, so he keeps going. He gives a loud yawn. It had been a late night. The reporters called it the Lawrence Heights Bloodbath. It covered the front page.

Four dead.

One undercover narcotics officer, Curtis Butler, 36, leaves behind a wife and two children...Police are searching for a suspect, Richard Bradley Squires, 38.

There was an inset photo of Rick Squires, his last mug shot on a drug charge in Wakulla County, Florida. Sandy-blond hair, reaching to the collar of his T-shirt, his jaw clenched, a dead look in his blue eyes.

Goode went to Butler's house last night to tell his wife the news. He didn't want some uniform she didn't know showing up. When you're the wife of an undercover cop in the Gang and Narcotics Division of the LAPD and a detective knocks on your door at three in the morning, you know it's not good news. She was already shaking when she answered. She burst into tears before he even said a word and covered her ears, backing away, trying to close the door on him, as if she could shut out the news. He had to gently push through. He held her in the hallway for fifteen minutes before she could breathe again. The kids woke up and stared at him from the dimness at the top of the stairs. It broke his heart. His chest still ached thinking about it. The funeral was being planned for Saturday. It would be a big one—line of duty and all—and Butler was well liked. But the flashy honor was little consolation to a young widow with two girls to raise on her own. He should try to check in on her before the funeral. Just to see if she's okay. She won't be—he knows that. But she'll pretend to be, the way they all will.

Goode finds a run-down burger joint and pulls up to a battered speaker. The voice crackles, tinny and small, like a harried cartoon character. "...take your order please?"

Goode peruses the faded menu. "Fried egg sandwich. Side-a hash browns. Got any Gatorade?"

"No, sir. Sodas, milkshakes, coffee, tea, orange juice—"

He interrupts. "Make it coffee, black."

"That'll be eight thirty-seven, please. Drive through."

Goode inches forward in line, opening the manila file on the steering wheel in front of him. It's full of crime scene photos from the mess in Lawrence Heights. Normally, he feels very little emotion about these kinds of shots. As if he's just wandering through a hardware store, calculating what he needs for a job.

Nails.

Putty.

Paint.

But this is different. It's not just his friendship with Butler. An official task force had been set up to deal with the situation, so the DEA and FBI were involved, too. Until recently the city had managed to avoid a lot of the opioid problems in the rest of the country, but now assholes were coming up from Florida with carloads of high-grade heroin laced with fentanyl. It was a deadly combination, and they were unloading it on the streets of his city. Squires was just another courier in a long string of them. So they set up the task force, called Butler, a young father, back from his promotion, into undercover work. Just to renew his old connections. They'd find the supplier and put an end to this shit. It was supposed to take a few weeks. That was six months ago.

Now? Four men dead, including Butler himself? He doesn't even want to count how many fatal overdoses there have been. And still no dope, no cash, and no Squires? If Goode didn't get some answers and put an end to the supply chain soon, there's every chance LAPD would be taken off the case.

That's not the worst of it, of course. The worst of it sits in his chest, an ache that won't go away, not since he held Fiona in that hallway. Saw her tears on his sleeve. Next time, he should bring something for the girls. What were their names? Savannah and— Sasha, that was it. He'll ask Dawes what they might like...She'll know.

The drive-through window slides open and the boy hands him a paper bag. "That'll be eight—" But he stops when he sees the bloody photos on the steering wheel. The gun on the seat.

Goode gives him a ten. "You should get Gatorade," he says. He closes his window and drives away.

6

CASSIE

Tuesday Morning

Cassie stands in the marble shower, letting hot water cascade over her skin. Using hotel shampoo, she lathers her long, dark hair, rinsing it under the stream. She knew they'd be looking for a blonde, so she dumped the wig last night. The memories, however, weren't as easy to forget.

Rick's lifeless body, drenched with blood.

That kid from the 7-Eleven tugging on her as she tried to escape.

The sound of gunshots.

She closes her eyes, fear lurching with every heartbeat. When is that going to stop? Or the ringing in her ears? Would it ever? She looks at her wet fingers, detecting the tremor still there. Layers of cords and bracelets on her wrists are soaking, but she never takes them off. Not even in the shower.

She hears a muffled voice and turns off the faucet. A shadow shifts on the other side of the shower curtain.

"Sorry to barge in on you—the door was open."

"No problem," she says, reaching for a towel.

He's at the mirror, smoothing his thinning fair hair, tucking in his shirt. "Wow," he says with a grin, watching as she dries herself. "Just—*wow*."

She forces a smile. His name is Matthew. *Matt*. She'd seen him having breakfast in the hotel restaurant downstairs. Of the several businessmen sitting alone, she singled him out for a few reasons: there was an empty table beside him, he was working on a laptop, and he had a newspaper folded on the table. She was hoping to find someone who'd been drinking with breakfast. Just a beer, to show he was bored with life, the way she'd always been, but it was barely nine in the morning and there wasn't a soul drinking anything stronger than juice or coffee.

She avoided the hostess, who glared at her as she dragged her suitcase and red duffel across the room, sliding into the banquette beside the stranger, bumping him with her knee.

"Sorry!"

"No problem." He smiled, going back to his laptop.

She glanced down at his newspaper. Folded the wrong way; she couldn't read it. His gold wedding band glinted on his finger. She wondered if it would help—or hinder—her plan.

The screens above the bar were tuned to a morning newscast. Talking heads. Flashy graphics. The weather report. Then a chaotic scene on a street. It was a moment before she figured out what she was seeing. A shot of the rental house, with police cars parked outside, reporters on the sidewalk. Then a mug shot of Rick, staring blankly at the camera. She had to remind herself to breathe, to blink.

A young man wearing a black apron came to the table carrying a coffeepot. "G'morning," he said, putting a menu in front of her.

"Sorry, I'm not having breakfast."

"Coffee?" He motioned with the pot.

"No, thanks. Just some ice water, please."

"Are you waiting for a room?" He was trying to be polite, but he was also a busy waiter during the breakfast rush. According to his badge, his name was Nathan.

"I *did* have a room booked," she began, frustrated. "But I left my overnight bag on the plane. So stupid of me. All my stuff was in there. My wallet, credit cards, my phone! I'm just waiting for them to sort it all out."

"Oh...well, I'm very sorry, but if you're not ordering, I'm not allowed to let you have a table."

"No?" A helpless little bleat.

"I'm afraid not. I'll have to ask you to wait in the lobby."

She gave a dejected sigh. "Great," she huffed.

"I'm really sorry."

"Don't worry about it. It's not your fault." She started getting her things together, hoping, waiting, for the stranger to interject.

"Excuse me," he began on cue. "I don't mean to pry. But it sounds like you're having a rough time."

She laughed tiredly. "Is it that obvious?"

"Kind of. Can I buy you a coffee while you wait? Maybe breakfast?"

"Are you serious?" she asked, her eyes brimming. She knew her black eyeliner was smeared, but it made her green eyes look even larger. Sometimes she didn't wash it off for days, just applied more. "That's so incredible of you. Thank you. You're the first person who's been nice to me since I got here."

"My pleasure," he said with a smile.

The waiter hovered. "What can I get you?"

"Actually, I could really use a drink," she admitted. "Can you drink in L.A. this time of day?" she asked, when she knew damn well that you could.

"Of course," said the waiter. "What would you like?"

"Maybe a Grey Goose martini." She winced. "A double?"

"Right away. Anything for you, sir?"

"Um…" He looked at his watch, glanced at Cassie. "Maybe I'll have a light beer?"

Excellent. He's game.

After the server left, he turned to her. "A double martini this early in the morning? You don't fool around, do you?"

"I know, but I just got back from London. My inner clock's all screwed up. It's probably five real time for me. And—actually, I do," she said, her voice teasing. "Fool around, I mean."

He frowned at her, not knowing if the double entendre was on purpose. She took off her leather jacket, letting it fall to the bench seat behind her. He couldn't help himself. His gaze darted down to her skimpy tank top. Then quickly away. Even when she was young, her teachers worried about how quickly she'd developed: precocious, they'd called her, mature for her age. It was "part of the problem." Over the years Cassie had learned this particular problem was a secret power she had over men. Whole conversations took place in an instant: dating, sex, marriage, divorce, and everything in between.

When the drinks came, she made small talk, flirting, laughing, reaching out to touch him. Working her way down a familiar path. Her footing wasn't as sure as it once was, and sometimes she thought she'd said the wrong thing. Even so, within the hour, they were in his suite on the ninth floor.

The martinis helped smear the memories away, let her mind be numb and her limbs drift across his body, over the sheets. It felt odd to be with someone other than Rick. He was always so rough, and he had so many tattoos that sometimes his biceps reminded Cassie of pythons coiling around her in the night. But this man had been so gentle, his pale arms like those of a nervous little boy's. Somehow a total stranger felt more loving than someone she'd been with for almost two years.

As she puts on a hotel robe, she tries to seem casual, glancing at the red duffel bag on the floor. *Girl stuff*, she'd told him, but she couldn't take a chance he'd look inside.

"The laptop's on the desk," he says, doing his tie. "The Wi-Fi code is just the hotel name."

"Thanks. I appreciate it." There are large mirrors on almost every wall, making the scene seem endless and unreal, the two of them just actors on a stage. "Such a hassle, losing my wallet. I have to cancel my cards. Call the passport office. I should get in touch with my family, too. They'll be worried."

"No kidding. Use the phone, whatever you need, okay?" He goes to leave, but hangs back. "Um—am I supposed to give you any—money?"

She widens her eyes. "Of course not! Please don't think that!"

"I'm sorry! That's not what I meant! B-but you lost your wallet, so maybe you need a little cash—or something?"

"I just needed a *break*."

"Oh, good." He exhales in relief. "I didn't know for sure. I've never done this before."

"Me neither," she lies.

"No?" He seems hopeful. "I—I'm here for the rest of the week. I've got to file this big appeal by Friday." He already told her he was some kind of consultant, and she tries to act interested, when all she wants him to do is leave. "I can't get away during the day, but you can stay here as long as you want. Maybe we could go to dinner tonight?"

"I'd love that. Thank you." She steps toward him, straightening his tie. "You're a real knight in shining armor, you know that?"

His skin reddens and he stammers, "J-just help yourself to whatever, okay? The bar. Room service. It's all on an expense account. I should be finished around six or six thirty. We can decide where to eat then." He glances at his watch. "I hate to leave you alone, but I have to go."

"No problem. I'll be waiting."

"See you soon." He points at her, eyes narrowed. "Cathy, right?"

"Cathy," she says with a smile.

7

RICK

Rick Squires is in his late thirties, with straggly fair hair, a thin beard, and blue eyes. The nails on his pinkie fingers are long and yellowed, his muscular arms covered in tattoos, more ink than skin showing.

He sits on the sagging brown couch, the cash counter on the coffee table in front of him. A gray blanket hangs over the curtain rod, doubling the thickness of the drapes, blocking the house from prying eyes. He has enough people watching him in this room already.

At a cheap dining table across from him is a man he knows only as Jules. Jules wears a white Adidas jogging suit, but judging from the size of him, he hasn't jogged a day in his life. He weighs kilos on a small scale he brought with him. He didn't trust the one Rick had. They never do. A small black road case sits open on the floor, the corners reinforced with metal. The case has a false bottom and is packed with Heat, a powerful combination of heroin and fentanyl from the Florida Keys. Using a band road case to transport the stuff had been Cassie's idea. "Nobody's going to stop us," she'd said, smiling. "We're just a band on tour!"

Behind Jules stands a second big black guy with a goatee, holding a gun at his side. Another sidekick, three hundred pounds if an ounce, watches Rick like a prison guard. Bobby, the skinny white kid who drove up with him and Cassie, is at the front door, facing the room, trying to look as intimidating as he can. Everyone either holds a gun or is within reach of one. Except for the soft tap of the scale and the *whoosh* of the cash counter, the room is silent. There's no music, no talking.

Rick unwraps an elastic from a roll of bills and inserts the cash into the hopper. The hissing and clicking begin. A red duffel bag, full of similar rolls of one hundred dollar bills, sits on the floor beside him. His heart beats almost as fast as the money in the counter.

$12,100 USD

$38,700 USD

$95,300 USD

The numbers on the LCD screen escalate silently. He wonders how long it will take to count this much cash.

Then he hears a faint clatter from the bedroom down the hall.

Jules freezes. "Somebody back there?"

"Nobody," Rick says. But Bobby tenses up, his gaze darting toward the hallway.

One of the sidekicks leaves his spot and heads out of the room.

"I said, nobody's there." But the guy keeps walking down the hall, the floor squeaking with each step.

Stay down, Cassie. Stay down or you'll get us all killed...

Then a shot explodes—so close, Rick's ears ring—and the guy in the hall tumbles to the floor. Rick sees Bobby's arms extended, the gun smoking in his trembling hands. Fuck! He must've been trying to protect Cass. There's an instant of nothingness when everyone looks around. Then things drag into slow motion. More shots explode, so loud and sudden, Rick feels his bones rattle. It seems to take him thirty seconds to grab his gun and it's just on the coffee table in front of him. Another minute watching bullets travel across the room. Furniture splintering. Mirrors shattering. Blood spraying. The gunshots just won't stop. But then the weight of a brick hits his shoulder, and he flies back, the noises starting to fade.

8

BETH

Tuesday Morning

Beth gets off the elevator at the Steinberg Academy in downtown L.A. The long halls are a din of piano scales and violin solos behind closed doors. She walks quickly, already late for her first student. She didn't even have time to stop for a coffee. She had trouble sleeping last night and she woke up in a bad mood— again. Every day she keeps thinking she's going to open her eyes in the morning and things will be different, but like the weather in L.A.—so unlike the seasons back home—nothing ever changes. It's just more of the same. The same. The same. She tries to tell herself that things are getting better. That *she* is getting better. That it won't be long now and she'll be her old self again. But she can't even remember who her "old self" was.

Maybe she's just tense about dinner tonight. That'll be two nights of socializing in a row, and getting together with her in-laws is always trying. She's still upset about Emily, too. She didn't even wake Jay this morning, tiptoeing around so she wouldn't have to talk to him.

Why is it still bothering her so much? Maybe she's just tired. She hadn't been able to sleep after that strange call last night. Cassie isn't a common name. It seemed such an odd coincidence. She tries to reassure herself it was just a wrong number, had to be. But then why did he know *her* name? *Is this Beth?* It makes no sense. It fills her with dread, a minor key running beneath her thoughts.

She steps into her small, stale music room, horrified to see a well-dressed woman and her little girl waiting by the piano. The receptionist must have let them in. The girl's a new student, too, with a helicopter mom who wants to sit in on the lessons. The woman glares at her with such derision, Beth feels a shiver run down her spine.

"I'm so sorry I'm late! Traffic was insane." She puts down her purse—a cheap knockoff, but passable—still sputtering apologies. Her cheeks are warm with a mix of shame and anger. "I hope you didn't have to wait long," she says, her heels clicking on the polished wood floor as she hurries to the piano.

"Ten minutes is long enough," the woman complains.

"I'll make it up to you. I promise." Beth tries to smile but just feels her cheeks aching. "Are you ready, Amy?"

"She's been practicing scales," says the mother, who sits straight-backed in a chair, a flashy Gucci bag clutched on her knees like a lapdog. "Nothing else to do while we waited."

Beth forces another smile, but she can't apologize any more, can she? She'll lose credibility, respect. She sits down on the piano bench next to the young girl, opens the sheet music in front of them, and turns on the metronome, setting it on the floor at their feet. The metronome *clicks*, *clicks*, *clicks*, like a mechanical heartbeat.

"All right, in one, two..."

Within seconds, the girl's hands are whirling across the keyboard of the Mason & Hamlin. She can't be more than eight or nine, but she's playing Tchaikovsky like it was "Chopsticks." The metronome beats steadily on the floor, goose-stepping straight toward her, getting louder. Closer.

She has impossible talent. Where did that kind of skill come from? Not in a little girl. It seems miraculous, almost magical. The tension starts to build in her throat, the heat behind her eyes, such a familiar sensation lately: wanting to burst into tears. But instead of bawling, she just nods to the music, occasionally smiles at the mother, trying to seem relaxed and professional. But that kind of talent—in a child? It's just so unfair. So damned unfair.

I'm wasting my life!

Isn't she? It had all been such a stupid waste.

As she sits there, listening to this prodigy, she remembers watching *Amadeus* in an elective class in college, Musical Drama 101, a "bird course," where they did breathing exercises and studied almost every musical from *Flashdance* to *Singin' in the Rain*. But it was *Amadeus* that stuck with her. She'd felt so resentful of Mozart's brash genius, and such a bond with the pathetic, envious Salieri. How he raged at God for giving him the desire to compose brilliant music but then denied him the talent to do so. Beth used to ask herself the same thing every day. But now she just wants to forget her dreams—and her failures. Now she just wants out.

9

JAY

Tuesday Morning

In the Hollywood Hills, Jay is out for his morning run, working up a sweat, helping to shake off his hangover. Around him, the rooftops of lavish homes peek through treetops and over walls, everything greenery, blue sky, and sunshine, not a hint of smoke or smog in the air. A perfect summer day.

But all he hears is a cash register.

Ka-ching. Ka-ching. Ka-ching.

The cars. The landscaping. The curb appeal. He likes to keep up appearances, too, but they can only afford the minimum right now and he resents it.

Don't wallow, he tells himself. Squeezes his eyes closed. Says his little mantra.

It's going to work out. It's a brilliant film. You're a brilliant producer. This is the one. Commisso is going to pull through. Just relax.

Jay can feel it's going to happen this time—like he's never felt anything before. He can picture it. *If you can dream it...*

A gleaming Mercedes drives by with a silver-haired man wearing a golf shirt behind the wheel. It reminds him of his father, off to another day on the links. If the deal fell through, he could always ask his parents for another loan, couldn't he?

Ka-ching. Ka-ching.

It isn't going to fall through!

He sees two young women, a blonde and a brunette, turn the

28

bend ahead of him. He passes them almost every morning, timing his own jog to bump into them somewhere along the route.
Barely dressed, ponytails—and everything else—bobbing. It's one
of the perks of living in a neighborhood like this: lots of models,
actresses, and trophy wives skipping about. He lifts his chest and
sucks in his abs.

"Morning, ladies!" He grins as he passes them, tipping his
black baseball cap.

"Hi there," says the blonde.

She's the only one who actually talks to him, but the other one
always smiles. They both seem friendly. So happy and carefree. He
twists around and jogs backward, watching them bounce away.
Real benefit to jogging backward. The rearview.

"Have a nice day!" he calls.

They lean into each other and giggle coquettishly, but don't
stop running. They turn the corner, out of sight, and he twists
forward again, pumped and energized. Flirting. Big deal. It meant
nothing. Why did Beth have to get so pissed off about it last
night? Did she have any idea what he'd been like before they
met? Hound Dog. That's what they'd called him at Princeton.
And now, they hadn't had sex in three months? At least. The doctor said that might happen, but still. He has needs! Big deal if he
ogles the neighbors a bit.

Had she really used that word? Ogling? She's always been
such a snob. All that Philadelphia Main Line breeding bullshit.
Jay's parents had money, lots of it, but they'd always drilled it
into his head that the worst thing you could be was a snob. It
was crass.

Beth's parents—judging from the pictures, the stories, that
big summer house on the ocean—had been the exact opposite.
WASPy snobs who looked down their noses at everyone. What
phonies. They didn't have a penny when they died. Beth had to
sell everything to settle their debts. She always complains about
how irresponsible *he* is with money—but what about them? He
and Beth wouldn't even be in this situation if her own parents

had a little more common sense. He's glad he never had a chance to meet them. He probably would've hated them.

Ogling.

God, how can she be so critical all the time? So what if he was a flirt? It was harmless.

10

CASSIE

Tuesday Morning

Cassie stands in the bathroom, hearing the clicks of his briefcase and four little *beeps* from the hotel room safe. She wonders what he's trying to hide from her. But then her focus splits and she sees his gold razor sitting on the sink, glinting like a watch in a jewelry store. She picks it up, feels its substantial weight, sets it down again.

"See you later!" he calls.

"Can't wait!"

As soon as she hears the hotel room door lock, she runs into the main room. Hurries to the desk for the newspaper. She's aware of the closed door in the corner, but it's not unbearable. Doors leading to sunlight and fresh air, or doors in public places, like the one in the hotel room? They're fine. But doors that open onto corridors, private hallways, dim spaces make her breathe faster. The fear isn't as bad as it used to be, but she's still aware of that door. In the instant she glanced at it, a mental picture snapped. *Four panels. Brushed-metal hardware. Emergency exit information in a laminated frame.*

The story made the front page: BLOODBATH IN LAWRENCE HEIGHTS: FOUR DEAD.

Robert Hackett, 28. Bobby was dead. She could tell that when she left the house. Poor kid.

Julian "Jules" Williams, 34.

Arkell Mitchell, 29.

Curtis Butler, 36, an undercover officer with the LAPD.

One of them was a narc? They killed a cop? Good God. If the police could connect her to the scene, they'd never stop looking for her. She may need more than a week to hide out. She may be running for the rest of her life. She grabs her purse, takes out a cigarette, and lights one with trembling hands, throwing the lighter down, pacing the room.

It was supposed to be easy. That's what Rick said. After it went down, they'd deliver a portion of the money back to Miami, then leave the country and hit a beach somewhere. Cassie loved to lie in the sun. It was another addiction of hers, easy and pleasurable, as the best highs were. But you could feel the light slipping away from you as the sun inched toward the leer of the horizon, pulling the darkness behind it like a black sheet. The high couldn't last forever. The sun had to set. The applause had to end. And eventually, everybody, absolutely everybody, had to go home.

Then the craving would begin again.

But that's what they'd come to L.A. for. That's why they'd driven so far. When they got that money, she wouldn't have to worry for a long time. They could do anything they wanted, go anywhere they wanted, find some dive in Mexico where she could stand on a stage in front of tourists at night and lie on a beach all day long. All they had to do was stay cool for one big drop. *One point two million, all unmarked bills. Almost a million of that cash was theirs.* It was too much to pass up, no matter how dangerous. But she knew Rick was getting nervous. He'd been so angry with her.

"You're in here singing?"

Summertime...

The article said they were searching for a "Richard Squires" in connection with the shooting. But she'd seen his body, lying in a pool of blood. She'd thought he was dead. Had he escaped? He must've, somehow. Oh God. How badly hurt was he? Would he be looking for her? For the money? Should she try calling hospitals and find him before he found her? Maybe he'd been admitted somewhere. But who would she ask for? It would just raise red flags. Maybe she should try calling him herself. She knew the number for his burner phone. She could try it. If he didn't answer, fine. If he did, she could tell him she'd been afraid. That was why she took off. She thought everyone was dead.

Would he believe her?

She'd taken that money. He might think she was trying to rip him off. He'd probably try to kill her.

She opens the laptop, unlocks the Wi-Fi, and taps on the keyboard, scanning the *L.A. Times* website. There's nothing new about Rick, but she keeps scrolling, almost against her will, checking for any news about the kid who picked her up last night. *Self-defense*, she reminds herself, *self-defense*. But there's nothing yet.

Even so, there's a building pressure in her chest. She can't stay here. She has to find a place to hunker down for a few days. An hour in a hotel room, that was nothing. They'd barely spoken. But another night together? She can't risk Matt being able to identify her, not with all this news. She needs somewhere else to crash until things calm down.

She thinks of Beth again. Her fingers tap the keyboard.

Beth Crawf...

It's not the first time she's Googled her old friend. She'd done it many times over the years. She hadn't been surprised Beth wasn't on Facebook or Instagram—she'd always been so reserved—so Cassie had to dig deeper, even calling the alumnae office at school; Beth hadn't been in touch there, either. But it was the name of that album that made the difference. Cassie finishes her search: "Beth Crawford" +"*The Lotus Flower*" + "Piano," and the same hit at the Steinberg Academy in Los Angeles comes up.

She follows her old trail, sees the lovely, serious photo of her friend on the website, next to her bio: *Crawford-Montgomery has a master's in music from the New England Institute of Music. She lives in Los Angeles with her husband, film producer Jay Montgomery.*

At first Cassie was surprised. Beth had become a music teacher? It was the last thing either of them wanted to be in college. But

Beth had always been so shy onstage. Maybe it was inevitable she'd slink off somewhere to teach. At least Cassie had been able to find her. She called the academy and used all her charm.

We were roommates in college.

I'd leave a message here, but I want it to be a surprise.

I haven't seen her in years . . .

But she can't call the place again—can she? *Sorry, I lost the number.* There's no way they'd give it to her again.

Fuck.

And then she remembers. She grabs her purse and empties it on the bed, wallet, makeup, and the broken bracelet tumbling out. There's the matchbook from that dive outside Miami Beach where she sang jazz standards at night for broke tourists. When they gave her the number, she scribbled it—there! The L.A. number is scrawled inside the flap, next to the name of the Steinberg place. But shit, she'd put all that info into her phone, too. She wasn't usually good about keeping up her contact list, but it was a sentimental thing to do, inputting her old friend's name and number. She'd taken the SIM card out weeks ago, because Rick wanted to use untraceable burners leading up to the deal. But Beth's number was still on that phone. Rick knew her old roommate lived in L.A., because Cassie had made them listen to Beth's CD on the way up, telling him and Bobby stories about freshman year. Maybe Rick would remember Beth's name and somehow track her down there. Maybe it wouldn't be safe.

Would Beth even want to help in the first place?

She's not sure, but she doesn't have a choice. She has to find someone she trusts. And for Cassie Ogilvy, that's a very short list indeed.

11

GOODE

Tuesday Morning

The morgue is chilly as Goode stares down at the face of his colleague and friend. A man twenty years younger than him. A young father. And a great cop. It isn't often Goode feels the need to use the word "tragedy"—but he does now.

His partner, Michelle Dawes, stands beside him, sighing heavily. Dawes is in her early forties and single. *I'm married to the job*, she always says. Goode never considered he was married to the job. But his ex-wife did. Which is why she isn't married to him anymore.

Dawes has a great figure—the kids call it "thick" nowadays—cocoa skin, full lips, the kind of girl Goode might've fallen in love with when he was younger. Plus she put up with him, no questions asked. She made going to work, and doing things like this, just a little easier.

The pathologist snaps off his latex gloves and covers Detective Curtis Butler's face with the blue sheet. He pulls his own face mask down to hang beneath his chin. "I'm only half done. You know how many we had last night?" He motions to a wall of stainless-steel crypts. "Eight. Eight OD victims. When the hell is this gonna stop, Frank? We can't keep up."

"I know. It's a fucking mess," says Goode. "It was supposed to be routine. Curtis wasn't even after Squires. He's just a courier. They wanted the supplier. Butler was just making his way up the chain."

"He didn't even have backup," adds Dawes. "Didn't think he needed it."

"By the time first responders showed, everybody was dead. Except Squires—who's gone. No money. No junk. A few grams on the floor maybe. But a total write-off."

"Damn," says the pathologist, shaking his head. He grabs a clipboard and a blank autopsy sketch, indicating the bullet wounds, absorbed like a disturbed kid scribbling in a coloring book.

Meanwhile, Goode takes a swallow of his Gatorade. Dawes frowns, motioning to the ABSOLUTELY NO FOOD OR DRINK IN MORGUE sign right behind him. Goode just shrugs, turning to the pathologist.

"You wanna hear a damn thing?"

The pathologist nods, finishing his sketch.

"Four bodies. Two handguns. One Kalashnikov. A house turned into firewood. Blood everywhere. I'm serious, you shoulda seen the place. But not one print."

"None we can use, anyway," Dawes says. "Doorknobs, light switches, cupboards, everything was wiped clean."

"Except for the empty beer cans," Goode says. "So we got Squires's prints. He was definitely in that house. They cleaned the rest of the place, but left prints on beer cans? They left in a hurry. Obviously."

"That explains it," says the pathologist, nodding to the crypts. "I found traces of ammonia on the skinny guy's hands and clothes."

"The Kurt Cobain look-alike?"

"Yeah. Ran a check. He was covered in window cleaner."

Goode nods, remembering the Windex bottle on the kitchen table, a sign they were dealing with professionals who knew how to cover their tracks.

"I don't suppose you got any pretty blondes in there?" he asks.

The pathologist looks up, frowning.

"According to the landlady," Dawes says, "a pretty blonde signed the lease on the place last week. Twenty-five. Thirty?"

"Sorry. No pretty blondes," the pathologist says. He wheels Butler's body away, slamming the door on the crypt. The ache in Goode's heart deepens, as if someone is leaning on his chest.

"Let's go," he says to Dawes, and she nods, putting away her notebook.

But he notices anger and frustration mingling in her expression. He feels it, too. The task force was breathing down their necks already, threatening to step in and take over the case. The spike in overdose victims was bad enough. Each one of those people had families with broken hearts, all pressuring the police to put an end to the crisis.

But now, with Butler's death, Internal Affairs would be involved, too. Everybody would be scrutinized, especially Goode and Dawes. That's why, over the next twenty-four hours, any clue, every clue—no matter how small—will become an obsession.

12

BETH

Tuesday Morning

The metronome, a tireless time bomb, ticks away the seconds of her life.

Click, click, CLICK.

"I can't do this," the boy huffs, banging the keyboard in a clumsy tangle of notes. "I hate it."

"Did you practice at all this week, Aiden?"

The boy doesn't answer, looking down at his hands, his dirty fingernails.

"I asked you a question. Did you practice at all this week? It doesn't seem as if you did."

He still doesn't answer, but she hears him sniff. In the sunlight streaming through her window, she sees the transparent tear glide down his cheek.

"There's no point if you don't practice," she says, trying to keep her voice calm, when she feels like crying herself. "If you want to get any better, you have to practice. When I was your age, I practiced for three hours every day. Sometimes four."

Three hours every day, minimum. It was true. She'd been devoted to her instrument and improving her talent. A very serious young girl, everyone said. So determined and disciplined. All Beth cared about was the piano back then.

"I got better things to do," Aiden says. "I hate it!"

He bangs the keyboard again, and she grabs his wrists. "Stop it!" she says, trying not to scream. Trying not to accidentally hurt him. "There's no reason to get frustrated. You just have to learn to make practice fun. *Pretend* that you're onstage in a great theater with hundreds of people watching me."

"What?" He squints at her.

"You. Hundreds of people watching *you*." Is she losing her mind?

"I don't want people watching me."

Then what the hell are you doing here?!

But she didn't like people watching her, either; she'd always had terrible stage fright. It makes her wonder what masochistic streak drove her to do this in the first place. She has a visceral worry that she's wasted every minute she's ever spent playing the piano, and it's basically all she's done with her life.

That's why becoming a mother had been so important to her. For a while, that dream made this—this studio, these kids, this monotonous life—bearable. Even pleasant sometimes. Now it feels as if she's in the middle of a suspension bridge, so terrified of falling, she can't take a step in either direction; she just has to reconcile herself to the fact she'll die here, petrified until her last breath.

Aiden is still sniffling. Poor kid. He's usually such an attitude case, but now he seems so much younger and vulnerable. She gets up, goes to her purse, and gives him a Kleenex.

"Please don't cry," she says. "But I want you to practice this week, okay? I want you to promise me. Even if it's only fifteen minutes a day, it'll help you improve. You'll enjoy it more when you get better, you'll see."

But he still won't look at her, sniffing and sullen. How many times was she going to have this conversation with them? Was it something about her? Could she do *nothing* right? She couldn't be a good wife. She knew Jay was miserable with her. Certainly not a good mother. Maybe she'd never even *be* a mother! She wasn't even a good musician. Her one CD had piffled out miserably seven years ago. All that money wasted on getting it produced, for nothing? Pathetic. And now she's even a bad teacher. She doesn't have the patience. Sitting with these kids, all the busy moms coming and going, so frazzled and condescending to the music teacher. It makes her feel like a hired nanny. She wonders if this was how Margaretta felt, being a housekeeper all her life.

She tries to keep the despair out of her voice. "Okay, let's try it one more time." She places Aiden's trembling fingers on the keyboard. But he snaps them away, quite viciously. She freezes. She can't touch him again. This is getting too rough. She could be reprimanded. Even fired. She looks at the clock. Still ten minutes left.

"All right, then," she says, folding her hands in her lap. "We'll just sit here and wait."

The metronome clatters. She turns it off. They sit in deafening silence.

13

JAY

Jay's in the kitchen making his post-run shake when the house phone rings. He rushes to answer, expecting a call from Karen. She sometimes phones the landline by mistake. But he sees the caller ID—OMNI PLAZA HOTEL—and backs away, letting the call go to the old machine, a clunker he brought home when they had to give up the production office last year. Another dent in his dignity. He grabs the blender as a woman's voice fills the room. Warm. Throaty.

"Uh...Beth...? Beth Crawford, right? I mean, of course it's you! I recognize your voice. This might freak you out a bit, but it's Cassie...Cassie O..."

He grabs his protein powder, opens the fridge for almond milk.

"It's been so long! Like, what? Ten, twelve years? Seriously, B, that's way too long."

Jay frowns, curious. He's never met any of Beth's old friends. There weren't any at their wedding. He had to insult his own frat buddies because she didn't have any bridesmaids to stand for her. When Jay pressed her about it, she said being around people from the past brought back too many memories of her parents. And he understood that. He's certainly never heard her mention this Cassie chick before. The woman continues, her voice unpolished and raspy.

"Anyway, I'm on my way to Monterey and I heard you moved out here, so I had to look you up."

41

Jay grabs a pomegranate from a bowl on the counter and the biggest Henckel from the knife block. He started adding fresh pomegranate to his shakes last year, pulverizing them in the blender. They were full of antioxidants and good for the prostate. A bitch to peel, but he's getting better at it. Saw how to do it on YouTube. He angles the knife over the center of the fruit, dragging the blade over it, opening a groove in the flesh that's so shallow, he doesn't even have to wash the blade.

"I'd love to see you, man...We should try to hook up or something. Go for a drink."

He pulls the two halves of the fruit apart, and they separate perfectly. It's a bloody mess scooping the seeds into the blender, red juices dripping, making him feel like he's Jack the Ripper disemboweling someone. He's never sure if the sharp twist in his stomach when he does it is disgust at the thought of hurting someone—or the desire to do it.

"Anyway, I'm in town for another couple days, but I'm a little hard to reach, so I'll try you later, k? Can't wait to see you! And, Beth? Great to hear your voice, even—"

But he hits the blender button and the message is lost beneath the whir of the blades.

14

BETH

Tuesday Afternoon

In the empty studio, Beth is on her cell, dabbing at her eyes with a crumpled tissue. She's between students, alone, pacing the room, her heels sounding like a metronome on the wood floor. She needs to find a way to snap out of this and get her day back on track. But her heart dips when she hears Jay's outgoing message.

"Hey, you've reached Jay Montgomery of BurMont Films. Leave your name and number and I'll get right back to you."

She hangs up. What was she going to say in a message? I'm jealous of one of my own eight-year-old students and I want to strangle the rest of them? He said he had a big meeting today. He doesn't need that stress right now. She's not even sure why she wanted to talk to him in the first place. They had such a bad night last night, and he never seemed interested in her music anyway—or her career. Cassie was one of the few people in the world who seemed to understand how she felt about music...

How strange. She's thought about Cassie so much since last night. She remembers that man on the phone, *Is Cassie there?* and a tremor runs through her.

15

GOODE

Tuesday Afternoon

The tan Ford had been in the back of a Walmart parking lot. Nobody even noticed it until after the store opened and the lot started filling up. Someone saw the passenger-side window, shattered into a silver spiderweb, pierced with a single hole. A young man buckled over sideways in the front seat, almost lifeless, but coughing, drenched with blood.

When Goode heard the man had been shot and a 9mm shell casing had been found at the scene, he was curious. An attempted homicide, only a few miles from the murders, with the same type of gun? Goode had to find out if the incidents were connected. He and Dawes watch as the team from the FSD traipse around the scene in white coveralls and booties, moving like astronauts on a strange planet.

"Name's Daniel Alvarez," says Dawes, consulting her notes. "Twenty-one. Critical condition. They've taken him to East L.A. It's a single shot, 9mm, basically point-blank. He's had some problems—assault, resisting—but not for a while. They found this beside him." She holds up an evidence bag containing a Taurus PT111, one of the cheapest semiautomatic pistols on the market. "Recently discharged."

"Is it registered to him?"

"No record of it."

He peers into the car, seeing the bloodstain on the seat. "Trafficking? Gangs?"

"Hard to say. Could be gang related. We found paraphernalia, too."

Goode's not surprised. This part of the world is mostly a middle-class neighborhood, but they still had their problems; the whole city seemed to. "Paraphernalia?"

"A broken pipe. Nothing too—"

But the roar of an engine drowns out her voice, and they turn to see a shiny black Dodge screech into the parking lot. A dark-haired young man climbs out from behind the wheel, moving quickly toward the scene. His eyes are glassy with tears, his jaw clenched.

"Detective Goode?"

He nods.

"Nico Alvarez." His voice is clogged with emotion. "I'm Danny's brother. They told me to talk to you. I think I know who did this. He was with a woman last night." The young man describes a white woman with long blond hair, carrying suitcases, who Alvarez picked up at a 7-Eleven not far from here. Goode doesn't have to flip back through his notes. He remembers the K-9 unit tracked a suspect from the rental house to the parking lot of a nearby 7-Eleven before losing the scent. Goode asks for more details—scars, height, what she was wearing.

"Jeans. Tank. She had lots of bracelets on her arms. I remember that." He rubs at his wrists. "I'm sorry, man. I gotta get to the hospital." He backs up toward his car. "This isn't his fault."

"Not saying it is."

"He's been keeping clean. Going to school. You gotta find this bitch."

"We will," Goode says.

16

JAY

Tuesday Afternoon

Jay wears a white towel around his waist as he scrolls through his phone. He sees two texts from Beth.

Please call!

It's urgent!

She left a voice mail, too. She probably wants to apologize for last night—or lay into him about Emily some more. Either way, he doesn't feel like talking to her. But he smiles when he sees Karen's number. He dials her back, sitting on the edge of the bed. He watches himself in the full-length mirror, his hair dripping. She picks up on the second ring.

"Howdy, pardner!" she chimes.

"Howdy, back." God, the smile on his face, it's so bright, reminding him of when he was younger. "Sorry, I was in the shower."

"No prob. I have a really important question for you."

"Shoot."

"Should I wear the blue suit or the red one?"

Jay laughs. "Really important, huh?"

"Everything's relative. So, what do you think?"

"The red one, no competition."

"Is that a personal preference?" There's a note of flirtation in her voice.

And in his. "All men like red. Come on, you look great in that suit. Trust me. You'll knock him dead."

"You're too kind," she says. "I'll see you at one. Don't be late!"

She hangs up without saying goodbye. They decided years ago life was too short for goodbyes. Nobody said goodbye on the phone in movies, did they? But it still takes a moment before he puts down the cell, as if he's holding a part of her and doesn't want to let go. He loved hearing her voice. Beth had a nervous edge in her voice lately, even when they weren't talking about money or work or starting a family. It was as if she was changing into someone new or was someone he hadn't known in the first place.

He looks at his reflection again, the toned arms, the hard-won six-pack, the shoulders and pecs. His towel falls open a bit on his thighs. He feels the pulse of warmth rushing there. He finally puts down the phone.

Has it really been over three months? Almost, anyway. He hadn't gone that long without sex since he was fourteen. Beth had never been the most hot-blooded woman he'd met, but he loved her, so he put up with it. He loved her, right? Things had been so full of hope when they met. She looked up to him. She enjoyed his energy, his confidence, and she made him feel good about himself. He was even able to curb his drinking a little bit, at least when they started talking about having kids last year.

But she was so desperate to start a family, it changed everything. He hadn't realized how desperate until life became all about the baby, ovulation, temperature taking. *Now, now, now.* He had no idea sex could feel like work. The last few months had been even more difficult. Whenever he tried to touch her, she'd practically flinch. Yes, the doctor said it would take time, but how much damn time? He's getting sick of it. It's bad enough he's having trouble raising the money for the film. He has to worry about a depressed wife, too?

It's going to work out. You're a brilliant producer. This is the one. Don't worry.

Maybe he should get himself off. That's what he needs. To relax before the meeting. The towel falls open farther and his hand slides down his abdomen. His thoughts travel to the meeting—and to Karen. They'd been partners for almost seven years, the longest "relationship" either of them had ever been in. More than twice as long as he'd known his own wife. "If this movie thing doesn't work out," they used to joke, "we could always get married." It made them both laugh.

The heat continues to work its way through him. He's just getting into it when his gaze travels to the framed photo on the nightstand.

Oh God...

The picture is of Beth and her parents, posing outside the big white house in the Hamptons. Beth was nineteen or twenty at the time, wearing a preppy yellow blouse, white shorts, her arms around her parents, both of them well dressed and slim; her father had a regal mustache, her mother, an elegant manner about her. Everyone smiled in the sunshine, the Great Gatsby mansion glowing behind them.

Every time he sees that photo, he feels a flash of regret, because he remembers how he teased Beth when they first starting dating, that her parents were even more stuck-up than his. To live outside of Philly and have a summer house in Southampton? "What? The Poconos not good enough for you?" he'd asked with a laugh. It seemed to make her uncomfortable. He thought it was because well-bred girls didn't like talking about money, but it wasn't just that. It was much worse.

A shiver runs through his body when he remembers making the gaffe shortly after they'd met. She'd been sweet when she told him the story, trying not to hurt his feelings for being so thoughtless. How she got through it, he wasn't sure. Losing both parents to a drunk driver one summer night? When you were just a college freshman? He'd been to the Hamptons. He knew what those roads were like. Narrow and winding, some of them so dense with tree cover, the GPS wouldn't work. It was like driving through an underground tunnel. Just deadly.

But he sees that big house in the background and his mind shifts on to another track. Money. How much would that place have been worth back then? Before the crash? Thirty million at least.

Maybe more. How had her parents gone through all that money?
If they'd just been more—

But he stops himself. His shoulders sag and he gives a dry laugh.
No way he feels like jerking off now. He closes the towel and
stands up to get dressed.

17

BETH

Tuesday Afternoon

In line at the Starbucks next to the academy, Beth tries to hold it together, waiting for her coffee, her eyes still red from crying, her throat aching and raw. She grabs a paper from the rack and skims the first page: BLOODBATH IN LAWRENCE HEIGHTS. She tries to read the article, tries to share in L.A.'s latest tragedy, but the words barely register, and finally she's next in line.

"Tall Pike Place Roast, please."

"Sure thing."

Beth pays for her coffee, still smiling. But it fades the second the girl turns away. God, she just needs Jay to call her back. To have someone, anyone, to talk to. She knows he had a big meeting today, but you'd think he'd pick up when she'd called and texted that many times. What if it was urgent? It *is* urgent. I'm dying here, she wants to tell him. And apparently no one cares. *Not even me.*

"Here you go," says the barista.

"Thanks." She forces another smile as she drops some nickels into the tip jar, hoping they make an impressive clatter. She takes her cup to the kiosk for milk and sugar. Her days of lattes are over. They're too expensive; even plain old coffee is an indulgence now.

She imagines Jay's going to pick up the tab at the meeting again today, trying to impress Commisso. He claims he splits all his business expenses with Karen, but Beth can't prove it. She doesn't go through his wallet. Maybe she should start. He and Karen are "such good friends." Have been for "so many years." Would there be hotel receipts? Flowers?

Stop! You're just torturing yourself!

A man walks up beside her, wearing a light beige suit and tie. He tries to fix his coffee but knocks the cup and it tips slightly, the fresh coffee burning his hand.

"Damn," he hisses, shaking out his fingers.

"You okay?"

"I think so," he says with a laugh. He grabs some napkins to wipe up the mess. As he turns, Beth sees his left arm is in a sling.

"Can I help you?" she asks.

"That would be great. Thanks."

"Say when." She picks up the sugar and begins to pour.

"When! Thanks."

She puts the jar down. But he's still staring at her.

"Um...I hate to be rude, but—aren't you Beth Crawford?"

She feels the cool weight of being recognized. It's something that never happens. She's so far from home.

"Yeah...Well, I used to be. It's Beth Montgomery now." She looks at him more closely. He's clean-shaven with dark hair, parted on the side, glasses. A welcome stranger, with kind eyes. But he doesn't look familiar. "Have we met?"

"Not officially, no. But I *thought* it was you! This is so incredible!"

"It is?"

"You're a pianist, right?"

Beth gives a dry laugh, feeling a dull kick in her heart. "Well, I used to be that, too," she says, going back to her cup.

"I knew it! I saw you play in Boston years ago. I forget the name of the place. I used to dabble a bit myself." He mimes playing a piano with his free hand. "But I was never good enough. Law school was next."

"I see. Well, wish I'd done that, too."

He laughs. "Don't even think about it. You're way too talented to waste your life behind a desk."

"Don't be too sure of that," she grumbles, half to herself.

"So—are you still playing?"

"Not professionally, no. I'm teaching now." Why is she telling a stranger that? She lets a moment of embarrassment pass. "The kids are great. It's very gratifying." She lets the lie sit between them. "But no, I don't perform anymore."

"That's too bad. Well, not bad that you're teaching! Your students are very lucky," he says, smiling.

"Thank you," she says, unable to muster another word.

Why hasn't she left yet? Why hasn't he? They're just standing there, staring at each other.

"Well, nice to meet you—um . . ."

"Tony," he says.

"Tony."

"You too."

She gives him one last smile and goes to walk away, but it's as if a string has connected them. She feels the knot around her heart loosen a bit and she hangs back, a natural smile broadening on her face.

"Can I just say—thank you?" she asks him.

"You already did."

"No, I mean—really. I needed this today. This new student of mine, barely eight, just played the ass off Tchaikovsky. She's so brilliant, I could be taking lessons from *her*. Then I had nothing but video gamers all morning. It was so damn depressing, I had to get out of there—and here you are, dusting off my ego. I can't thank you enough."

"My pleasure," he says. "I'd dust off your ego anytime."

18

JAY

Tuesday Afternoon

Cecconi's on Melrose is busy for lunch as usual, with fashionable tables clustered amid hedges as tall as fortress walls. Jay sits on the patio, a champagne bucket chilling beside him, an empty scotch glass on the table, his second since he got here. He wanted to arrive early and have a drink, to relax and get his bearings and to make sure they got a good table.

He senses movement and looks up from his phone. The hostess leads Karen Burns over. She does look fabulous in that red suit, which fits snugly around her curves, professional but sexy. She's not wearing a blouse underneath, and her long, dark hair is smooth and gleaming. Commisso follows behind. As usual, he wears expensive pinstripes and his hair is slicked back, his gold watch and tie clip glinting in the sun. A real estate developer Karen knew, he wanted to get into the film business, but he looks more like a gangster than anything else.

Jay juts out his hand. "*Ciao*, Vito, so good to see you again."

"Yeah, right," Commisso grunts, but he won't even meet Jay's eyes before sitting down.

Jay and Karen don't kiss cheeks, as they usually do. They're keeping it professional today. They have to focus.

Jay grabs the champagne out of the ice bucket and pastes a big smile on his face. "Call me optimistic," he says.

The waiter heads over to recite the day's specials, while another server pours the champagne. They all listen attentively, even though

Jay's already decided he'll order the spaghetti Bolognese, one of the cheapest dishes on the menu. Karen orders frugally, too—Margherita pizza—and they both skip the appetizers. Jay hates all this scrimping, but he doesn't have a choice, especially when Commisso orders carpaccio to start and Maine lobster at market price. Jay is adding up the tab in his mind.

Ka-ching.

He picks up his glass to make a toast, but Commisso ignores him, taking a swallow of champagne and turning to Karen. "Did you talk to Kate Hudson yet?"

Jay interjects with a laugh, making it sound good-natured. "Not yet, but it's incredible Milla's interested. She looked at the script and she loves it. We're in negotiations with her agent right now."

But as Jay smiles and tries to act charming, another voice runs through his head: *All we need is for you to give us the up-front money you promised, asshole. Then we can attach her, for chrissakes. You have no idea how this business works.*

Karen, meanwhile, has a hopeful lilt in her voice. "Actually, we're really lucky Milla's considering. She's perfect for the part, don't you think?"

Jay nods and sips his champagne as they dissect the actress's credits. He's drinking faster than the others and his glass is almost empty. He picks up the bottle and refills it, shifting his focus to the conversations around him. The laughter and the watches and the suits and the multi-million-dollar deals that must be getting made.

Ka-ching.

Don't worry, he tells himself. It's gonna work! Commisso will cave. If not today, then tomorrow. Just stay cool. So he sits there grinning like an idiot, trying to drink to take the edge off, when all he wants to do is jump down the bastard's throat and scream: *Give us the money, you prick! Stop dicking around!*

19

CASSIE

Cassie wipes her fingerprints off the hotel pen and adjusts the notepad on the dented pillow.

Dear Matt,

I had to go! Thanks for everything!

Love, Cathy xo

She can't risk him getting back early and finding her here. She hikes the red duffel bag over her shoulder, grabs the suitcase, and looks around, making sure she hasn't forgotten anything. The suite is littered with miniature bottles of vodka and empty snack bags. She didn't want to take a chance ordering room service and seeing anyone, so she subsisted on fare from the mini bar. Her gaze travels to the laptop, and she resists the urge to steal it, as much as she needs it. She doesn't want him reporting anything to the police. He has to remember this as a sweet dream, something that almost didn't happen.

The way the shooting at the house didn't happen.

Or the kid in the car.

She takes a deep breath and opens the door, peeking out. There's a housekeeping cart in the hallway and a maid vacuuming somewhere, but otherwise the corridor is empty. She hurries toward the elevators, letting the door lock behind her.

There had still been no news of the kid. Maybe she'd imagined it. Jesus, she wishes she had, but she knows it happened. She has muscle memory of that shove in her shoulder from the recoil, the passenger window shattering. She thinks she can still hear the ringing in her ears.

The elevator comes and it's packed; she gets on, not making eye contact with the other guests. She wheels her luggage through the busy lobby, averting her eyes from a security guard, and walks out into the sunshine. The airport shuttle bus is waiting out front. She'd timed her exit to catch it. There'd be no record of a shuttle ride, no cabdriver to identify her, fewer witnesses than a bus, just an anonymous shuttle that would take her on a route from here, through shopping malls and other hotels, to the airport. But she isn't going to the airport. She's waiting for a chance to call Beth again.

She climbs onto the shuttle with a family of tourists and a handful of business travelers, everyone so clean and fresh, she feels like a bag lady in comparison—even though she showered. Twice. She drops into a seat at the very back, her knee pumping with nerves.

She's used to living life on the edge, not knowing for sure where her next meal was coming from, her next high, sometimes not even sure where she'd sleep at night. But this is much worse. A churning in her mind, chewing down possibilities. It's too quiet! She needs her iPhone playlist, with everything from Ella Fitzgerald to Eminem, to take her mind off things. But there's only the murmur of strangers.

Bang!

She jumps. A man has simply unlocked the handle of his rolling suitcase—but it sounded like a gunshot to her. It reminds her of last night. She had no intention of shooting him. But then he drove to that dark parking lot, *Fucking bitch*, reaching out for her, his hand grabbing her breast. He wasn't afraid of her. He must've known she wouldn't shoot him.

She tried to push him off, but he grabbed something out of the back of his jeans. His arm curled, and she saw the silhouette of a gun. He struggled to aim it on her, but she grappled with his arm, their guns clanking against each other. She saw his wrist tense. Blue veins popping. What sounded like a grenade exploded next to her head. The window splintered beside her, like an instant winter's frost. Another shot. But this time she felt the vibration in her own arm, the ache in her shoulder. He toppled toward her, wailing in pain.

She tried to back out of the car, grappling with the duffel bag, reaching for the door handle, but he flailed for her and managed to grab the ends of the wig. If he'd actually caught her hair, she might not have gotten away. She yanked it back from him, clutched the door handle, and tumbled backward out of the car, the red bag rolling out with her. He was still sprawled sideways on the front seat, gasping, choking. She scrambled to her feet and yanked open the back door. Grabbed the suitcase. She slammed the door— *bang*—and ran off through the darkness. She heard that ringing in her ears, tasted smoke in her mouth. She waited in different chinks in the night, listening to sirens come and go, and to silence, wondering if she'd killed him.

20

GOODE

Tuesday Afternoon

In the living room of the rental house, everyone works methodically, blotting, measuring, collecting. Goode stands at the broken window with the blanket over it, looking back over his shoulder, analyzing the angles of shots. He's waiting to hear from the task force about Butler's field tapes. He needs access to them for the investigation, but they were tangling him in red tape. Maybe they didn't trust him anymore. Maybe they were already talking about taking him off the case.

He tries not to think about it. Tries to focus on the scene, the mayhem he remembers when he arrived last night.

Curtis Butler's body was behind the table, beneath a window. He must've been shot by someone on the couch. There's a large bloodstain on the carpet in front of it, and the blood type matches Squires's. They need to run DNA to be certain, but he's probably injured. Judging from the angle, Squires shot Jules Williams at the table, as well.

The floor squeaks as he walks down the hall to the large bloodstain outside the bedroom. Taking into account the angle, the spent shell, and Robert Hackett's body in front of the door when he arrived, Hackett must've been the one to shoot Arkell Mitchell from behind.

Why was Mitchell walking away from the room?

Then there's that ragged hole in the plywood door, another in the hallway where the bullet lodged into the wall. Someone was

58

inside the bedroom, shooting out, as well. They're running ballistics to be sure, but there's a good chance this gun is a match to the Alvarez shooting. It's the same caliber bullet, same general neighborhood, and both incidents occurred within hours of each other. For a Monday night, that was a lot of action—even in L.A.

He steps into the bedroom. Fingerprint powder blackens the walls and furniture, and the striped bottom sheet has been placed into evidence. Dawes, speaking with an investigator, notices him and comes over.

"They found this on the bedding." She hands him a small, clear tube. "Blond hair. But Forensics says it's a synthetic polymer."

Goode squints at the tube and the long fibers that resemble curled fishing line. "From a wig?"

"Exactly. She's in disguise for some reason. She and Squires must be worried she'll be recognized."

"Check Squires's associates again. We're probably not looking for a blonde anymore."

"I'm already on it. So, what do you think happened? The kid's brother didn't see anyone with her last night."

"They probably knew she had a better chance of getting a ride if she was alone."

"True. Maybe Squires was waiting for them somewhere. Alvarez pulled the gun when he realized he'd been set up. Gets shot in the process?"

"It's plausible. But it's sloppy. Risky." He lets out a long, frustrated sigh. Then he frowns, sniffing the air, a familiar scent tugging at his senses. He leans next to the light switch and inhales sharply. Beneath the scent of harsh resins in the fingerprint powder and stale gun smoke, he smells it. Windex. It's an ironically happy smell for Goode, reminding him of his grandmother cleaning house on Saturday mornings.

But as he glances down, he sees something on the floor behind the dresser. He eases the piece away from the wall and picks up a small round object about the size of a pea. He holds it up to the light, peering through a hole drilled in the center. It's a wooden bead.

21

BETH

Tuesday Evening

Beth stands in front of the bedroom mirror, blotting her red lipstick. She hasn't worn such a bright color in years, but she feels energized tonight. Bumping into that old fan of hers at Starbucks turned her whole day around. It was like kismet or something. To be so depressed about work, about Jay, about everything. *Your students are very lucky*, he'd said, with that warm smile on his face. Men still notice her sometimes. Even if Jay doesn't.

He's in the bathroom, shaving for the second time that day, going on about how they have to prepare for another grilling from his parents about the film tonight. That movie is all he thinks about anymore. She didn't tell him about Tony, but he'd noticed she was in good spirits when she got home.

"Somebody's in a good mood tonight," he said when she came in the door.

She just smiled and waltzed passed him without saying a word. Part of her wanted to tell him, to see if he'd get jealous. But what if he didn't even care? That would be the worst of it. To try to get her own husband jealous, only to realize it's impossible. Besides, it feels more exciting to keep it to herself.

What was his name again? Tony? Maybe he works in the area. Maybe I'll see him again.

Jay comes into the bedroom to put on a fresh shirt and finish a tumbler of scotch. She bristles, as if he can read her thoughts.

"Can you see the price tag on this?" she asks, turning to face

60

him, adjusting a blue floral scarf around her neck. "I want to wear it one more time before I bring it back."

He frowns at her. "But I thought you loved that scarf."

"I do. I do. But we can't afford a two-hundred-dollar scarf right now, and there's still time to get a refund."

"Beth, we can afford a two-hundred-dollar scarf."

"No, we can't."

"Then why did you buy it?"

She sighs forlornly, remembering the sick feeling in her stomach as she stood in Barneys justifying putting the scarf on her Visa card. "Because the girl said it brought out the blue in my eyes."

"It *does* bring out the blue in your eyes."

That horrible tension, where she both wanted—and didn't want—something, floods through her, as if *wanting* itself was a dangerous state. "I still have to take it back. I don't need it right now."

"Whatever," Jay mumbles, as if he can never win.

The house phone rings, and he goes to the nightstand to answer.

"Pay phone? Welcome to the nineties." His voice is sharp as he picks up. "Yeah?" But then it softens into a laugh. "Oh, right... Sorry, yeah. Just a sec." He turns the receiver toward his chest, wincing a bit. "I forgot to tell you. Some chick called for you today."

"Who?"

"Cassie Somebody."

Beth feels a small tremor. "Cassie—Ogilvy?"

"I guess, yeah. She said Cassie O."

There's a moment when Beth feels nothing. She can't even move, the way a lone doe might freeze after sensing a predator in the woods.

"You okay?" Jay asks, frowning.

She nods. *I think so.* She walks slowly across the room and takes the phone. She holds it for a moment before sitting down on the bed.

It can't be...

"Hello?"

A raspy voice calls out, "Hey, B!"

Beth can't believe it. It's her. There's no question. After all these years? "Cass?" she says, a quaver in her voice.

"Who else? This is so awesome! I can't believe I found you!" She seems breathless. Excited. Different. The same. "I'm not getting you at a bad time, am I?"

"No, no, not at all. Not really." Her heart squeezes in on itself. She's had this dream many times in her life. *This nightmare.* She knew it would happen. They were inseparable in college. That's what everyone said, like sisters.

As Jay goes into the bathroom to splash on cologne, Beth lowers her voice. "Cass, what's going on? Where are you?"

"I'm in town, man. I'm in L.A.! I got a gig coming up in Monterey. Thought I'd give you a buzz on my way through. Was that your husband who answered?"

"Yeah…" *In L.A.? Good God.* But then she can't help herself. She falls into her old pattern of worrying. "Is—is—everything okay?"

"Sure!"

"I mean, okay-okay."

Beth hears that smoky, inside laughter she knew so well. "I'm not in any trouble, if that's what you mean. I just wanted to say hi."

"Well…*hi.*" She tries to laugh. Tries to sound normal and happy. This can't be happening. Beth took Jay's name. How did Cassie find her? She thought she said goodbye to this girl ages ago. She's been trying to avoid her all these years. The drugs. The drinking. All these thoughts, pressing together, nothing making sense, like the din of an orchestra warming up. Then her old friend's voice cuts through, a cymbal crash that stops everything, and the curtain rises on the opening scene.

"Why don't we go for a drink or something? Catch up?"

"Now?"

"No, not now." Laughter again. "Like not this minute. I mean, later."

For the first time, Beth is happy about their plans for the night. "Sorry, Cass, I can't. We're on our way out to dinner with my in-laws."

"So—how about later, then?" Cassie presses. "I can't come out all this way and not see you, Beth. Come *on*. Don't break my heart."

She looks at Jay, who's dabbing gel in his hair in the bathroom, lifting up the little pieces, twisting them this way and that, absorbed with himself.

"I'm serious. I miss the hell out of you. Dude! Come on! For old times' sake. Pretty please?"

Beth thinks about it. What choice does she have? Cass never could take no for an answer.

"Sure," she says finally, but it feels as if she's just stepped off a cliff. She lowers her voice and says, "It'll give me a good reason to leave early."

Cassie laughs. "Awesome! How about this place called Foot-sie's? You know it?"

"I can find it."

"Great! Say ten-ish?"

"Yeah, that should work."

"Excellent! Can't wait. See ya then! Love you!"

"Love you—too."

Beth hangs up, but she doesn't move from the bed. She lets the phone fall into her lap.

"Blast from the past?" Jay comes into the bedroom, buttoning his cuffs.

"Yeah. An old friend of mine."

"Old friend?" He raises his eyebrows at her.

She shakes her head as if to clear it and stands up. "Yeah, freshman year at college, we shared a dorm room," she says, still stunned. "She was in the vocal program. Such a talented singer. Jazz mostly. Some people thought she sounded like Amy Winehouse. Are you sure I never told you about her? Cassie Ogilvy?"

"Nah. I'd remember that name. Any relation to the advertising people? Ogilvy. They're huge."

"Not that I know of. She never talked about that, anyway. I don't think she was very well off at all. She was there on a scholarship. Dropped out after the first year. She was *so* irresponsible. A real party girl." She motions to the photo of the beautiful white mansion on landscaped grounds, the ocean in the background. "She spent that last summer with us in Southampton. God, how long ago was that? Twelve years, I guess. We had a fight that summer; I don't even remember what it was about. We lost touch after that."

I lost touch after that.

Beth has braced herself for this for years, Cassie coming back into her life, but now that it's happened, she's not sure how it makes her feel. Stripped. Vulnerable. But not alone anymore.

"To tell you the truth, I'm surprised she's still alive."

Jay gives a dark laugh. "What?"

"Nothing," she says. "But I really wish you hadn't answered."

"How come?"

She sighs heavily. "There are some people you just want to forget."

22

CASSIE

Monday Night

The blue suitcase sits open on the bed as Cassie throws in crumpled T-shirts, jeans, and flimsy underthings. Her blond wig sits on the dresser, next to the gun. She hasn't turned on a lamp—they might be watching the house—so she works in the light of the setting sun. She's already packed Rick's bag, with everything he needs, in the SUV, but she has to finish her things, too.

No hos, he'd told her. Fucking ridiculous. *No hos.*

"They're here," Bobby says, from the living room. "Three of them."

She closes the suitcase, snapping the locks, setting it on the floor.

"Stay cool!" Rick barks down to her.

"I *am* cool," she mumbles.

She goes to the edge of the bed, resting the gun on her thighs. She takes a deep breath. Stares at the partly opened door. Even now, she didn't want to close that door. Rick told her as long as she didn't make a sound, it would be okay. Probably trying to make up for their fight.

She hears footfalls from outside. A dull knocking. The front door opens and the house wheezes with the presence of new bodies. She hears the men in the living room. Mumbled voices. Thumping. Footsteps.

She sits with her back straight, staring at the door, hands sweating as they grip the gun. All she hears are soft *clicks* of the road case being opened and the *clunk* of the money counter being set up.

The sun sets completely and the amber glow on the wall turns dusky blue. The bedroom is stifling on the hot summer night. The window doesn't open, and the AC hasn't worked since they got here. Her back starts to ache from sitting in the same position.

How much longer would they be?

A drop of sweat makes its way down her forehead, into her brow, and she wipes it with the back of her hand, careful to keep the gun away from her face. But she hears a sharp clatter, not from the living room, but from her feet. In a panic, she looks down to see a wooden bead bounce across the floor and hit the door.

"Somebody back there?" A stranger's voice, deep, threatening.

"Nobody," says Rick.

She hears creaking from the hallway, and Rick's voice again.

"I said, nobody's there."

Her heart pounds. The footsteps get closer. She squeezes the gun handle, lifting it toward the door.

Stay cool.

Suddenly, the world is nothing but thunder and banging. The door jolts in its frame as a ragged hole explodes in the wood. She's not fully aware of pulling the trigger, only the numbness in her shoulder from the recoil. She separates the din of her ringing eardrums from the gunshots in the living room. It feels like a war zone: bullets blasting, glass crashing, the walls vibrating. She has to get out of here. She doesn't want to die. She stumbles to the window and tries opening it, but it's just a panicked instinct. She knows it's painted shut.

Another blast.

Then another.

Then...nothing.

She waits.

Silence.

Nothing but the smell of gun smoke hanging gray in the air.

She creeps to the door and listens. After a moment, she peers out into the hall. She flinches when she sees a body on the floor in front of her, the back of his white T-shirt blooming crimson, everything else about him absolutely still. She leans out further. Sees Bobby on the floor by the door, unmoving, covered in blood. Bobby's the only one who had a clear shot of the guy; he must've shot him to protect her. *Fuck.* She sees the lifeless, bloody hand of someone leaning across the table. But there were three coming. Is the other one dead, too? Or is he waiting for her?

And where's Rick?

Still holding the gun, warm to her touch, she creeps into the hallway, stepping over the body. She slides against the wall, the floorboards creaking as she moves toward the carnage. She smells the metallic smoke that hovers in the air, notices a fine mist of white powder settling in the light from an overturned lamp.

Then she sees them.

One lying face forward on the table. Bobby in front of the door. Another big guy down by the wall. Rick is lifeless, too, fallen between the couch and the coffee table, his tank top and arms so covered in blood, he looks splashed with red paint. She holds her breath for a moment, then feels something she wasn't expecting.

Relief.

The cool rush of relief.

She exhales for what seems like the first time in weeks.

Then she sees the money. Rolls on the coffee table, splattered with blood, much more in the red duffel bag on the floor. She works so quickly, she can barely see her hands moving in the dimness. She grabs all the loose cash she can and stuffs it back into the duffel, hiking it over her shoulder. It's damn heavy, but she can manage. She stumbles clumsily into the hall, nearly tripping on the body because she's afraid to look down. She hurries into the bedroom for her things. She steps over the corpse one last time. At the very last second, she remembers: fingerprints. And turns back to wipe the bedroom doorknob with the hem of her top. She stumbles into the kitchen, then shoulders open the screen door. It slams behind her as she hears the first siren in the night.

23

BETH

The main dining room of the Rosedale Park Country Club over-looks the landscaped gardens where Beth and Jay posed for their wedding pictures. She remembers feeling giddy on champagne that night, her cheeks aching from smiling, her voice hoarse from meeting Jay's family and friends. It had been so romantic. A happy new beginning for her, with a new family, a new life. But her focus shifts and she sees her reflection in the window, like a ghost of herself, dissolving into the darkness.

"So what does he do, exactly? This Italian fellow," Jay's mother asks, cutting her steak.

Ellen Montgomery is in her early sixties, white hair, a Chanel suit, her perfume cloying around her in a little cloud. She switches the fork to her other hand before taking a nibble of the steak. It's an old-fashioned way to eat—not even the most cosmopolitan. But it's one of the things she liked about Jay when they first met: he had good table manners. It was a silly thing, but it said a lot about how a person was raised.

"He's an investor," Jay says in the tone of voice he uses when he's trying to con somebody. Light. Casual. He had a couple scotches at home, and more here, along with the wine; he's getting overconfident. "He made a fortune in real estate. Now he wants to get into the business. He's gonna put up some of the money. In this case, two million. And that triggers the whole rest of the operation. We can start making offers. Writing checks. That kind of thing."

"*Start?*" Jay's father asks with a sarcastic laugh. John Montgomery is fit, wearing a navy suit and tie, with the same shade of white hair as his wife's, but brushed back. Beth has not seen his hair change from that stiff wave in all the time she's known him, regardless of the occasion or the weather. "How long does it take before people in your business actually start getting paid?"

"It might be slow, Dad. But when it happens, it's big. And this time it's gonna be huge."

Beth sees the phony smile on her husband's face. The eagerness to please his parents is transparent, but it's an impossible task with them. She doesn't even know why he tries.

"Did I tell you we're in talks with Milla Jovovich right now?"

"Is she the one with the orphans?" Ellen asks.

"You're thinking of Angelina Jolie."

"Has she signed a contract yet?"

"Dad, I said we're *in talks*. That means we're negotiating with her agent."

"Why do you act as if *negotiating* is a good thing?"

"Because that's the way the business works!" He gives a forced laugh. "Look, I'll send you the deal memo, okay? You can see what I mean. I'd love your opinion on the budget, too."

Ellen turns to Beth. "Business, business," she whispers. "It's always business with boys, isn't it?" She taps her mouth in a mock yawn.

Beth tries to smile, sipping her wine.

"You seem a little quiet tonight, dear. Are you feeling all right?"

"Of course. I'm fine, thanks." At the best of times, Beth feels like an outsider with her in-laws, but she's so nervous about seeing Cassie, it's even worse tonight. She's barely been able to talk. She has no idea what to expect. Cass was always so unpredictable, always getting into trouble. Getting *her* into trouble, too.

"Are you sure?"

"Absolutely."

"Just don't force anything, darling. If it's not meant to be, it's not meant to be. It doesn't matter to us if you have children. We have plenty of—"

"Ellen." Beth puts down her wineglass, more forcefully than she expected, and it *clinks* the side of her plate. Jay glances over, frowning. *Why does she have to bring that up again?* She did it every time they got together. "Just don't worry about it, okay? I said I'm fine. We both are."

"Yes, yes, of course you are." A few silent slices of Ellen's steak. The men are still talking contracts, but Jay glances over again, as if checking up on her. "You know I was out with a friend the other day who went to Bryn Mawr. Didn't you go there?"

"No, Mom," Jay says. Beth doesn't know if she's grateful or pissed off that he's been eavesdropping. "She grew *up* in Bryn Mawr. The town. She went to college in Boston. The New England Institute of Music. Remember?" He gives Beth a wink. "It's the best music school in the country."

"What about Juilliard?" his father asks.

Beth tries not to roll her eyes. Every time her education comes up, Jay reminds his folks, *Best music school in the country*, and every time, one of them says, *Better than Juilliard?*

Jay is always forced to add, "Well, it's *one* of the best."

"That's what they told us, anyway!" Beth says, trying to laugh.

"At any rate, this friend of mine," Ellen continues, "she's from Philadelphia. And *she* went to Bryn Mawr. Do you know her by any chance? Celia Barnes?"

"No, I don't think so," Beth says.

"She doesn't know everybody, Mom."

"No, I suppose not. Good family. Anyway, I had lunch with her last week and we were talking about this time I visited her for homecoming. I had to remember that little limerick, or whatever it was, for all the stops along the Main Line."

The Main Line was the name for a collection of wealthy villages along the Pennsylvania Railroad that once served as grand country estates for Philadelphia's richest old-money families. The stops were distanced exactly two minutes apart on the railroad tracks, and locals created a mnemonic device to remember all the names.

"What was it again?" Ellen asks, squinting. "Old maids never wed and...hmmm?"

"Old maids never wed and have babies," Beth says in a dull monotone.

Is that why she brought it up? Beth thinks. *Because it's about babies?* She feels a stab in her heart, so sharp and painful it's as if Ellen leaned over the table and wedged her steak knife between Beth's ribs.

"Right! How does it go again? Old was for Overbrook. Maids was for Merion. Never was for Narberth. But what was—"

"Wynnewood, Ardmore, Haverford, and Bryn Mawr," Beth says. "Wed and have babies."

"Oh, that's right! I've got to tell Celia. She'll get a kick out of it. She couldn't remember it either."

Almost as if Ellen is testing her, Beth goes on. "Really vicious retrievers snap willingly."

"Pardon me?"

"It's not finished. There are about ten other towns. Really for Rosemont. Vicious for Villa Nova. Retrievers for Radnor..."

Jay and his father are looking over now.

"Snap for St. David's. Willingly for—"

"Beth," Jay says, with a little laugh. "I think she gets it."

"Really?" There's a sarcastic note in Beth's voice as she regards her mother-in-law. "Do you get it?"

Ellen just gives her a cold smile. Jay goes back to his conversation with his father, but glances over at Beth, clenching his jaw as if to say, *Take it easy.* Beth sighs and looks at her watch. As nervous as she is about seeing Cass, she can't take it anymore. She needs a few minutes to decompress by herself.

"I'm sorry," she says, dabbing the corners of her lips with her napkin. "I really should go."

"Oh, that's right. You're meeting an old friend, are you?"

"Yes. From college." Beth grabs her purse and stands up from the table; the men stand up, too. Jay glares at her for leaving early, but she knows he won't make a scene.

"Well, have a nice time," Ellen says. "I love that scarf, by the way. Is it new?"

"Yes, it is, thank you."

Ellen places her hand next to her mouth in a mock whisper. "You might want to sneak to the ladies' room first. The tag is showing, dear."

24

Boston, Twelve Years Ago

Cassie is wasted again. She leans on Beth's shoulder, her whole body weight pressed against Beth as they squeeze through a crowded corridor, black light making everything glow, music blaring behind them. Cassie's skirt is so short, the gauntlet of men seem not just entitled to stare, but invited to do it. They glance at Beth, too, but it makes her uncomfortable. Cassie is like a different species. She has instincts that Beth doesn't have. Even drunk out of her mind, she uses her sexuality to get attention. She leans over, yelling in Beth's ear to be heard.

"I need a pit stop!" she announces.

"Can't you wait? We have to get back." They couldn't miss curfew again. But Cassie has already pulled away. She zigzags toward the women's washroom. Black leather skirt barely covering her ass, fishnets ripped, cleavage on display. She's a walking cliché.

Beth follows her into the dank room. There's a small line of women waiting, but one stall is broken and there's no door. Cassie stumbles into the stall, lifts her skirt, drops the fishnets. Beth blocks the doorway, looking over her shoulder, giving Cass at least some privacy. There are a couple of women doing lines on the edge of the counter, others fixing their hair in front of the mirror, but nobody looks at them. Nobody cares.

Cassie flushes, stands up. But she doesn't pull up her stockings. She's standing there, her pussy on display, the fishnets digging into her thighs. She had no shame in the dorm either, always walking around nude. It had taken only two days before Cassie confessed to wondering if she was bisexual. Now Cassie hooks her hand around the back of Beth's neck and drags her in, stopping just before their lips meet, her breath smelling like beer.

Beth lurches back. "Cassie—you're drunk."

"Not that drunk," she says with a laugh.

It wouldn't be the last time Cassie tried to come on to her. But it never worked. Beth was perhaps the only person Cassie Ogilvy couldn't seduce.

25

BETH

Tuesday Night

She pulls up outside Footsie's, a low brick building surrounded by discount stores closed for the night. A cringe works its way up her spine as she surveys the bar. It looks like just the sort of dive Cassie loved going to. Gritty. Rough. The last time she'd been in a place like this was with Cassie herself.

Why are her memories of that time so clear? Like photographs laid out on a table.

Cassie on her single bed in the dorm room, laughing.

Sitting around the turquoise pool in Southampton, drinking wine.

Dancing in a club, mascara smeared.

Cassie with her microphone. Beth at her keyboard.

Music was everywhere back then. It was how they connected. On a soul level, drawn to each other through their love of music.

But this isn't good, Cassie showing up like this. What happens if she meets Jay? Beth knows she can't trust her old friend. Back in college, she seduced every guy Beth was remotely interested in. She isn't sure she can trust Jay either, not with a woman like Cass.

Stop it. This is just drinks with an old friend. Cassie's probably changed, grown up a bit. She's just being paranoid.

She takes a deep breath and grabs her purse. She twists the rearview to freshen her lipstick. That's when she sees the scarf

around her throat—and the little tag poking through the silk. She
unties it and shoves it into her purse.

The lighting is dim, billiard balls echoing, the smell of stale beer
thick in the air.

"Hey, B!"

Beth squints in the darkness and sees a figure at a table near the
back. The swing of an arm. "Over here!"

Beth walks toward the woman with long, wild dark hair. Something about the stubborn tilt of her head is so familiar, she'd
recognize Cassie anywhere—even in silhouette.

"You look great, man!" Cassie says, engulfing Beth in a hug.
Feeling her exotic curves is like stepping back through time. She
still smells the same, too, like booze and cigarettes and musky perfume. "Grown-up life must agree with you."

"Oh, thank you," Beth says, genuinely shy. "But *you're* the
one who looks great. You haven't changed a bit. You're still gor-
geous!"

Cassie just shrugs off the compliment. "Forget it. I'm a wreck.
Got up on the wrong side of the bed, like, five years ago. Haven't
slept since."

Beth laughs, but she's more than a little surprised her old friend
looks so good, especially considering she still "lived hard," judging from the smudged black eyeliner, leather jacket, and tight
jeans. Not to mention the empty beer bottles and shot glasses lined
up on the table. But her olive skin is clear, full lips frame her perfect white teeth, and if she's gained a pound, it's in all the right
places. Maybe there are a couple of new lines around her big green
eyes, but no worse than Beth's. Otherwise she *seems* the same. Still
entirely "Cassie." Beth is inwardly stunned. She feels so different
than she did back then, the preppy blonde with a ponytail, now a
married music teacher feeling middle-aged.

"Siddown, siddown," Cassie says, moving a blue suitcase under
the table. She shoves a red duffel bag onto the empty seat beside
her and plops her big black purse, full of buckles and fringe, on

top of it. She raises her hand for the waiter, who heads over, thumping in combat boots. His head is shaved, his neck tattooed, gold hoops in his ears.

"A glass of sauvignon blanc, please," says Beth.

"Pinot okay?"

"Fine."

"And another round for me."

"Sure thing." The waiter collects her empties and heads off.

"Guess no use specifying the vintage in a place like this, right?" she whispers.

"Probably not," Beth says, laughing. The girl always did know how to make her laugh.

"Sorry to drag you out this way. But fuckin' L.A. They say you need a car, but you don't really believe it till you get here."

"Yes—you definitely need a car." Beth smiles, studying her old friend like a movie come to life. Despite the tension of the night and dinner and Ellen, despite everything, Beth feels more relaxed right now than she's been in months. Maybe years. She remembers now why they became friends in the first place. It wasn't just that they were thrown together in that tiny dorm room— Beth had been used to new roommates—and it wasn't just that Cassie was the first person she'd ever known who loved music as much as she did, though that was part of it. What really amazed Beth was Cassie's way with people. She was so comfortable with everyone, so at ease in her own skin, treating everyone the same: custodians, the school dean, club owners, teachers, drug dealers. Waiters. She had no filters. No censors or shame. It's why she was such a brilliant performer. Beth always admired that about her. How she could truly be herself anywhere, anytime.

"I can't believe I found you," Cass says. "I checked Facebook for you, like, a million times over the years."

"Sorry. I never got the hang of it." She pauses, curious. "So, how *did* you find me?"

"I Googled you. Saw you on that school's website."

"Ah..." Beth remembers her boss insisting they hyphenate her name, *Beth Crawford-Montgomery*, so they could put the shot of the album cover next to her bio. But then she wonders aloud, "Okay, but how did you get my *home* number?"

"Wasn't hard. I called that Steinberg place and conned them."

"I see." Beth is secretly annoyed they'd give out personal contact information, but she also knows how convincing Cassie can be.

The waiter brings their drinks and the women *clink*, as they had countless times before.

"So—you decided to become a teacher, huh?"

"Yeah," Beth says, trying to smile.

"Bit the bullet?"

"I know, I said I never would, but I love it. It's a good school. Great kids." Beth has choked down the lie so many times, it has somehow come to seem like the truth.

"So you're not playing at all anymore?"

"Not really, no."

"That sucks. You should be playing. You're brilliant. *The Lotus Flower* was amazing, by the way. I downloaded it."

"You're kidding? You and about two other people. How did you even *know* about it?"

"I told you. I look you up every now and again. Saw you released it. So what happened? Why'd you give it up?"

Beth stares at her a moment. *What happened?* What a stupid question.

"Nothing! That's what happened. Nothing. I had to move on." She wants to change the subject. It's too painful. Cassie wouldn't understand. She takes a sip of wine and brings lightness to her voice. "So, what about you? You said you've got a gig coming up in Monterey?"

Even as Beth asks it, she feels a stab of envy. Naturally Cassie's career would turn out so much better than her own. She didn't have the same fears Beth had. Beth loved—and hated—that about her friend since the day they met.

"Not a big deal," Cassie says, shrugging. "Just some little dive. Fake it till you make it, right?"

Beth smiles at the mention of the old motto. Jay uses it, too. She'd forgotten it was one of Cassie's favorites. How strange. Jay would probably love her. They'd get along. They both love drinking and partying so much. Her heart clenches as Cassie keeps talking, never at a loss for words.

"This friend of mine's picking me up. We're gonna head out tonight. Get some rehearsing done. It's been a while." She touches her throat and makes an off-key sound. "She should be here any minute. I can't wait for you to meet her. I've told her all about you."

"That's sweet." Beth doesn't know if she's relieved, or disappointed, that they were being joined by someone. "So? What about you? How are you doing?"

"I'm great."

"No, I mean—*really*. How are you feeling?" Beth reaches out, almost putting her hand on Cassie's, but stopping at the last moment.

"You mean, am I taking my meds?" She widens her eyes dramatically.

"Don't put it like that."

"It's what you meant, right?"

"I just care about you, Cass, that's all. I just want to make sure you're okay."

"Of course. Don't I look okay? My insurance ran out, so I'm self-medicating now. Otherwise, it's all good."

"You're not!" Beth fears the worst. Heroin. Opioids. Meth.

"Not the hard stuff!" Cassie laughs, holding up her drink. "I'm too old for that shit. *And* too smart. Look, I'm fine. Seriously. How about you? You got married, I see."

"Yeah, almost three years ago now."

"Noticed I didn't get an invitation to the wedding." She grins, teasing.

"I would've loved to invite you, but it was just family. Very small."

"Any kids?"

Beth refrains from touching her stomach, a dead giveaway. "No, not yet. You?"

Cassie almost chokes on her beer. "God, no!" And Beth envies her loose attachment to family. "Hooked up with a roadie for a while. But it's over. Nasty dude."

Beth knows that when Cassie Ogilvy called someone a nasty dude, you could believe her. "You always did like roadies."

"What can I say? I have a soft spot for stoners with great arms and tattoos. Who else do you meet playing bars, anyway? Or street corners."

"No!" Beth gasps.

"Kidding! About the street corners, anyway." She raps the wooden table. "Listen, I should call Lily. Find out what's up. She should be here by now. Where are the phones around here?" She twists in her seat. "I lost my damn cell."

"Here, use mine." Beth reaches in her purse for her phone. She can't help but offer her friend a favor.

"Thanks, man." Cassie gets out her wallet, messy and overstuffed as it always was. Pictures, receipts, and scraps of paper spill out. As she rifles through the mess, Beth notices her wrists are still layered with mismatched bracelets, some of them familiar from the old days. Beneath the leather, the silver, and beads, she catches a glimpse of the faint slashes on Cassie's wrists; the scars aren't as clear as they were when the girls were in college, pale ghosts of themselves. If Beth didn't know what to look for, she may never have seen them. But like all bad memories, they would never fade completely.

"Remember that?" Cassie tosses a photo to her. Beth picks it up and sees the two of them standing outside the big white summer house. The ache in her heart is palpable; she'd forgotten they all took pictures that day.

Meanwhile, Cassie finds a chit of paper and taps the screen. She blocks one ear as she speaks. "Lily? Hey, it's me...Where are you? Why is it so loud?"

The shot is of Beth and Cassie, standing with their arms around each other. Cassie's in a scruffy T-shirt and shredded jeans, that familiar old knapsack on the ground at her feet; Beth wears a crisp yellow blouse and white shorts, her hair in a ponytail. The girls looked so different from each other—even back then. She thought that day would be the last time she saw her old friend.

"No, no, I checked out already...Really...?"

Her friend's voice fades as the image pulls Beth into its own world, away from the sound of pool tables and clanking beer bottles. Instead she hears the breakers pounding on the beach outside, the ocean so rough they couldn't even swim without getting sand thrown into their faces from the waves. She hears the rising notes of her own fingers on the keyboard of the grand piano in the conservatory, can even smell the lawn and the sea and lemon oil on antiques. These were memories she'd been afraid to relive for years, yet here they all were.

She remembers those long summer nights in the big yellow bedroom overlooking the ocean, while she and Cass drank and smoked and talked about their music careers. It was so different from her bedroom in Bryn Mawr, with its shelves full of untouched, collectible dolls. She was allowed to play with them if she wanted to, but she never did. She never even took them out of their boxes. They were for looking at and keeping safe.

But life was different at the summer house. Instead of plastic dolls in their packages, the shelves were crammed with old, musty-smelling stuffed animals, some missing eyeballs or tails, leaning this way and that, as if they were all drunk, the way the girls were that summer. Beth had never drunk so much as she did that year with Cass. Cassie was always the one to instigate things, dragging the madness long into the night, until the clubs closed or Beth was so tired she insisted they go home. Cass was usually hungover in the morning, sleeping past noon most days. But Beth had always been an early riser, so there'd be long, quiet talks in the kitchen before Cass woke up.

"You've got to expect some problems that way, Beth. Growing up in foster care presents a lot of challenges. Especially if there's been some form of abuse. It's heartbreaking, really..."

Beth looks over at her old friend, still on the phone—that crooked smile, that wild hair—and she's surprised by the fondness she feels.

"Nah, really, Lil, no problem...Yeah, okay, see ya then...For sure...Love ya, too." She hangs up and looks over at Beth. "Shit. Now she can't make it till Friday."

Beth feels pressure in her throat. *Don't say it. Don't say it.* But she feels trapped. "You have a place to stay until then?"

Cassie gives a little shrug. "I'll think of something. I always do."

26

RICK

Tuesday Night

The only light in the dingy motel room is the shifting haze of the television. Rick sits propped up in bed, breathing heavily, trying to ignore the searing pain radiating from his shoulder. He takes a swig from the whiskey bottle.

The motel room is fetid with the smell of mildew and dust. And something else, a sickly smell. He knows it's coming from the wounds, two of them, straight into his left shoulder, red veins mapping outward, blood and pus oozing around the dressing. He knew gauze wouldn't stanch the bleeding. He'd gone through this before, years ago, so he bought gel patches instead, and taped gauze over them. But even with the air-conditioning on, he's sweating and jittery, his head pounding. Were the wounds getting infected? Must be. He knows he should get to a hospital, but he can barely get out of bed. The cops would be on him within minutes anyway, especially now that a narc was killed. He grits his teeth, riding out the rage. How could he be so stupid? Letting himself get set up like that.

It's been twenty-four hours since the "bloodbath," and the story has moved farther down into the newscast. Without any breaks in the case, the world has new catastrophes to consider. A terrible accident on a freeway. A missing child. A suspected gang member shot in his car. But he can't move on so easily. He needs that money. He has to find Cassie. She must know he's alive. Why isn't she looking for him? She has the number for the burner phone he's using. Why hasn't she called?

He tries to focus on every detail after the shooting. He remembers hearing the back door slam at the house, sounding like another gunshot. It took a moment before he realized where he was. The back of his head seared with pain, and he thought he'd taken a bullet there, too. But it was just a large, sore lump, not even bleeding. He must've been thrown back into the wall after the first shot and gotten knocked out.

Then he heard sirens approaching, distant but getting closer. He struggled to his feet, his shoulder and chest aching so badly, he could barely breathe. He saw Jules hunched over the table. Bobby down by the door. The guy with the goatee on the other side of the room. *Butler.* He was the narc. Rick saw his picture on the news.

He remembers glancing around for the red duffel bag—but the money was gone.

He grabbed as much of the junk as he could, dragging the black case with his good arm. There was another body in the hallway outside the bedroom. A bullet hole in the door. Worried about Cassie, he checked the room—but it was empty. He ripped the top sheet off the bed and held it against the blood oozing from his shoulder. He limped into the kitchen, pushed open the screen door.

"Cass?" he hissed into the night. She'd been angry at him after their argument. Maybe she was hiding somewhere. "Cass?"

But there was no sign of her. By the time he stumbled to the black SUV parked in an alley behind the yard, the sirens were right out front, car doors slamming. He pulled away into the darkness and spent the next two hours scouring the streets for her. He wasn't worried about the car being identified. An uncle of Bobby's had died recently and left the car to him in the will. As long as they didn't get stopped for a busted taillight or speeding, and the cops learned that Bobby hadn't changed the registration yet, they'd be fine. He was more concerned about Cass. He kept checking his phone, expecting her to call—but she didn't.

He'd been bleeding so badly, he had to stop at an all-night drugstore for first aid supplies, covering the stains by slinging his denim jacket over his shoulder. After that, he needed a place to stay. Two motel managers had turned him away because he didn't have a credit card. But the third place, a run-down, sunbaked dump called the Seahorse Motel, accepted a cash deposit. Thank God he had enough for that.

When he let himself into the dingy room, the first thing he did was turn on the news. The next, he finished half a bottle of whiskey. Then he tended to his wounds. He was numb with shock. The only way he knew one of the bullets had gone right through him was the bloodstain above his shoulder blade when he turned around to check. He could see the slug of the other one, so he dug it out with trembling fingers and his pocketknife, then bandaged himself up. He was even lucid enough to be able to track down that friend of hers, the one who played the piano. *"Is Cassie there?"*

"Who?"

She sounded so shocked and confused, as if she'd never even known a person named Cassie. He wonders if Cassie lied about that, too.

Then he got drunk, waiting for her to call.

Are you okay, baby? Where are you? I've got the money.

But his phone was silent. Cassie's phone was useless, too, without its SIM card. But at least he'd been able to find her friend. He didn't have her home address yet, but it was only a matter of time.

He woke early the next morning. Was able to move around and do everything he had to. Shave. Change his hair. He'd even been able to leave the motel and function for a couple of hours.

But he must've been running on adrenaline, because the pain is much worse now than it was earlier in the day. *Much worse.* It feels like a really bad flu settling in. Day one, you feel like shit, but you can deal with it. Day two, you feel like you're going to die. By day three, you actually want to.

The room starts to spin. He feels nauseous. He slams the bottle down and stumbles to the dingy bathroom, throwing up.

Fuck.

He grabs a towel, wipes his face. His head pounds and there's a ringing in his ears. A concussion maybe? From his head hitting the wall? He got concussed after a fight a few years ago. It felt like this...

There is one blessing to the pain: it takes the edge off his rage. Because every time he thinks of Cassie running out on him, his blood starts pumping and he has to force himself to breathe deeply, trying to relax.

He stumbles to the nightstand, grabbing a small vial, digging white powder out with his yellowed pinky nail. He snorts it, lies down, and waits for the ache to subside, the room to stop spinning.

He can't stay here much longer. There are probably three bounties on his head right now. One from the cops, one from Jules's posse, and one from his supplier in Florida. What if they think he set them up and took the money himself? Betrayal was the worst crime in this business. It didn't stem from any kind of honor; it was all about optics. He owed them money for the deal, two hundred and fifty grand. How would it look if they let it go? They couldn't—and they wouldn't. He needs to get that money back. He has to find Cass or they'll both be dead.

27

JAY

Tuesday Night

Jay is at the fridge, wearing his robe, drinking orange juice from the carton, when Beth and Cassie stumble in the door, shoes and luggage thumping. The clock on the wall reads 1:35 a.m. He's surprised; Beth hasn't been up past midnight in a year.

He wears boxers, but the robe hangs open, and he quickly yanks it closed, not expecting company. Beth didn't even text she was bringing anyone home. The girl hangs off Beth's shoulder, her hair disheveled, her makeup smeared. She's exotically beautiful, everything oversized and lush: eyes, lips, breasts. She can't possibly be wearing a bra, he thinks as she stumbles and laughs, a tight T-shirt visible beneath her black leather jacket, her jeans faded and frayed. Jay just can't picture Beth hanging out with a chick like this. Yet here they were, together again.

"Jay, I'd like you to meet my old friend Cassie Ogilvy."

Jay extends his hand, and it takes a moment for Cassie to focus on it. When she does, her skin is soft, and so warm, it's almost fiery.

"Nuh-hice to meet you," she hiccups.

"You too." And because it's been on his mind all night, he asks right away: "Any relation to the ad people?"

Cassie just burps, her eyes hooded and dazed.

"She can't get any money for your film, if that's what you mean," says Beth.

Jay feels a jerk of anger. "That's a shitty thing to say," he snaps. Three hours with an old friend and she's already giving him attitude?

"I'm just *kidding*. Help her with the luggage."

Jay grabs the suitcase, but Cassie keeps the red duffel clutched close to her.

"Thanks, man," she says, slurring. "You're a real genn-elman."

They all tumble out of the room.

The extra bedroom is at the end of the hall. It's messy and mismatched, with a basket of clean laundry on the single bed. Ever since he gave up the office last year, Jay's been working out of this cluttered space. The desk lamp is on, papers scattered about, his laptop open, an old printer set up. As Cassie stumbles into the room, she bumps the chair and the desk rattles.

"Careful!" he says, annoyed.

"Hold on to her for a sec." Beth eases her friend toward him. Jay feels her weight, and the softness of her curves, so different from the slim, narrow frame of his wife.

"Hope you don't mind the mess, Cass," Beth says, grabbing the laundry, setting it aside. The moment the mattress is clear, Cassie pulls away from Jay and flops face forward into bed.

"Doesn't look like she minds anything right now."

Beth laughs softly. "She won't care. She was never a clean freak to begin with."

Beth bends down to pull off the girl's beat-up black boots. Jay notices how natural it looks, as if she's done it a hundred times. How strange. Beth usually wasn't so loving or maternal.

"How long is she staying for?" he asks. He's bitter about the interruption, despite how hot she is.

"Just until Friday." Beth tries to pull the blanket out from under her, but she won't budge.

"Are you kidding? Friday? But all my stuff's in here, and I have a big meeting tomorrow."

"Seems like you have a lot of big meetings lately," she says.

"Yeah? So?" What's she implying? That things aren't moving

fast enough on the film? He's frustrated too, but does she have to bring it up?

"So get it, Jay," she says. "Just be quiet. And leave the door open a bit."

"Why?"

But Beth tiptoes out of the room without answering. Jay huffs, irritated. Houseguests weren't supposed to just drop in like this. For days at a time? How inconsiderate. Who was this chick, anyway? Why did Beth suddenly act so friendly? He'd never even heard her mention a Cassie before. This is all so unlike her.

He goes to the desk, grumbling, gathering up his things. He closes the laptop and grabs his papers. He resents being inconvenienced the night before a big meeting. She'll be here tomorrow, too, when he's getting ready. It'll throw off his energy. He's used to having the house to himself during the day. Is Beth going to take off work to keep her company? Or just leave him here—alone—with her? A stranger? It didn't make any sense. What is he supposed to do with her all day?

He turns off the lamp. The room goes dark. He's just about to leave when he hears rustling on the bed. He freezes. Light from the window shines in, illuminating Cassie in a silver-blue pool. She's on her stomach, but she's pushed herself up on her elbows. She struggles for the edge of her T-shirt, trying to pull it off. She makes helpless little moaning noises. Jay doesn't know if he should help her or get the hell out of the room.

Instead, he watches in the darkness, holding his breath. Cassie squirms on the single bed, awkwardly pulling up the edge of her tee, revealing her bare back and the tan lines of a bikini top across her skin. Jay feels strangely proud that he'd guessed right: she isn't wearing a bra. She twists in bed to pull the shirt over her head, turning toward him, and as she does, he sees her breasts. Firm and round, candy-pink nipples going hard from the friction.

Good Christ.

He feels a tingling rush. But then she flops forward again, on her stomach, arms limp, her hair falling across her face. He lets out a long breath and shakes his head. He tiptoes out of the room, about to close the door, then remembers to leave it open a bit. He has to stand in the hall a moment, composing himself, as a shiver works through his body. He hears Beth shuffling around in their bedroom and goes to the doorway. She's in her blue nightie, pulling decorative pillows off the bed, piling them on a chair.

"Why does she have to stay here?"

"She's broke, Jay. She can't even afford a hotel."

"And that's *our* problem?"

"She's a *friend*, okay? And I owe her. It's only for a few nights. She's got to be in Monterey for the weekend." She stops for a moment, regarding him. "Just be careful with her. She has"—Beth searches for the word—"issues."

"Issues? What do you mean?"

"Not tonight. I can't get into it. Just be careful with her, that's all."

"Don't worry. I plan on it." He watches her climb under the duvet, pulling it around her shoulders. "You're not going to read?" He's used to seeing his wife tuck in every night with one of her romance novels. To look at her, you'd think she'd have her nose in Tolstoy or some other classic all the time, but she always said she needed the happy endings in romances.

"I'm too exhausted," she says, yawning, reaching up for the light. "You coming to bed?" There's no hint of invitation in her voice.

"Got work to do."

"Okay, g'night." She turns off the lamp and the room sinks into darkness. The same streetlight that illuminated her friend's bare breasts only moments ago now shines on the shoulder of his wife's blue nightgown.

28

BETH

Tuesday Night

Beth lies in the darkness staring at the surface of the nightstand. She didn't want Cassie seeing that old photo, so she's put it away, hidden it in the drawer. It seems strange to want to hide things from Cass. They shared all their secrets in school. She remembers those nights with Cassie in the dorm room, their beds barely four feet apart. Everything they talked about. Their dreams. Their fears. Their failed relationships. Night after night. They came from such different backgrounds, it was hard to believe they could ever be such good friends.

"You're a damn prodigy," Cassie said after she heard one of Beth's exam recitals. "Come play with me at Wally's."

Beth's heart clamped with panic. She loved to play, but an audience terrified her. Her stage fright had almost prevented her from auditioning for the school. Cassie, on the other hand, was one of the few freshmen who were talented and gutsy enough to get paying gigs on the weekends. Beth admired—and envied—her for that.

"You're wasting your time on these teachers, B. You gotta get out there. You gotta play in front of people. There's this quote I love. Something about talent and happiness?" She snaps her fingers, trying to think of it. "I can't quite—"

"'The person born with a talent they are meant to use will find their greatest happiness in using it.'" said Beth quietly. "It's Goethe."

92

"I should've known you heard it before." Cassie laughed. "Except we should put *chick* in there, right?"

"We should," said Beth with a smile.

Late the next night, she got a call from the manager of the bar where Cassie performed. Voices and music were so loud in the background, she could barely hear, but it seemed Cass needed her. It was a fifteen-minute walk to the bar, but Beth ran it in half the time, squeezing around students on the sidewalk. Out of breath, she ducked into a street-level pub with a black sign above the door, WALLY'S CAFÉ (EST. 1947).

The small room was crowded, with a bar along one side, air ducts in the low ceiling. The cramped stage at the back was empty, and the stereo played canned jazz. The clientele was mixed: black and white, young and old. The bartender recognized her—this wasn't the first time she'd had to rescue Cass—and pointed to the end of the bar. Beth pushed through the crowd to find Cassie with her head down on the counter, a cluster of men surrounding her.

"Cass!" she said, shaking the girl's shoulder.

"Hey, B," Cass growled, looking up.

Beth glanced at the men. "Would you excuse us for a sec?" They seemed disappointed at the interruption as she turned Cass on the stool, staring into her bloodshot eyes. "What happened to Alex?"

"Screw him," she said, flapping her hand. "Second time he ditched me. That's it for that prick."

"But you can't skip tonight, Cass. They probably won't have you back. Are you able to go up there now?" Beth was dubious, but she had to ask.

"Yeah," Cass said, a playful smile on her lips. "If *you* come with me."

"Oh, for chrissakes. You planned this, didn't you?"

"I'll never tell!" she said, grinning. She finished the beer with a gulp and rolled off the stool with more finesse than Beth would have given her credit for.

"Don't *do* this!" Beth hissed at her. "*Don't!*"

"The show must go on!" Cassie said with a grin.

She walked to the middle of the small stage area, grabbed the mic from the stand, and faced the crowd. The canned music turned down. A smattering of applause grew louder, and a few of the customers whistled. Cassie Ogilvy was a popular draw at the club. Young as she was, she was beautiful, talented—and sexy as hell. She seemed like a star in the making.

"I'd like you all to meet a good friend of mine tonight," Cass began.

Beth felt the ground warp beneath her feet. A wash of sound reverberated in her ears, making Cassie's voice seem distant and unreal.

"She's going to accompany me on the ivories."

A few more whistles and cheers filled the room, taunting Beth.

"She's a really talented musician—and my BFF. Ladies and gentlemen, Beth Crawford."

The walls throbbed and colors blurred. Beth felt pressure, like an undertow in the ocean, lifting her up and pressing her down at the same time. There was applause; she could hear the wash of it beneath the pounding in her head.

"I'm gonna kill you for this," she hissed as she passed her friend.

Cassie's laugh rang over the microphone. It was amazing how lucid she suddenly seemed. But Cassie had a gear meant just for performing. A real pro. Beth sat down at the keyboard, her legs shaking, her hands sweating.

Haydn got stage fright.

Chopin.

She put her fingers on the black-and-white keys. It was just a battered old upright, with sheet music already laid out, and a set list with Cassie's scribbles. "Stormy Weather." "Ain't Misbehavin'." "Summertime." Beth first thought Cass would prefer rock or pop music, with her black eyeliner and wild hair, but jazz was her forte, throaty, sexy, and layered.

Barbra Streisand got stage fright.

And Adele.

Cassie counted her in with nods of her head. Beth focused, taking a deep breath. She started to play the opening bars of the first song, her fingers trembling on the keys.

"Slow it down," Cassie whispered, leaning into her, putting a hand on Beth's shoulder. Beth took the pace down a bit. The direction helped her focus.

Cassie's throaty voice filled the room, sultry and magnetic. "Stormy Weather," nearly a hundred years old, felt contemporary—and strangely alive. It lived in Beth's fingers. It breathed there, seeping out of the keys into the ether. Or was it out of the ether into the keys? She wasn't sure, but it was another force communicating through her, melding with everyone in the room.

The jazz standard felt simplistic compared with the classical music Beth preferred, but she appreciated its purity, and Cassie was a gifted performer, enough to make you forget everything—including stage fright. The further she got into the song, the more she found her rhythm fusing with that of her friend. The keys seemed to vibrate beneath her fingers, almost lifting up to meet her.

With the red exit light glowing from the back of the room, the two freshmen from the New England Institute of Music mesmerized the audience that night, and Beth's whole world changed. She realized she could perform in front of a crowd—if she had to. Her fearless new roommate had helped her be stronger, too.

29

JAY

Late Tuesday Night

Jay's neck is stiff, the budget spread out on the coffee table in front of him, the laptop open, a single lamp on. His gaze travels from the screen to the pages and back again.

It's after three in the morning when he hears footsteps in the hall. Not the shuffle of Beth's slippers, but the padding of bare feet. The guest bathroom door opens. The sound of splashing. Good God. She didn't even close the door to pee? A moment later, a flush, the faucet, more creaking, and suddenly she's there, eyes half closed, hair tousled.

"Shit!" She jumps when she sees him. "I didn't know anyone was up."

"Uh...yeah...sorry," he says, closing the laptop. "Didn't mean to scare you."

"Had to take a badass whiz."

"Uh...yeah."

She's not naked, but she might as well be. She's put on an old Rolling Stones T-shirt, Mick Jagger's oversexed lips gobbling up her voluptuous breasts. The shirt barely covers her ass, and the fabric is so threadbare, it's almost transparent, ripped at the neck so it hangs off one shoulder. He remembers the episode in the bedroom, panicked that she might recall how he stood there, watching her. But she appears unaware.

"Got anything to drink?" she asks, yawning.

"Help yourself." He motions to the wet bar in the corner.

"Nah, just a beer or something. I'm parched."

"In the fridge." He watches her pad barefoot into the kitchen. Except for the counter, the rooms are open concept, and the fridge light illuminates her figure. He tries not to look down the length of her body, but he can't help it. Her legs are toned and tanned, her curves silhouetted beneath the thin cotton.

"Want one?" She grabs a beer and twists it open.

"No, thanks. Gotta keep a clear head. Big day tomorrow."

She closes the fridge and the silhouette is lost. Jay almost salivates watching her take her first swallow. He really could use a drink. But Karen would be angry if he's hungover for the meeting at the bank tomorrow. Cassie walks back into the living room, looking around. Considering how drunk she was a couple hours ago, she seems awfully sober right now. Had it been an act? He suspects everything about this woman right now.

"So, uh, I asked before if you were any relation to the ad people? Used to be Ogilvy and Mather, something like that?"

She shrugs. "Not that I know of," she says, looking around. "Great place. You guys own or rent?"

"Own."

"Cool." She says the word lazily, like a teenager: *Cuhl.*

She takes a few steps to the entertainment unit and peruses their vast wall of vinyl and CDs. "You like music?"

"Who doesn't?"

"True." She leans over to read the spines, casually running her fingers along the cases. Bent over like that, Jay can see her panties—skimpy and black—and a shudder rocks through him. He flounders for something to say.

"Um, Beth tells me you're a jazz singer?" he stammers. "Like Amy Winehouse?"

"Did she say that?" She straightens, seeming pissed.

"Uh, no. She said *other* people said that about you."

"Yeah, well, I got the Amy Winehouse thing from people with no imagination. *About Town* called me a young Sarah Vaughan."

"Wow. That's great. I love Sarah Vaughan."

"*I* don't," she says. She sees a CD and pulls it off the shelf. "Oh my God! I can't believe you have this! Well, of course you do. But I haven't heard it in ages."

She turns the case around, presenting Beth Crawford's first and only classical CD, *The Lotus Flower*. On the front cover, Beth—in her twenties—sits at a white grand piano, looking slightly off camera. She wears a floor-length white gown with a deep V, her long blond hair in full waves, her pearls clasped around her neck. Her face is young, serene, unreadable. A ghostly white lotus blossom floats above her like a pale cloud. Jay hasn't heard the CD since he and Beth were dating. She didn't like listening to it. Her "gory days," she called them.

"Can I put it on?" she asks, opening the case without waiting for an answer.

"Sure, but use the headphones. Beth's a light sleeper."

"She didn't used to be." Cassie inserts the disk and hits Play. The opening notes of a strong piano solo ring through the house. "Shit, sorry, sorry!" But she doesn't seem very sorry, casually scanning the unit for the volume button. Jay can't find the remote, so he rushes over to turn it down. Cassie winces, a cute expression, like a little girl who knows she can't get into serious trouble. "Sorry," she says again.

Jay's heart is pumping. He steps away from her as she closes her eyes, listening to the music, swaying on her feet.

"Man, doesn't she sound great? She's so talented. She could play anything when we were kids."

The silence between them is filled with Beth's music. Rhythmic. Studied. Beethoven or something. Maybe Bach. It's all the same to Jay, always has been. He peeks down the hall to check if Beth woke up. The door's still closed, so he returns to the couch, his heart thumping hard. Cassie walks around the room, looking at things, touching whatever she likes. She lingers over their wedding picture.

"Cute," she says, but it sounds sarcastic.

There's something he doesn't trust about this girl. It goes beyond

Beth's warnings. Instinctively, he knows she's trouble. He's met crazy chicks like this before, wild party heads who seem to want fun but then cause nothing but grief.

"So, how long you guys known each other again?" he asks, trying to keep the suspicion out of his voice.

"Me and Beth? We go way back. Used to be super-tight."

"That's funny. She never even mentioned you. Not until you called."

"Ouch. Was that on purpose? Cuz it hurt."

She walks around the coffee table and sits down right beside him, her bare thigh close to his. He straightens, shocked. There's a chair across from him, lots of room on the far side of the couch, and there she is, right beside him? He smells the stale booze and her unfamiliar, musky perfume. She stares at him with frank green eyes.

"We shared a dorm room in college for a couple years," she finally says. "So you do the math."

"I thought it was just one year. Then you dropped out."

"Did I only last that long?" She snaps her fingers. "I keep forgetting. So I hear you're making a movie with Milla Jovovich."

"That's a bit preemptive. But she liked the script."

"Past tense?"

"She *likes* it. We're negotiating."

"*Cuhl.*"

He feels anxious sitting this close to her, so he gets up to pour himself a drink. It won't hurt, just one. But he's so nervous, his hand shakes, the scotch bottle nicking the lip of the glass. He takes a quick slug and remains standing, afraid to sit beside her again.

"Mind if I smoke?"

And of course he minds, but she's pulling the cigarette package out from beneath her T-shirt as she asks it. It was tucked into the back of her panties, like a gangster hiding his gun. As she grabs for them, he sees the curve of her hip, her bare thigh. He swallows as she watches him, the T-shirt dropping back down. She pulls out a cigarette, sliding it between her lips. There's a lighter in the package and she uses it, the flame making her eyes glow. A wisp of smoke curls upward as she exhales.

"That an ashtray?" She points to a dish on the end table.

A wedding gift from somebody or other, nobody's used it as an ashtray since their housewarming party, but he doesn't want to seem uptight in front of her so he just nods. She grabs the dish, puts it on her bare thigh. Rests one foot on the table.

"So, too bad about the baby," she says.

"What?"

"The miscarriage."

"She *told* you?"

"Uh-huh. We had a lot of catching up to do tonight." She takes a drag. The smoke now feels like another intruder in the house, a wispy apparition she's brought with her.

"Weird," Jay says. "She hates talking about it. Nobody even knew we were pregnant. Except for my parents."

"Maybe we're closer than you think," she says. "We never keep secrets from each other." Smoke rings curl out of her lips as she pumps her jaw. Once, twice. It looks obscene, as if she's giving head. "So you guys trying again or what?"

It was amazing how rude she was being! His parents had a term for girls like this—coarse. Such an unassuming word, yet it said so much. They'd used it about that chick from college, too.

"Yeah, I guess," he finally says. The tension clamps harder, a vise inside his chest. He drains his scotch, feeling it burn and twist going down his throat. "Listen, I'm kinda tired. Can we pick this up in the morning?"

"Sure thing, man. By the way, you mind if I use your laptop for a bit?"

Such an innocent question, but he looks at his work spread out on the coffee table and his precious MacBook. Of course he doesn't want her to use it, but he can't say no. It would make him look too suspicious. She must notice his reticence.

"Don't worry. I won't rack up your porn bill," she says with a laugh. "I just want to check flights back home."

"Oh, sure..." What a relief that'll be. When she's back at her own home and out of his. "Just—just let me close a few things down first." He has to step over her legs to get to the computer. It's awkward; they're much too close together, but she doesn't move— she just watches him. "There." Relieved, he steps away from her. "Just be careful with that cigarette."

"No worries. I've been smoking in bed for years and nothing's ever happened."

He's in the hall when he hears her say, "*Yet.*"

His heart pounds as he creeps through the bedroom. Beth is fast asleep, breathing peacefully. He tiptoes into the bathroom, closing the door. The room is dim, streetlight shining through a small frosted window. He opens the medicine cabinet and grabs his Ambien bottle, a natural instinct when he's nervous. But he reconsiders. It's too late for a pill. He'll be groggy for the meeting. Goddammit, he shouldn't have had that drink. He wanted to stay totally sober tonight.

But how can anyone blame him? He felt so awkward around her. Why had he been so nervous? Because she was like that girl? Jen? Jane? He can never remember her name. How could she walk around half-naked, in front of her friend's husband like that? Even Beth puts on a robe to wander around the house. Yet there's something so sexy about her. He's always been drawn to women who weren't ashamed of being sexy. They're a weakness of his. But he wonders about this one.

Issues, Beth had said.

He opens the door and quietly crawls into bed, not wanting to wake Beth. She doesn't even move. He lets out a big breath of air. The scotch rushes through him, finally helping him to relax. Through the closed door, he hears music, very faintly: Beth playing piano, her old friend listening, barely dressed.

30

CASSIE

As soon as she hears the bedroom door close, Cassie logs onto the *L.A. Times* website. She scrolls past the old articles she read at the hotel. There don't seem to be any breaks in the case, and the police are still searching for Rick.

But she gasps when she sees a breaking story about the shooting of a young man named Daniel Alvarez. The inset photo clutches at her heart. She hates knowing his full name and, especially, how young he was. She remembers being twenty-one, those years of feeling invincible. *Self-defense*, she reminds herself. She forces herself to read on. Her eyes grip each word like finger holds in a steep climb.

A huff of relief rushes out of her. He's in the hospital, critical, but alive.

Thank God. Thank God.

The article says the shooting is suspected to be gang related and that they're investigating a possible link to the Lawrence Heights murders. It also quotes the kid's brother. "He left with a blond woman, carrying suitcases." The police are asking the public for any information from witnesses who may have seen someone matching that description Monday night. She's wanted in connection with the attempted homicide.

Fuck.

She clears the recent searches and inputs: *Flights to Miami*—in case Jay checks.

31

GOODE

Goode feels something nudge his shoulder. He opens his eyes, squinting at bright light. It's morning. But everything's sideways. He looks up to see Michelle Dawes standing above him, holding two Styrofoam cups, uniforms milling about the squad room.

"You been here all night?" she asks, putting a coffee down for him.

Goode leans back, stretching and yawning. "Nah. Went home last night to change my briefs."

"You're kidding, right?"

"Why? You thought I was a boxer man?"

She just shakes her head. "You get clearance yet?"

"Nope," he says. He'd been at the station all night, waiting for Butler's field tapes to be released to him. The task force said they were working on it, but he had to be at his desk, on a secure server to listen to them. So far, nothing.

"I got ballistics," she says, sitting down. "What they have, anyway."

She shoves a file over, sipping her own coffee as Goode scans the documents. "Three guns found at the scene," she begins, pointing out the results. "But five different bullets found altogether. Including the 9mm that went through the bedroom door. The casing's a match to the Alvarez shooting."

Goode shrugs, not surprised; they already assumed it was possible the same gun was used at both scenes.

"Any sign of Squires?" she asks.

"Nothing. He hasn't had a registered cell phone for years. We can't get a fix on a vehicle either. Total washout so far. We need to find that blonde. Fake blonde, I should say." He sorts through another file. "They found hair fibers on the front seat of Alvarez's car. But it's synthetic polymer."

"A match to the wig from Lawrence Heights?"

"Looks like. Same fiber length. Same color. But it's a common type. Available in just about every wig shop in the city. Doubt we can narrow it down."

"I've been busy, too," she says. "Running his associates again."

She goes to her desk, only a few feet away, and taps at her keyboard. Goode rolls up his chair, and she angles the screen toward him.

"Richard Squires," she says, "this is your life."

The monitor glows with the felon's considerable criminal record, from drug charges to aggravated assault to armed robbery. Among the thug's associates, Goode sees Robert Hackett's mug shot, the young man who'd been found dead at the scene. There are various seedy-looking characters, all male. On his file are only three known female associates, two of them blond. One is in prison, where she's been for the past six months, serving time for solicitation; the other died of a heroin overdose last year.

The third is a brunette. She was arrested with Squires last year on the drug charge in Florida. Squires had been convicted of possession at the time and sentenced to one year, serving nine months. The woman got off with probation.

Hair: Brown

Eyes: Green

Goode studies the woman's face in the mug shot. There's something about the way she stares at the camera, stubborn and pissed off, for sure—but not scared. They have to get this photo to the Alvarez kid, see if he recognizes her. Goode jots the woman's name down: *Cassandra Anne Ogilvy.*

32

JAY

Wednesday Morning

Jay wakes up thinking of her. Her voice and her legs and her breasts and her lips... His eyes blink open and he sees Beth at the closet, her back to him as she gets dressed. The visions disappear. He tries to sit up, his voice cracking. "What're... you doing?"

"I'm late."

He sits bolt upright. "You're going to *work*? I thought you'd take some time off to"—he stops, looking at the wall, lowering his voice—"to be with *her.*"

"I can't, Jay. Not until Christmas. You know that. This is my busy time."

"So you want *me* to babysit her all day, is that it?" Now he's irritated. "I told you, I've got a meeting."

"You don't have to worry about Cass. She was so hammered last night, I doubt she'll be up for hours."

"Probably not," he says. He doesn't want to say he saw Cassie in the middle of the night. Or that they talked. Listened to Beth's CD together. It feels somehow clandestine. As he straightens up in bed, he notices the surface of her nightstand. "What happened to the picture of your folks?" He's accustomed to the happy three-some grinning back at him from behind the pretty frame.

After a moment, she says, "I hid it."

"You *hid* a family picture?" He laughs. "Why? You think she'd steal something like that?"

"Of course not," she says, continuing to get dressed.

"Then what is it?"

"I don't want to talk about it."

"Beth—we *have* to talk about it."

But she ignores him.

"I have a right to know who's staying in my own home. Don't you think?" He crosses his arms. She sighs heavily, seeming to consider it, then comes to sit on the bed beside him.

"When I said she had *issues*," she begins, her voice a whisper, "I meant emotional issues. Mental health issues. That's what the doctors told her, anyway. She said she was diagnosed—or misdiagnosed, as the case may be—with all kinds of things growing up. ADHD, bipolar, dissociative disorder, or something like that, depression. They kept telling her different things. Putting her on different drugs. Remember when I told you I'm surprised she's still alive?"

He nods, on edge.

"Well...she tried to commit suicide when she was a teenager."

"God," he whispers. He wasn't expecting that. The woman seemed unshakable.

"I know, so sad. But you can hardly blame her. She had such a rough life. Her mother died when she was very young. An addict or something—heroin, meth, whatever. Cass wasn't even sure, but it was an overdose. And she never even met her father. Anyway, she got adopted after that—into quite a good family, or so they thought. He was a doctor. They had lots of money, apparently. But then the man..." Beth hesitates, shivering. "Oh, I shouldn't be telling you all this. She'd kill me."

"Did he abuse her?" Jay asks. "Sexually?"

Beth closes her eyes tight. Nods. "For years," she says, lowering her voice even further, barely audible. "Since she was a little girl. Cass was about eleven or twelve when it all came out. The guy went to jail, but the wife was devastated. After that, Cass had to go into foster homes. God knows how many different places she lived or what happened there. But at one of the homes she was in for a while, they'd lock her in her bedroom when they couldn't handle her. That's why she doesn't like closed doors." Beth glances at their own bedroom door, giving a sad smile. "I don't know how she got through it, poor thing."

"Jesus. That's awful."

"Mmm..." Beth nods, but she's quiet for a moment, her fair brow working over memories. In the silence, Jay tries to reconcile the woman he saw last night with this horrific story. He's not sure if it fits perfectly—or doesn't jibe at all.

"I still don't understand why you had to hide that picture," he says.

She turns to stare at the nightstand. "That last summer in the Hamptons, when Cassie stayed with us, she got really... *attached* to my parents."

"What do you mean—attached?"

"Well, she kind of adopted them. Or vice versa. I don't know. It got very confusing."

"Is she psycho, Beth? Just tell me."

"God, no! And it's not her fault! She just glommed onto them, that's all. I think she wanted what I had. She loved the idea of a *real* family, you know? Mom, dad, nice house, square meals, everything like that. My parents really liked her, too. I think they felt sorry for her. You didn't know them. They were very generous people. My mother especially. She was always looking for a new charity case, and she had a soft spot for Cass. Anyway, when they..." She hesitates again, swallowing a lump in her throat. "When they died, Cass took it almost as hard as I did. I think they sort of became *her* parents that summer, you know? So I just don't want her seeing any pictures of them hanging around. She doesn't need any reminders." She holds up a finger. "But don't tell her I told you any of this! She'd be livid with me."

"Are you kidding? I'm not gonna get into this shit with her. She sounds like a nutjob and I'm no shrink."

She laughs weakly. "You have such a compassionate heart, you know that?"

"One of my great qualities," he says, grinning.

"And very humble, too." She laughs. "I better run. I'm already late, and I want to leave Cass a note." She leans over to kiss him, trying to brighten the mood. "Good luck at your meeting."

"Yeah, thanks." He watches her hurry out of the room. But he's surprised. She hasn't kissed him goodbye in a long time.

33

CASSIE

Wednesday Morning

Cassie sits up in bed, smoking a joint, peering out the window as Beth leaves the house. Getting into her Audi, she sees Cass in the window, and her face breaks into a wide smile. Cassie waves and blows her a kiss. Beth *smooches* her lips, then climbs into the car and drives away.

Cassie glances up and down the block, craning her neck to see every shadow. A swell of relief washes through her. The street is quiet. There's nobody watching from a parked car, no one hiding in the shadows, only the happy details of her friend's privileged life. The flowers, the palm trees, the shiny Mustang in the driveway. Cassie isn't surprised Beth settled down long before she did, because getting married and buying a house was what you *should* do. Beth always worried about what she should do. Always wanting to be perfect, always trying to do the right thing. As if that were even possible.

She lets the curtain drop closed.

How will she be able to stay cooped up in this house? How long will she have to hide? She's not sure, but she's already restless. She tamps out her joint and immediately lights a cigarette, feeling jittery. She needs something to do while she waits for Jay to leave and she can check the news again.

She grabs her makeup bag and fishes out the broken bracelet. Maybe she can restring it, just to occupy herself. But when she sees the leather thong and the loose wooden beads, her heart catches on a memory. She remembers the way Beth used to stare at her wrists when she didn't think Cass could see. She didn't ask about the scars, not for weeks. And Cassie didn't say anything, either. If she had a few secrets she wanted to keep, that was up to her.

Finally, one night after they'd been drinking, Beth said the room was spinning so fast, she might throw up. Cassie could tell her new friend wasn't used to overindulging, so she told Beth to put one foot flat on the floor and that seemed to help. But the alcohol had given her more nerve, and she asked the inevitable question. Cassie looked down, fussing with the tangle of bracelets, the ember of her cigarette glowing.

"What do you think happened?"

There was a long silence and then a single word, breathed in the darkness. "When?"

"When I was fifteen, sixteen. Something like that." It shocked her how casual her voice sounded, as if she were just saying what she had for lunch. She tossed her cigarette out the window, then crept across the room to open the door a crack. She was in the habit of shutting it when she smoked, so she wouldn't get caught. She crawled back into bed, and they were quiet for a moment, but Beth couldn't let it go.

"How come?"

"I don't know. Don't you ever think about it?"

"Think about it, yeah, but...to actually...try it?" She fought a yawn. "You're not afraid of anything, are you? Not even death." She took her foot off the floor, obviously feeling better, and rolled over, her voice muffled by her pillow. "You don't even get stage fright...I'm so jealous..."

"You shouldn't be," Cassie said. "Nobody should be jealous of me."

But Beth didn't seem to hear. "Do you think there's a finite amount of fear in the universe?"

"What?" Cassie smiled. *Finite.* It was just the sort of word Beth would use.

She continued, her voice groggy and faint. "...And that some people get more than their fair share and other people don't get enough?"

"Is that what you think?" Cassie said with a laugh. "Just because I don't get stage fright that I'm never afraid?"

There was no response.

"Beth?"

But she was breathing heavily, already passed out.

Cassie smiles at the memories. Maybe Beth was right. Maybe there was a fixed amount of fear in the universe and she was one of the luckier ones. But it didn't mean she was never afraid. She was terrified Monday night. Hearing gunshots. Sirens. Dogs barking in the night.

But now that she's here, in her old friend's house, the fear has eased. It might even have something to do with Beth herself. Cassie had always been the brave one between them, the strong one—even the crazy one. Beth was so much more delicate and vulnerable. But they complemented each other, and in a way, they must've needed each other to define themselves back then. Maybe they still did.

She senses movement from the next room and puts the bracelet away, taking one last drag and crushing her cigarette. She hurries into the hall just as Jay comes out of the bedroom in a nice gray suit.

"Morning," she says brightly. "Don't you look dapper!"

He stops in his tracks. She notices him suck in his gut. He's a good-looking man, but he still feels self-conscious in front of her. She can tell.

"Hey," he says, turning away.

"Going somewhere?" she asks, following him.

"Got a meeting. Back soon."

Back soon. In other words, don't touch anything. "Are you taking your laptop?"

"Yeah, I need it." His jacket swoops as he hurries through the kitchen.

"All right, well, have a—" But the door slams as he leaves the house. "Nice day."

She hears the growl of the Mustang; it all but shakes the walls. She peers out the blinds—the dark wood slats bar the California sunlight—to see the car roar out of view. She checks the street again. Nothing.

34

GOODE

Wednesday Morning

East Los Angeles General sprawls across four city blocks, its clean, modern lines giving the impression of a cruise ship gone aground. Goode stands outside the door to a room in the ICU, peering through a small window. Danny Alvarez is unconscious, an oxygen mask on his face. His chest rises and falls uneasily. The bullet had passed through the young man's ribs on the right side, punctured his liver, and exited the body, lodging into the driver's door. The boy is still in critical condition, but he's expected to live. His brother and mother sit on either side of the bed, wearing surgical masks and blue latex gloves.

"Ready?" he asks Dawes. She nods. Goode taps the window. Nico Alvarez looks up, then says something to his mother. She nods but doesn't take her eyes off her unconscious son. Nico rises, pulling off his mask.

"Hey," he says, walking into the hall, looking drained but relieved. The *beep* of the heart monitor fades as he closes the door behind him. "You find her yet?"

"Not yet," Goode says. "But we're making progress. Forensics found fingerprints on the passenger-side handles of your brother's car—and they got a hit." He presents the mug shot of Cassandra Ogilvy from the Florida arrest. "Do you recognize this woman, Nico?"

He squints at the photo, considers it, shrugs.

"Take your time. Maybe you've seen her around before? Maybe she knew your brother?"

"I don't think so," he says, shaking his head. "Never saw her before."

Dawes's phone rings, and she excuses herself, stepping away to answer.

"Nico, we believe this is the woman your brother left with Monday night," says Goode. "We found a cluster of long blond hairs on the front seat of his car. But they were synthetic, so we think she may have been in disguise." He rests a blank page of his notebook against the photo, covering the woman's dark hair with the white paper. "Take another look."

The boy glances at the photo, cocks his head. "Shit, yeah, that's her. Could be, anyway."

"Excellent. You said she had bags with her. Did you get a good look at them?"

"No. It was dark. I wasn't paying attention to her goddamn luggage."

"Was she injured, as far as you could tell?"

"No, not at all."

Dawes winds up her call and heads over, giving Goode a meaningful look.

"Thanks, Nico. If you think of anything else, you let us know."

The boy nods and opens the door to the room, but before he disappears, Dawes reaches out. "I know this is tough, Nico. But it could've been a lot worse. Your brother's gonna be okay. He's a lucky guy."

"Yeah? Why? You gonna pay his hospital bill?" He throws her an angry glare, then disappears into the room.

Dawes stares at the door and sighs heavily. "That was a stupid thing to say, wasn't it?"

Goode shrugs. "Serves you right for trying to be nice. Was that the judge?"

She nods. "We're all set."

Goode swells with his own brand of reserved optimism,

pocketing the photo. As soon as they got a hit on the prints on the door handle of the Ford, they called their favorite judge to rush an arrest warrant for Cassandra Ogilvy. She is no longer just a possible suspect in the Butler case. They have hard evidence she was involved in the Alvarez shooting, too. Ogilvy is now wanted for attempted murder.

35

BETH

Beth fixes her coffee in Starbucks, glancing around for the man she met the other day. Tony? She hopes she sees him again. It's been a long time since a guy made her feel attractive, and she could use another ego boost. Especially now that Cassie is here, sexier than ever.

She recalls the shock at seeing her friend wave from the guest-room window, her face seeming to float between the curtains, ghostly and unreal. She'd expected Cass to sleep in for hours, the way she always used to, so it had been such a surprise that she was awake. Beth chews her lip worriedly; she hopes Cass hadn't overheard any of her and Jay's conversation this morning.

I think she wanted what I had . . .

Her phone rings and she gets worried when she sees the screen; her mother-in-law never calls her. "Ellen? Is everything all right?"

"Of course, dear. Everything's fine." But she has an edge in her voice. "Jason called earlier. He'd sent his father some film documents and needed advice."

"Uh-huh?" Beth says, irritated.

"He said he met that friend of yours last night. She was a bit wild. And that she was very drunk."

"She had a few drinks, yes. We both did." *What business is it of yours?* She carries her coffee out into the sunshine. The relentless California sunshine.

"And you're leaving her alone in the house all week?"

116

"It's only three nights. She's leaving Friday. And she's *not* going to be alone."

"Well, she'll be alone today, won't she? When Jason goes to his meeting and you're at work? He told me you said the girl had—"

Beth interrupts her. "Ellen, can we talk about this some other time? I've got a student waiting."

She hangs up without saying goodbye. She can't defend herself right now, not against this, because part of her isn't even sure why she let Cassie stay with them in the first place. It was such a risk.

She gets to her studio with only a few moments to spare before her student comes in—a young girl of twelve, dedicated but untalented. They sit on the piano bench and the metronome starts.

Click, click, click.

The girl begins the first of a series of endless, repetitive scales. As Beth turns the page of the music book, she's so angry, her hands tremble. Why did Jay have to mention anything about Cassie being drunk last night? He knows how critical Ellen can be. She'd been so wrong about his parents—and so damned naive—it still humiliates her.

She remembers the night they announced their engagement, over dinner at the country club. She'd only met Jay's parents a few times, and she wanted to make a good impression, so she sat straight backed, smiling, trying to be the good girl. Jay was even more eager to please them than she was, exchanging his cool, confident persona for that of an eager little schoolboy. She barely recognized him.

When they finally got past the inevitable *That was fast!* and *Are you sure you don't want to wait?* Ellen turned to her.

"Congratulations."

"Aren't you going to congratulate *me*?" Jay asked, laughing.

"You don't congratulate the groom-to-be," she snapped. "It's bad form."

All through dinner, Beth felt them regarding her, sizing her up, making her feel like a damaged antique they were only half interested in buying. Then the questions started in full force.

So sorry about your parents, they said, the picture of sympathy. *How awful for you.*

We understand they weren't in a very good financial situation when they passed. That must've been so difficult to deal with—on top of everything.

Beth couldn't believe their nerve, or how rude they could be. Jay obviously told them the story. She saw him glaring at them to shut up, clenching his teeth. As the night went on, the questions got more subtle, but they didn't stop.

Did they travel much?

Did your mother do any charity work?

Where did your father golf?

It was obvious they were trying to learn the fundamentals of her upbringing, and it appeared her answers helped her pass the test. They were especially happy she was taking Jay's name. "I love that you're so traditional!" Jay's mother said, one of her few pleasant statements of the night. But Beth wasn't changing her name because she wasn't a feminist. She'd been anxious to forget "Beth Crawford"—the failed pianist—and become someone new for years.

But if Beth thought she was marrying into a warm, loving family, she was wrong. Because the next day, Ellen invited her to the house for lunch. Beth was excited to talk about wedding plans. She also wanted to explain that she and Jay had decided to foot the bill for the reception themselves. The groom's side of the family wasn't responsible for paying for a wedding, and since Jay's parents were so interested in "good form," she thought they'd appreciate that. She didn't know at the time that the small, elegant reception would become the first foothill in their growing mountain of debt.

She remembers driving to the tasteful mansion in Beverly Hills, white and glowing in the sun. Big white houses had such a special energy: peaceful and powerful at once. A dark-skinned maid answered the door. She had a kind smile, reminding Beth of Margaretta, as they entered through the large foyer. The house was beautiful, luxurious, filling her with melancholy and longing.

She stopped in her tracks when she got to the kitchen. It wasn't just Ellen waiting for her; Jay's father was there, too. She smiled awkwardly as everyone shook hands.

"We're just waiting for someone else to join us," John told her.

Beth wondered who it could possibly be. A wedding planner? A minister? The maid set out sandwiches with the crusts cut off, tea, and a bowl of store-bought potato salad. She then vanished without saying a word, without either of the Montgomerys acknowledging her presence. It was very different from Margaretta, who had been a loving part of the family for years.

"I love your pearls," Ellen remarked as they waited.

Beth was so nervous, she'd been toying with them. "Thank you."

"Are they Mikimoto?"

"Tiffany, actually."

"A gift?"

"They've been handed down through the family. They were my grandmother's to begin with. My mother left them to me."

"They're just beautiful. Pearls always look perfect, don't they?" She glanced at Beth's dress. "No matter what you're wearing."

Finally, there was commotion in the foyer as the maid answered the door and another gentleman walked into the room, carrying a large briefcase. He had thinning silver hair and wore a pin-striped suit. When he sat down, he pulled out a thick legal document, and Beth read the front page. It was a prenuptial agreement. The sight of it made her stomach clench. They didn't even go into John's den for the discussion. They sat in the kitchen. This was grunt work.

"Don't mind us for being candid," John had said. "But we have to insist on this. Standard practice. We have to protect ourselves. Our investments. Our son."

Even in her shock, Beth couldn't help but notice the order of their priorities, with Jay being last on the list. The lawyer went to work, outlining each page of the document. Every minute that went by, Beth felt more stupid and depressed, more self-conscious of the wedding magazines she'd brought sitting on the table, the pretty brides looking vapid and unaware. She had dressed up for this, done her nails, spritzed on her best perfume, thinking she'd be discussing menu options and bridal gowns with her future mother-in-law. But it was all legalese. There would be no alimony or settlement in the event that the couple divorced, and only legitimate children would be provided for.

Legitimate? How archaic, she'd thought.

And of course they wouldn't be responsible for any debts incurred under her or her family's name.

"This wasn't Jay's idea, by the way," Ellen had said. "Please don't blame him. He was angry about it, but it's what's best for everyone."

Everyone but me, Beth thought.

"Of course, I understand," she'd said. But as she signed the agreement, she was heartbroken.

"Mrs. Montgomery?" The young girl stops playing, looking up at her. Beth is pulled from the memories, realizing she's in the music room. "Do you want me to turn the pages now?"

"No, that's fine. I'm sorry." Beth flips to the next exercise in the music book, and another endless scale begins.

36

JAY

Wednesday Afternoon

Jay and Karen sit in big leather chairs in an immaculate office. They're at her bank, not his—he'd drained the charity out of his own bankers long ago. Beth thought he was at another meeting with Commisso about the film, but he couldn't tell her the truth. If she knew they were applying for another business loan, she'd kill him.

Karen wears her black suit, her hair back in a sensible ponytail, cleavage under wraps. Jay chose a nice suit himself, and took it easy on the hair gel. As nervous as he is about the loan, he still can't stop thinking about Beth's old roommate being alone in the house. She was already smoking drugs before he left this morning. She's probably going to rip them off and skip town. He should've hidden his watch collection. He makes a mental note to do that when he gets home.

Unbidden, Karen reaches out and takes his hand. "I'm nervous," she whispers. They must look like a young couple waiting to be approved for their first mortgage.

"Don't be," he says, but he sounds more confident than he feels.

"We *need* this money, Jay."

"Don't worry. We'll get it."

"I hope so," she says, chewing her lip. "This would save our asses. We wouldn't look so desperate. I just hate feeling beholden to that jerk."

"Me too. Just relax. I'm sure everything'll be fine."

He gives her hand another squeeze and kisses it; they smile at each other in a way that's supposed to seem fraternal, as they tell their respective partners, "We're like brother and sister!" But they both realize it's much more than that.

He knows Karen understands him better than his own wife does. They certainly have more in common. He and Karen both grew up in L.A., both went to Ivy League schools, both were drawn into the movie business by a creative pull neither of them could resist. There had been "encounters" over the years. Several of them, in fact. But it had been a while now, not since Beth was trying to get pregnant. They decided it made them feel too guilty. For Jay, sex was now something that had very little to do with pleasure. He'd learned so much about ovulation and optimal days, it felt more like a night course than intercourse.

Karen didn't question the change in their relationship. She had a long-term boyfriend herself. But he still thinks about her, and he knows she thinks about him. Sometimes he remembers their little pact—*if this movie thing doesn't work out, we could always get married*—and wonders if he would be happier if he had married Karen instead.

The door opens and they unlink hands. A blond woman in her late forties comes into the room, well dressed and friendly looking. She specializes in business loans. It's not the first time she's lent money to BurMont Films, and Jay hopes it won't be the last.

"Can I get you guys coffee or anything?" she asks, smiling. She has a stack of files with her, his budget sitting on top.

"We're good," Jay says.

The woman scratches her chin as she peruses the files in front of her. Jay feels his heart suspend beating.

37

CASSIE

Wednesday Afternoon

Cassie drags the red duffel bag out from under her bed and unzips it. The gun is a cool, dull weight in her hand. She has to get out of the house. If she gets some fresh air and sunlight, it might help her relax. She can't sit inside watching basic cable all day, and she jumps at the sound of every car going by. Not even the Montgomery music collection can entice her. She noticed the backyard was private and fenced in, surrounded by greenery; nobody would see her tanning back there. But she can't take any chances, so the gun is a safety precaution—just in case.

She begins snooping around for supplies. After opening a few doors in the hallway, she finds the laundry room, and next to it, the linen closet. Beth was just the sort of woman to have a nice linen closet, matching sheets and towels neatly folded. She sorts through the stacks for a beach towel, throwing one over her shoulder. She hesitates when she sees a small pile of pastel cotton tucked on the bottom shelf. Curious, she lifts one out. It's a little flannel blanket for burping newborns; the sale tag from babyGap is still attached.

Why does she keep all this stuff around? Beth always did like torturing herself.

In the master bedroom, she sees the pillow shams, the mocha bedding, the polished furniture. It's a serene room, yet there's something almost too calm about it. It reminds her of the living room at the rental house, full of all those bodies and blood.

Because this is the scene of a crime, too—the place where happiness went to die. Certainly her old friend's happiness had gasped its last breath here. Cassie knows Beth well enough to realize she's miserable—as much as she tries to hide it. But Cass sees through her old friend's "perfect" act. She always could.

She creeps to the dresser, opens a drawer. Jay's T-shirts are neatly folded. Another. Beth's underwear a study of neutrals. She walks to the bed and opens the nightstand. Sees a couple of romance novels tucked away. The shelves in the guest-room closet are stacked with these books, too, mauve and pink covers, with couples in swirling embrace. She laughs to herself. She can't believe Beth still reads this stuff.

But as she closes the drawer, the paperbacks shift and she sees something glinting beneath them. A picture frame. She reaches in and turns it over. She gasps when she sees the photo from that last day at the summer house, Beth with her arms around her parents. She remembers Beth asking Cassie to take the shot of them together.

But *this* is the photo her old friend chose to frame from that day? And not the two girls together? Cassie's pretty sure Beth hasn't been carrying around a picture of them in her wallet all these years either.

Cass isn't sure why Beth didn't stay in touch, as the girls promised to do that summer. She guesses it's because Beth never approved of Cassie's lifestyle, the drinking and the drugs. Cass still feels judged by her old friend that way. She suspects if it were up to Beth, they never would've seen each other again. She sighs, touching the glass, then quietly puts the photo back.

She steps into the en suite and opens the medicine cabinet. Judging from the shaving cream and hair gel, she sees what must be Jay's shelf. She notices a prescription bottle. It brings back the memory of manicured fingernails shoving pills into her mouth. Urging the glass of apple juice to her lips. The door locking. The knob hot and slippery in her hands as she tried to pull it open. Her throat aching from screaming, the fury and fear mixing in her gut.

Then slow stillness would seep through the walls, bringing with it relief, then finally, sleep.

She shakes off the memories—or tries to, at least. She notices the prescription is in Jay's name, for a fairly heavy dose of Ambien.

Everyone has their problems, she thinks, putting the bottle back.

Another shelf is full of drugstore finds: hair spray, moisturizer, hand cream. Beth doesn't appear to be using designer skincare right now, but Cassie would've guessed there'd be lots of sunblock—and there is. Beth was always protective of her fair skin. During that summer, Cassie remembers Beth slathering on SPF 30 every hour on the hour. Cassie didn't worry about that so much. She tanned well. Rather than sunblock, she grabs a half-empty bottle of baby oil, then pours herself a strong drink.

The back door is stiff on its hinges and takes a moment to open, as if no one has used it for a while. She steps out into the sunshine. The yard is angled into the hills, with a high cedar fence. She'd always imagined Beth would end up in a house like this. She glances around as she spreads a towel on a lounger. The patio furniture is classic, but the navy chairs are fading and the barbecue is covered in a film of dust. Overgrown frangipani bushes rim the yard, red flowers blooming, but it's clear they don't have a gardener coming in, and this would be one of the few houses in the neighborhood without a pool. It's like a dream perfectly set up, but then stalled in mid-flight. She feels a combination of envy and sympathy, two things Beth could always make her feel.

She packed bathing suits, but didn't bother digging them out, settling on her mismatched bra and skimpy panties. She takes off her robe and rubs baby oil on her chest and stomach, down her legs, her skin gleaming. She takes a sip of her drink, then lies back, tucking the gun beneath the towel.

She tries to relax, feeling the sun warm her skin. The languid pleasure of just lying in the sun both soothed and excited her, the way drugs did, the way applause did. It was such an easy way to bring ecstasy. She wishes she didn't need the constant excitement, the way Beth didn't seem to need it. Fake, romantic happy endings were enough for Beth, but not for Cassie. She needs the real thing. She'd turn the stereo on and blast it loud enough to reach the backyard, but she doesn't want to attract attention. She could use a blunt, too, but she needs to stay alert—just in case.

Then suddenly something cuts through the silence. A car pulling into the driveway. Her heart constricts. It's not the throaty growl of Jay's Mustang.

Rick?

She sits up, reaching for the gun. A car door closes. She holds her breath.

38

CASSIE

Monday Afternoon

Her earbuds are in. She hears nothing but music. Not the *squeak* of her rubber gloves on the cupboards, not the *click* of the nozzle as she squirts the door handles, the gloves making her movements clumsy and childlike, as she wipes with paper towels. "Summertime" is on her iPhone, the Janis Joplin version. She still uses the phone for music, and this is one of her favorite songs. She remembers performing it with Beth at Wally's all those years ago. It makes her smile. She misses her old friend. Maybe she can call her from the beach when this is all over. She squirts the cupboard again.

She tries to ignore why she's cleaning now, and the danger if she misses a spot, leaves fingerprints that can tie them to this house. They can't get caught again. But all the driving, all the planning, all the waiting will be over soon. When Rick finishes the deal, there'll be nothing but beaches and music for a very long time.

As she twists her wrist to scrub the backside of a handle, she feels something whack her, hard, in the back of the neck. Her vision blurs for a second from the impact. She turns to see Rick glaring at her from the back doorway, the screen door open, Bobby's eyes locked on hers with worry and fear. They'd gone out for pizza, leaving her to clean the fingerprints off the cupboards and doorknobs.

He's yelling at her, but she can't hear him, only the music: Janis's growl, like something wounded on the street, dragging its way to safety. She touches the back of her neck, and her fingers come away wet. Beer. The half-empty can rolls on the floor at her feet, dented from where it made contact with her spine. She's frozen in place. Rick's face is contorted, pink lips moving, eyebrows furrowed, spit flying from his mouth. He takes three long strides toward her, but she doesn't even flinch. Why doesn't she defend herself? Bobby's just staring at her like a scared kid.

Rick yanks one earbud out of her ear. "—the fuck are you doing?" His voice overpowers the music, and the beach, and the piano bench with Beth vanish. Janis is only half alive in her head.

"You gotta get this done!" he yells, his face reddening as he motions to the cupboards. "You should be finished by now!"

Her eyes dart to Bobby, but he still hasn't moved.

"Are you packed yet?" Rick demands.

Her iPhone cord still swings from one ear, Janis grappling with the closing bars of the song, her voice dying and faint.

"There's so much to do and you're fucking singing to yourself? Just having a good time?"

She hadn't realized she was singing out loud. She hadn't meant for him to hear.

"Get this shit cleaned up and get in the goddamn bedroom! They said no hos when they get here!"

Your bedroom. Get to your bedroom. The words hit her like a slap. Before she can move, Rick grabs the cord and yanks the other bud from her ear, pulling the phone from where she's tucked it into her waistband. There's only quiet now. Unless the sun, starting to slant through the door, makes a noise she can hear. A kind of soft whisper, like distant applause. The sound of the sun.

Get to your room!

Rick is right up in her face, chin out as he wraps the cord around the iPhone, daring her to stop him. She smells beer on his breath. She could hit him. She *should* hit him. She should smash his nose into his brain.

Summertime...

She knows he's got a temper, but he's never hit her before. What the hell is wrong with him? Maybe he's just stressed about the deal tonight, but they all are. That's no excuse. She's not going to take this crap, not from him, not from anyone. As she stands there, not speaking, just glaring at him, her chest heaving, she watches his mood change, anger now replaced by a dim confusion. He knows the truth, that she wants to hurt him and that she could do it. That she may not be able to stop herself from doing it. Poor Bobby's still watching from the doorway, blinking, staring at them both, waiting—as she is waiting—for somebody to get hurt.

Rick finally speaks. "Did you at least get the suit?"

"Yeah, I already packed everything," she tells him, almost spitting in his face. "Do the rest of this shit yourself. I'm not your maid."

She slams down the Windex bottle and reaches for her cigarettes on the counter. She walks into the backyard, the screen door banging shut behind her. The two men stand in the shadows of the house, staring after her.

She drops into the plastic lawn chair, trying to grab a cigarette from the pack. The rubber gloves make her too clumsy. She pulls one off, then the other, but the second one sticks and she has to tug hard. The pressure snaps the leather thong on one of her old bracelets, and wooden beads patter to the dusty ground.

"Shit!"

The bracelets are her talismans. Her armor. She quickly scoops up the beads, clutching them in one hand, blowing off the dirt. She finally manages to bring the lighter to the tip of her cigarette, inhaling long and hard. She hears Rick stomp farther into the house, slamming things, still swearing because her suitcase isn't packed. She sees Bobby at the screen door, watching her.

"You okay?" he whispers.

She forces herself to smile, then shrugs as if it doesn't bother her. She knows Bobby has a crush on her—Rick's even brought it up himself. But she doesn't want him to worry, so she shoves her middle finger at the house, where Rick is still on his tirade. Bobby smiles, relieved, backing into the shadows. Through the screen, she sees him pick up the Windex bottle, squirting the cupboards, wiping quickly. How sweet of him.

She hears Rick yelling again and her muscles coil. What's wrong with her lately? She's not like this. She doesn't let anyone treat her this way—especially a man. What's happened to her? Is she losing her mind?

She looks down at the dusty beads in her hand, the frayed thong curled like seaweed on a beach. She made the bracelet years ago; she can't even remember when. At first the hobby was to cover her scars—even though sometimes the bracelets just seemed to draw attention to them. She remembers Beth asking about how she got them.

You're not afraid of anything, are you?

She's been thinking about Beth so much lately.

"Hey!" It's Rick's voice, sharp and cutting. She looks up as he opens the screen door. He's brandishing a handgun, letting her see what it is before he points it at her. He cocks his head, a cruel grin on his face. "Come on in, honey. There's still *so* much work to do." Then he mocks pulling the trigger. "*Click.*"

39

CASSIE

Her hand trembles as she grips the gun, holding it down at her side, beside the chair. But she's ready to fire if she has to, her finger hovering over the trigger. Through the narrow slats of the fencing, she sees a tall figure approach from the driveway.

The gate opens.

Her wrist relaxes when a man with silver hair, wearing a yellow golf shirt, steps into the yard, carrying a manila envelope. She carefully slides the gun beneath the beach towel before he can see it. He freezes when he notices her in her bra and panties, lounging in the sun.

"Hi there!" She stands up, putting on her robe, aware the movement emphasizes her bust, as he stares at her, his jaw agape. Male attention is another dependable drug. With the envelope in his hand, she assumes he's some kind of messenger. "Can I help you?"

"I—I must be at the wrong address," he says, backing out of the yard.

"No, wait a minute!" She runs after him, following him to the gate. He's already opening the door of a gold-toned Cadillac, but she stops, leaning out. "Are you looking for Beth or Jay?" she asks, a little out of breath.

"Yes. I'm looking for my son, Jason."

Of course. No messenger drives a Cadillac. "You've come to the right place!"

131

"I thought so." But he seems confused, frowning at her with a mixture of suspicion and curiosity. "Oh! You must be the friend who's staying."

"Yeah," she says, trying to seem casual, but she's anxious Jay's been talking about her already. The fewer people who know she's here, the better. She glances back and forth, checking the street, then walks into the driveway, the stone warm on her bare feet. "I'm Cassie," she says. "Great to meet you."

The silk robe clings to the moisture of the oil on her skin, and the man can't help himself: he glances down, then up again.

"John Montgomery," he finally says, shaking her hand. But he still seems uneasy. "I was just coming to drop something off for Jason, but it's too large for the mailbox."

"I'll make sure he gets it," she says, holding out her hand for the envelope.

"I'd rather leave it for him, if you don't mind. It's confidential. I was going to put it next to the back door."

"Door's open. You could leave it inside yourself."

As he considers it, the deep lines on his forehead worsen; they're from a lifetime of squinting at golf balls across a fairway, no doubt. Judging from the expensive car and the big gold watch, the Montgomery clan has money. She wonders why the yard here is so overgrown, then. Something deeper is going on in this family.

"Maybe I'll do that," he says, in a decisive way, as if he's come up with the idea himself.

She smiles her most unassuming smile. "Fab. This way." She walks into the backyard ahead of him, the gate shutting behind them. "Just leave it in there," she says, pointing to the door.

John gives a nervous smile, before disappearing into the shadows of the house. Cassie feels a hot twist between her legs, enjoys the feeling of impending mischief. She follows him into the house, the hallway dim and cool after the bright sunlight, as if they've stumbled into a network of caves. He's in the kitchen, writing on the envelope with a gold pen. He notices her and immediately gets ready to leave.

"Thank you so much," he says. "I should get going."

"Aw, do you *have* to go?" Cassie asks, though she knows it's a trick question. This man's ego is bound to be huge—probably bigger than his son's—and nobody like that wants anyone to think he "has" to do anything. It's an easy trap, and he doesn't know how to answer. "How about a drink? I was just having another one," she says, going to the bar.

He glances at his watch. "I don't think so."

"Oh, please. Nobody's here, and I hate partying alone. Just one?"

He looks toward the back door, then at her, uncertain. "All right, fine. Thank you."

"Scotch? Vodka?"

"Scotch and soda, if you have it."

"Sure thing. Go on out. I'll bring it to you."

He seems eager to leave the room. She doesn't bother looking for soda. Instead, she pours two generous doubles. She sees the envelope on the kitchen counter and quickly checks it. It's sealed, with a CONFIDENTIAL sticker glued to the flap. The logo on the top left corner reads: *John R. Montgomery, President, Montgomery Holdings, Inc.* Interesting.

When she gets outside, Jay's father is inspecting the dusty barbecue. He accidentally knocks over the bottle of charcoal lighter, then sets it upright again. Cassie smiles and hands him his drink.

"Thank you." He waits to sit down until she does.

"Such a gentleman. I like that." She's aware of the gun just beneath her towel.

He takes a sip and winces.

"Sorry. There was no soda."

"Fine," he mutters, unable to meet her eyes.

She doesn't say anything, watching him, waiting for the inevitable questions. Men like this always have questions.

"So—you're an old friend of Beth's? Are you from Philadelphia?"

"No, New York. But we went to school in Boston together."

"Oh, that's right. You're a musician, too?" And the way he uses the word, he might as well have said, *So, you're a worthless layabout, are you?*

"I'm a singer."

"A singer?" His silver eyebrows pump up.

"Jazz mostly."

"I see. I like jazz, actually."

"That's good." She sips her drink. Even a few sips of alcohol have emboldened him. He meets her eyes now.

"How long are you staying for?"

"A few days. I have a show coming up in Monterey. I thought I'd see Beth while I had the chance." She leans back and points her toes, observing him like a Cheshire cat stretching in the sun. "So, what do you do, John?"

"I'm in banking."

"I could've guessed. You just have that powerful aura about you." She circles her fingers in a bewitching move. "I can sense things like that about people."

He laughs, flattered despite himself. He takes another loud swallow. Half the drink is already gone. Cassie doesn't know if he's trying to get drunk, or hurrying to get out of here. She doesn't really care. Either one is fine with her.

"This might seem forward," she begins, "but would you do me a favor?"

"Of course."

She pauses a beat and locks eyes on him. "Would you put some baby oil on my back?"

"Um..." He hitches, surprised.

"I want to flip over and I can't reach," she says, her voice light and casual now. She picks up the bottle, holding it out for him. "Please?"

He takes the oil in slightly trembling hands. Cassie turns around and lets the robe fall off her shoulders. She lowers her bra straps, then reaches back and unclasps the bra, letting it drop into her lap. She can tell by the hesitation that he's just staring at the curve of her bare back. She has to hold her breath not to laugh out loud.

"I'm sorry," he murmurs. "I h-have to go." He sets the bottle down without even touching her.

"Wait, John?"

But when she turns around, he's already halfway across the yard, walking quickly, the nape of his neck flowering red. He doesn't look back as he strides through the gate, letting it bang shut. The door of the Cadillac slams, and the motor starts up. She hears a little screech of tires as he pulls away. She wonders what he'll tell his wife about this little errand—or Jay.

Serves them right for talking about her.

She drains her drink and lies back, closing her eyes against the sun. But the yard is even quieter, even emptier, than before.

40

GOODE

"I didn't want to touch it," says the woman, shuddering in distaste. She's in her midforties, wearing yoga gear, her frizzy hair up in a high ponytail. She holds a small Yorkshire terrier in her arms, a rhinestone leash hanging loose. According to her 911 call, the dog found something suspicious on the street. "When he pulled it out, it scared me. There's so much blood, it looked like someone was murdered."

"Thanks for calling it in," Goode says. "Looks like you got a little K-9 officer in training here." He lets the dog sniff his hand, then scratches its head. "If you could just give Detective Dawes your statement, you'll be free to go."

"Right this way, please," Dawes says, leading her to a cruiser parked down the block, where officers hold back a few onlookers.

Goode slips on black latex gloves and crouches down to examine what appears to be a pile of garbage on the sidewalk next to a string of newspaper boxes. But it's not garbage. It's someone's home. A tangled mess of blankets, used clothes, old shoes, and plastic bags full of empty wine bottles and beer cans. A large piece of cardboard, acting as a lean-to, is scrawled with black marker: ANYTHING HELPS. GOD BLESS.

Next to the mess is a crumpled pile of striped cotton—covered in so much blood, the pattern is almost obscured. The sheet was found less than three miles from the shootings, and the officer who responded to the woman's call about it had been one of a dozen uniforms at the rental house that night. She recognized the distinctive striped pattern of the fabric and called Goode, almost embarrassed to be bothering him over bedding. But her hunch had been right. It isn't a fancy Egyptian cotton sheet either, but faded and threadbare, like the one at the house; it appears to be an exact match. And it explains why the heavy trail of blood that led to the bedroom had stopped there; clearly someone had used this sheet to stanch a severe wound.

Goode remembers that big bloodstain in front of the couch in Lawrence Heights. They're still waiting for DNA results, but the blood type matches Squires. If he took the sheet, he'd just escaped from a crime scene. Would he drop evidence with his own blood on it in the middle of a busy street? Goode doubts it. Even in a panic, nobody would be that stupid. The homeless person who lived here probably found it somewhere else and brought it back.

Goode scans the small group of onlookers on the sidewalk. There's no sign of anyone who might call this place home. But maybe Squires is in the crowd somewhere, watching, hiding in plain sight. But then he sees something else that gets his attention. Across the street is a drugstore, with dumpsters lined up along one side. What does a wounded drug dealer need after escaping from the scene of a shootout? First aid, of course.

41

JAY

"Take it easy, for chrissakes!" Karen says from the passenger seat, hanging on to the dashboard.

But Jay ignores her, swerving through traffic. "What a bitch! Can you believe that? Not up to her. Then who the hell *is* it up to? Isn't that what she does for a living?"

"I know. I'm sorry."

"It's not *your* fault," he grumbles, trying to calm down. But it had been a degrading experience. Jay was his most charming self, a first-class car salesman, and Karen was note perfect, too, but still, the woman had so many concerns.

If it were up to me, it wouldn't be a problem. I believe in you guys. But the house is already remortgaged, and your debt-to-asset ratio concerns my manager. He has to sign off on these things, too.

"Screw her," Jay says. "She's just passing the buck."

A Trans-Am squeezes into the fast lane in front of him. Jay leans on the horn so long and hard, it makes his head ache. "Fuck you, asshole!" he screams, racing past the guy, giving him the finger.

Fuck you, too, asshole! the other guy mouths through the window, a character muted on-screen.

"Jay, calm down!" But he keeps leaning on the horn. "Stop!" Karen yells. She pulls his arm away from the wheel and the car swerves into the next lane, everyone barely missing one another, more horns joining the fray.

"Are you trying to get us killed?"

"Are *you*?" she demands. "Just chill out, okay? I can feel your heart beating through your arm!"

"All right, okay…" He takes a deep breath, then another, trying to relax. He turns to her, hopeful. "Can we go somewhere for a drink? I could really use one, and I don't want to go home yet."

"No, we can't."

"We'll just talk." But Jay is already trying to think of a bar in a hotel, where maybe he could convince her to get a room. He needs to be with her, to reconnect with her, the way it was when they got together, so young and full of passion, for the business, for the future, for each other.

"There's nothing to talk about. We just have to be patient. We have to wait."

"For what? Commisso? Are you kidding me? Do I have to remind you we have to come up with three hundred and fifty grand before Friday or our star is going to walk? We can't keep stringing her along like this. If she passes, we're back at square *one*. Less than square one!"

"You think I don't know that?" she snaps. "You're such an asshole sometimes."

Jay lets a beat pass, his mood softening. He feels bad. It really isn't her fault. She's doing everything she can.

"I'm sorry," he says. "*Please*, let's just go for one drink. I really don't want to go home yet. Beth's…*friend*"—he can't seem to think of a proper insult for her—"is still there. She's a weirdo. I don't want to be alone with her."

"Such bad timing."

"Tell me about it. This week of all weeks? I smelled her smoking pot at barely ten in the morning, if you can believe that."

"And she's Beth's friend?" Karen seems shocked.

"From a long time ago, college." He remembers the sharp scent wafting through the house, lingering in the air. She had such gall. Such nerve. He almost admired it, remembering what Beth told him about her. *I don't know how she got through it, poor thing.* "Whatever," he says, hopeful again. "It's not my drama. So

139

where do you want to go? The Standard?" A favorite old haunt of theirs.

"I told you, I can't. I have to go home and work on a way to get an extension."

She means she'll get in touch with Milla's agent again. The actress liked the script, but she had other offers and she'd have to take one if there wasn't at least some money on the table soon, as an act of good faith.

"Let's do a conference call, then," Jay says. "I can be there when you talk to him."

"He doesn't like conference calls."

"That's bullshit!"

"All right, then, he doesn't like *you*. Okay? He says you're too aggressive."

Jay laughs, a sharp and bitter sound. "A Hollywood agent is calling *me* aggressive? That's hilarious! I'm flattered!"

Jay looms up on a transport truck ahead of him. It sputters along, holding things up. He goes to pass on the left, but the transport eases over, not letting him by. Jay swerves back to the right and floors the engine, leaning on the horn.

"Will you *relax*?" Karen yells. "He was just letting you pass!"

"Bullshit! He was trying to cut me off!" Jay roars ahead, still blasting the horn, barely in control of the steering wheel. Why the hell did everything—absolutely everything—always have to go wrong for him?

42

BETH

The Barneys store in Los Angeles is surrounded by palm trees, bristling with red awnings. As Beth enters the store, she's so nervous, the marble floor seems to dip and swirl beneath her. She carries a crinkled shopping bag that barely weighs an ounce, but somehow it feels as if she's dragging an anvil.

She has to bring the scarf back now more than ever. They'd be feeding and entertaining Cassie for the rest of the week, and even without a houseguest, they were on a tight budget. She doesn't want Cass to know how much they're struggling. It's humiliating that she'd come so far and had attained so little in her life.

Why does she still want to impress Cass so much? Nothing had changed. She's already planned on picking up more beer, but with the money from the scarf, she can buy some nice wine. Maybe she should stop at that expensive butcher shop she used to go to. She wouldn't even have to pay for parking. Or maybe they could go out to dinner for a change.

But as she approaches the counter where she bought the scarf last month, her hands begin to shake and her mouth feels dry. She hates bringing anything back for a refund, and she's had to do it so much lately.

Couldn't she make up her mind?

Don't you know what's right for you?

And the most embarrassing judgment of all: *Can't you afford to keep nice things?*

141

Behind the counter, she recognizes the sleek brunette who waited on her. She'd just been browsing at the time, something to do on her lunch hour, fantasizing, pretending she could afford any of the pretty things on display. But the woman had been so adamant about the scarf—*"That really brings out the blue in your eyes!"*—Beth felt roped into buying it.

She approaches the counter, each step requiring great effort. The girl looks up, smiling. "May I help—oh, hello! Nice to see you again."

She's surprised the woman remembers her. People rarely seemed to. "Hello," she says, smiling, then pretends to peruse the display case, trying to get up the nerve to dig out the scarf. What would she say? It's the wrong size? No. She'd have to admit she couldn't afford it or otherwise insult this woman's taste.

"We just got these ones in," says the girl, running her hand along a selection of textured silk. "They're going fast."

"Thanks, but I'm just browsing right now."

"Of course. Take your time." The woman smiles and heads for greener pastures, a glitzy redhead on the other side of the counter.

Beth's bag feels even heavier. Her forehead breaks out in pinpricks of sweat. The cloying smell of perfumes from nearby counters bombard her. She wants to burst into tears, stomp her feet, curse Jay, Cass—herself—everyone, for putting her in this position, being unable to entertain an old friend for a few days. The weight of humiliation is almost enough to make her pass out. She takes a deep breath, steeling herself. "Excuse me," she calls, a little too loudly.

The girl turns around. "Yes?"

"I think I do need your help, after all."

"One moment." The girl smiles, excusing herself from the redhead, who seems absorbed with her own reflection and the task of choosing a new scarf herself.

"I hate to trouble you." Beth wills her hand to stop shaking as she pulls out the scarf. "But I'm not sure I want to keep this."

"Oh? Was there something wrong with it?" The girl inspects the piece of blue silk, the price tag, the stitches.

"No. My husband didn't like it, that's all."

"Oh, what do husbands know?" she says, laughing.

Beth tries to laugh, too, taking out her wallet. "What can you do, right? There's no accounting for taste."

"So true. Well, no problem at all. Do you have the receipt?"

"Of course." Beth focuses on the task of retrieving the chit of paper, handing it to the girl, who turns to the cash register and begins tapping at keys. The redhead looks at them with disdain, then drops the scarves she's considering and walks away. A jolt of regret surges through Beth. Did she make the girl lose a sale? She hopes not.

The tapping stops. "I'm sorry, but the grace period has elapsed."

"Excuse me?"

"You only have thirty days to return merchandise for a refund. It's been thirty-two. Would you like store credit? Or maybe an exchange?"

But Beth can't answer. She snatches the scarf and hurries out of the store, trying not to cry.

43

GOODE

Wednesday Afternoon

The cool air-conditioning makes the drugstore a respite from the heat of the sun. But it's the closed-circuit security cameras that get Goode's attention, hidden in mirrored domes suspended from the ceiling. He flashes his badge at the nearest cashier, a woman with a long, dark ponytail, and asks to speak to the manager. She picks up a phone, her voice crackling on the intercom as she calls the manager to the front.

"So—what's going on out there?" She nods to the commotion on the street. "Is the doctor okay?"

"Doctor?"

"That's what we call the old guy who lives there, anyway."

"You know his real name?" Goode takes out his notebook.

"No, sorry. But he's always rummaging through our dumpsters for recycling. Coming in for wine or beer."

"So he's been around awhile?"

"Yeah, I mean, at least since I started here, and that was about two years ago."

"When's the last time you saw him?"

"He was just in this morning. He comes in every day. Sometimes twice. Is he okay?"

This afternoon? The bloodstains on the sheet were much older than that, but Goode pushes it just the same. "When you saw him, did he seem injured?"

"Gosh, no. He seemed fine. Why? What happened?"

144

But before Goode can answer, they're interrupted with a cheery "Hello there!"

A smiling African-American woman in a white lab coat walks over. "Is there something I can do for you?"

Goode flashes his badge and the woman's smile collapses.

The cramped security room at the back of the store is long and narrow, with one wall covered in a messy bulletin board, the other, a bank of CCTV monitors. The security footage is grainy and black-and-white. The manager flicks a tracking wheel and stops on a frame with a time stamp of 11:38 that morning.

"There he is." She points to a frail-looking man in a tattered blazer and baggy pants, opening a cooler at the back of the store. His white hair is long and straggly, his shoulders hunched. As he turns to the camera, clutching a six-pack of beer, Goode sees his gaunt face and sunken eyes. He couldn't weigh more than a hundred pounds, and he was obviously alive a few hours ago.

"Has he ever shown any violent tendencies?"

"Not at all! He's sweet as anything. What happened? Is he in trouble?"

"You just call the next time you see him, okay?" Goode hands her his card and points to the screen. "How long do you keep security footage for?"

A few minutes later, Goode is sitting by himself in a squeaky chair in front of a black-and-white monitor. The manager was kind enough to offer him something to drink, so he sips a cold Gatorade. He showed her the mug shot of Squires, and she apologized that she didn't recognize him, but he was free to check the footage himself.

His fingers work over a small control panel of buttons as he cues the video up to Monday night, watching customers zip in and out of the store in fast motion. The first 911 call about shots fired at the rental house came in at 9:52 p.m. If his hunch is correct, the striped sheet was taken from the scene around that time, used to stanch a bullet wound—or wounds—and dumped near this store when whoever was injured came in for some DIY emergency medical care. And it must've been Squires, because according to Nico Alvarez, the "blonde" was uninjured.

The gray figures continue to dart and swirl. Just after midnight, he sees what he's looking for. A man walks in with a jean jacket draped over one shoulder. Goode freezes the frame, narrowing his eyes to peer more closely at the scraggly fair hair and patchy beard.

Play.

Goode waits, tracking forward to another camera, as the man grabs a cart, using only one hand to push it. He picks up beer and two bottles from the liquor aisle, again favoring the arm beneath the jacket. He doesn't look up at the camera, but what convicted felon would?

He's wearing a dark T-shirt and, as he turns down the first aid aisle, loading up with supplies, Goode gets a better view of his free arm. His biceps and forearm are covered in ink. Tattoos are considered as individual as fingerprints when it comes to identifying suspects—and designs were now kept on file as distinctive features, like scars and birthmarks. He can't get a good look at the tats, but his skin is clearly inked in a full sleeve, like the suspect's.

At the cash register, the shot of the man's face is better, clearer, with fewer shadows. As he grabs his bags, he turns in the direction of a camera at the door, the best angle yet. Goode freezes the frame, recognizing his personal most wanted: Richard Bradley Squires. Alive. But he's alone. And he's not carrying anything else. He's certainly not dragging a million plus in drugs or cash with him. Since nothing was found at the place in Lawrence Heights, either, where had Squires hidden everything?

If Ogilvy had escaped the house with him, Goode assumed, in tracking her down, he'd find Squires, too. Was she waiting outside for him, guarding the loot in a vehicle? It's a possibility. But Squires wouldn't have risked coming into the store by himself if he had a partner. Would he? Especially if he was injured. He would've sent Ogilvy in alone and guarded everything himself.

Nico Alvarez said the blonde had been on her own. Another consideration is that the pair split up.

Was that part of the plan? A mistake? An argument?

Alvarez said she had heavy bags with her. Did she have the money? The junk? Would it still end up on the street somehow?

Goode looks at the photo of Cassandra Ogilvy again. He feels like he's been trudging up a great jagged ridge of mountain, only to find there's nothing on the other side but more mountains. With four men dead, including a fellow officer, and at least one killer at large, he's now reduced to watching security footage at a drugstore?

Fuck.

He's just about to punch the wall—or something else—when his phone beeps with a notification. It's from his captain. He has clearance on Butler's field tapes. Finally. But he has to get back to his desk to access them. He stands up, rushing out of the room so quickly, the chair spins and hits the wall behind him.

44

JAY

Wednesday Evening

Next to sex, video games are one of the few things in the world that help Jay relax. While Beth is at work, he can spend hours on the couch, racing sports cars in exotic countries or shooting terrorists in abandoned bunkers. After such a rough day, all he wanted to do was come home, put his feet up, and kill some bad guys. But he couldn't, because he didn't want to be alone with *her*. Women usually didn't intimidate him like this, not even beautiful ones. But with Cassie, it's different. It's not just that a part of him wants her. Any man would. He just doesn't trust her. She's up to something; he can feel it.

So after he dropped Karen off, he went for a drink at the first bar he could find and texted Beth to let him know when she got home. He sat in the dimness, drinking doubles and flirting with the bartender, who was pretty and busty and uncomplicated. He was attracted to her and he could tell she was attracted to him. Yet at the same time, he couldn't stop thinking of *her*. Cassie Ogilvy roused in him sensations he hadn't felt in a very long time. Desire. Confusion. Anger. Frustration. By the time he heard from Beth, he'd finished two doubles and two beers.

When he got home, the girls were in the living room, playing cards on the coffee table, laughing and drinking.

"Hey, Movie Man!" Cassie called. The first thing he did was open the fridge for a beer, surprised to see the shelves full of Heineken. Heineken? He hadn't bought that brand in a while.

"Hey," he said when Beth came in to refill a bowl of nacho chips.

They exchanged a dry peck. "Finally," he whispered, motioning to the fridge. "She contributes a little something to the cause."

"Oh—I picked that up after work," she said, seeming preoccupied. Jay was shocked. He didn't think Beth had the nerve to buy beer in the first place, let alone drink it. What the hell was happening to his prim and proper wife?

And now, there they are, giggling and chattering right next to him, while he lies on the couch, trying to play Xbox. They're making so much noise, it's hard to concentrate. They sit on the floor, a deck of cards stacked between them on the coffee table, beer bottles sweating on coasters. Cassie wears a tank top and denim shorts that are so tiny, the bottom of her cheeks hang out when she gets up on her knees to lay down a card. Her ass is *right* there, in front of him, and Beth doesn't even notice. Cassie's not wearing a bra either; he can see practically *everything*. He's repulsed and enticed at the same time.

"Change to diamonds!" Cassie exclaims, slapping a card on the table. "Woo-hoo! Pick up five!"

"Damn," Beth complains. "You always got the five of diamonds."

"I know!" Cassie says, sitting back down, finally out of his field of vision.

"But guess what?" Beth narrows her eyes and lays down her own card.

"Shit. And *you* always got the two!"

The women start laughing, picking up their cards, counting together.

"One, two, three..."

Jay grimaces, trying to concentrate, the controller extended as he maneuvers back and forth.

"Four...five..."

"Can you guys try and, ya know, keep it down a bit, please?"

But they don't stop counting.

"Six...seven..."

Jay heaves a breath of relief when he hears a soft *ding* from down the hall.

"That'll be the dryer," Beth says, standing up. She points a finger at her old friend. "No cheating."

Cassie holds up her hands in mock innocence. "Who, me?"

"Yeah—*you*. Keep an eye on her, Jay."

He grumbles something.

"Want me to help you fold?" Cassie asks.

"Ha ha. Very funny." Beth shuffles out of the room in her slippers.

"It's a joke," Cassie says to Jay. "I never fold things. What's the point? Everything just ends up wrinkled again. Total waste of time."

He just gives her a look. She makes a showy deal of picking up cards and looking at them. "Hey, you're supposed to make sure I don't cheat."

"You're a big girl."

"What are *you* so grouchy for?"

"*Grouchy?*" He almost laughs. She has a child's mind.

"Yeah, grouchy." She slides back to lean against the couch next to him, her knees up. "Bad day?"

"Nothing but lately."

"Aw, that sucks. You want to tell me about it?"

"Not really."

"Your loss." She watches the game for a bit. "You're pretty good at that. You play with yourself every day?"

He grits his teeth but doesn't answer. She grabs her cigarettes and lights one right beside him. He stops breathing through his nose. Because of the cigarettes? Because of her perfume? He's not sure. But he's glad she's shut up at least, just watching him. Beth never watches him play video games. She thinks it's juvenile. He hears her leave the laundry room and head down the hall to the guest room.

"On your six!" Cassie suddenly yells.

Jay hammers the controller as a horrid monster leaps at him from a purple cliff. He's so distracted, he wasn't prepared.

"I said your six, your six! Behind you!"

But his character dies a horrible, bloody death.

"Ah, too bad. You died. Can I buy you a beer? Cheer you up?"

"Still working on this one."

Cassie gets up from the coffee table.

"Help yourself, though," he says, a note of sarcasm in his voice. Even so, he can't help but glance over as she wiggles into the kitchen. God, she is so damn sexy. Fuck. He waits for the game to reload. One of the things he resents is that he doesn't have the newest version of Xbox; their tech budget went to upgrading his phone. He hears her fussing about in the kitchen, getting a beer from the fridge. There's suddenly a hollow crash.

"Shit!" Cassie says.

He gets up from the couch and hurries into the kitchen to see her limp away from the fridge, her foot bleeding. A broken beer bottle lies in a puddle of foam on the floor.

"You okay?" he asks, surprised he even cares.

"I don't know..."

"Beth! Situation here!" he calls down the hall.

"Be right there!" she calls back, but he can tell by her voice she's preoccupied with the laundry.

Cassie hobbles to a stool and sits down, pulling her bare foot up. "I can't see anything. Can you look? Is it deep?"

He kneels down in front of her as she lifts her leg so he can see the bottom of her foot. It's a strangely intimate position. He's never been on his knees in front of a woman like this, not without going down on her.

"How does it look?" she asks, wincing.

Her heels are dirty from walking around in bare feet, and a thick rivulet of blood oozes across her skin. But he can also see between her thighs, the thin thong of frayed denim doing very little to protect her modesty. She doesn't appear to be wearing panties.

"I—I don't know. I can't tell."

"Do you think I'll live?"

"P-probably," he stutters. He's wearing shorts, and she rests her uninjured foot on his bare leg.

"Thanks...Doc," she says with a smile, running her foot up his thigh. Heat floods through his body. He stares at her in confusion. Is she hitting on him?

"I'll get the Band-Aids," he says, standing up.

In the bathroom, he opens the medicine cabinet and grabs a box of bandages. As he closes the door, he sees his reflection in the mirror. He stares at himself a moment, his heart still beating hard.

Thanks...Doc...

He hears Beth go into the kitchen, her voice distant and concerned. "Oh no! What happened?"

"Battle wound," Cassie says.

That look in her eye. The feeling of her warm toes on his leg. Was she really flirting with him? Does she flirt with everyone?

Good God, what did Beth do, bringing this girl into their house? Only two more days, he tells himself. Two more days.

45

GOODE

Wednesday Night

Goode wears headphones, hunched over his desk. His notebook is open, a burger getting cold in front of him. But he can't eat. He can only listen to the quiet voice of Curtis Butler on the field tapes. The voice of a ghost in his head.

Sunday, fourteen hundred, MB1, MB2, and I arrive at location three.

Male Black One and Two: Jules Williams and Arkell Mitchell. The location was a diner where a quality check would be performed and details of the exchange drawn up for the following evening at the house in Lawrence Heights.

MB1 takes table by himself. MB2 and I sit behind him in separate booth.

The voice is monotonous. Completely without fear or emotion. In such contrast to the laughter Goode remembers. Whether in training sessions or grabbing a beer, Butler was always so quick to laugh.

Fourteen hundred twenty, black SUV circles parking lot. Stops out front. Tags obscured.

Most field reports are filed at the end of each day, so there's no information about the day and night of the shooting itself. Butler had no idea what was going to happen to him the next night. He was just doing his job.

MC1 and MC2 exit vehicle and enter location. Sit with MB1.

Male Caucasian One is Squires; MC2 is the "Kurt Cobain lookalike," Robert Hackett.

Observed FC1 in driver's seat of vehicle, waiting outside. Blonde. Late twenties. She lit a cigarette and watched the building.

There she is again. That blonde in the center of all of this. It has to be Ogilvy. The problem is, he doesn't know if he's getting closer to her, or if she's already slipped away.

46

BETH

Thursday Morning

Beth wears a robe, her hair up in a towel as she makes coffee, squinting against the bright sunlight. Her head throbs and her stomach roils. She shivers involuntarily. It had been one hell of a night. She and Cassie were up late, holed up in the extra room, talking and laughing and drinking the way they used to in school. Jay had to yell at them to keep it down. But the whole time, Beth was trying to find out more about why her friend was back in her life. And what she was really doing in L.A. Because she knows Cassie is lying to her about something. Maybe about everything.

Nerves clench her body when she sees Jay coming up the driveway, back from his run. The door opens and he invades the room with his pounding energy and the smell of sweat.

"You look guilty," he says, out of breath.

"I think you mean hungover."

"Both." He grabs his blender for his post-run shake. "What the hell time did you guys get to bed last night?"

"I don't remember."

"No kidding." There's a sharp note in his voice. "Is she up yet?"

Beth shakes her head, and just that small movement sends a shriek of pain to her skull. She reaches in the cupboard for some aspirin, swallowing two. Her hands are shaking. She can't bear the idea of going in, listening to the metronome, not today.

"I smelled you guys smoking grass in there last night," Jay says with derision.

"So? You were smoking last night."

"Yeah, but till all hours? I just can't believe you. You're acting like you're still in college or something."

She almost laughs; he doesn't know how right he is. "Don't worry. I can't take much more of this, either. She's leaving tomorrow, so just don't—"

There are footsteps in the hallway.

"Shhh!" Beth hisses, and they both shut up, going about their routines. It feels strange to be whispering in her own house, but she doesn't have a choice. She doesn't want Cassie to hear them, especially after last night, because she knows Cassie's not telling her everything.

A moment later Cass appears in her threadbare Stones T-shirt. It's like a living flashback: Cassie padding around the dorm in bare feet and oversized tee, her cigarettes in one hand. It takes a moment before Beth can reconcile the past and the present and bring a smile to her face.

"Hey, sweetie, I didn't expect to see you up this early."

"I'm not. I'm the walking dead." Cassie holds out her arms and pretends to be a zombie as she thumps toward Beth, giving her a kiss on the cheek.

"Did you sleep okay?"

"Like a baby." Cass lights a cigarette and props on a stool at the counter. Beth sees Jay tense up; he hates cigarette smoke, and the house smells sour with it already. Like everything else about her old friend, it makes her feel young again. She doesn't know whether that's a good thing—or not.

"How about you?" Cassie asks.

"Ugh. I'm not used to these late nights. I could use a few more hours." She sets down a fresh cup of coffee for her friend.

"So? That just means you had fun. And you, Movie Man? We were a bit rowdy last night. Hope we didn't keep you up."

But Jay just flat ignores her as he reaches for his protein powder. Watching him gather the almond milk and a pomegranate, Beth can't believe it. She's always nice to *his* friends when they come over.

"Don't worry about Jay," she breaks in. "He sleeps like a log. Now he does, anyway. I made him get a sleeping pill pres—"

"Beth!" Jay slams down the butcher knife.

"Well, it's *true*, Jay. You were snoring like a bear when I came to bed." She turns to Cassie. "He normally has the dizzy legs."

She laughs. "The what?"

"The dizzy legs."

"Hey!"

"What the hell are dizzy legs?"

"His legs move around a lot when he sleeps. Unless he takes the pills."

Jay stands there, his eyes wide, trying to compute her betrayal. "Are you still drunk or something?"

"Oh, Jay, who cares? It's nothing."

"So?" he says sharply. "It's *personal*."

"Jay, my man," Cassie begins, "crystal meth is personal. Crack cocaine—also personal. But sleeping pills?" She shrugs her lips. "Not so much."

Jay just tosses his blender in the sink with a *bang*. He stabs the knife back into the wooden block and storms out of the room. Beth winces, waiting to relax until she hears the bedroom door slam shut and the shower turn on. She hasn't seen Jay go without his post-run shake since she met him.

"Uh-oh. I think he's pissed off." She smiles at Cassie apologetically. "Sorry about that. He's just really been stressed lately."

"I don't blame him. I show up here unannounced, drink all his beer. Smoke him out of house and home."

"He'll get over it," she says, forcing a laugh. She wipes down the counter, looks at her friend, this apparition in her life, and wonders if she should ask. She always used to worry if she should pry into Cassie's life, afraid of what she'd find.

"I keep forgetting to tell you," she begins, her voice casual. "I think some guy called here for you the other night."

Cassie freezes. "Here?"

"Yeah. I'm sorry I didn't mention it. I guess I was just so caught

157

up with seeing you, I totally forgot. Does that make any sense? Monday night? Like, three in the morning?"

"A guy? Did he leave a name?"

"No. He hung up, actually."

"I have no idea who it could be," she says, shrugging. But her knee starts to pump.

"Could it be that ex of yours?"

"No way. He doesn't know where—oh, wait. I know, it must be Lily's brother."

"You gave him this number?"

"Yeah. Just in case." Cassie stabs out her cigarette, but her knee still jumps like a piston. "That reminds me, I should get in touch with her. Just to arrange everything. You mind if I make some calls this morning?"

"Of course not. But when, Cass?"

"When what?"

"When did you give this guy my home number?"

"Couple days ago, I guess. When I knew I'd be coming through town."

So Cassie already guessed Beth would let her stay here? She's been planning this all along? As she stares at her friend, there are a thousand questions she wants to ask.

What's going on, Cassie?

What are you really doing here?

More than anything, she wants to know: *Why are you lying to me? Because I know you are.*

47

CASSIE

Fuck.

Cassie flicks nervously at her lighter until she finally gets a cigarette lit. She inhales deeply, pacing the guest room. It had to have been Rick who called. There's nobody else who knows about her connection to Beth. He must've remembered her name and seen the number in her contacts.

But he hasn't found the address yet, thank God; otherwise she'd already be dead. Cassie tried doing a reverse lookup on Beth's number herself many times but could never find a corresponding address. That doesn't mean Rick wouldn't have better luck. If he knows she's here, it's only a matter of time before he tracks her down.

She has to get the hell out of here.

She hears Beth leave the house and get into her car. She goes to the window, peeking out. Beth glances over, but Cassie shifts into the shadows so she can't be seen. She notices Beth's forehead scored with worry lines as she drives away. Cassie has seen that look on her old friend's face many times before. She knows something's wrong.

But this changes everything, Rick tracking her down so soon. She has to find somewhere else to go. She grabs her suitcase, throwing it on the bed, starting to pack.

She should leave the country. That would be the best thing to do. But the cops have probably already flagged her name and they'd get her at the airport.

There was a guy, outside of Vegas—she and Rick were going there for new IDs after the drop. Was it worth the chance? Or would Rick be waiting for her there? One way or another, she can't stay here any longer.

She gets an idea and digs in her purse for the business card she took from the hotel room the other day. Cupping the phone to her ear, she dials the number.

"Hi. You've reached Matt Addison of Nor-Star Biochemical. Please leave a message and I'll get back to you."

She takes a deep breath, trying to sound natural. "Hey, Matt. It's Cathy. Remember me?" A sexy laugh. "So sorry I had to take off the other day. It was an emergency. But I'm still in town and I'd love to grab dinner tonight. What do you think? My treat. I'll try you again in a bit."

She hangs up, moving quickly, tossing more of her things into the suitcase. Her makeup bags. Her scattered clothes.

The handset rings. She sees OMNI PLAZA HOTEL on the call display and answers. "Hey!"

"Hi there." His voice is sullen. "I didn't expect to hear from you again."

"But that's why I'm calling! So I can make it up to you. So what do you think about dinner tonight?"

"I think that's—doable," he says, playfully grudging. "I'll be out of here around seven or so. We could meet in the lounge for—"

"Actually, can you come get me?"

"Uh, sorry, I don't think so. I don't have a car here."

"Maybe you can rent one?"

"Well, maybe later. But I'm swamped right now. I can't get away. The appeal's tomorrow and—"

"Shit." She cuts him off, chewing her lip.

"Why? What's wrong?"

"Nothing. I just needed a ride. That's okay. I'll see you in the lounge at seven."

"Okay, sounds good—but, Cathy? Please don't ever call my cell number again. Promise me. Next time, just call me at the hotel."

"Yeah, whatever." She hangs up.

Just an average married man trying to cover his tracks. Asshole. But she needs him tonight. She can't stay here, and she has nowhere else to go. If she meets him at seven, she has five hours to wait. Should she go to the hotel and wait there? Or somewhere else?

Can she stay here for the day? Or is it too dangerous? Because it's not just Rick she has to worry about. If he's alive, he knows she took that money. What if he's hooked up with the supplier from Florida? Or the guys who bought the junk? Cassie knows what men like that do to people who steal their cash. Rick could be with them already, trying to set her up right now. They'll find her eventually. If the cops don't get to her first.

48

JAY

Thursday Afternoon

Glock 19 instructions.
   Pizza Kitchen delivery.
   SAG scale rates.
   Flights to Miami.
Jay sits on the couch in the living room, stunned by the recent searches on his laptop. They ordered pizza last night while they were playing video games, but *Glock 19*? He inputs the term, just to make sure, and three hundred thousand hits come up, complete with menacing shots of a pistol with a deadly black profile.
   Jesus.
He's even more concerned why Cassie isn't up and about yet. He heard her in there earlier, shuffling around, could even smell her smoking through the inch of her open door. But she hasn't been out in hours and he needs to use the printer. He has a vague worry that she's being so quiet because of the Ambien news. Maybe she's judging him. *Dizzy legs.* How could Beth be so rude?
   But now everything is so silent, it's as if she's already gone. He tries to imagine this place without her. But she was like fire damage: the smell of smoke will always be in the walls.
   He goes over the notes his father had dropped off about the budget one more time, then slides the pages back into the manila envelope. Cassie told him she met his dad yesterday. *You guys look so much alike*, she said. But she wouldn't explain more than that. He's almost afraid to hear what his father thinks; Cassie

Ogilvy isn't the kind of woman you want your polite daughter-in-law hanging out with.

Finally, he hears footsteps from the hallway. Thank God. He waits until the shower turns on, then hits print, making five copies of the updated budget. He hears a faint *click* as the first page catches in the extra room. He creeps into the hall. The door to the guest bathroom isn't quite closed, resting against the frame. Over the running water, he hears her humming.

He hurries down the hall, bracing himself for the steeplechase of junk. Beth warned him this girl was a slob when they were roommates, but when he peeked in the room yesterday, it was beyond comprehension. Clothes everywhere, cheap lingerie hanging about, empty beer bottles, dirty ashtrays. To be a guest in someone's house and care so little about keeping the place neat?

Still, there was something about that attitude he admired. The coolness of her. So unlike Beth, with her suits and her pumps and her early-morning alarm. Cassie was just so *herself*. Frank and honest and in-your-face. If they were movies, Beth would be like a Bergman film, all subtext and hidden meanings. But Cassie was a summer blockbuster, nothing but explosions, car chases, and gunfights.

When he gets to the room, he's surprised. Her blue suitcase sits upright and closed. The makeup tubes and hairbrushes are packed away. She must've decided to leave early after all. He doesn't know if he's pleased or disappointed. He tries to shake it off, waiting for the aggravating old printer to spew out the remainder of his documents. His father's suggestions actually helped. He was able to trim another hundred grand off the bottom line. He grabs the stapler and turns to leave the room, but freezes when he sees Cassie in the doorway. He hadn't even heard the shower go off. How did she get here so fast?

She wears only a towel wrapped around her body, and not a big one, it barely reaches her thighs. She holds the edge, tucked in at one corner, but the tops of her breasts heave over it. Her long, dark hair is dripping wet as she runs her fingers through it, shaking it out, just watching him. For a moment he can't speak, can't move, unable to believe any woman would let herself stand half naked in front of a friend's husband like this without even blushing.

"You spying on me?" Her eyes narrow as she looks around the room, seeming suspicious.

"Uh, no, sorry. I just needed to print something." He motions with the papers, but almost drops the stapler at the same time, having to clamp it against his body to catch it from falling.

"No prob," she says. "*Mi casa, su casa.*"

He tries to laugh, but thinks, *Only it's mi casa to begin with.* He walks toward her, expecting her to step aside, but she doesn't move, blocking the doorway. He clears his throat, a manly apology, he thinks, and tries to step the other way. But she shifts so he can't get by. She's not holding the towel anymore, and it loosens, threatening to fall. He moves the other way, but she does it again, stepping in front of him.

"Don't you hate when this happens?" she says. "I'll stand. You go."

Jay moves one way, but she shifts her weight again, this time grazing him with her breasts. He freezes, staring down at her, heat prickling his cheeks.

"You musta been lousy at hoops," she says.

"Wasn't my game."

"No kidding." She grins and finally steps out of his way. He hurries out of the room.

His hands shake as he works at the coffee table, collating and stapling the new budget. But it's hard to concentrate. A physical memory tingles on his skin where her breasts touched him. He feels self-conscious, as if he's done something wrong.

He hears the blow-dryer whir for a couple minutes, then her bare feet in the hall. His chest tightens as she walks into the room. She's changed into a short white robe and her hair is still slightly damp.

"You can work in there if you want. I'll stay out of your way."

"It's all right. I'm fine here." He doesn't look at her as he gathers up another sheaf of pages, tapping them straight. Shit, why is he so tense? Is it the Glock search on his laptop? Or is it because she's naked beneath that robe?

"Mind if I watch, then?"

"Nothing to see."

"Don't be too sure of that. I'm fascinated by the movie business." But she doesn't seem fascinated. She seems tense, going to the window, peering back and forth through the blinds.

"You waiting for someone?"

But she ignores him, twisting the blinds closed. The room goes dim. "Want a drink?" she asks, walking to the bar.

"No, thanks."

"Come on. It's our last day together." She pours a strong drink, then grabs a second glass.

"Last day? I thought you were leaving tomorrow."

"I'm not sure. Things are sorta up in the air right now. Scotch, right?"

"I said I'm fine."

She pours him a double anyway. "Don't be a party pooper. Your dad had a drink with me yesterday."

"He did?"

"Yeah, when he dropped that off." She puts his drink down, pointing to the manila envelope on the table. But Jay's puzzled; his father hadn't mentioned staying for a drink. "What're you working on?" she asks.

He's relieved when she doesn't sit on the couch beside him, but pulls up the leather chair, adjusting it on the other side of the table. He senses that something else is going on, though. She still seems preoccupied, her knee pumping.

"Just budget shit," he says, stapling another copy of the document.

"So you're not too busy, then? You think you'd have time to give me a ride somewhere? I mean, if I had to go somewhere, could you drive me?"

He gives a dry laugh. "I'm not sure. I guess it depends on when—and where. What's up?"

"It's nothing. If you're too busy, forget it," she says, lighting a cigarette.

As she leans forward to put the package on the table, she dips low enough to reveal her cleavage. Jay freezes when he notices the view. She sits back and puts one foot on the coffee table, revealing more of her bare legs. He can't understand his response to this woman. Twenty minutes ago he was worried she was judging him about something. Now that she's here, he wishes she were back in her room.

"Seriously, Cassie. What's wrong? Where do you have to go?"

"Doesn't matter," she says, exhaling. "So, you don't play basketball. What *is* your game, then?"

"I don't know. What's yours?" he answers, his mouth dry.

"I'm pretty open-minded."

"You don't say. So what did you and my—"

But the house phone rings, cutting him off. Cassie tenses, as if she's afraid who might be calling. It doesn't seem like her to be so nervous. What's wrong with her today?

"It's just Beth," he says, checking the display.

She heaves a sigh of relief. "I'll get it." As she leans over to answer, Jay catches the swell of her breasts again. And the first blush of her nipple. He takes a deep breath. Holds it.

"Hey, working girl," she says, answering. She finds the speaker button on the keypad and hits it.

"...doing okay?" He bristles as his wife's voice fills the room. She sounds small and distant, as if she were on a space station, a million miles away.

"Totally," Cassie says. "Just took a shower. Borrowed your blow-dryer. Hope you don't mind."

"No problem. Listen, is Jay around?"

Cassie grins, staring across the table at him. "Actually, *no* ... He's not."

He cocks his head in confusion.

"Where'd he go?"

"I don't know." She blows a smoke ring, her mouth moving in a lush, agile circle. She's performing for him. "He was gone when I got out of the shower. I didn't see him."

"He must be at a meeting. He's had such a busy week." Beth's voice again, punching through the pounding in his head. "Anyway, I think I might be a bit late tonight. There's a birthday thing here. I'm going to try to get out of it, but if I can't, I should be home around seven. We'll get takeout or something. Unless you feel like going somewhere? It's your last night. We could do something special."

"Whatever. I'm easy." She gives Jay a wink.

"Actually, Cass. I'm kind of glad Jay's not there. I wanted to talk to you alone."

"You did?" She arches an eyebrow, curious.

"Yeah. I have to ask you something, and I want you to be honest with me."

She laughs. "*That* I can't guarantee."

"I'm serious, Cass. What's going on with you? Really."

She jerks back, surprised. "What are you talking about?"

Jay feels embarrassed for Cass, and ashamed of his wife. Beth doesn't usually pry like this.

"It's just a feeling I have. I know you, Cass. I know you better than anyone. I think something's up with you and you're not telling me everything. I just—I just want you to tell me the truth. You can trust me. You know that."

"What the *hell* are you talking about?" Cassie asks, sitting forward, her mouth fixed in a snarl. Her robe shifts open, gaping all the way to the knot in the belt. If she's aware of it, she makes no attempt to adjust the silk.

"I'm just worried about you, that's all. I haven't heard from you in years, and all of a sudden, out of the blue, you need a place to stay. I think you're hiding something, Cass. Maybe you're in trouble or—"

"What the fuck?" Cassie interrupts, stabbing out her cigarette.

"You don't think I'm ashamed enough I can't afford a hotel? That I've got to sponge off you like some charity case? You want to rub it in or something?"

"No. It's just that—"

"Bullshit. I don't know why you always think the worst of me."

"I don't!"

"You do! You always did!"

Jay feels awkward overhearing the spat, but he's fascinated, too, watching their codependent relationship play out, seeing Beth so helpless in front of this bully.

"Cassie, please, I—I'm sorry! I didn't mean it like that. I just—"

"You're just what?" Cassie mocks her.

"I just want to make sure you're okay! I didn't mean to start a fight. That's the last thing I want to do. I'm so sorry. Really..." A desperate groan. "Will you forgive me?"

"I don't know," she grumbles.

"Come on... Just forget I brought it up. It's nothing. We'll have fun tonight, okay? I promise." But Cass doesn't say anything. Beth sighs heavily. "I should go, try to track Jay down. If you see him, ask him what he wants to do for dinner, okay?"

Cassie looks at him, cocks her head. "I will."

"Love you."

But Cassie hangs up, and the connection is broken. The living room is quiet again, the two of them more alone than ever.

"Your wife wants to know what you feel like eating for dinner," she says. She tilts her knee inward, allowing her robe to fall open on one side. He glances down to see a hint of a tan line and the bare curve of her hip. But no panties. "I was kind of wondering that myself." She starts rocking her knee open and closed in a rhythmic, lazy way, the hem of the robe slipping down further each time. He can almost see... almost...

Why is she acting like this? Is she trying to trick him or something? Is she just mad at Beth? What the hell is he supposed to do?

His cell phone rings on the table, and it makes him flinch.

"Oops. That'll be her. I wouldn't answer if I were you. I'm not sure you're that good a liar."

Jay swallows and picks up the cell, checking to make sure the speaker isn't engaged. "Hey..."

"Oh, good!" Beth says. "Glad I caught you. I'm trying to find out what to do for dinner tonight. I don't have the energy to cook. Unless you feel like barbecuing?"

"Doesn't matter to me."

"Maybe we'll just order in. But there's a birthday thing here. If I can't get out of it, I might be a little late. Seven or so?"

"Sure, whatever."

Cassie throws something at his crotch. He fumbles for it. It's a large, unlit joint.

He looks at her in confusion. She covers her mouth, trying not to laugh. Beth is still talking.

"Oh, man, I'm dragging myself around today. I'm so exhausted! I can't believe how that girl can still party."

Cassie nods and gives a thumbs-up.

She can overhear Beth's voice?

A tired laugh. "To tell you the truth, I can't wait for her to leave. I'm getting so sick of her bullshit. I think she's—"

Cassie's expression drops. Jay cuts her off with a tumble of words. "Hey, Commisso just got here. Gotta go." He moves toward the kitchen out of earshot.

"What?"

"Gotta go. See you tonight."

He hangs up without saying goodbye.

"I guess I was wrong," Cassie says, gritting her teeth. "You *are* a good liar. And so is Beth." He sighs helplessly, returning to the couch. She gets up to pour another drink. "Your wife is so fucking two-faced. I can't believe it. First she tells me she's just worried about me. Then she tells *you* she's sick of me?"

"She's just hungover, that's all. She doesn't party much, and this is all just..." His voice trails off. Too much for her? Too much for him?

"You don't have to make excuses for her, Jay. I know what she's like. I lived with her, remember? She's a fucking uptight bitch, and she's been judging me since the second we met." Without asking, she grabs his glass and fills it again, too.

"Don't say that. She loves you."

"Oh yeah? Is that why she didn't reach out to me for twelve years? I tried getting in touch with her so many times. And never *once* did I hear from her. Not *once*."

"Didn't you guys have a fight or something?" He doesn't want to get into it, but he feels strangely defensive about his wife.

"I don't remember any fight. Did she say that?" She hands him his glass. But this time, she walks around the coffee table and sits beside him on the couch. His whole body goes rigid. "I don't know why she'd lie about something like that."

"Maybe I got it wrong. Seriously, drop it. Cheers."

He holds up his drink in a quick toast and they *clink*. He takes three big gulps, needing it badly. She takes a sip, too, licking the vodka off her lips. As she adjusts her hips to face him more squarely, she tilts one knee on the couch. He can't help it. He looks down.

Does she know?

That he can see everything?

"I was thinking," she begins, "when I go, we're probably never going to see each other again."

"I guess not." He drains his drink. Puts the empty glass on the table.

"Doesn't that bother you?" She runs her tongue along the edge of her front teeth, dragging one finger downward, toying with the edge of the robe. He feels a strange tilt in his internal axis, as if the room has shifted. Her hand finds his bare knee, and she runs her fingernails along his skin. "Jay? I asked if that bothered you? Cuz—"

He grabs her wrist. "W-what are you doing?"

"Nothing," she says, shrugging, the picture of innocence.

"I told you, I have work to do." He pushes her hand away,

turning back to his papers, tapping another pile quickly. But his thigh feels scorched where she touched him.

She laughs, grabbing the stapler. "Don't be such a bore!" she says, leaping up from the couch, bounding to the other side of the room.

He huffs in frustration. "Come on, Cass. Give it." He holds out his hand.

"Then come get it, Movie Man," she teases, holding the stapler above her head.

"Cassie, don't be—like that." Irritation. Anger. Desire.

"It's right here," she says, waving it. "Come and—"

Energy springs into him. It explodes so suddenly, it's as if his bones have burst from his skin. He tries to leap over the coffee table, but his foot catches on it, and he stumbles forward, awkwardly righting himself at the last moment. But the table jerks out of place and everything slides off, his papers scatter, his cell tumbles, the empty glass rolls across the carpet. He catches his laptop at the last moment. She just laughs.

"Don't fuck around, okay?" he warns.

"You call *this* fucking around?" Her voice is getting sharper.

He stomps over to her and grabs her wrist in one hand. "I said, give it *back*." He twists the stapler away from her.

"Ow!" She glares at him, her teeth clenched.

"Why are you screwing with my head like this?"

"I'm not!"

"You are and you damn well know it." He throws the stapler behind him onto the table, but it slides off, bouncing under the couch.

"Let go!" she demands, yanking out of his grasp. But she doesn't step away from him. Instead, she gives him a crooked grin and moves closer. She gets up on her toes, whispering in his ear, *"Didn't she say she was gonna be late?"* Her voice sends shivers across his skin. *Is this really happening?* Is she trying to get him in trouble?

He tilts his head slightly, the sweetest, smallest movement he's ever made in his life—and their lips graze. It's electrifying. He shifts back, watching her mouth. But she doesn't pull away. Good God. He feels how rock hard he is. He doesn't know when it happened, no recollection. But right now it feels as if every cell in his body is centered between his legs and there's only one way to release it and she's staring at him right now.

"She's got you jumping, doesn't she? You don't deserve it, Jay... You don't..."

Another kiss, this one deeper. Her lips are lush. Erotic. Unfamiliar. His heart pounds as her tongue flicks out, wet and supple. She doesn't have to encourage him much more. He grabs her head and pulls her in to him, kissing her roughly, like a dying man gorging at a water spout. He feels her teeth against his, the soft cushion of her lips. She asked for it. She wants it. She doesn't care about Beth.

Right now, neither does he.

He grabs her shoulders and pushes her down on the thick carpet, the chair falling over as he kicks it. He hears the air jerk out of her as she hits the ground, scattered papers ripping and crinkling. She seems to love the roughness of it, a soft moan escaping, her eyes fluttering closed. His hands run along her body, splitting open that little robe, tearing at the knot in the belt, pulling it away. He looks down at her. The tanned skin still moist from the shower. The breasts that rise up toward him, rocking with each rough jerk. He begins dragging his mouth down her body. The fullness beneath him, the warm, eager skin...

It's not even his fault, really. How can anyone blame him? Three days alone in the house with her? So sexy. So hot. How could Beth do this to him? What did she expect? You can't leave a man alone with a girl like this. Not if you're not going to have sex with your husband for months at a time. It's too much to ask. It's Beth's fault really. Beth's fault all along...

And then the thoughts disintegrate, replaced only by red-hot impulse. He can't stop himself anymore. It's as if he's falling into her. God, she's hot. His hand slides between her legs. Bare skin. Wet flesh. It feels as if his arm will burn up.

But suddenly she grabs his hand. "No...stop," she says, breathless. "Stop."

He's heard those words before. Pretended not to hear them. *Shit.*

"What's wrong?" He's panicked now. Did he do it again? Was he being too rough? Not reading the signals right? He's supposed to know better!

"Not here," she breathes. "Not here..."

He looks at her questioningly, feeling helpless.

"I want to do it in your bedroom," she whispers.

Jay hears a relieved whimper escape from his throat. "Why are you doing this to me?"

"Because it turns me *on.*"

He picks her up in his arms and carries her down the hall, throwing her onto the bed. She bounces onto the mattress, laughing her smoky laugh, the mocha sheets twisting beneath her. He slides down on top of her, kissing her more deeply, rubbing against her, tugging the robe right off. She helps him rip off his own clothes. His T-shirt goes up over his head in an easy arc. His shorts are rumpled on the ground in seconds. She's an expert. A whore. He shoves his wife's fancy pillows off the bed. Collapses on top of her. His blood pumps so hard, his veins surge like pipelines. He sees the skin on her neck, beautiful, vulnerable, her lips parted, her breasts heaving...Then the rest of the room vanishes, lost in the fog beyond his pleasure.

49

GOODE

Thursday Afternoon

Goode stares at the sympathy card, reading the names of the other officers until his eyes lose focus. What is he supposed to write? *Deepest condolences? Keeping you in my prayers?* In the end, he scrawls his signature, *Francis X. Goode,* and hands the card back to the rookie who's making the rounds with it. He doesn't even look at her. He doesn't want her to see the emotion in his eyes. Only after she walks away does he realize *Francis X. Goode* was too cold. What's wrong with him? He should've put *Frank.*

Even *Love, Frank.*

Fuck.

He shakes his head, going back to work. Work is the only thing that helps him forget the people involved in this case. Butler, Fiona, their daughters. It's not the first time he's lost a friend on duty. It won't be the last. Over the years, he's tried everything to get his mind off that part of the job. Boxing. Kickboxing. Meditation, briefly. Yoga, even more briefly (Dawes dragged him to a class). Karate. Running. Pumping. Squash. Booze. The only thing that works for him is to stop trying to forget. Because it never happens. So instead, he works.

He listens to Butler's voice on the field tapes. Follows up his scant leads. Takes phone calls from the task force, his captain, and Internal Affairs. He tracks Ogilvy's recent Visa purchases.

Compares notes with Dawes. He hears himself make bad jokes trying to get her to laugh. Or maybe to make himself laugh. Sometimes it works, but not often. The whole time, he tries not to smash his desk, the computer, and the entire squad room. He doesn't want to admit it, but it's Butler's laugh he wants to hear.

50

JAY

Thursday Evening

"Jay?"

He opens his eyes. Sees the ceiling of their bedroom.

But it's not Cassie's voice he hears.

It's Beth's.

She's at the closet, taking off her blazer, frowning with concern. He rips the sheet across himself, his heart leaping in his chest.

Pieces of reality fit together clumsily.

The bed is empty. Cassie is nowhere in sight.

Orange sunlight slants through the window.

The clock reads 7:22 p.m.

He was so goddamn exhausted, he must've passed right out. He feels the memory of the pleasure sliding along every inch of his skin, then off it, into the sheets, onto the floor, draining away. Only ice-cold fear is left.

He got carried away, didn't he? He remembers the tender flesh of her neck beneath his hands. He doesn't want to think about the rest.

"You okay? You were out like a light." Beth's voice is only mildly critical, maybe even concerned.

"Uh, yeah. I'm just—exhausted."

"Me too," she says, yawning.

She walks into the bathroom, and he hears the faucet turn on. He sits up in a panic, his heart pounding so hard, it's as if he's come in from a run. *Where the hell is she? Where did she go?*

He looks around. Notices the pillows on the floor, quickly picks them up, sitting back in bed, catching his reflection in the mirror. Good God, he looks pale. And his eyes are blinking too fast. He feels the first dogged pull of guilt. Then another, digging into his heart like a spade into the earth.

"Sorry I'm a little later than I thought. They had cake." Beth walks back into the bedroom. "Then I decided to stop for some wine on the way home. Some nice bottles. It's her last night, I thought, why not splurge?" She laughs tiredly. "I can't take any more beer."

"No p-problem." *Her last night.* What a relief. It can't come soon enough.

"Where is she?" She gets undressed, stripping to her bra and panties, getting into sweatpants, his Princeton T-shirt. Jay doesn't know if he's turned on or embarrassed.

"Uh, I—I don't know. Isn't she out there?"

"I didn't see her. Was she here when you got home?"

"Home?"

"From your *meeting*. Jesus, did you take a pill or something?"

"Yeah, I didn't sleep well last night."

"How'd it go, by the way?"

"With Commisso? Fine, fine." Another lie. His life is nothing but lies now. "But we're seeing him tomorrow for lunch and..."

His voice drops off when he sees Beth freeze, staring in the mid-distance beside him.

Shit. They've left evidence behind. No condom wrappers—it was all bareback—but something else. Terrified, he follows her eye line. But she stares at the nightstand, and the photo of her with her parents, angled neatly to face him. He hadn't noticed it when they tumbled into bed.

"Did you put that back there?" she asks.

"Of course not. Why would I?"

She rushes out of the room, down the hall. He twists the sheet around himself more fully, still searching the room for clues. The setting sun dips below the treetops, and the room is suddenly in shadow.

"Jay!" Her surprised voice from the next room.

"What?" His adrenaline spikes. It could be anything. She's left a written confession for Beth. Hanged herself out of guilt. He sees Beth hurry down the hall, checking the rest of the house.

She returns a moment later, looking stunned. "She's gone."

"What?"

"Her things, they're all gone. She must've just—left. I guess that Lily friend of hers showed up. Did she say anything?"

"No. She mentioned needing a ride, maybe, but—she didn't even call to tell you she was going?"

"No," she remarks, shaking her head in disbelief. "Not even a thank-you." Jay watches emotions flood across his wife's face. Anger, frustration, resignation. "That girl, she never changes." Beth gets into her slippers and shuffles out of the room.

Jesus, she just left? Is she trying to freak him out? Play head games? Or maybe Beth's right. Maybe that friend of hers just came early. Maybe it's nothing to worry about.

He gets out of bed, leaning into the hall. "I'm gonna take a shower. Might wake me up."

He hears her distant voice. "Okay!"

He turns on the faucet, the hottest water he can stand, and steps under the stream. He grabs the soap bar and begins to scrub, hard and fast. He's relieved she's gone, actually. It's the only respectable thing for her to do in this situation. Maybe she has some decency in her after all.

Even so, he's nauseated. His own thoughts feel like fists inside his skull, and he has to defend himself against them. *You prick, you bastard, you son of a bitch. How could you do that to your wife?* With her best friend, too.

But the defense batters back, blow for blow. Best friend? Are you kidding? It's not even his fault. The bitch. The slut. How could she do that to him, anyway? Seduce him like that. Take advantage of him when he's weak and alone. It must've been all that shit she went through as a kid. Spiteful bitch. She must've planned this all along. What a slut. He fills with hatred, unable to believe what happened. He could kill her for what she's done to him. They had a good marriage...Beth was a wonderful wife. How could Cass do that to her? How could she do that to *him*? He's just glad she's gone and this whole nightmare is over. He never wants to see her again in his life.

51

CASSIE

Thursday Afternoon

"*Jesus Christ, Jay!*" Cassie growls. "*Get off me!*" She pushes his chest, sweaty and rigid against her palms, but he won't budge. "I said get the fuck *off!*" Another shove, and he finally rolls away. She scrambles to sit up, leaning over the edge of the bed, coughing.

"I'm so sorry," he says, breathless. "Are you okay?" She doesn't answer, bent over, rubbing her neck. "I didn't hurt you, did I?"

She just glares at him and grabs her robe, storming out of the room.

"Cassie?" she hears him call after her, but he doesn't follow her.

She marches down the hall to the living room, needing a cigarette. Figures he'd be a freak, into all that asphyxiation bullshit. Beth told her they hadn't had sex in months—and it was obvious. He'd been ravenous. But what an asshole, choking her like that. Poor Beth, married to a—

At the thought of her friend, her pace slows. She imagines Beth in her music studio, going about her day, and she feels a stab of guilt. But she shakes it off. It's not even her fault. She was just teasing. She didn't mean for it to go that far. She tried to stop him— didn't she? He just wouldn't listen.

The living room is still a mess of scattered papers, the chair knocked over. She finds her cigarettes and lights one, inhaling heavily. The smoke scorches against her sore throat. She goes to the kitchen, cupping her hands over the sink, slurping cold water.

She still has to get out of here, now more than ever. Should she take Jay's car? He wouldn't report her, would he? He wouldn't dare, not now. But she can't take that chance.

In the guest room, she yanks the red duffel bag out from under the bed, feeling the deadweight of the money. She unzips it, making sure the gun is still there, too. She gets dressed quickly, a leather miniskirt and heels. She gathers up the rest of her luggage and sneaks out of the room, hurrying down the hall, stopping at the master bedroom one last time. Jay's on his back in a twist of sheets—but his eyes are closed and he's snoring.

How can Beth stay with that bastard? For *this*? She looks at all the suburban touches her old friend cherished so much. It's a mausoleum. Beth's hiding behind all these trappings. But she can't hide anything from Cass. Not even that old photograph. Cassie knows who she really is.

Moments later, she drops her bags in the kitchen and rifles through drawers, looking for a phone book, a flyer, anything with a cab company number. She could go to Footsie's and wait there, have a few drinks, then take the shuttle to meet Matt at the hotel. As long as Rick's not already outside, watching the house, then nobody could trace that route, not if she took the shuttle. She could spend the night with Matt, then figure out the rest from there. She's just got to stay a step ahead. She can do that.

"Fuck." She grits her teeth, unable to find a number for a cab. Nobody has a fucking phone book anymore these days.

She needs a drink, a toke. Something. She dropped that joint in the living room. She hurries in to search for it among the papers on the floor. Her gaze focuses on Jay's cell phone. She picks it up, swipes the glass, smiles to herself when there's no password. Maybe he has an Uber app she could use...

But she gets a better idea when she sees his recent calls. She scrolls through them, tapping a number.

DAD.

A moment later, John Montgomery answers, sounding irritated. "Yes, Jason?"

"No, John, it's me—Cassie." Her throat still feels sore; she touches it lightly.

"Oh, hello again." There's an uncomfortable beat. "Can I help you with something?"

"Yes, actually. I have to ask you a huge favor." She's not sure he'll go for it.

"What *kind* of favor?" He sounds suspicious.

"I need a ride somewhere."

"I don't think I can today, Cassie. I'm—"

"Oh, please," she pleads, her voice pitching higher. "I have to get out of here."

"Why?"

"I'll explain when you get here. I can't talk about it right now."

"Can't Jason drive you?"

"No. And Beth's at work." She pauses, lowers her voice again. "And you're the only person I trust."

"What's wrong, Cassie? What happened?"

"Please, John. Just come."

She hears him sigh. She closes her eyes and waits.

Twenty minutes later, his gold Cadillac pulls into the driveway, but John doesn't get out of the car. Cassie imagines he opens the door for his wife, but not for a strange young woman who "needs a ride somewhere." He can't be seen doing that.

She quietly lets herself out of the house, hurrying down the driveway with her bags. She wishes he'd pull closer. She feels so exposed. She tries the door, but it's locked. She knocks on the tinted window, looking around, noticing every flower, every bird, the vague outline of Los Angeles in a summer curtain of smog. There are trees and bushes everywhere. Rick could be watching her right now.

The lock clicks open. She throws her bags in the backseat, then climbs in the front. Jay's father blinks at her, his blue gaze taking in her skimpy ensemble.

"Okay if I smoke?" she asks, but she's already lighting a cigarette, her hand trembling.

"I suppose," he says, backing out of the driveway. "Do you mind telling me what the urgency is?"

She draws deeply, closing her eyes, tilting her head back in relief.

She shouldn't have done it. If Beth finds out, she'd never forgive her.

"Cassie?" The car swerves slightly. "What happened to your neck?"

She doesn't answer. She considered covering the marks with makeup, but realized it was better to keep them visible.

"Did Jason do that to you?" His voice is more worried now.

"What do you think?" she asks him.

"Well, I'm sure he didn't mean it. Tell me, what happened?"

But Cassie doesn't answer, sinking down in the seat, putting on her sunglasses. They pass a dog-walking park, and Cassie sees people jogging, nannies with strollers, young mothers with their kids. She fidgets with her bracelets, staring out the window, seeing Rick in almost every face that turns her way.

"Could you at least tell me where we're going?" he asks.

"I'll tell you where to turn."

He sighs, helpless, and keeps driving. He'll soon learn what both his son and daughter-in-law already know—Cassie Ogilvy doesn't take no for an answer.

52

JAY

Thursday Evening

Jay's hair is still wet from the shower when he finds Beth in the kitchen, smelling the wine cork. Two glasses of red wine breathe on the counter in front of her. He notices the coffee table shoved out of place, the chair knocked over, the papers on the floor. It's just a slice of memory.

"What the hell happened in there? Looks like a cyclone hit. Were you guys drinking or something?"

"Of course not!" He hurries to tidy up, righting the chair, picking up the glass. "I just couldn't find a page in the new budget and..." His voice trails off as he glances around the room. Was there any other evidence? "I just got frustrated, that's all."

"Well, we can relax now. She's gone. And we're relatively unscathed. *Relatively*," she adds with a laugh. She comes in with the wine, handing him a glass. "*Salut.*"

He tries to smile. "*Salut.*" He takes a sip, relishing it: "This *is* good."

"I know. It wasn't even on sale. I just felt like splurging for a—" The phone rings, and Beth checks the screen. "The Omni Plaza?"

Jay's stomach clenches when he remembers the first message from that hotel. *This might freak you out a bit, but it's Cassie...Cassie O...*

Beth puts the phone on speaker and answers. "Hello?"

"Um, is Cathy there?" It's a man's voice, nervous.

184

Beth frowns, snapping to attention. "Did you say *Cathy* or *Cassie?*"

"Uh...I'm not sure, actually."

"If you're calling for Cassie, maybe—"

But he hangs up quickly.

"Weird," she says, staring at the receiver. "I guess she was meeting some guy tonight. Maybe that's where she went. Who knows? I can't keep track of that girl."

"Yeah, she's insane." But he surges with—what is that? *Jealousy?*

"I warned you she was trouble, didn't I?" she says, straightening the coffee table.

"You certainly did," he says, his voice glum.

Tidying up, Beth finds the joint Cassie threw at him this afternoon. "Of course, wherever Cassie goes, there must be marijuana." She sets it in the ashtray and turns to him. "You still feel like ordering Thai? I really don't have the energy to cook tonight."

But he doesn't answer her. He can't. Because he notices her CD case on the shelf where Cassie had left it the first night. Before it all happened. He realizes now, life will always be *Before Cassie* and *After Cassie.* He picks up the case, handling it as if it were a precious artifact. His wife looks so beautiful at her piano, so innocent and brave. The tenderness that floods through him could almost drown him on the spot. She is such a good person! She doesn't deserve any of this.

"Jay—" She seems irritated that he's not listening to her. "Do you still feel like—what's that?" she asks, frowning.

He turns the case around to show her. "We were listening to it the other night."

"You and Cass were listening to *my* CD?" She narrows her eyes on him. "Isn't *that* cozy."

He's trapped, caught in an even worse intimacy than adultery. "She just wanted to hear it, that's all," he stammers. "So did I. You sounded so beautiful. I forgot how—"

But before he has time to finish, the phone rings again. This time it's Beth's cell, chirping on the kitchen counter. She walks over to answer, glancing at the screen, then holds up the display. JAY. "Did you lend her your cell or something?"

He rummages through his papers, lifts the pillows on the couch. "She took my *phone*?"

"Hello...? Hey, Cass? What's going on? Where are you?"

He waits, breathless, for the nightmare to begin. For the yelling and the fighting and the demands for divorce. How stupid could he be? The crazy bitch can torture him now.

"Just a sec. I'll check." Beth turns to him and whispers, "She forgot something." Momentary relief as she heads down the hall, her voice fading. "Were you supposed to meet someone tonight, Cass...? Yeah, some guy called from..."

Jay watches her disappear into the guest room, moving out of earshot. His stomach churns with nerves. What if she's just getting Beth alone to confess? What if she tells her everything? A slice of fear cuts through him.

What if she wants to blackmail him? Or press charges?

He listens for the screaming, the banging. But a moment later he hears Beth's voice again as she walks back into the hall, returning to the living room. He watches her for any clue that she knows, but she seems normal.

"Uh-huh... well, I can't find it. Are you sure you left it here...? Maybe... Okay, whatever. Call if you need a ride, okay? I'm serious... You, too." She hangs up and sighs again, loudly. "I can't keep up with her."

"Why? What's wrong?"

"She left something here. A gym bag? I don't know, but she's coming back for it."

"She's coming back? *When*?"

"I'm not sure. Before she leaves town. I told her to call if she needed a ride."

"Well, is she coming tonight—or not?"

"Jay—I just told you, I don't know. She's playing it by ear. She sounded strange, actually."

"Strange?"

"Yeah, when I told her that guy called, she sounded sort of nervous. I think she's in some kind of trouble. She's not telling me everything, that's for sure."

No, she's not. Thank God.

"She said thanks for the phone, by the way. She'll drop it off when she comes."

"Whatever." He doesn't even care about his phone anymore. Not if it means he has to see her again. But if Cassie didn't say anything just now, maybe she never would. Maybe she regretted it as much as he did. Maybe everything would be fine.

"I just can't believe how inconsiderate she is," Beth says, pouring more wine. "First she leaves without telling me. Then she wants to come back, but she's not sure when. I love her, I really do, but things are always so chaotic when she's around. Why do I still have to deal with all this? I can't look after her for the rest of my life, can I?"

"No, you can't."

"I've done enough for her already, haven't I?"

"You certainly have."

"Good. I just want to forget the whole thing."

"Me too," he says.

She smiles at him, a friendly little *Oh, well, we'll get through this together*, and it makes his stomach churn.

"Can we just smoke this?" she asks with a weak laugh, picking up the joint. "I could really use it."

"Good idea."

She flops onto the couch and grabs the lighter from the coffee table, the same one Cassie used this afternoon.

"This is ridiculous," she says with a laugh. "I haven't smoked this much dope since college. I'm ashamed of myself." She chokes slightly as she passes it to him, a shy smile on her face. "She's always been such a bad influence on me."

"No kidding." He tries to laugh. He takes a long, deep draw on the joint, waiting for the calming effect he needs so badly. But now the room is too quiet, the air prickling with tension, questions, fear. "We need some music," he says, grabbing the remote for the stereo. A piano sonata fills the room, each note drifting after the other in perfect sequence. Perfect timing.

"Turn that *off*." Beth groans, reaching for the remote, but he holds it away from her.

"No, leave it. I love it. You sound so beautiful."

"Don't get too sentimental on me, Maestro. I know you hate this stuff."

"That's not true! I just hadn't heard it in so long, that's all. I forgot how brilliant you are." He takes her hand, kisses the back of it. "You're so talented..."

"What's *wrong* with you tonight, anyway?" she asks, frowning. "Why are you being so sweet?"

Because I love you. Because I need you. Because I'm sorry.

But instead he smiles at her and nods for them to finish the joint and just listen. He watches the emotions play across his wife's face as music fills the room and smoke fills the air, leaving no space for conversation. She seems suddenly moody and complex. He loves this other side of her, the Bohemian side all artists seem to have. It's the Beth Crawford he met three years ago, that strong, independent musician with the tight body and great hair.

What has he done?

Beth can never find out about it. Never.

53

GOODE

Thursday Night

It's almost midnight and Goode is still in the squad room, his brain numb from coffee and a lack of sleep. Time feels like a noose squeezing around his neck. Every minute, it gets harder to breathe. Harder to think. But then a call comes in about a dumpster fire downtown. Nothing to worry him personally—until a local shopkeeper finds an abandoned handbag containing ID for one Cassandra Anne Ogilvy.

When Goode gets to the scene, the street is blocked off by cruisers and fire trucks, lights flashing, smoke thick in the air. He steps over the yellow police tape strung across the end of an alley and makes his way toward a dumpster, where firefighters train a hose on the smoldering mess. The smell of burned garbage is thick in the air, sweet and acrid, but there's also the unmistakable scent of burned meat. He sees Dawes taking notes from bystanders, everyone silhouetted in light from the shops behind them. Dawes notices him and heads over. There are no pleasantries.

"There must've been a struggle," she says. "The butcher said his garbage bags were all over the place. And he found this in the mess."

She hands him a black purse that seems to be nothing but a tangle of buckles and fringe. He puts on latex gloves and reaches in, pulling out an overstuffed black wallet, shining his flashlight on an expired New York State driver's license. Cassandra Ogilvy looks considerably cheerier at the DMV than she did in her mug shot, but it's definitely her.

An officer in uniform, a burly young man with a brush cut, approaches them and produces his phone. "Saw blood when I got here, sir. Thought hoses might wash it away, so I documented it before Fire arrived."

The young officer's name is Sanchez; he holds up his screen for Goode to watch. Police video was admissible as evidence, and almost as helpful as the real thing. In the tiny image, Sanchez walks down the alley, recording the pavement at his feet, his heavy shoes clumping in and out of frame, the glow of the fire pulsing. The shot closes in on a pool of blood gleaming red, smeared on the asphalt.

"And where was that?" Goode asks.

"Next to the dumpster, just left of it."

Goode takes a step toward the smoking bin, but feels something underfoot. He looks down to see he's kicked several small, round beads across the grimy asphalt. Different colors scatter like little billiard balls after a break. He crouches down to have a better look. There's a broken leather thong on the ground, strung with a few wooden beads, like the one he found at the house. He remembers Nico Alvarez: *She had lots of bracelets on her arms, I remember that.*

"Make sure these get tagged," he tells Sanchez.

"Yes, sir."

The wind shifts, blowing smoke in their direction. Goode bats the air with his hand, then carries the purse to the end of the alley where the streetlight is better and at least they can breathe.

He sets the bag on the hood of a cruiser and digs inside, as the scent of a musky perfume battles with the smell of smoke. He finds messy makeup containers, a hairbrush, cigarettes.

"You think the purse was planted?" Dawes asks. "Seems awfully handy that it was just left here."

"Could be," he says. "Or maybe it's a message. Squires's supplier hurting his girlfriend, trying to flush him out."

"Or it could be Squires himself. Maybe she'd double-crossed him."

"Maybe. What about those bags the kid said she had with her? Any sign of those?"

"Nothing so far. Maybe robbery was a motive."

"Could be. But they left behind a brand-new iPhone and sixty dollars in cash." He shows her the other items he found in the bag.

He looks back down the alley, wondering if Ms. Ogilvy met her match tonight.

A crime scene investigator heads over, wearing a white coverall and wet booties. She pulls down her mask, revealing brown eyes, a prominent nose.

"Did you locate the body?" he asks.

"Nothing so far, sir. It's still too hot to get inside. It's gonna take at least a day or two to sift through this mess. Doesn't help that we've got all kinds of bones and animal tissue in there, from the butcher shop."

Goode nods, looking back at the smoking bin. He expects they'll find dental remains in the next day or two, when this will officially become a murder investigation. Right now, there's enough evidence to move ahead as if it is.

He addresses the others gathered around him. "This guy's panicked or stupid—or both. If he's left something behind, I want every piece of garbage turned over for ten blocks until we find it."

He watches as the team spreads out. He hates the term "crime of passion." It sounds too romantic. But there's something not sitting right with him. He looks down at the iPhone and goes to power it up, but then stops. There's something smeared on the screen. It looks like dried blood. He swipes the glass to engage it and checks the last number dialed.

54

RICK

Thursday Night

He stands in front of the bathroom mirror of the motel, tending to his wounds, the fluorescent light discoloring his skin yellow-green. His shoulder aches, but it's manageable. Better than yesterday. At least the throbbing has subsided and he can rotate his arm. He's healing. The headaches have stopped, too. Wincing, he pats a last piece of tape over the fresh gauze, then checks his reflection more closely. Perspiration films his forehead, his upper lip. The dye job is holding up, but his blond stubble is coming through. He should shave before tomorrow...

The muddy blare of a bullhorn makes him flinch. He snaps off the bathroom light. A smear of noise clutches at his heart—sirens, yelling, pounding. Blue and red lights strobe outside the bedroom window, making the thin drapes glow like drive-in screens. He dashes out of the bathroom, sliding against the wall, moving quickly. He switches off the TV as he passes, the only light in the room. He grabs his gun and a fresh ammo clip and spins toward one side of the window, dropping to a crawl, his shoulder screeching with pain.

The voices are clearer now:

"Step out of the room!"

He straightens, flattening his back against the wall, snapping the fresh magazine into the gun. He leans toward a crack in the drapes, sees chaos in the parking lot, hears sirens as more cruisers pull up, screeching to a halt.

Fuck. How did they find him?

Thumping on the concrete walk outside the door as shadows fly by the window.

Was it Cassie's phone? He sees it sitting on the dresser across the room, the earbuds curled. Can they trace a smartphone without a SIM card? They must've been able to.

A commanding baritone from outside. *"Step out of the room! Walk back toward the sound of my voice!"*

He braces himself, his finger slippery on the trigger, the safety off. He leans toward the break in the curtains, training his gun barrel on the parking lot outside. There are a dozen uniforms, a wall of cruisers behind them. But the cops aren't looking in his direction. Their guns all point toward a room farther down. Rick almost laughs. They're not even here for him.

"Keep your hands up! Walk back toward me!"

He sees a skinny white guy with no shirt walking backward toward the line of cops. The man is drunk, stumbling, barefoot.

"On your knees!"

When the man doesn't obey, they rush at him. He resists, struggling, yelling. It takes three uniforms to push him down to the asphalt and cuff him. Rick smirks as they shove the guy into a cruiser and slam the door. The next few minutes are a sheer delight, watching the police officers clap one another on the back, get in their cars, drive away, leaving darkness and silence in their wake. It's a comedy acted out just for him.

When they're gone, he moves away from the window, heads toward the dresser and Cassie's iPhone. He powers it up, seeing the cover of her friend's album on the screen. SIM card or not, it's still too much of a risk. He lifts the butt of his gun and drives it down onto the glass. The screen shatters, mineral veins of white slashing through the image of the blonde at the grand piano.

55

BETH

Late Thursday Night

Loud pounding on the front door wakes Beth up.

Bang, bang, bang, bang, bang, bang, bang, bang.

She sits up and squints at the clock. It's after two in the morning. Jay's side of the bed is empty.

Bang, bang, bang, bang! Gruff shouting that she can't quite make out. She sees blue and red lights flashing against the curtains. Her heart constricts with panic.

Bang, bang, bang!

She grabs her robe, turning on lights as she makes her way through the house. She hears shouting now, too.

"LAPD! Open up!"

"I'm coming!" she calls, her voice crackling with nerves.

She gets to the living room. Jay is passed out on the sofa, both bottles of wine on the coffee table, one of them empty. She nudges him awake, and he groans.

"Get up," she hisses.

His eyes open, blinking.

Bang, bang, bang, bang, bang, bang, bang!

He sits up, rubbing his head, groggy. "What the hell was in that stuff?"

"Jay—get up. The police are here," she says, hurrying into the kitchen.

"What?"

Bang, bang, bang!

He stumbles up from the couch and joins her by the door. "What happened?"

"I don't know."

"Is it her? Is she in trouble?"

"I hope not," Beth whispers, her hand trembling as she reaches for the lock. She sees more than one silhouette through the blinds, tall shadows shifting. She glances at Jay, her eyes round with tension. He shrugs, looking just as surprised. She leans toward the door but doesn't open it. "Yes? May I help you?"

A man's voice is muffled. "Detective Francis Goode of the LAPD, ma'am. Does Jason Montgomery live here?"

Beth frowns at Jay, who goes rigid with fear. "Yes..."

"We'd like to speak to him for a moment."

She moves to unlatch the door, but he stops her.

"Check his ID first," he whispers.

She opens the door a crack and sees the detective's badge already offered. There are two uniformed officers standing behind him. Beth rides out a wave of fear, takes another deep breath, and opens the door.

56

GOODE

As he steps into the kitchen, Goode notices the modern perfection of the place, everything gleaming and showy. He turns to the couple, who stare at him with open confusion.

"I'm Detective Francis Goode with L.A. Homicide," he says. The woman goes pale as a picket fence; the man looks stunned, blinking at them. "This is Officer Layton and Officer Sanchez." He motions to the two burly officers thumping in behind him. He turns to the man. "Are you Jason Montgomery?"

"Yeah," he says, nodding. "Jay, actually. People—call me Jay."

Goode observes him for a moment. "So you want me to call you Jay? Is that it?"

"It doesn't matter. You can call me—I'm just—" He tries to back off the ridiculous cocktail-party banter. "W-what's going on—sir?"

There it was. Feigned politeness. Layton and Sanchez walk farther into the kitchen, their heavy shoes clumping.

"Do you know Cassandra Ogilvy?" he asks, holding up the driver's license.

"Yes. She's a friend of ours." The woman wavers on her feet, leaning into her husband. "Is everything okay?"

"When's the last time you saw her?"

She squints, holding her head. "This morning, but we spoke on the phone...about...uh...uh..." She looks up at her husband.

"Seven thirty maybe?"

"Does she live here?"

"No." The woman's blue eyes fill with tears. "She's an old friend. She's been staying with us for a few days." She puts a hand on his arm, clinging. "Please, tell us—what happened? Is she okay?"

"That's what we're trying to find out, ma'am," he says, measuring how to share the news. "We have reason to suspect foul play."

A sob escapes from her throat, and she covers her mouth, as if it were some bodily function she should be ashamed of. The man tenses up even more, his jaw muscle working.

"You mind if we take a look around?" But even as he says it, they've started spreading out, moving through the kitchen, into the living room, observing what is in plain sight. The woman stares blankly ahead, waxen, in shock, but the man appears territorial, glancing around.

"Don't you need a warrant or something?" he asks, a fake laugh in his voice.

"No, actually. Not if you're cooperative. And you look like a cooperative guy—*Jay.*" Goode gives him a crooked grin. "Have either of you seen or heard anything unusual tonight? Any strangers in the neighborhood or—"

"Excuse me, sir." Layton walks over, holding an ashtray. There's what's left of a large joint sitting in the ashes.

Jay steps in. "Hey, that's not ours! We never do that stuff. Hardly ever anyway."

Goode gives him a dubious look, making a show of it, reaching in his pocket for a black latex glove, shaking it out, slipping it over his fingers. He plucks the roach from the ashtray, brings it to his nose, smells it, raises an eyebrow, drops it inside an evidence bag.

"You got any other illicit substances in the house?" he asks, his voice lowering an octave. "Any needles? Weapons?"

"Of course not!" he insists. "It's legal, anyway. And it's not even *ours.*"

"It's true," the woman says. "She—she left it. Cassie's the one who—" But she can't finish, touching her head, wincing as if she's in physical pain.

"Wait," Jay volunteers. "Some guy called for her tonight. From the Omni Plaza Hotel."

"That's right!" says Beth. "I think Cassie was supposed to meet him somewhere. I tried to take a message, but he hung up. It was around the same time. Seven thirty or so?"

"We'll run a check on your phone records, if you don't mind."

"Of course," she says.

"Mrs. Montgomery, please show the officers where your friend was staying. I'm afraid we have to search her room."

"She took all her things with her."

"Still, it might help."

She nods, unsteady on her feet, leading the other men down the hall.

"There someplace we can talk, Jay?"

"Sure." He motions to a leather chair, taking a seat on the couch himself, looking around, unable to make eye contact for more than a second at a time. Goode notices the chair is on an odd angle and he has to straighten it before he sits down.

"So—your wife said she talked to her friend at around seven thirty tonight. Did you speak with her?"

"No."

"When's the last time you saw her?"

"Uh...this afternoon, I guess. Four maybe? Something like that."

"What time did she leave the house?"

"I don't know. I was passed out."

He frowns.

"I had a nap, I mean. I work from home and it's a busy time for me."

"What do you do, Mr.—sorry, Jay."

"I'm a film producer."

"Yeah?" His tone lightens. "I love movies. Done anything I'd know?"

"Not really. Probably not. But we've got Milla Jovovich attached for our next project."

"Milla? I like her. *Resident Evil.* Great flick."

"Right. But she's been in a lot of other things, too."

"That's true." Goode reaches in his pocket for the evidence bag and holds it between them. "Is this your mobile phone?"

"Yes, it is!" He goes to grab it, but Goode pulls it back.

"Please don't touch it."

"But I need my phone."

"So do we. For another day or two. It's evidence." Goode loves the effect the word "evidence" has on people. Even innocent people. "It appears there's blood on it." Goode holds up the bag, revealing the smear on the screen.

"Well, it's not mine."

"You just said it was."

"I mean, the phone's mine. But the blood's not. She stole that, anyway. She didn't even ask. Is that how you found me?"

"Found you?"

"The phone."

Goode watches him for a moment. "We traced the number to this address, so yes, that's how we *found* you. You mind if we run through the recent calls with you?"

"Sure." He rubs his hands together, clamping them between his thighs.

"Sure, you mind, or—"

"No, no. Go ahead."

"Thank you." He consults his notebook. "There were two outgoing calls to a Karen Burns yesterday morning."

"Yes. I called her. She's my business partner."

"One incoming call from Beth Montgomery at 2:43. That would be your wife?"

"Yeah." Goode notices his Adam's apple bob as he swallows.

"You called your father, John Montgomery, at 4:23 p.m."

"What? My dad? No. I didn't talk to him yesterday."

"Well, somebody called him from your phone. The outgoing call was almost five minutes long."

"Are you saying *she* called him? From my cell? Cassie?"

"It appears so."

The man frowns at the thought of Ogilvy talking to his father. *Interesting.* But he sputters, "What does it matter, anyway? If she talked to my dad or not?"

"It *all* matters at this point."

He sighs. "Yes, of course, sorry."

"There's another call to your wife's cell around seven thirty. She mentioned that one."

"Yeah, Cassie said she forgot something."

"Did you speak with her?"

"No."

Goode keeps his pen poised over his notebook but watches the man carefully. "How long have you known Ms. Ogilvy, Jay?"

"Um...three years or so."

Goode jots that down. "How'd you meet?"

"At a friend's party."

"She stay here often?"

"No. Just this once. I never even laid eyes on her before this week."

"Okay, either I'm confused or you are. I thought you said you met three years ago."

"I met *Beth* three years ago. Sorry, are we talking about Cassie—or my wife?"

Goode lets a moment pass. "We're talking about the missing person, Ms. Ogilvy."

"Oh, yeah. Right. I met her just the other night. She came here—uh, Tuesday night. Listen, do you mind if I get something to drink? My throat's a little dry."

"Not at all."

He stands up and moves toward the kitchen, then hangs back. "Sorry. You want something?"

"Got any Gatorade?"

"No."

"Then I'm fine, thanks."

Goode watches him walk into the kitchen and pour himself

water. He notices a CD case on the coffee table and picks it up. Sees the blond woman on the cover, sitting at a grand piano: *Beth Crawford, The Lotus Flower.* He raises an eyebrow, impressed. There are bottles and wineglasses on the table. Crumpled papers in a pile. Then something metallic glinting beneath the couch gets his attention. *A gun?* He angles his head to get a better look.

Jay comes back into the living room with a glass of water. "Sorry," he says, sitting down, trying to smile. "I don't know what's—"

But Goode interrupts him, holding out a hand. "I don't want you to reach for it, Mr. Montgomery," he instructs, back to last names. "But what's that, under the couch?"

"What?" He leans over to look.

"I said, don't reach for it. Just tell me what it is."

"It's just a stapler," he huffs, grabbing it anyway, plopping it on the table. "I was working and I got frustrated—and dropped some things today."

"Frustrated about what?"

He sighs loudly, but doesn't answer.

Goode watches as the man keeps glancing around the room, his hands working together between his knees. "You okay, Jay? You seem nervous, you don't mind my saying."

"Do I?"

"Very."

"Well, the cops are here," he says with a tense laugh. "That could put a guy on edge."

"True. But there you go again. The fidgeting. The sweaty brow. You sure you don't have something to tell me?"

"N-no." He wipes his forehead with the back of his hand.

"I'm just saying, I'm trained to pick up on things like that. If you're hiding something—and it seems to me you are—it'll be much better for you if you just come clean now."

Jay looks toward the hall, swallowing loudly.

"Jay, if you know something that might help us find your friend, it's a very serious crime to keep it from us. A felony."

The man takes a deep breath, steeling himself. Goode waits.

"You could be charged with obstruction, tried, jail time, the whole—"

"Actually, I *do* have something to tell you." He says it quickly, like air escaping from a balloon.

"I thought so."

"But I don't want my wife to know."

"I won't tell her."

"You sure?"

"Yes, I'm sure."

"This afternoon, something happened...Me and Beth"—he shakes his head—"I mean, me and Cassie...we, uh..."

Goode notices him glance down the hall one more time.

"We, uh...we had—" Jay finally decides on a word. "*Relations*," he whispers.

Goode lets a beat pass. "Intercourse?"

Jay nods guiltily.

"You and Ms. Ogilvy?"

He nods again.

"When?"

"Today—I mean, what time is it? Yesterday. Yesterday afternoon."

"Where?"

"Here."

"Here?" Goode motions to the couch.

"No. In the bedroom."

"Her bedroom?"

He shakes his head, guilty again.

"You and your wife's bedroom?" Goode doesn't bother to keep the derision out of his voice. Jay nods, and Goode makes a note.

"Don't write that down!"

But he keeps jotting. Does *this* explain the shifty eyes? The trembling hands? An affair?

"You say your wife doesn't know?"

"God, no! And I don't want her to!" His voice is a desperate whisper. "I'm just telling you because if she's been hurt or, y'know, something like that, and you find a body and there's, there's DNA or s-semen or whatever...maybe...maybe it's mine."

"Good chance of that," he says. "Why? You kill her?"

"God, no!" Jay blurts. "Of course not!"

Goode doesn't say anything at first, just watches the man.

"I'm telling you the truth! I didn't touch her!"

"Now, *that's* not true, is it?"

"I mean, I didn't hurt—" His voice halts in his throat. He blinks, staring ahead.

"Mr. Montgomery?"

"Sorry?"

"You were saying you didn't hurt her."

He swallows again, so long and hard, Goode feels he's watching a snake digest a rat. "No, I didn't. I didn't hurt her. I don't even know where she went."

Goode continues jotting.

"Does this look bad?"

"I'm afraid so."

"Well, I swear I didn't do anything to her. You gotta believe me. I wouldn't lie about a thing like that."

Goode looks up, a small grin on his face. "Not about a thing like that, huh?"

57

BETH

Beth stands in the doorway as the two officers move about the guest room, tall, broad-shouldered men who make the house seem so small. The dirty ashtray is still there, the empty beer bottles. She hasn't tidied up yet, and it embarrasses her. But the rest of the room seems echoic, vacant, except for the lingering smell of Cassie's stale perfume.

"I think she took her things with her when she left," she says.

The men nod, clumping around.

Why is she so cold? She pulls her robe around her more tightly, glancing at the unmade bed, remembering Cassie sitting cross-legged on it, rolling joints, singing to herself.

Is this really happening?

Sanchez picks up a blow-dryer from the desk. "Is this hers?"

Just took a shower. Borrowed your blow-dryer. Hope you don't mind.

"I'm sorry, no," she says, reaching out with a shaking hand. "It's mine." God, it sounded so pointless. Why not just let them take it? She doesn't know what to say.

It's my only blow-dryer?

How stupid. Jesus, Beth.

What the hell did that mean compared with everything else? She shouldn't even have mentioned it. What's wrong with her? But the officer hands her the appliance just the same, as if it were some piece of her old friend. Beth imagines Cassie's hand wrapped

204

around it, her long, dark hair fluttering as she used it. Then Cass bent over in the dorm room, fluffing her hair. Or in the bathroom that summer, brushes and makeup everywhere, as they got ready to go to a club.

"We need something with her fingerprints on it," says Layton.

Beth points to the beer bottle on the nightstand. *Jesus.* She's so damned cold. Shivering as if she's been locked out of the house and left to wait in the snow after school.

"Can we take this, too?" One of the officers lifts the ashtray, overflowing with butts and burnt roaches.

Beth nods, watching as he slides the entire mess into an evidence bag. She can't do this anymore. She can't watch the police stand in her extra bedroom, bagging and tagging what little her friend left behind.

"Excuse me," she says, and hurries down the hall to the master bedroom.

Gasping for air, she closes the door, runs to the bed, and sits down. She's still holding the blow-dryer. It suddenly feels as if it's on fire. She has to put it down.

She remembers seeing her friend in that dim bar with the pool tables. The smile on her face: *Got up on the wrong side of the bed, like, five years ago. Haven't slept since.*

How did a few drinks with an old friend turn into this nightmare, police crawling all over the house, Cassie God-knows-where right now? She leans forward, putting her head in her hands. She hasn't even seen the girl in twelve years! They hadn't stayed friends. She hadn't even *wanted* to stay friends with Cassie. She always made life so complicated, always taking them to the edge of disaster like this. Now Beth is part of it, too.

And yet. She has to admit she hasn't felt this alive in as long as she can remember. She's always lived in a world where Cassie lived, even when they weren't together. She's always been aware of Cassie, always so connected to her. God, what a dull, throbbing void life had been without her all this time, like the atmosphere on

Mars. Looking back, Beth realizes, everything's she's done in her own life has been a shadow, all of it in response to that one year with Cass. It didn't matter that they hadn't talked for more than a decade. Best friends were best friends. When Cass showed up, trouble on her heels—that's when Beth was finally reminded who she really is.

58

GOODE

Goode walks slowly down the hall to the back of the house. He notices things when he moves slowly, things he might not if he were always in a rush. He sees the happy wedding photos on the walls. Oil paintings that don't look like garage sale finds. He hears Layton and Sanchez in the bedroom at the end of the hall and leans in.

"Don't touch anything else," he says. He doesn't want to screw anything up with an illegal search. "We'll get a warrant and come back in the morning. We could lose him."

"Yes, sir."

But Goode's not sure who he's afraid to lose anymore. Squires—or the nervous husband.

The detective knocks lightly on the door to the master bedroom. There's a muffled voice.

"Come in." He opens the door to find her sitting on the side of the bed, facing away from him, but he can see her reflection in a full-length mirror in front of her.

"You okay to answer some questions, Mrs. Montgomery?"

"I think so," she says, her voice sounding stuffy.

He steps into the room, closing the door. As he moves to the bedside, he notices the matching drapes and pillow shams. The sparkling bathroom through an open door. Great care and a good deal of money seems to have gone into the decorating. But he also notices the twisted bedsheets and he remembers the husband's words:

We had...relations.

When he circles the bed, she finally looks up at him. Her blue eyes are round and glassy, her skin reddened around her nose. There's a crumpled tissue balled in one hand, a box of Kleenex on the nightstand. Beside it, he notices a framed photograph, recognizing Beth as a younger girl. A beautiful white mansion in the background. A happy family photograph, like the ones in the hallway. Goode knows it's not fair, but he doesn't trust happiness. Families were messy business. The odds you'd end up in one where everyone got along were about a billion to one.

"I keep expecting her to walk in the door," she says vaguely.

"I'm sorry?" He steps to the window, glances out.

"It's just that she always stayed out late. You could never tell what she was up to. But something happened to her—didn't it? Something bad?"

"I'm afraid it looks that way, Mrs. Montgomery." He takes out his notebook, pulls up a chair, angles it near her. "Your husband said she came here Tuesday night. Did she stay with you often?"

"No, actually. I haven't seen her in years. Not since college, anyway. We didn't keep in touch."

"You haven't seen her in that long and you let her stay in your house?"

She sighs. "I know, but we were roommates back then. She was always a little wild. I used to feel responsible for her. Still do, I guess." She shrugs helplessly. "When she didn't have a place to stay, I thought, why not? We have the room." She looks down at the Kleenex shredded in her hands.

Goode picks up the box and holds it out for her. She grabs a fresh tissue, thanking him silently. He puts the box down on the nightstand and the photograph catches his eye again. Is it fake happiness or real happiness in front of that enormous white mansion? He'd need to be there. He would be able to tell if he'd been there.

"It's just so awful," she says. "I still can't believe it. I always knew she was trouble—but this?"

He nods, trying to seem understanding, to be patient. When he feels anything but right now. "How long was she supposed to stay with you?"

"Until Friday. Today, actually. I'm sorry. It's so late. But then she left early—I think to meet that man who called. She wasn't sure when she was coming back. A friend of hers was supposed to pick her up. They were going to Monterey. Cass had a gig."

"Gig?"

"She's a singer. Wait!" She snaps her fingers. "She called this woman from my cell. Her name was—" She tries to think, closing her eyes. And then it comes to her. "Lily! Yes, Lily. She was supposed to take Cass to Monterey. Maybe she knows something."

"You got a last name?"

She shakes her head. "Sorry, no."

"Mind if we run a check on your cell records?"

"Go ahead, yes. If it helps."

Goode reaches in his pocket for the mug shot of Rick Squires. "Do you recognize this man?" he asks, passing her the photograph. She holds it for a moment, her hand shaking. She studies the straggly fair hair, the patchy beard, the blue eyes.

"I don't know. Maybe. He looks a little familiar."

"You might've seen his face on the news."

"I guess? I'm not sure." She hands the photo back. "Who is he?"

"His name's Richard Squires. He's a convicted felon. Not a nice guy. He's the focus of our investigation into your friend's—" He's about to say "death" but stops himself. "Disappearance," he finishes. "We think he's gotten her involved in some serious trouble."

She frowns at him.

"You heard about the shootings in Lawrence Heights? Where an undercover cop was killed?"

"Yes, I remember."

"Squires was at the scene. By all accounts, he should've been apprehended. Or dead, at least. But he escaped. We know he's armed and dangerous. We think Ms. Ogilvy was involved in the incident, too."

She narrows her eyes on him. "What do you mean—involved? How?"

"That's question number one on a pop quiz that gets longer every second that goes by. We ran a routine check on your friend's Visa card. Just to trace her movements over the last while." He consults his notes. "According to their records, she made a few cash withdrawals recently. Including one for twenty-two hundred dollars. And my dead guys were found in a rental house that required a deposit of twenty-two hundred dollars—cash. The house was rented under a phony name, but we're pretty sure Ms. Ogilvy was involved."

"Because she withdrew some money?" Her tone is dubious.

"Not just that." He consults his notebook again. "In the days leading up to the shooting, she picked up some items at a Walgreens two blocks from the scene. Hair dye. Rubber gloves. Window cleaner. Paper towels."

"That doesn't sound like Cass."

"Those last items are used to clean drug houses."

"I see," she says quietly.

"She also stopped at a wig shop on Wilshire, where she spent eighty-five dollars and ninety-nine cents on a blond wig. And the landlady rented the house to a blond woman. All that is circumstantial, of course. But we also have her fingerprints in a vehicle where an attempted homicide took place Monday night. And we have a witness who can identify her as leaving with the victim."

"Cassie hurt somebody?"

"We believe so. There's an arrest warrant out for her in connection with the shooting."

"My God." Her eyes, already glassy with emotion, drop tears as she shakes her head in disbelief.

"But our main concern right now is her connection to Squires.

He's considered armed and dangerous, and we have reason to believe he'll be after your friend. Be careful, is all I'm saying." He hands her his card. "You call if you see or hear anything unusual. Anything at all."

She nods, his card trembling like a leaf in her hand.

59

JAY

Late Thursday Night

Jay takes off his shirt in the bedroom and stares at the unmade bed. It's after four in the morning. The police have just left. Beth is in the adjoining bathroom, her voice echoing against the tiles.

"It's so awful," she says. "And to think she was just here, in our bed."

Jay flinches. "What?"

She comes into the room, looking exhausted, rubbing cream on her hands. "I mean, that she was just here last night, sleeping in our house." She shivers, taking off her robe, her blue nightgown beneath. "I think something happened to her, Jay. The cops do, too. I knew she was in some kind of trouble. I had a feeling..." But then her tone changes, becoming sharp and accusatory. "Why the hell did you let her leave the house?"

"Excuse me?"

"She doesn't know L.A. well. Why did you let her leave by herself?"

"I didn't even know she left. I was—passed out!" He looks back at the unmade bed, remembering her passion and her skin and her lips and her breasts and her legs. "I couldn't have stopped her, anyway."

Her voice and her hands and her tongue and her—

But it's only smears of images twisting in his mind now, like the aftershocks of a nightmare.

"You're right," she says, sighing. "I'm sorry. Nobody could ever stop Cass from doing what she wanted." She drops to the edge of the bed and grabs another Kleenex, sniffling and blowing her nose. "What were you and that detective talking about before he left?"

He's still staring at the bed.

"Jay?"

"He—uh—he wants me to go down to the station tomorrow morning."

"What for?" She frowns, waiting. An unbearable silence floods the room. "Jay? What is it?"

When he finally speaks, it's not even his voice he hears. "We have to talk, Beth," he says. He goes to the bed, kneeling in front of her, taking her hands in his. He tries to think how he'll tell her. He has to come clean with her. He doesn't have a choice now. If he tries to cover it up and she finds out somehow, it'll be even worse. That detective might tell her anyway. And then what?

"Beth," he begins, "you have to believe me. I didn't kill her."

"I know that!" she says, laughing with nervous surprise. She watches him a moment. "Jay... what's wrong?"

He looks down, unable to meet her eyes. He won't tell her everything. He can't.

"Jay?"

"Today... no, yesterday... something—something happened with Cassie," he begins.

"What happened?" she asks.

He closes his eyes and forces himself to speak. "We... Cassie and me... we..." But he can't finish. He doesn't know how.

"What're you saying, Jay?" He watches her features sag, her eyes fill with tears. "What're—you and Cass?"

He doesn't even nod, just looks at her, waiting for her to understand.

Realization floods over her, and she stands up in a rage, yanking her hands from his. "Jesus Christ, Jason!" she yells. She only uses

213

his full name when she's furious—and she is. Her chest heaves. Her cheeks bloom red. "What're you telling me?" she demands. "That you—that you—*fucked* her?"

He looks down in shame.

"Are you kidding me?"

He still can't look at her.

"Where?"

He doesn't answer.

"Tell me *where*!" She stomps her foot.

He can't help himself. He glances at the bed.

"Here?" she screeches. "In our *bed*?"

He still can't face her, but he doesn't have to answer. She knows.

"Jesus Christ," she says, bristling with rage. "What are you telling me?" She grabs her head, begins to pace. "I can't be hearing this! This can't be happening!"

Jay forces himself to look up at her, but the fury in her eyes is excruciating. He's never seen her this angry before, not about money, not about his folks, not about work.

"Oh my God! I keep expecting things to get better, and every minute I spend in this marriage, it just keeps getting worse! I knew it! I knew if I got you two together, this would—"

But he interrupts her. "I didn't hurt her, Beth! I swear! If something happened to her, it's not my fault."

"That's supposed to make me *feel* better?" she shrieks. She begins stripping the sheets, tearing them off the bed. He joins her, trying to stop, trying to help, he doesn't even know. "You prick!" she says bitterly. "I always knew you were going to do this to me. I always knew it! But I thought it would be Karen or Emily or somebody! Not my best—"

"Beth, come on, please." He tries to grab her, but she pulls away from him.

"I hope you had *fun*!" she yells. "I hope it was worth it!"

"You have to calm down," he says, reaching for her again.

"Do not touch me!" She yanks away angrily, on the verge of tears. "Do not come near me! The two of you can have each other!

Fuck both of you!" She storms out of the room with the dirty sheets, Jay following on her heels.

In the laundry room, she throws the sheets into the washer. He comes to stand in the doorway. He feels so tired, he has to lean against the doorjamb to hold himself up. "Beth, please calm down. We have to talk about this. I could be in trouble."

"You're damned right you're in trouble." She dumps in the detergent.

"No, I mean, that detective. That's why he wants me to go to the station. To give a DNA sample."

"DNA?" She slams the lid closed. "What for?"

"Because—he knows."

"Goode?"

He nods, ashamed.

"You *told* him?"

"I had to!"

"Why? Why did you have to say *anything*?" She jams the controls on the machine and pushes past him out of the room. "Tell the cops something like that? Are you insane?"

"What choice did I have?" He follows her to the linen closet. "He said if I didn't tell them everything I knew, they'd charge me with obstruction of justice or something. And if she's dead somewhere and they find her, they can do those tests, you know? They'd find out I was with her anyway."

"How?"

He doesn't answer.

"Jay—how would they..." And then she understands. "You—you didn't use a condom?"

Jay lets out a frustrated sigh, and it's answer enough for her. He sees her actually buckle over, holding her stomach, as if someone just kicked her. She leans against the wall for a moment, seeming in agony. But then she grits her teeth and the anger forces her up again.

"Are you crazy?" she screams. "Do you have any idea where

215

that girl's been? Or the people she's involved with? How could you *do* that? How could you be so stupid?"

"I know…I know…" And he does feel stupid, like an idiot; he thought he'd made mistakes before. In college, he was such a prick, always so arrogant, such a bully, so many mistakes. All the women. All the stupid decisions. The drunken parties. The laughter, the anger, that horrible night with Jill or Jen or whatever the hell her name was. But it's nothing compared with this.

"You're going to have to go to the doctor," she says. She opens the linen closet, reaching blindly for fresh sheets. "Just to be safe. You'll need an STD test and—"

Suddenly, his blue gym bag tumbles out of the closet onto the floor, thumping at their feet. Beth leaps out of the way just in time. Jay looks down at the familiar bag.

"What the fuck is that doing in there?" he asks, chills flooding his body.

"You didn't put it there?"

He shakes his head. "I haven't used it since I canceled my gym membership."

"I don't get it. Why would she hide your gym bag in there?"

"Who knows? But she said she forgot something, right?" He gives it a light shove with his foot. The bag is packed to the seams, and it's been empty for months. *What the hell was Cassie up to? Some crazy head game?* He bends down to open it up.

"Jay, careful. Maybe we shouldn't touch anything."

But he ignores her, unzipping the bag, pushing the flaps apart. They both freeze. The bag is crammed with large rolls of cash wrapped in elastic bands.

"Jeezus," Beth breathes.

Jay pulls out one of the rolls, his hands shaking; it's all hundred-dollar bills. He's never seen anything like it before. It takes him a moment to process it, but when he does—*my God*. His head begins to spin, as if he's floating up into the clouds. He digs back into the bag, rooting through yet more thick rolls of bills. It's packed so densely, he can't feel the bottom.

"Beth... there's a lot of money here."

"Why would she have that much cash on her? Where did she get that kind of money? Is it that drug-deal thing the police talked about?"

"Who cares?" he says. He picks up the bag and carries it down the hall.

60

BETH

Late Thursday Night

Beth follows him into the living room as he checks the window, peering into the night. He's acting so furtive, yet it seems natural to him. He's excited by this. Energized. The bastard.

"Jay—what are you doing?"

He twists the blinds closed. "Get the kitchen."

"What?"

"The blinds. In the kitchen."

"Jay, don't scare me. We have to—"

"Just *do* it," he orders, glaring at her.

The look in his eyes. So cold and demanding. Hours after he cheated on her with her best friend. Did she know this man at all? But she doesn't argue, going into the kitchen and closing the blinds, hurrying back to the living room. Jay sits on the couch, pulling money out in fistfuls, setting it on the coffee table. Some of the packets are spattered with reddish-brown droplets.

"Wait! Jesus, Jay, is that blood?" She hears her own voice rising in panic.

But he doesn't answer. He doesn't seem to care. The way he didn't care about having sex with Cassie. He doesn't seem to care about her or anything else anymore—except money. He keeps grabbing handfuls, stacking it on the table.

"Jay, we can't keep it," she says firmly. "It's not ours. We have to call the police. Goode told me Cassie might be involved with what happened at that—that drug thing the other night. Where all

218

those men were shot? The money's probably got something to do with that."

"You don't know that for sure."

"But what if someone comes for it?"

"Who's gonna come for it?" He goes back to rifling through the bag. "Shit, Beth. There's gotta be eight hundred grand here. Maybe more." A smile builds on his face, making him look almost crazed; it frightens her, as if he could hurt her after all. Or Cassie. She always knew he was selfish, maybe even stupid sometimes, but she didn't know he was filled with such darkness and greed. He suddenly seems capable of anything. Cheating. Stealing. Even violence.

"Stop it, Jason," she urges him. "Something's happened to her. I just know it. And it's got something to do with this money."

"Maybe, but she's not some innocent little flower girl. She was researching goddamn Glocks on my laptop."

"What?"

"Guns! She was researching guns!"

Her hand trembles as she covers her mouth. "God, Jay. Goode said she was wanted in some kind of shooting this week. We have to tell him about all this."

"No—we don't. It's not our problem. I don't want to get involved."

"You're *already* involved! We *both* are! We could get dragged down with her! We have to call him *now*!"

She reaches for the phone, but he lunges at her and grabs her wrist, squeezing hard enough that she flinches in pain. "What's wrong with you? You're hurting me!" She yanks away from him, rubbing the pink imprints on her skin. But he's pried the phone from her hand, setting it down.

"I'm sorry," he says. "I'm sorry. We just gotta think about this first." It's a tone of voice she's never heard him use before, sharp and calculating. He goes to the bar, pours a drink, gulps it all back. He doesn't look at her as he paces the room in tight turns. She watches him stride back and forth.

"Jay, listen to me. Goode says Cassie was with some felon. He could be out there right now. Waiting to kill us."

"Don't be paranoid, Beth. We need this money."

"Yeah, but I don't want to die for it!"

"We're not going to die!" he yells, loud enough that the walls seem to vibrate. It makes her jerk with surprise. "If somebody knew where this money is, we wouldn't have it right now. We'd already be dead. So just calm down! I have to think."

Trembling, she sits on the couch, still rubbing her wrist, wondering what he could do next. He begins to pace the room again. Back and forth. It's almost frightening how much the money has changed him already. He's not the man she married at all. He's a stranger.

"I know," he says, stopping in his tracks. "I know what we have to do...I'm gonna call Goode tomorrow morning and tell him I'll go to the station. But this is how it's gonna work..."

61

GOODE

Friday Morning

By seven a.m., Goode is waiting in a small queue at the entrance to the lobby restaurant at the Omni Plaza Hotel. He's already asked the front-of-house staff if they remember seeing either Ogilvy or Squires recently. A security guard recalled seeing the woman get off an elevator and leave the hotel earlier in the week, but otherwise, there are no witnesses.

A pretty hostess with long hair zips around the busy restaurant, seating guests. He waits, watching people on laptops, drinking coffee, reading newspapers. He notices the televisions suspended above the bar, some tuned to sportscasts, the other to the local news. The story has been rotating throughout the morning. *Butler's photo. The mug shot of Squires. The photo of Cassandra Ogilvy, the missing woman now wanted for attempted murder.*

As usual, Dawes is handling the publicity, taking questions in front of the precinct, surrounded by microphones; she looks calm and professional, even though they don't have all the answers yet. Squires is definitely a suspect in Ogilvy's disappearance, but now so is Jason Montgomery. His name hasn't been released in connection with the case, but it's possible he was trying to cover up the affair with his wife's friend. Was that conceited prick actually capable of killing someone?

The hostess smiles, plucking up menus. "Table for one?"

"Actually, I have some questions," he says, showing his badge.

The girl hesitates but seems cooperative. Goode presents the photos of Ogilvy and Squires.

"I recognize *her*," the girl says. "She was in the other morning. I think Nate served her." She points to a fair-haired waiter in a black apron, notepad poised as he smiles, taking orders.

"I totally remember her," Nate Langley says when he sees the photo.

"You sure?"

"Absolutely. I've never served anyone double martinis at nine in the morning before."

A moment later they've squeezed other servers out of the way and stand at a computer terminal, where Nate taps on the keyboard, flipping back through his orders for the week. "It was a couple days ago. Monday? Tuesday?" More tapping. "Here she is."

Goode sees an order from Tuesday morning for coffee, toast, two double martinis, and a beer. His instincts perk up when he sees the name of the guest who signed for the tab. *Matthew Addison, Room 915.* When he ran a check on the Montgomery landline, there was an outgoing call to a cell phone registered to this man yesterday afternoon. A San Francisco number. It also explains why the couple received two incoming calls from this hotel yesterday.

"Was she staying with this guy? Addison?"

"No. She came in alone, but he was having breakfast. They ended up talking."

"Did they leave together?"

"Yeah, after about half an hour or so."

"Have you seen him since?"

"For sure. He's been here all week. Must be for a conference or something. He always comes in for breakfast. Just left a little while ago, actually."

"Was she with him?"

"No. He was alone."

* * *

Goode moves through the lobby of the hotel, past fountains and chairs, to a set of doors indicating conference and meeting rooms. He steps into a wide, quiet corridor. Along one side is a table of pastries, with a few tired-looking businesspeople lined up at the coffee terrine. On the other is a series of doors, some closed, some open. He sees a sign outside one of the rooms: NOR-STAR BIO-CHEMICAL INC. The name of the company on the Visa Business card Addison had been using all week.

He peers in to see a man in shirtsleeves setting up a PowerPoint presentation at the far end of the room, the screen covered in what looks like Greek symbols. Two women in suits arrange folders around a long boardroom table.

"Are you lost?" one of them asks, smiling. The man hasn't noticed him yet, still fussing at the screen. He's prematurely balding, wearing glasses, his suit jacket off.

"I'd like to speak to Mr. Addison," says Goode, motioning to him.

She calls down, "Matt?"

The man looks up. "Sorry, this is a closed session," he says to Goode. He doesn't seem sorry, but rather put out.

"Could we have a word?" asks Goode, holding up his badge. Even across the room, the shield must register because the man freezes, then turns to the woman nearest him.

"Can you finish this up?"

The woman nods and goes to the end of the table, looking curiously at Goode.

"I won't be long," he murmurs, putting his suit jacket on. "This is nothing." It's obvious the gentleman didn't mean to be overheard, but the acoustics are so clear, Goode caught every word. The man approaches with an awkward smile. "May I help you?" His face, already pale from a life spent inside boardrooms, is now blanched.

"I just have a few questions."

"Can it wait? I'm getting ready for a busy day here."

"Shouldn't take long." Goode holds the door for him.

223

In the corridor, he gives Addison his business card. He likes to present his card, especially to people like this. Business cards were familiar, responsible, they gave a person credibility. When the man reads the card—HOMICIDE—he seems to deflate and tense up at the same time.

Goode motions to low couches set up around an empty coffee table. "Have a seat, Mr. Addison."

They sit down at an angle to each other, sunlight filtering through potted plants around them. Goode notices the wedding ring, the darting eyes, the stiff posture.

"Can I ask why you're staying at the hotel, Mr. Addison?"

"I'm a biochemical engineering consultant," he says. "I live in San Francisco, but I've been hired by a firm here to handle an appeal on a ruling by the EPA against them. District Court of Appeals is just a couple of blocks away. I'm sorry I can't tell you more. It's confidential."

"That's fine," Goode says. He doesn't even want to know more, but "biochemical engineer" explained the Greek he'd seen on the screen. He produces the photo of Ogilvy and lets him look at it in silence for a few beats too long. "Do you recognize this woman?"

The man stares at the image, takes a deep breath, and hands it back. "Yeah, I think I saw her on the news this morning."

"Mr. Addison, I know you had breakfast with her on Tuesday, so please don't—"

He interrupts, looking around. "I can't talk about this here."

"No problem," he says, standing up. "We can go down to the station instead."

"No, I don't want to do that either!" He manages to smile at a passing suit, who disappears into the meeting room.

"All right." Goode sits down again. "How do you know her, Mr. Addison?"

The man's gaze shifts around, his voice quiet. "I met her the other morning. In the restaurant."

"Tuesday. Yes, Nate told me."

"Ahh." Goode notices Addison's jaw clench. It seems Nate

wouldn't be getting any more big tips. "He also told me you bought this woman drinks, and had one yourself, at barely nine in the morning. Then you left the restaurant together. I'm assuming to go up to your hotel room. Correct?"

"It's not something I do on a regular basis, trust me."

"You didn't answer me."

"We went to my room, yes," he says, his voice barely a whisper. "It was stupid, I know. She could've—could've robbed me. Worse. But she seemed to need my help. She told me she lost her wallet, her phone, didn't even have enough money for a coffee."

"A real damsel in distress."

The man shrugs, seeming rueful.

"Ms. Ogilvy is involved in an ongoing murder investigation, Mr. Addison. One that involves the death of an undercover narcotics officer. And the attempted murder of a young man. She's associated with some very dangerous people and now she's missing. In order to find her, we have to know everything she's been up to the last few days. Everyone she's talked to. Everyone she's been in contact with. So—tell me what transpired between you two?"

The man seems reluctant.

"I could subpoena your statement, but that might get messy. And public."

He sighs and sits forward, still keeping his voice lowered. "I wasn't in the room with her very long. Only an hour or so. I had to leave, to come down here."

"You left her alone in your room?"

"I felt bad for her! She had nowhere to go. That's what she said, anyway."

"Was she a prostitute?"

"No money changed hands, if that's what you mean. She made that absolutely clear." He lifts his chin as if he's proud he didn't cheat on his wife with a hooker.

"Exactly what time did you last see her on Tuesday?"

"About ten thirty, I guess. I rushed back to the hotel room after my session was finished that day. About six or so. I even picked up flowers for her." He shakes his head. "Stupid, I know. But she was gone when I got back. She left me this."

He reaches in his jacket pocket and retrieves a small piece of hotel paper. Goode unfolds it and reads:

Dear Matt,

I had to go! Thanks for everything!

Love, Cathy xo

"She said her name was Cathy?"

"Yeah. For a minute I thought maybe it's not the same person. But it's her, isn't it?"

Goode doesn't respond. There's no mistaking this woman's face.

"Any phone calls since Tuesday? Any other contact?"

"No. Nothing. That's it." He glances back and forth; there's another pained smile at a colleague. "If you don't mind, I really should be going. I've got a lot left to do today."

"Are you sure you didn't see her or talk to her yesterday?"

He nods, but swallows a large lump in his throat.

"Because we have reason to believe she called your cell at four twenty yesterday afternoon. There was also a suspicious phone call coming from this hotel to the residence of Jason and Beth Montgomery last night."

"Who? I never even heard of them."

"Ms. Ogilvy was their houseguest this week."

"Oh—well. Okay."

"Were you supposed to meet Ms. Ogilvy last night, Mr. Addison?"

His lips tremble; his breathing is shallow. He closes his eyes and nods. "She called me yesterday afternoon," he says. "She said she needed a ride somewhere, but I couldn't get away."

"Where was she going?"

"She didn't mention. We were supposed to meet in the lounge last night. But she stood me up."

"What did you do when she didn't show?"

"I had a couple drinks, I tried calling that number. When I couldn't find her, I went back to my room by myself."

"Were you alone all night?"

"Yes."

"No witnesses?"

"How can there be witnesses? I said I was alone." His voice is rising again, and he catches himself, settling down.

"Without witnesses, that's not so much an alibi, Mr. Addison. More like a story that I should take your word for."

"Alibi? You think she was murdered?"

"We're investigating the possibility."

"You don't think I killed her?" He slaps his chest with one palm. "I barely knew her!"

"That doesn't exactly let you off the hook."

His shoulders slump, but then he looks up. "Room service! I ordered room service. The guy who brought the food would remember me. He'd be a witness, right?"

"What time did you order?"

"About eight thirty, I guess." Goode makes a note so he can confirm that. "But I couldn't even eat. To tell you the truth, I've been feeling damn guilty about being with her ever since it happened. Now *this*? Talking to the police?"

"Timing sucks, doesn't it? Having a missing woman on your hands?"

"*My* hands?"

Goode grins, but doesn't respond. "That should be fine for now, Mr. Addison. Meantime, I think I better take this note." He motions with the folded chit.

The man seems forlorn. "Do you need it?"

"Could be evidence. And just think—this way your wife won't find it in your pocket when you get home."

227

62

BETH

The alarm goes off, and Beth reaches over to turn it off, feeling anxious and drained at the same time. She lay awake all night, fighting bouts of nausea. Bouts of tears. Bouts of panic. Jay was restless, too, shifting and fidgeting, his legs working as if he were on a stationary bike. He didn't take a sleeping pill; it would've knocked him out for the meeting with Goode. But he didn't talk to her, either, so they lay in the quiet darkness, sometimes pretending to be asleep, other times not even bothering, just rustling and sighing and waiting for morning.

The sheets were clean—she knew that—she'd changed the bedding herself, but her skin crawled to touch them, as if they'd been rotting in a landfill and were infested with maggots.

This bed. Her bed. Their bed.

Screaming.

Panting.

She tries to push the images from her mind. She gets out of bed, seeing her reflection in the mirror. The bones of her chest stick out like ripples in beach sand. She looks as if she's lost weight since yesterday.

Did they eat dinner last night?

No. No, they didn't. She can't even remember the last time she ate.

She looks back at Jay, staring up from his pillow, not smiling. He just nods. His "plan" from last night runs through her head.

I'm going to go for my run, as usual. And you're going to get ready for work. Just like always.

She looks away from him and goes into the bathroom. Everything had to be normal, he'd said. That was important.

She has to make coffee now.

She washes her hands, walks out of the bathroom, sees him sitting on the edge of the bed, as if he were trying to find the nerve to jump off a high cliff. Neither of them says anything.

She goes to the kitchen to start the coffeemaker. Pours water. Measures the coffee. Turns on the switch. But she feels disconnected from her hands, the way she often felt onstage. Sometimes she could watch her hands on the keyboard, but they didn't really look like hands at all. Disjointed, nonsensical things.

Staircases.

Snakes.

Coils of wire.

But not hands. And especially not *her* hands. This is the way it is as she tries to make coffee. Her hands are something else and they belong to someone else.

She thinks of her husband's hands on her friend's body.

She wants to forget it, but she can't. Guiltily, she realizes Jay's infidelity bothers her more than anything Cassie has done. She is used to forgiving Cass for things. She had to do it countless times back in college. But she can't forgive Jay. He was willing to sleep with her best friend inside of three days? In their *bed*? He's a worse person than she could ever have guessed.

She hears him fussing about in the bathroom, getting ready for his run. She waits, as she always does, by the coffeemaker for the first cup to drip out. She can't believe the way Jay fixated on that money, splattered with blood. He'd acted like some conniving, guilty villain. How had he changed so much since they met? She remembers seeing him at that party, laughing, taller than everyone, smiling, flooded with energy. When he spotted her, she felt electrified by him, and flattered as he made his way through the room toward her. She felt an instant connection to him. It was his confidence. She was always so anxious herself, she was attracted to confident people. It was one of the reasons she loved Cass so much. She was drawn to the strength and energy of people who seemed at ease with themselves. She remembered seeing his Princeton school ring, his expensive watch, talking to him about his production company and his big plans for Hollywood. It helped that he was from a good family. A wealthy family. She could tell by the things he talked about, even the things he joked about. *What? The Poconos not good enough for you?*

They started dating later that week and were engaged within six months. Beth thought, finally, everything was going to be okay. Like the heroines of her romance novels, she'd found her handsome prince. She could settle down, start a family, put the past behind her.

Of course, it wasn't a happy ending at all. How wrong she'd been about everything, especially him. How stupid she'd been to trust him. She had hoped, for a short while, that things were going to get better when she got pregnant, but it was over now, and she won't feel it again. She's sure of it. Hope had a shelf life, turning rancid, becoming something else on a molecular level. Cynicism? Depression? Despair?

But then she floods with anger again. God, he's selfish. Vain and shallow and selfish. How could he do this to her?

And Cassie, too?

Then again, she *knew* this was going to happen, didn't she? When she sat in Footsie's, deciding. She remembers the pressure in her chest. *Don't say it. Don't say it.* But she felt trapped. She'd always felt trapped by Cassie.

She sees Jay come into the kitchen, pulling on a tank top. "Everything *normal*," he repeats in a soft, dangerous voice. She doesn't respond.

She watches him jog down the driveway and disappear. He seems taller than she remembers. Different. His energy is unfamiliar. She wonders when this started happening. How long ago had he stopped being her husband and become this stranger? Would she feel this way if Cassie hadn't shown up? Or had she been on a path all along, looking for an excuse to leave him?

No, she screams at herself.

She can't worry about those things now. She has to focus. There's too much to do, too much to think about. She has to stay calm. Jay's words run through her mind as she hurries down the hall, past the wedding pictures, carrying her coffee cup.

We're going to do whatever they want, he'd said, pacing the living room, that crazed energy coursing through him. *We're going to cooperate in any way they want. DNA, whatever. I know they can't do anything to me, because I did not kill her. And I have no idea where she is. So as long as we stay on the same page, everything's gonna be okay.*

She tries to focus, tries to concentrate. She's just performing. Just watching something called her hands do what they were supposed to do next. But Good God, she's nauseated, as if she's been rehearsing a performance for months and today is the big day. Every instinct in her body tells her to run the other way, but at one point it's too late—gravity takes over and there's no going back. She has to perform. If she doesn't perform, she doesn't exist. The show must go on.

You can do this, she tells herself. *You're a lotus flower. You can survive anything.*

Just act normal.

That's what Jay said. But it's a lot to ask of her. Because whatever "normal" had once meant, it's something she can never be again.

63

GOODE

Goode is at the window overlooking the North Wilcox parking lot when the Montgomery cars pull in. After talking to Addison, he came back to the station and gave Dawes the details on the meeting, then went to wait at the window. He wanted to see them arrive, to observe how they interacted when they didn't know they were being watched.

Even from a distance and through bulletproof glass, he hears the throaty growl of the red Mustang as it pulls into the lot. The navy Audi follows behind. Goode is fascinated by how much of an extension a person's car is of themselves. Not just the color or the style, but the way someone handles a vehicle. The red Mustang owned by a wannabe film producer almost screeches at a ninety-degree angle into a parking spot, decisively stopping on a dime. The navy Audi belonging to a music teacher slows down, hesitates, then turns in slowly, nudging to a stutter of small stops, before finally settling in.

The lot is busy on a Friday morning, so they can't park side by side. As soon as they get out of their cars, Goode notices them look around and seek each other out. They meet halfway between the parking spots, even though it means a longer walk to the main doors. He narrows his eyes, straining to see their mouths moving, but their beige faces look still. He doesn't believe they say a word to each other as they take matching steps toward the entrance and out of view. But he noticed they came in separate cars. Could be force of habit. Or it could be a sign of something amiss.

Dawes comes up behind him. "They here?"

"Eight minutes early."

"Impressive."

He knows Montgomery will be in Processing for at least half an hour. His cheek will be swabbed for DNA. His fingerprints will be taken, and his photo. His dutiful wife will sit in the waiting room outside, like he's seen a thousand wives, mothers, and hookers do.

"I got more on them." She holds up two thin files. "Interested?"

"Very."

They walk toward the squad room side by side, Dawes holding a file open. There is a symbiotic dynamic in the station, and everyone understands it. Two homicide detectives working on a breaking case get the right of way, so uniforms step aside to let them pass, as if for a cruiser with its lights flashing on the interstate.

"Not much on the woman," Dawes says. "She's a music teacher, has been for six years. Used to play piano professionally. Recorded one CD."

"Saw that."

They reach their desks, barely ten feet apart in the squad room.

"I don't have her full history yet, but check this out. The guy? Originally from Beverly Hills. Went to Princeton. Producer now. Nothing big." She stops and looks at him, grinning.

"Sounds like there's a *but*."

"Oh, there's a but, all right. There are actually some *big* buts."

"Fantastic. Nothing I like more than big buts."

Dawes sighs. He loves the expression she makes when she's trying not to smile, the way her lips purse, making her cheekbones pop. He also loves that she perseveres without commenting.

"Not counting the million plus they owe on the house in the hills, he's into the bank for over four hundred grand. There's an eighty-grand second mortgage on the house. About seventy grand on credit cards. He also has a business loan for two hundred K with his partner, Karen Burns of BurMont Films."

Goode can't decide if he's surprised or not. He remembers that house, the gleaming furniture, the happy photographs he didn't trust.

"I never woulda guessed they were so broke. They looked so...I don't know. *Pink.*"

"They're not pink," she says. "Not even close. I'm saving the biggest 'but' for last."

"You spoil me."

She hands him another file. His eyebrows shoot up when he reads it. "That's a big but, all right."

He senses their presence before he actually looks up, a sort of hesitant shadow in his peripheral vision. In the squad room, absolutely everyone moved with practiced authority. Nobody dawdled. Everyone had somewhere to go. But victims and criminals didn't enjoy being in a police squad room. The victims were confused and the criminals were nervous, so they both behaved the same way, like tourists without a map in a bad neighborhood, trying not to get mugged.

"Good luck," Dawes says, noticing them, too. She wheels her chair back to her desk.

Goode waves and they see him, both lifting their heads and smiling, as if meeting someone for a dinner reservation. They seem aware of the inappropriateness of their expressions and their smiles fade as they walk over.

"Mr. and Mrs. Montgomery," he begins, back to the formalities, "thank you so much for coming."

"Of course," says Jay.

"Have you heard anything from her yet?" Beth asks.

"I'm afraid not. Please have a seat."

They take two chairs across from his desk, and Goode sits down, too. He observes them without saying anything at first, crossing his fingers on his belly, leaning back, stretching out his legs. Don't speak unless you have something specific to ask them. Just let them talk, because sooner or later, if they were hiding something, they'd give themselves away. Guilty people always did.

As the silence draws out, the awkwardness of the situation mushrooms before everyone. Jay looks back and forth between Goode and his wife. Goode just sits there, waiting.

"I told her," Jay says finally.

"About...?" Goode lets his voice drag out.

The guy didn't expect to have to be specific. It would seem too rude. But Goode will make him be specific. He just sits there. *About...?*

"About...about yesterday," Jay says. He clears his throat and sits up a little straighter, shifts his weight in the chair. It's an awful lot of fidgeting. Meanwhile, his wife sits with her back straight, her hands clutching the handle of the purse in her lap.

"You mean, about you and Ms. Ogilvy having intercourse?" Goode asks. Sometimes he can't believe his own nerve. He should've been a standup comic. He has no fear, no boundaries. He isn't proud of it—he can't help himself—which is why he's slightly remorseful when he sees the woman's eyes widen in shock. Clearly, she's trying to forget things. She may not know it yet, but she won't be able to forget, no matter how hard she wants to.

"I felt I had to tell her," Jay continues, "especially after everything that's—that's happened."

"Well, that's very big of you, Mr. Montgomery," Goode says. He turns to Beth. "And you're okay with all this?"

She cocks her head on an angle, as if considering it. "That's not exactly the word I'd use, but—"

"But we're gonna *be* okay," Jay interrupts. "We're gonna work it out."

Goode looks briefly at Montgomery, then turns to the wife. "That true?"

A moment passes and she nods in resignation. Goode sighs, then winds the conversation around. No use torturing them. He isn't a marriage counselor. He moves on, sliding the crime scene photos out of the way, opening another file.

"We ran a check on that number you said your friend dialed from your cell," he tells Beth.

He sorts through the photographs, searching for the single sheet of paper he needs. He doesn't have to do this—he could've been prepared—but he wants to see their reaction, so he pushes the gory crime scene photos from Lawrence Heights back and forth across his desk. He notices them look down, then quickly up again, as if they were on the roof of a skyscraper and the height might make them pass out.

He slides a piece of paper over to Beth and circles a line on the page. "Ten twenty p.m. Tuesday night, your friend didn't call a 'Lily.' Or anyone else that night. She called a pay phone at LAX that never picked up. She must've been listening to it ring."

"Why would she lie about that?"

"Maybe you can tell me."

She seems to think about it. "Maybe this Lily friend of hers—doesn't exist?"

"That'd be my guess."

"What about the club in Monterey?"

"She's not listed anywhere that we could find. She's not playing the Jazz Festival, that's for sure."

"So she lied about that, too?"

"Looks like."

The woman lets out a breath, as if she's been holding it for years. She actually seems relieved.

"Speaking of phones," Goode says, retrieving Jay's cell from his desk drawer. Still in an evidence bag, it's smeared with fingerprint powder, but the blood has been scraped off for analysis. He places it on the desk between them.

Jay picks it up, handling it gingerly. "The battery's dead," he says.

"Sorry about that."

"That's—that's okay," he says, still happy to be reunited with his phone.

Everyone is quiet for a moment, before Dawes breaks the silence, right on cue.

"Got that info you asked for," she says, dropping a file in front of Goode.

"Thanks. You two ever meet my partner?"

"Michelle Dawes," she says, shaking their hands. Beth smiles weakly, but Jay barely looks up. "I'm doing a coffee run. You guys want anything?"

They both shake their heads. Of course they don't want anything. They just want to get the hell out of here.

Goode says, "Gatorade."

"What color?"

"Surprise me." She leaves the three of them alone again. Goode watches the couple for a moment. "You like Gatorade? I don't know what it is about that stuff, but I can't stop drinking it. It's like I'm addicted or something."

"It's the electrolytes," Jay explains.

"The what?"

"Electrolytes. I drink it sometimes myself, too. It's manufactured that way. So you keep drinking more. Helps replenish your fluids after workouts."

"So it's like you can never get enough? No matter how much you drink?"

Jay nods. "Kinda, yeah."

"That explains it."

There's another awkward silence. Goode looks down at the file Dawes gave him, peruses it a moment, then takes a big breath as if he's not sure how to proceed.

"Mr. Montgomery, you have a criminal record?"

"I'm sorry?" Jay laughs. "I don't have a record." He glances at his wife, who frowns at him.

"That's true. I guess you don't. The charge was expunged."

"Exactly," Jay says.

"What charge?" Beth asks, frowning. "What's he talking about?"

"She doesn't know?"

"Know *what*?" she asks.

"It doesn't matter," Jay says.

"I think it does," Goode says. "This isn't the first time that you've been involved in a violent crime against a woman."

"Jay—what is he talking about?" She turns to him, her cheeks reddening.

"I'm not involved in anything," he says. He rubs his eyes hard, clenching his jaw, then bunches his fists up on the arms of the chair.

"What is going *on*?" she asks, looking back and forth between the men.

"It was a mistake!" Jay says. "A misunderstanding!"

"What is this *about*?" Beth demands, her voice rising.

"Shhhhh," Jay says. "Jesus, do we have to talk about this now?"

"I can't imagine a better time," says Goode. "Would you like me to tell her?"

"I will. I will. I don't have a record, though. Right?" He looks at Goode challengingly. "I think that's unfair. Saying I have a record. It was expunged."

"That's true. I'm sorry to offend you."

The woman seems baffled, blinking, her cheeks still flushed.

"I'll explain it to her, okay? It has nothing to do with this. It was years ago. We can do this all in private." He stands up. "Now, I'm afraid I have a meeting. So if that's everything..."

"Actually, it's not," Goode says. "There's one more thing. We need your car."

The guy sits down again. "Mine?"

"Routine search. No big deal."

He sighs loudly, turns to his wife. "Can I borrow yours? I have to be at the Ivy at one." She nods, still preoccupied. He reaches in his pocket for his keys, handing them to Goode. "It's a red Mustang."

"License?" A needless question.

"J-A-Y-M-1."

"Cute," Goode says. He twirls the key chain on his finger. "Shouldn't take long. Couple days at most. Thanks for coming by."

They stand up quickly, but then hesitate, as if they've just given condolences to someone at a funeral and aren't certain if they've done enough and can leave now. Finally, they turn away. Goode watches them walk to the elevator, wait. Maybe they speak. Maybe they don't. But if they say anything, it isn't much. The elevator comes, they step inside, turn around. Neither of them looks at him as the doors close.

Goode stands up and goes to the window again, watching as they emerge from the lip of the building. They move quickly, straight toward the Audi. They're talking, he can tell, the way they tilt their heads toward each other. Jay tries to grab his wife's arm, but she pulls away from him. He's the one who goes to the driver's side. He talks over the roof of the car. No question about it now; he's not shutting up. They get inside. Goode watches the car make quick, decisive moves out of the parking lot before disappearing into the steady, seeping stream of traffic.

64

BETH

"Answer me!" Beth says, glaring at her husband. "What was he talking about? What record?"

"I *don't* have a record!" Jay insists, swerving through traffic.

"Then what did he mean?"

"Never mind. We can talk about it later."

"I don't *want* to talk about it later! I want to talk about it *now*!"

She can't believe any of this. It feels as if she's stepped into someone else's life. As if it wasn't bad enough waiting outside a place called the Processing Department before they met with Goode. The shabby people who came and went, street bums, prostitutes, drug dealers. It terrified and humiliated her. And now Jay's a criminal, too? It's too much.

"*Jason!* What was he talking about? Tell me!"

Jay's driving fast, aggressively, veering back and forth through traffic. It makes her want to throw up.

"In school," Jay says, "years ago, something happened."

"In college?"

"Yeah, this crazy party, off-campus. A girl, she was drunk. So was I." He's still swerving and speeding.

"And?"

"And it got—a little rough. But I didn't do anything she didn't want me to do! I'm *serious*." He looks at her. "We were both so drunk, I barely remember any of it. But I know one thing. I didn't

240

hurt her or anything. I *didn't*. Anyway, the next day, she said—she said..." His voice trails off.

She narrows her eyes on him. "That you raped her?"

"Date-raped, okay? There's a difference."

"Are you kidding me, Jay? I can't believe you! There's no difference!"

He turns to her, adamant. "Beth, you weren't there!"

"Watch the road!" Her heart is hammering.

"She was into it!"

"You said you were drunk! How do you even know?"

"Because there are—snippets. Memories."

She puts her hands over her ears. "I don't want to hear this!"

"You said you wanted me to explain, so I am! She was *into* it! I'm telling you, she was into it!"

"Stop!" Her hands are still on her ears, but she can't drown him out.

"How was I supposed to know she'd call the cops the next day? Stupid bitch! She set me up!"

"Oh my God, my God..." She looks out the window at the baked palm trees, the sun-bleached buildings. "*My God...*"

"It was just a stupid misunderstanding, that's all! She was a liar!"

Beth looks at him, his chest heaving, his face blotched red. How did she know nothing about the man she married? "Who the hell are you?" she hisses at him.

"It was years ago! You're overreacting! It was nothing!"

"Nothing? Are you kidding? How can I believe anything you say anymore? How am I supposed to believe you didn't go somewhere and hurt Cass, too?"

"Beth, stop! There's no way I'd—"

They're talking over each other.

"Maybe you had a plan to take that money or something?"

"Jesus Christ, you're imagining things!"

"You and Cass, maybe. And then you changed your mind! Did you do something to her? Tell me!"

"Beth, you're acting crazy! I said no!"

"Why should I believe you? You're a fucking liar!"

The emotions, the rage, the car careering back and forth, it makes her so dizzy, she feels sick.

What the hell is happening to her life?

She wants to vomit. She hasn't felt this way since...*since*...

Since she was pregnant.

Could it be?

No. It's impossible. They haven't had sex since the miscarriage. She doesn't even want his child anymore. She wants to get away from him—forever. That's all she wants. He's still trying to explain.

Nothing...she was drunk...she was into it...years ago...

She suddenly feels as if she's not in a car, but in a boat on a roiling ocean. There's no perspective. She can barely hear her husband's voice. When he pulls up in front of the academy, it startles her. She can't believe they're here already. The car idles.

"Normal, remember. Everything normal."

"Jesus, Jay..."

"Re-*lax*!" he snaps. "We can talk about it later. Everything's going to be fine. What do you usually do when you get to work?"

Beth can hardly think. She points to the Starbucks next door. "I—I usually get a coffee."

"Then you're gonna get a coffee."

She puts her hand on the door handle to get out, but stops. "Jay, this just feels so wrong."

"Don't worry about it. Everything's gonna be fine. Just don't do anything out of the ordinary. Not until we know for sure what's going on. Call me when you're done," he says. "I'll come get you."

"Okay," she says, feeling weak. "What are you going to do?"

"I'm meeting Commisso for lunch later. But right now I'm gonna do something just for fun."

"What's that?"

He cracks a wide grin, revving the engine a bit. "I'm gonna go home and finish counting our money."

Beth can't believe the smile on his face. He never seemed able to make that expression before. It's as if he's had some kind of stroke. He leans forward to kiss her, but she lurches away. She doesn't want him to touch her. She opens the door and the warm air wafts in. How strange it feels to be getting out of the passenger side. She slams the door closed. As she watches him drive away, there's a sharp tug low in her stomach. She hates seeing him behind the wheel of her car, because it's happened only twice before.

On the way to the hospital when she started bleeding.

And on the way back from the hospital when it was all over.

She didn't even take the day off. She had students. She had to walk upstairs, into her studio, sit on the piano bench, bleed into the strange, bulky sanitary napkin they'd given her at the hospital after the miscarriage. She had to sit there and feel empty.

65

JAY

Friday Morning

Jay hurries into the house, his cheeks aching from smiling so much. What a break. His luck is changing; he can feel it, like a piston in his chest, gaining momentum. It takes guts to do what he's doing, but sometimes you have to push yourself; sometimes you have to do things you never dreamed of doing to get ahead in life.

To be successful in business, you have to be ruthless. That's what his dad always said. If you let an opportunity slip by—no matter how risky—you might as well just curl up and die on the spot because there's no guarantee another chance is going to come by anytime soon. You just have to have the courage to see it through.

But how lame Goode mentioned that bitch. He could tell the news had freaked Beth out. It pissed him off. He thought he was done with all that. Alistair said his record was expunged. Nobody would ever know. A mistake. Could happen to anyone.

Yet the memory was so much like yesterday with Cassie. The pressure of his hands on her flesh. She wanted it. Cassie wanted it, the way that girl wanted it, too. Beth wasn't like that, but some girls were. She wouldn't understand. None of this was even his fault! Cassie was just another random slut trying to bring him down. Well, she couldn't, could she? No matter how hard she tried. Neither of them could. And now it was all going to be worth it.

He pulls off his suit jacket and grabs a beer from the fridge, pops it open, and takes a long slug. It's early for a drink, but he has to calm his nerves. He hurries down the hall to the linen closet. Grabs the blue gym bag from the shelf and carries it back, setting it on the coffee table. He unzips the bag, astounded all over again by the sight of that cash. He dumps the bag onto the coffee table, where the money lands in a sliding mound of green, some of it falling onto the floor. It feels like winning the goddamn lottery.

If you had asked him a week ago if he was capable of the plan he was pulling off now, he would've said "in another life" maybe. Yet now that it's happening, it all feels so natural, it invigorates him. It's the biggest rush he's ever had. It makes him feel like someone else. Or maybe someone he's always been, if the people around him had only seen his potential from the beginning.

Funny, he isn't even afraid of getting caught. Not really. He'd never been a fatalist before, but he's starting to believe that things happen for a reason. Seeing this money made him think that. Meeting Cassie made him think that. As horrible as it all was, as bad as he feels about everything, if Beth hadn't invited Cassie to stay with them, he never would've found this money. And now with Cassie gone, it's theirs. His. Things were rolling his way. Finally. He takes another slug of his beer and begins counting the cash.

Every time he picks up a roll of money and unwraps the elastic, he flips through the stack quickly, like a blackjack dealer handling cards. After a while, he doesn't have to count each bill because he knows the pattern.

A hundred bills per roll.
That's ten thousand dollars.
Twenty stacks.
Thirty stacks.
Forty.

He uses the calculator on his laptop, as if he's working on the film budget. When he looks up from the money, it's later than he thought. It's time to leave for his meeting. The crick in his neck is painful and his back is stiff, but at the same time, he feels elated. Pain is something different now. Like everything else, it seems to energize him. He zips the bag back up and shoves it onto the shelf of the linen closet. On his way out of the house, he texts Beth.

66

BETH

Friday Afternoon

Beth sits on the piano bench while one of her students murders the memory of Mozart. She feels her blazer pocket vibrate with a text. She pulls out her phone, checking the screen. She grits her teeth when she sees it:

Over $1M!!

"Keep playing," she says, standing up, letting herself out of the studio, closing the door behind her.

The hall is empty. She's alone. She rarely hears what the hall sounds like during a midday lesson. The din of instruments is bizarre and muffled, as if she's walked into an invisible circus. She can't tell if it's a happy sound or a depressing one, but it's monotonous, so many scales, up and down, pointlessly, endlessly, the same notes she'd played all her life, that they all played over and over again. The absurd but necessary practice of a language that made no sense.

She checks the cell again, and an inward peal of anger rushes through her. How stupid can he be? He's telling her to try to be normal and he's *texting* this kind of information? She can't believe it. She dials and Jay picks up.

"Hey, babe! Isn't that incredible?" He's laughing. She can tell by his voice that he's in the car. "We're millionair—"

"Jason, not on the phone!" she hisses. "Don't be stupid!" She looks over her shoulder, making sure she's still alone. She is. So alone. She paces the hall, wondering when she became such an expert at how to handle all of this.

"Sorry, man, sorry. Stupid, I know. I'm just so blown away."

She rides out another wave of rage. Her head pounds—*blam, blam*—like the metronome inside the room. All she wants to do is scream at him right now, but she can't because she's so angry, she'd yell over the instruments, and everyone would hear.

"Babe? You okay?"

He doesn't call her "babe" much anymore. It drops her into a different time in her life, a year ago or more. Back then, their life wasn't perfect, either. They had money problems, but not nearly as bad as now. Things were starting to heat up on Jay's film. He was so excited and confident about it. She hadn't gotten pregnant yet, but she was sure it would happen soon. Watching the little blue lines on the pregnancy tests, taking her folic acid, buying baby things on sale. It was all still potential. Their marriage was full of hope.

But it had been such a bad year.

"Beth?" He prods her again. "You okay?"

"I'm having trouble concentrating."

"Well, no kidding. So am I. But you're gonna have to try. Everything normal, remember? Nothing out of the ordinary."

"Why did you text me at work, then? You say act normal, but then you do this? When's the last time you even *thought* about me during the day, let alone—"

"Beth, calm down. Please!"

She takes a deep breath.

"Have you had lunch?" he asks.

"*What?*"

"Lunch. Have you gone for lunch?"

"I'm not hungry."

"You're supposed to—"

But he stops. He must know how ridiculous he sounds, because if he says "act normal" one more time, she'll throttle him.

"Look, you need to eat," he insists. "Go grab a sandwich or something."

"I said, I'm not hungry!"

"Then go get some air! Get a coffee! You need to chill *out!*"

His tone of voice shocks her. Yes, she has to calm down or this would all go wrong. She should go out for a coffee, get some fresh air, clear her head.

"I'm serious," he continues, in an "in charge" mood, the way he was last night when he hatched the plan. The way he used to be. As strange as it is, she misses that about him. He'd been so dashing when she'd met him, so confident. But he'd been floundering for so long that now she was floundering, too. Both of them treading water, trying to reach a life raft that keeps floating away the harder they swim for it, unable to save themselves, losing strength, out of breath. They couldn't even help each other anymore. If they so much as linked hands, they'd pull each other under and drown.

She kept telling herself, just be strong, just be patient, just keep going—she's a lotus flower. She'd been through worse than this. And there is an escape hatch now. That cash would help. They say money can't buy happiness, but neither do poverty or debt. She can vouch for that.

He continues—the confident, charming Jay. "Beth, I know this is hard. And I'm sorry. I really am." She feels as if he's in a pitch meeting, the way he's acting so smooth. "I hate having to put you through this."

"Why didn't you tell me about that girl?"

"What was I going to tell you? That some slut tried to blackmail me in college?"

"Jason!"

"I'm serious! That's what happened. Just forget it, okay? We can talk about it later. We have to stay cool right now. We're on the same team, remember? Everything's gonna be okay. I promise. Look, I gotta go. I've got to—"

"Wait!" she says. "Wait!"

"What is it?"

She holds her head, which aches so badly, it feels as if her skull is crushing her. But she has to ask him. She has to know.

"Have you ever done this before?"

"Done *this*?" He laughs. "Of course not!"

"No, I mean, have you cheated on me before?"

"What? Are you kidding, Beth? Are we really talking about this *now*?"

"I don't mean Cassie. I mean before that. With Emily or Karen. Or someone else."

There is a moment of silence on the phone. Nothing but the bizarre, muffled circus around her.

"Beth, please, I told you to—"

"I asked, have you ever slept with Emily or Karen?"

"Beth, they're my *friends*!"

"So? You slept with *my* best friend! Why wouldn't you do it with yours?"

"She's *not* your best friend! Are you—"

"Just answer me!"

"Of course not!" he barks.

"It's just Cassie, then?"

His voice is quieter, soothing. "Just...yes...of course. Look, I can't get into this now. I'm almost there. Let's talk about it—"

"Did you fall for her?"

"*Who?*"

"Cassie."

"God, no!"

Her voice softens. "Did you hurt her?"

"Beth, please..."

"Just tell me, Jay. I have to know."

"I told you already—no, goddammit! Just please try to relax, okay? I'm serious. I know I fucked up, but everything's gonna be all right. I promise. Everything's gonna be great. I'll see you after work. We can celebrate in style."

And then he's gone. Beth looks at the screen. *Call Ended*.

67

GOODE

Friday Afternoon

Goode's line of work doesn't normally take him onto the palm-lined boulevards of Beverly Hills, but he has to talk to John Montgomery. It's been almost seventy-two hours since the shootings, and their only lead—Cassie Ogilvy—has vanished. If he doesn't find her, or some other connection to Squires's supplier, the task force will close in. The LAPD might be one of the largest police forces in the country. But it's still dwarfed by the feds.

Which is why he wants to talk to Montgomery. To confirm the phone call from yesterday. Did he speak with Ogilvy? Did he see her? Does he know where she is?

He also wants to learn more about the son. They say the acorn doesn't fall far from the tree. Are both men capable of violence?

He follows the bends in the dark asphalt, staring out at the mansions. When he gets to the right address, there's a gate, but it's open, so he drives through. The big double door is white and carved. There's a doorbell and a knocker, but Goode forgoes both. He likes to announce his arrival manually, pounding on the door with the side of his fist.

Bang, bang, bang, bang, bang.

A moment later, a short Latina woman opens it. She wears a pale blue uniform with an apron. Goode thinks the getup is ridiculous and immediately feels sorry for her.

251

"Is Mr. John Montgomery in?"

"No, sir," says the woman, smiling. She has a Spanish accent. She seems polite, but Goode notices her gaze flit toward his car, then a furrow forms between her dark brows; when she looks at him again, her eyes have narrowed and she's not smiling anymore.

"Could you tell me where he is, please?"

"I don't think so, sir," the woman says, starting to close the door.

But at the same time, another voice joins in. A woman with silver hair emerges from the shadows above the maid's shoulder, a questioning look on her face.

"Who's there, Isa—" When she sees him, a deflated sound comes out of her. "Ooooh." Goode can tell she distrusts him immediately.

"Mrs. Montgomery?" he asks, taking a little bow. He crosses his hands in front of his crotch and plasters a big, fake smile on his face.

"Y-y-yes?" She's so nervous, her voice stutters and that one small word—yes—has about six syllables.

"My name is Detective Francis Goode. I'm with the Los Angeles Police Department." He presents his badge, then gives her his card in a move so slick, it's almost a magician's sleight of hand. She sees the word "Homicide," and her wrinkled throat jerks like a bobbing apple core as she swallows. She goes back to stuttering.

"Y-y-yes?"

"I'd like to speak to your husband, please."

"I—I'm afraid he's not in."

"Do you know where he might be?"

"He's golfing."

"It's very important that I speak with him as soon as possible. Do you know where he's golfing?"

"At the c-club," she says. "The Rosedale Park."

"Thank you kindly," he says, clicking his heels as he backs away. "I appreciate your cooperation. Have a nice day."

He feels her watching him as he walks back to his car. He could question her about Montgomery's whereabouts last night, but it would be too much of a tip-off. She might call and warn him Goode was coming. She might do that anyway, but no use supplying the details of the case. As he gets behind the wheel, she's still standing in the doorway, staring at his card. He roars away, giving the gas a little extra kick so the tires squeal before he gets to the gate.

The Rosedale Park Golf and Country Club appears out of the greenery, an elegant Georgian estate. Goode glides up to the curb, where a valet is waiting for him, opening his door.

"Welcome to the Rosedale, sir," he says, smiling.

Goode has no idea how to navigate this situation. He's never interviewed anyone on a golf course before. He flaps open his badge. "I'd like to speak with a member, please. Could you tell me how I might do that?"

"Maybe you should talk to the concierge, sir," the young man says. "She's inside."

"I'll do that. Thanks." Goode strides up a broad set of white steps, where another helpful lad smiles.

"Welcome to the Rosedale, sir," he says, opening the big double door.

"Thank you. That's very kind," Goode says, surprised. He prepared himself for some resistance, maybe even a fight.

He enters a large lobby featuring the kind of polished wood and high ceilings he associates with cathedrals. A pretty brunette sits at an antique partners desk ahead of him. The girl smiles in such a welcoming way, he would've approached her even without the sign on her desk.

Concierge: Ashley.

"May I help you, sir?" she asks. She has the kind of face that was made to smile. Must be clothespins in her cheeks holding up her lips. Goode introduces himself, shows his badge, mentions that he's got to talk to Mr. John Montgomery. The smile doesn't falter as the young woman picks up a phone and says she'll call the assistant manager. "Mr. Sullivan, I have a guest here who'd like to speak to Mr. Montgomery...Thank you." She hangs up, still smiling. "He'll be right out."

Goode nods, looking around at the polished furniture; everything's so huge—chairs, tables, mirrors—it's as if giants live here. There's a shop of golf clothes across the lobby, full of blues and yellows and ridiculous greens. Beyond the jungle of pastels and primary colors, another young woman is visible, like something camouflaged in the forest: she sits at a counter, flipping through a magazine.

Less than a minute later, a blond man in his forties, wearing a very crisp suit, appears from the hallway. If not for the fact he wears a brass name tag that reads WILLIAM B. SULLIVAN, M.A., ASSISTANT MANAGER, Goode would've thought he'd just come from a wedding, standing as someone's best man.

"May I help you, sir?" he asks, smiling with perfect white teeth.

Goode goes through the routine.

"I'm sorry, sir. But we can't interrupt members while they're on the course. Especially since the mayor is in the Montgomery foursome today."

"The *mayor*?" Goode asks. He's impressed.

"I'd be delighted to have you wait in the club room if you like. They probably won't be more than forty-five minutes."

"That'll be fine." He nods goodbye to Ashley as the assistant manager takes him through yet another set of double doors into a large dim room full of brass and glass and empty tables. A young man sits folding napkins in the corner, and another pretty girl is behind the bar, polishing glasses.

"Please have a seat," says the manager, pointing to the tables and chairs. "Holly, get Mr. Goode something to drink while he waits."

"Of course," she says, coming out from behind the bar. She's obviously gone to the same smiling tutor as Ashley. "What can I get for you, sir?"

"Got any Gatorade?"

"Sure. What flavor would you like?"

He's surprised. Most restaurants don't stock Gatorade. "Which ones do you have?"

"All of them," she says.

"Like, twenty-one of them?"

"Well, maybe not *that* many." She laughs. "But several."

"Surprise me, then," he says with a grin.

"Of course." She turns and whisks back behind the bar.

Goode looks around, noticing a set of French doors leading outside. Despite the fact the restaurant is empty, the large veranda is full of guests at tables, various shades of silver, white, and dyed-blond heads bobbing and turning and nodding. Of course everyone would be out there on a beautiful Friday afternoon.

It's a little hard for him not to join them. He's a curious person, and he's never been to a private country club before. He crosses the portal from the dim room into the brilliant, bright outdoors. The plates are full of succulent burgers and salads and poached fish. The silver heads bob and smile. Some people look at him curiously, but not as many as he'd think. He finds an empty table and sits down. Adjusts another chair and puts his foot up on it, leaning back. He surveys the domain. Rolling green grasses and manicured trees, tiny figures moving around at a relaxed pace. White golf carts seem to float like sailboats on an emerald sea. He's never seen anything like it. It's a secret paradise inside of Los Angeles. He grew up here, thought he knew every inch of the city, but this is totally new to him. How were they keeping this from him? From all of them? He always suspected that rich people had secret places like this, but it seemed more like a conspiracy theory than any possible truth. If it weren't so damned impressive, he'd cry.

The girl named Holly comes over with a blue Gatorade. "How's this?" she asks. She sets down a glass and pours it for him.

"That's just marvelous."

"Enjoy."

"I'm sure I will."

His drink is half gone when he notices the assistant manager get into a red golf cart—the only red one Goode can see—and roar toward the eighteenth hole. Goode sits forward as Sullivan gets out and approaches men rolling up in two white carts. There is some discussion. All four heads turn in the direction of the clubhouse. Goode still can't get over it. He better tread carefully. The mayor may have time to golf with the one-percenters, but he's also on the task force.

The assistant manager collects him a few minutes later and brings him down a paneled hallway to his own office.

"Mr. Montgomery will be here momentarily," he says, then bows away.

Goode waits. The office is imposing. Banker's lamps, paintings of horses, lots of leather furniture and photographs of men and women posing for group shots.

Ladies championships.

PGA tournaments.

Fund-raising balls.

"Hello?" A man's voice behind him. Goode turns to see a tall man, very fit for his age. His smile is practiced, his handshake firm. "John Montgomery. May I help you?"

Goode intuits this is someone accustomed to controlling every situation, even when he doesn't know what the situation is yet. Goode introduces himself, handing over his card. There's no immediate fear in Montgomery's expression, though age spots on his forehead shift slightly as he frowns. Regardless of who you are—a drug dealer from the streets or a rich bastard in a country club— there's never a good reason to be visited by a homicide detective. Goode motions to a leather club chair.

"I think you should have a seat, sir."

The man seems to consider it, unaccustomed to taking orders, but he finally sits down. Goode takes the liberty of going behind the assistant manager's desk, sitting in the big leather swivel chair. He slides the DMV photo over to the man. "Do you know this woman?"

Montgomery glances at the shot. "No, I don't think so."

"Are you sure? Cassandra Ogilvy. Maybe you spoke with her on the phone."

"I told you, I don't even know her. Why would I have spoken to her?"

"Because we have a record of a call to your cell phone, from your son's number—and we believe Ms. Ogilvy made that call."

"Oh, that's right!" He laughs uncomfortably. "She's a house-guest of theirs. I dropped something off the other day and met her briefly. I'm sorry. I didn't recognize her. I don't have my glasses on. I shouldn't do anything without my glasses." He tries to laugh again. "Especially golf."

Goode doesn't even smile. "So, *did* you speak on the phone with Ms. Ogilvy yesterday—or not?"

The man's lower lip droops, gleaming with a fleck of spittle. He looks down at the card again. "This says *homicide*. Do they think something happened to her?"

"Do *we* think something happened to her?"

"Yes, of course. That's what I meant."

Goode gauges how best to share the news, deciding on short but sweet. "Ms. Ogilvy is missing and we have reason to suspect foul play."

The man leans back as if he were pushed. Goode hopes there's no heart condition involved, because it looks like he might have to perform CPR any minute. When Montgomery speaks again, his voice is so weak, it's as if he's acquired a case of laryngitis.

"I—I was just golfing with my lawyer," he stammers, motioning to the veranda. "May I bring him in? I think I should bring him in."

"You can bring him in."

"Thank you," he whispers. He gets up and leaves the room.

So the blustery act was gone. Humility reigned supreme. About time. The guy was no saint himself. John Montgomery had been charged with DUI in 1998 and again in 2007. Both misdemeanors, without jail time, probably because he traveled in powerful circles. But no history of violence.

Goode watches through the big windows as Montgomery walks out onto the veranda and approaches a table of men having lunch. They're all wearing golf shirts in cupcake colors: pink, mauve, yellow. He wonders if they know how ridiculous they look. But he recognizes the mayor, looking up, listening. It's strange to see him without a suit and tie on. Goode probably wouldn't have recognized him if the assistant manager hadn't tipped him off. A few words are exchanged, but not many, and one of the gentlemen stands up.

A moment later the two men enter the office. Montgomery looks at least ten years older than he did when he first walked into the room. The lawyer, on the other hand, is stiff and abrasive—or as stiff and abrasive as a grown man can look in a bright pink golf shirt.

"My name is Alistair Briggs," he says, presenting a crisp business card. Goode's never dealt with the fancy law firm before, but he's heard of it. "You may speak to my client through me, Detective. How may we help you?"

Goode is happy to turn the big leather swivel chair toward the mouthpiece.

"I'm investigating the case of a missing woman," he begins. "I'm trying to establish what your client was doing between four p.m. and ten p.m. last night."

The two of them confer behind a web of tanned, wrinkled hands. Gold wedding bands and watches flash in the light.

"He had various errands to do. Then he spent the evening with his wife."

"Did he, or did he not, see Cassandra Ogilvy yesterday?"

Conference.

"Yes, he did."

"When?"

Whispering.

"Around five p.m. yesterday."

"What did you—what did *they* discuss?"

More with the conference.

"Oh, for chrissakes!" Goode feels as if he's playing a children's birthday game. "I'm sick of this bullshit. A woman is missing, probably dead. Don't waste my time." He turns the big chair toward John again. "You've lied to me already, Mr. Montgomery. You said you didn't know her, but you do. So stop fucking around and answer my questions."

They both stare at him, blinking bookends in leather chairs.

"All right," says John, defeated.

The lawyer seems displeased, as lawyers tend to be when you cut them out of the equation.

"I did meet her the other day. Briefly. I had to drop something off for my son. But she called me yesterday and told me she needed a ride downtown. So I—I picked her up at the house."

"That's very thoughtful of you, Mr. Montgomery. Driving all the way from Beverly Hills to offer a young woman a ride."

"I was just trying to be helpful."

"Of course. Did you not think it was odd that she didn't ask someone else? Your son, perhaps?"

"Not—really."

"Before you go any further, Mr. Montgomery, I should tell you, your son has already confessed to having sexual intercourse with Ms. Ogilvy yesterday."

The man glances at his lawyer, then back again. "That's none of my business."

"Maybe not. But it might be ours." He lets a beat pass. "Your son was arrested and charged with sexual assault, was he not?"

The man stiffens, his lips pursing. It's clearly a sore point with him. "That's not exactly true. His record was—"

"Expunged, yes, I realize that." Goode has done some more digging into the case, so he knows the details. "But it looks like you came to his aid. You bought the girl off and the charges were dropped?"

The lawyer steps in. "That's a distasteful way of saying that we settled out of court. It happens all the time. Kids make mistakes. Look, Mr.—"

"*Detective* Goode."

"Detective Goode, this was all settled a long time ago. My client's son made a mistake. The girl was drunk. He didn't realize how drunk. There's no reason he had to suffer his whole life for one mistake anyone can make."

"How do you even know about it?" John asks. "It was so long ago and his record was expunged."

The Montgomerys seem to like this word, "expunged."

"Yes. I realize that. But under the circumstances, I'm investigating the possibility your son may be involved in Ms. Ogilvy's disappearance."

"That's ridiculous! Jason didn't *mean* it! I told her that a dozen times. She wasn't badly hurt, anyway."

"Hurt?" Goode's skin prickles.

"She told me what happened between them. Her neck was a bit pink, but that's all. Jason can be a little rough sometimes, but he's not capable of really hurting anyone."

"What about you? Are *you* capable of hurting someone?"

His forehead wrinkles, shooting his white hair up like a snowdrift. "Absolutely not!"

"Did you have sex with her, too?"

"God, no!"

"That's enough, Detective," says the lawyer. His jaw tenses so visibly, it looks as if he could chew concrete to dust. "Do you have any official charges against my client?"

"Not yet." He looks back at Montgomery. Allows the silence to play out. Did this man have what it took to kill someone? Was he protecting his reputation? His fortune? His son? It seemed at least possible. Rich people had been doing a lot worse to keep what they had in life.

"Don't say anything more, John. It's not—"

But Montgomery doesn't listen. "I want you to know, I've been faithful to my wife for over forty years."

"If I had a dime for every time some guy told me that, I bet I could afford a membership at a place like this." He motions around the room.

"No need to be facetious, Detective," says the lawyer.

"I'm telling you, nothing happened," John maintains. "She seemed upset. She wanted to go for a drink. I told her I couldn't— I mean, I can't be seen having drinks with a young woman like that. When I told her no, she still wanted to be dropped off at a bar."

"Do you remember the name of the place?"

"Tootsie's? Footsie's? Something like that."

Goode is familiar with the old landmark club. "What time was that?"

"Five thirty or six. She asked me to take her inside, so I did. But I didn't stay for a drink. I just helped her get a table, and then I left. I didn't even sit down."

"You left her alone in a bar?"

"She was hardly alone. One of the waiters even recognized her. That young lady is more than capable of looking after herself."

"Let's hope so," Goode says. "Did you see or hear from her again after that?"

"No. I went straight home. That's where I was all night. At home with my wife." He delivers the information like irrefutable proof of his good character.

"Your son was at home with his wife last night, too, sir," Goode says. "But that doesn't make him innocent."

"It doesn't make him guilty of anything, either," says the lawyer.

"That's true," Goode concedes with a smile. "I'm just saying, it's no medal of honor to be at home with your wife. Let's not act as if it is."

The lawyer grumbles, unable to respond.

"I swear to you, Detective," Montgomery begins, "I did not hurt that girl. I left her at that place safe and sound. My son wouldn't really hurt anyone either. He's not perfect. I realize that. He can be hotheaded and he makes mistakes. There's no doubt about that. But he's not capable of really hurting anyone. I promise you."

"How do you know that, sir?"

Montgomery shrugs, as if a lifetime of disappointment has come crushing down on him. "He's too weak."

68

BETH

On her next break between students, Beth hurries out of the studio. She tries to smile at the receptionist as she passes her desk. "Just going out for a coffee, Kelly."

"Enjoy. Nice day out there." The girl smiles and goes back to her ringing phone.

Waiting for the elevator feels like an eternity to Beth. She's still angry at Jay for texting her, but at the same time, she's so nervous, she thinks the receptionist can see her heart beating through her clothes. She knows Kelly gave Cassie their home number. When she found out, she'd considered confronting the girl about it, but now she's glad she didn't. What if she saw the news about Cassie's disappearance? How she's wanted in connection with all these shootings? Would she recognize the name? It seems like a long shot, but Beth can't be sure. If things don't go according to plan—and even if they do—she'll have to worry about everything from now on.

Finally, the elevator comes. It's empty, thank God. She gets on and the doors close. She feels the perspiration on her palms, rubs them against her skirt. She still seethes about Jay. How can he be so stupid? He's going to get them caught. And why did she ask if he's ever cheated on her before? What's the point now? She knew he'd lie to her. Why does she even care? She doesn't. Not anymore.

The door opens and she crosses the lobby, heels clicking quickly. The metronome of her life. How many times has she walked through this lobby, bored, frustrated, or holding back tears? Everything feels so different now. She wonders what would've happened if Cassie hadn't called. Is it possible everything would've been fine between her and Jay? What if she had eventually gotten pregnant again? What if his film eventually got made? They could've just gone on with a normal life, the one she longed for, the one she thought she was getting when she married him. But now everything has changed. All the scheming is getting dangerous. And Jay is being such an idiot, he could get them both in serious trouble. She might still end up in jail over it. And if not, she'd have to worry about that for the rest of her life.

How could she have been so gullible, to think there'd ever been a gig, ever been a Lily on the phone? None of this would've even happened if Beth had just stood her ground and said: "I'm sorry, Cass, we don't have room." Or "I'm too busy." Or "I can't see you. The past is the past. I don't want to get involved."

What would Cassie have done? After all these years, would she really have come out and said, "You told me you owed me," expecting Beth to do her bidding?

Of course, if Cassie hadn't shown up, they wouldn't have that money, and that money was the best thing that had happened to Beth in as long as she could remember. That money was her way out.

69

JAY

Friday Afternoon

Traffic moves swiftly past the low white picket fence of the Ivy. On the patio, Jay and Karen sit across from each other. It was natural for them to hold hands as they talked about it. Such old friends, she was a comfort to him at a time like this. He told her the story about Cassie's disappearance and how the cops had come to the house in the middle of the night. Karen gasped at all the right places, covering her mouth as if watching a thriller on TV.

"You're kidding? What a nightmare!"

"Tell me about it. The police think she's involved in that drug-deal thing the other night. You read about it? Four guys dead or something?"

"So she's a criminal? On top of everything?"

"Looks like."

He'd left certain details out, of course. His afternoon dalliance with Cassie, for instance. Karen wouldn't take *that* well. And he definitely didn't tell her about the cash. As business partners, they were into everything fifty-fifty. If she knew he had more than a million dollars sitting in a bag at home, she'd want to have a say in how it was spent. But until he knows exactly what he's going to do with it, no use complicating things.

"Is Beth okay?" Karen's voice is intimate, soothing. She's so thoughtful. Of course she'd be worried about Beth. But Jay doesn't want to talk about his wife. It was her fault for bringing this woman into their lives in the first place. None of this would've even happened if Beth hadn't been so trusting.

Of course, behind every curse is a blessing. He's never believed it before. But he's seen the money. Touched it.

"She'll be all right," he grumbles, remembering how cold she'd been on the phone. Criticizing him, like always. *Don't be stupid!* He was excited, that's all. Happy for the first time in a long time, and all she did was cut him down. "You invite people like that into your home, what do you expect?"

"Still. Do they really think she was murdered?"

"They're not sure, but with a chick like—" But before Jay can finish, the roar of a black Ferrari cuts him off. On the street, Commisso gets out of the car and hands his keys to the valet. Jay leans toward Karen as they stand up.

"Let's leave the cops out of the pitch, okay?"

"Great idea," she says with a laugh.

70

GOODE

Goode pushes the door open, stepping into the dim room. Billiard balls tumble and *clack* as two figures stand by a pool table, perusing a fresh break. A few lonely souls sit at tables or at the bar, hunched over their drinks. Goode thinks there's nothing more depressing than a bar during the day, when you can see all the stains on the floor.

A cocktail waitress with a blond brush cut is wiping down tables, greeting him with a smile. "Hey. Sit anywhere you like."

He holds up his badge. "I have a few questions about a customer who was in last night," he says.

"Sorry, I was off yesterday," she tells him, seeming relieved to stay out of it. "But Ryan was working." She points to a man with a shaved head, carrying a case of beer behind the bar. Goode nods *thanks* and heads to the counter.

The young man is muscular, crouched by the beer fridge, setting the case on the floor. Small gold hoops gleam in his earlobes, and tattoos encircle his neck, up into his shaved skull. The man senses Goode behind him and twists back. "What would—" But he stops when he sees the badge and stands up, grabbing a bar towel, drying his hands. "How can I help you?" His tone is firm, flat.

"Was this woman here at any point yesterday or last night?" He holds up the photo of Cassie, watching the man for his reaction.

A smile brightens his face. "For sure. She's been in a couple times this week." He wipes the counter down as he speaks. "Why? What's up?"

"Actually, she's missing, and we're trying to find out where she might be."

His features drop. "What happened?"

"We're not sure. What time did she come in?"

He squints, thinking. "Six or so. Around shift change. I'm covering for someone this week, so I've been pulling doubles."

"Was she with anyone?"

"An old guy came in with her, but he didn't stay."

"You said she was in a couple times this week?"

"Yeah, the other night she was in with a friend. Tuesday, I guess. A blonde. I'm glad she wasn't alone. She got sort of—loaded."

"Did she drink much last night?"

"Not at all. Not nearly as much as the last time. She seemed a bit quiet, actually. Worried. I asked her if she was okay."

"And?"

"She didn't get into it. She was sort of preoccupied. Not as bubbly as the other night, that's all. I think she was waiting for someone."

Compression tightens Goode's chest. "Did she mention any names? Jay? Rick? Anything ring a bell?"

"Sorry. She didn't say. And Thursday nights are busy. I didn't have much time to chat."

"Did anyone show up?"

"No. She was alone the whole time. She went outside to blow a couple smokes. She left in a hurry, around nine or so. I thought maybe she got stood up, cuz she seemed pretty pissed off all of a sudden."

"Pissed off?"

"Yeah. She didn't say bye or anything. She was so friendly the other night. This time she just stormed off."

"Did she have anything with her? Bags? Cases?"

"She had luggage with her, yeah. Like the other night. Two bags, I think."

"How'd she pay for her tab? Cash or credit?"

"Cash. I remember it was a C-note. She left me a nice tip, too. I didn't even get a chance to thank her."

"I don't suppose you have that bill?" The money from Lawrence Heights was all hundred-dollar bills—unmarked, but there still may be something traceable.

"Sorry, no. The manager deposits everything at closing. Man, I knew something was wrong. She's such a sweetheart. I hope you find her."

"I do, too," says Goode.

71

BETH

Friday Afternoon

In Starbucks, Beth takes her place in the long line. She sees today's paper on the rack and grabs it quickly. Nothing on the front page. But on the bottom of page three, there's a small photo of Cass. God, she even looked beautiful on her driver's license. She scans the article. *"Police are searching for a thirty-two-year-old woman in connection with the shootings in Lawrence Heights on..."*

She jumps as the paper jerks toward her.

"Boo!"

She lowers the page and sees a man standing on the other side, his index finger extended where he tapped the paper. She only vaguely recognizes him at first.

"Hey, Beth!" he says with an exaggerated smile. He's not as clean-cut as the last time she saw him, his hair disheveled, his jaw peppered with whiskers. He wears the same jacket and glasses, but there's no tie, and instead of suit pants, he wears jeans.

Despite all that, she would've recognized him if he were wearing the sling, but it's gone. He seems different without it, stronger.

"Sorry. Didn't mean to scare you," he says with a citric grin. She feels like she should be glad to see him again, happy for the ego boost he offered before. But she doesn't want to talk to him right now. She doesn't want to talk to anyone.

"It's o-okay," she stammers, going back to the article. He's right beside her, staying even with her as she shifts forward in the queue.

"Can you stay for a coffee?"

"I'm afraid not. I have to get back to work." She can smell him now, a foul odor—sweat, liquor, and something else, something putrid. Something is definitely different about him. It makes her uneasy. She feels him lean over her shoulder to read the article.

"Cassie was always getting into trouble, wasn't she?"

Chills tighten her skin. She gasps, despite herself.

Is Cassie there?

She recognizes the voice from the phone call that night. That call. The one that started everything. She turns to him, heart pounding. There's still a cruel smirk on his lips. When Goode showed her the photo in the bedroom last night, she knew he looked familiar, but she couldn't quite place him. The dark hair and the glasses were so different from the scruffy man in the mug shot. But she recognizes him now.

Her "fan."

He grabs the paper from her and puts it back on the rack. She tries to rush away, but he snatches her arm, stopping her. She feels pressure against her ribs. Glances down to see the metallic barrel of a gun. Her heart flies so high into her throat, she can almost taste it.

I used to dabble a bit...

Why had she been so eager to trust him before? How could she have been so stupid? She didn't have any fans. Her own idiocy makes her want to be sick. If she'd just recognized him from the photo, she could've told Goode about him. Maybe the police would've protected her. Had her guarded until he was caught. Now it's too late.

"Can we skip the coffee?" he asks, tucking the gun into his suit jacket pocket but still gripping the handle. "I'd like to talk."

"I t-told you, I have to get back to work."

She doesn't know what to do. Goode said he's a killer and he's after that money. He isn't going to let her go now.

"I'm afraid you're not going back to work today," he says, taking her elbow and easing her away from the line. With a bent arm, in his jacket pocket, he can keep the gun well hidden. As he urges her across the room, customers tap on their laptops. Chat at tables. Wait in line like zombies. Nobody even glances over.

She should scream. Why can't she scream? It's as if he's stepped on her windpipe. He pushes her toward the front of the shop, murmuring in her ear.

"Take out your phone, Beth."

"*What?*"

A stranger coming in stops and smiles, holding the door for them. She tries to scream again, but her lips barely open. Rick pushes her into the sunshine. On the sidewalk, he shoves her toward the wall, getting close, as if they were lovers. He smells so awful. Sweat, whiskey, and that rancid, horrifying stench.

"I said, take out your phone."

Trembling, she gets her cell out of her bag.

"You're going to call the school right now and you're going to tell them you're not feeling well."

"But they just saw me. I was—"

He talks over her. "Something you ate maybe. Had a long night. Whatever. You're going to tell them you're not coming in this afternoon. Do it."

But she can't move. He gives her a threatening jab from the gun.

"*Now.*"

Shaking, she dials the front desk. The sun is so hot. Blinding. Blistering. The line rings in her ear. She tries to turn away from him, but she can't; he's too strong. The gun jabs into her ribs. The people walking by, why aren't they looking at him? Why can't they see what's happening to her?

The receptionist answers. "Good afternoon, Steinberg Music Academy. May I help you?"

"Hey, Kelly. It's Beth..."

"Hey, Beth, what's up?"

"Well, all of a sudden I'm not feeling very well, actually. I don't know what happened."

"Oh no!"

"Yeah, it just came over me...I'm kind of nauseous."

"Maybe you're pregnant!"

Beth lets out a little sound, part laugh, part sob, but she doesn't comment. "I should go home. Can you get someone to cover the rest of my students this afternoon? Sheila said she has a quiet week."

"Absolutely! Get better soon, okay?"

"Thanks so much." She hangs up, feeling as if she's let go of a life preserver on a rough sea.

"Good girl," says Rick. "Now turn it off. *All* the way off." He watches her power the phone down, then propels her away from the wall and back onto the sidewalk. "You know how to drive, right?" He takes out a fob. Half a block down, parked at the curb, a black SUV chirps to life.

72

GOODE

In the Vehicular Forensics Impound Room of the LAPD, two crime lab technicians work on Jason Montgomery's Mustang. Goode watches from behind the big window in the viewing room, a monitor documenting the search behind the glass. They'd already found a cigarette butt in the ashtray, same brand as the package in Ogilvy's purse. But the major discovery was blood. Goode sees a dark pool of it, looking almost black against red carpet in the trunk of the car, an elongated stain the size of a football.

The speaker *clicks* again. This time, the woman with the prominent nose regards him. "It's B-positive. We also have dark hairs, with the follicles still attached."

Goode nods. "See if you can expedite the DNA."

"Sure thing."

But there's not much doubt the blood belongs to Cassie Ogilvy. Only ten percent of the population had the blood type B-positive.

Dawes walks into the room, smiling. She holds a rolled-up evidence bag. "Just talked to the manager at the Omni. Addison's alibi checks out. He signed for two scotches in the lobby bar, leaving by himself just before eight last night. The locks are computerized, so we know when he got back to his room. The kitchen confirms he ordered room service—a burger, a Coke, and a chamomile tea. But once the food was delivered, nobody entered or exited the room until seven thirty this morning, when he went to work."

Goode's disappointed—but not surprised—the smarmy bio-chemical engineer is just a luckless bystander to this mess. "Okay, so then why are you grinning?"

"Because you were right to check the alley. They found this in one of the garbage cans down the block."

She holds up the evidence bag to reveal a large butcher knife. Goode takes it, inspecting it more carefully. Dried blood smeared on the blade, collected in the wooden hilt.

"They thought it might be from one of the restaurants," Dawes says. "Or maybe the butcher shop. But it doesn't look commercial, so they just brought it in. They're running the blood through Forensics now."

"Good work," he says. "But I still don't see why you have such a big grin on your face."

"Because there were prints. Partials, but they were enough. And we got a match."

73

BETH

The smell of his breath, the heat of it, makes her skin crawl. "What are you so afraid of, Beth? Have I hurt you?"

The gun jabs into her back as she stands at the door of a run-down motel surrounded by baked-out strip malls. Her hands tremble so badly, she drops the key trying to unlock the door. He knows about the money. He must.

"Just calm down," he whispers.

She picks up the key, focuses, manages to slice it into the lock, throwing open the door. He pushes her, and she stumbles over the threshold into the room. He locks and chains the door behind them. The blinds are closed, light slashing the walls like cell bars. The double bed caves in the middle, the twisted sheets stained with dried blood, empty beer bottles everywhere. The whole place smells of garbage, liquor, fetid drains—and something else. It's the smell of rot itself.

"Have a seat," he tells her.

When she can't move, he pushes her toward a chair. Her shoe catches on a heavy case—black with silver rivets—and she nearly falls, righting herself at the last instant. He shoves her again, and she stumbles into the chair, turning to face him. He grins as he throws something at her. She has to duck not to be hit. His keys clatter on the dresser behind her, skidding to a stop against the wall.

He goes to the nightstand, putting the gun down. He uncaps

a half-empty whiskey bottle and takes long swallows, his throat bobbing, but his eyes never leave hers. He puts the bottle down, digging in his pocket, pulling out a tiny vial of white powder. He snorts straight from the tube, knocking his head back, his eyes closed for a moment.

She should lunge for the gun now. This is her chance. She feels her thighs tense up to run, but he's glaring at her again. She has to calm down, she tells herself. She has to calm down, or she's never getting out of this.

"I think you know why you're here, Beth." He takes off the glasses, setting them on the nightstand, an almost gentlemanly move.

"No, I d-don't. I have no idea." She hears the quaver in her own voice. She hates the sound of it. So helpless.

"I think you're lying."

"I s-swear, I'm not. I don't know what you want."

He pulls off the suit jacket, and she notices the dried bloodstain on his shirt. He unbuttons the shirt, strips it off. Tattoos blot his skin, but there's also a gauze bandage between his chest and shoulder, bruises radiating like a purple starburst.

"Well then, *Beth*," he says. "I'll get you up to speed. It's about the money. I want my money. And I really don't want to have to hurt you for it. But I will."

"What money?"

A dry laugh, mocking her. "What money?"

"I don't have any—"

He lunges across the room and grabs her by the hair. Her scalp burns as he yanks her to her feet and swings her around, throwing her facedown on the bed. She tries to scramble off, but he grabs the gun from the nightstand and gets on top of her, holding the barrel to the back of her head. He adjusts his weight and jabs his knee into the small of her back, pinning one arm behind her until it feels like her shoulder blade will snap.

"Don't be stupid, Beth," he hisses in her ear. "The money Cassie stole from me. Where is it?"

"I told you, I don't know what—"

"Don't lie to me!" He knees her in the back again and she gasps in pain. "Trust me, Beth. You do not want to screw with me. I've had it with being screwed over by chicks this week. What is it with you two? Both of you? Cass shoulda known better. But you—"

But before he can finish, she slams the back of her head up into the bloody patch on his chest. He lurches away, grunting in pain. She twists onto her back, bracing herself with her hands. Scrambling forward, she kicks the bloodstain, this time with the heel of her shoe. He cries out, stumbling backward off the bed.

She tries to rush for the motel phone on the nightstand, but he's on her in a second, grabbing her ankle, yanking her back. She's only able to pull the cord, snapping it toward her. The phone hits the open whiskey bottle and it tumbles to the carpet, splashing liquid. She looks up just in time to see him swing the gun down at her, butting her across the face. A dense focus of pain on her cheekbone, burning and cold at the same time. The strength goes out of her and she collapses onto the bed. She sees the sheet turn red beneath her cheek before everything goes black.

74

JAY

Friday Afternoon

Jay watches Commisso nattering away with Karen. He's taking a different tack today. No begging. No champagne. And no cheap meal for himself. It's a welcome change. Jay hasn't felt this confident in front of the guy since they met. It's like he's had an adrenaline hypo to his heart. He's in control now, like his old self, all swagger and shine.

He finishes his double scotch, the warmth sliding through him, stinging and soothing at the same time. He catches the server's attention with a flick of his hand and orders another. His third. He doesn't need it. He deserves it. The longer he stews here, baking in the heat, smelling exhaust from traffic, listening to Commisso's excuses about the money, the more his mind drifts. And the angrier he gets at Beth.

Not on the phone!

She acts as if all that cash is hers. If she had it her way, she'd probably want to put it all toward the bills. But did she have a right to *any* of that money in the first place? It was his idea to keep it. She just wanted to call the police and give it back. Shouldn't *he* be the one to decide what to do with it? Absolutely. He's going to have to talk to her tonight. He's going to put his foot down.

That money will go into his film. It's the most important thing. With that cash, Jay can start attaching people. He can get a bank draft after lunch and bring a check to Milla's agent personally, before the end of the business day. It's enough to start preproduction, on a small independent film at least. He can get office space. Hire someone to answer phones. This is just the kind of windfall they've been waiting for. How can Beth be so selfish? What is wrong with her? If she doesn't watch it, she's going to screw everything up.

As they speak, the grumble of a brown Chevy, very different from the Ferrari or any of the other luxury cars pulling up out front, interrupts the quiet afternoon, stopping at the curb. When Jay sees Goode climb out of the car, something snatches at his heart. Quick and cold. The detective looks across the patio. Their gazes meet over the low fence. Goode smiles, in a threatening way. Jay's in the middle of a mouthful of scotch, but his throat feels clogged and it takes him three tries to swallow. Goode climbs the steps to the restaurant.

Karen's still trying to sweet-talk Commisso.

Is it possible, is it remotely possible, Goode is here to speak to someone else?

At the hostess station, Goode flashes his badge and points to Jay's table. It's over. That's it. He's not here for someone else. How stupid to think that. Goode walks across the restaurant toward them, winding around tables. Jay hears his own blood pounding in his head and then the sound of Karen's voice.

"Jay?"

"Huh—what?"

"He's got a point. Unless we can get someone to sign off on—"

But she stops as Goode approaches the table, a sly grin on his face.

"Hi there, Mr. Montgomery. I remembered you said you had a meeting here today."

Jay clears his throat. "Yes, hello, Detective."

Karen and Commisso frown at the intruder, then glance curiously at Jay.

Goode looks around the restaurant. "Nice place. I drive by all the time, but I've never been."

"Yeah, it's…nice," Jay says. His heart squeezes when he sees two more cruisers and an LAPD van pull up in front. "Can I h-help you with something?"

"Yeah." Goode motions to the free chair. "You mind if I join you?" But he sits down without waiting for an answer. Karen's and Commisso's eyes are wide. Goode looks at Jay's plate. "What're you having?"

"Uh...sea bass," Jay says, though he's barely touched his plate.

"Looks good. Don't let me interrupt." He picks up a piece of bread from the basket and begins buttering it.

"Uh...we're just finishing up some important business here, Detective. If you could just wait somewhere—*else*—I'd really appreciate it."

"Actually, this is important, too. It won't take long. I just wanted to go over one more time where you were last night between four p.m. and ten p.m."

"I told you. I was at home all night. I passed out."

"You sure about that?"

"As sure as anyone can be—who's *sleeping*." Jay can't help it; he's pissed off. They have nothing on him. What were they doing here, humiliating him like this?

"Maybe you don't remember. You were under the influence of drugs last night, after all. And drinking quite a bit."

"I'd remember leaving my own damn house and—and hurting someone."

"Would you? Do you remember what happened last time? Back in college?"

"Goode—that has nothing to do with this and you know it!"

The other guests in the restaurant start to stare as three uniformed officers and Detective Dawes pass the hostess station and make their way through the tables. Dawes has a clear plastic bag in one hand, something gleaming inside.

Goode says, "You remember my partner, Detective Dawes."

"Yes, we met at the—place," Jay says. He doesn't want to say "the station." More people are looking over now. "Look, could we go...somewhere?" He needs this not to be happening, not here.

Goode ignores the question. So does Dawes.

"Nice to see you again, Mr. Montgomery," she says. She holds out the bag.

"You wanna have a look at that, Jay? See if you recognize it."

Jay stares at the bag—and the large, familiar butcher knife inside.

"Take it out if you're not sure."

Jay sees the blade and the smears of blood. "I don't want to touch it," he says.

"Why not?"

"Looks like there's blood on it."

"Of course there's blood on it. That's why we suspect it's a murder weapon. And it's not just blood. It's full of prints, too. Guess whose?"

"How the hell should I know?" he says, heart pounding.

"They're *your* prints, Jason."

"*What?*"

Karen and Commisso seem to have stopped breathing, their only movements the occasional blink of an eye. Neither of them will even look at him. With all these cops around the table, Jay feels trapped in shadow, yet his skin has opened up, pouring a billion pinpricks of sweat.

"Looks like you tried to wipe it clean. But you didn't quite make it."

"I have no idea what you're talking about. No fucking—"

"Were you in too much of a rush?" Goode presses, ignoring him. "Or was she struggling too hard?"

The dusty hills of Hollywood seem to swing above his head. The blood rushes to deafen him. His prints? Did he leave the house last night? Did he do something to her? No, it's impossible.

"Maybe somebody came into the alley and saw you starting the fire?"

"What are you talking about, Goode? You can't do this to me. I know my rights. This is harassment!" he says, jabbing the table with his fingertip. "Police harassment!"

"Thing is, Jason, if you're not gonna clean a murder weapon properly, you should at least dispose of it safely, ya know? Don't just leave it where we can find it."

"Find it?" Jay's scared now. He tries a different tone of voice, a little laugh. "There's been some mistake, Detective. This is crazy. I didn't do anything to her."

"Come on, Jay. After everything that went on between you two? Her cigarette butt's in the ashtray of your car. Her hair's in the trunk. A lot of blood, too. Bet the blood on your phone is a match to hers, too, right?"

"Goode, I'm telling you I had nothing to do with—" But Jay feels the strong hands of another cop on his arms as he's pulled from the chair.

"Jason Montgomery," Goode begins, "you're under arrest on suspicion of murder."

"What the hell?" Jay's being manhandled, so he fights back, elbowing one cop in the chest. But it doesn't help. The hands clamp down even harder on him.

"You have the right to remain silent..."

"You're insane! I told you, I didn't do anything!" But Jay feels the sharp chill of the handcuffs around his wrists. Everyone in the room is staring now, some people rising to get a better view of the commotion, others taking out their phones to record it.

"Should you give up the right to remain silent—"

"I didn't kill her, Goode! I swear! I told you what happened!"

"—anything you say can and will be held against you in a court of law."

Jay knocks chairs and tables, struggling as they weave him toward the entrance. He looks back over his shoulder to see everyone standing, staring, speculating, a loud murmur of judgment in his wake. To Jay, the humiliation is almost as bad as the panic. Maybe worse.

75

RICK

Rick flips through her wallet, finally seeing the elusive address on her driver's license. *What money?* she asked, so innocent and confused. But if she and Cassie were as close as he thinks, she knows where that cash is. He's sure of it. He hears groaning from the bed as she raises her head, blood smeared across the side of her face, soaking the sheet.

"Look who's up," he says, shoving her wallet back into her bag. She's bewildered, glancing around, uncertain where she is.

"The famous pianist," he says, then mocks a tune. "Blah, blah, blah, blah, blah! I hated your music, by the way. What a joke. Cass made me listen to your shit on the drive up. What a fuckin' has-been." He grabs the gun from the back of his waistband and handles it, checking the magazine. She watches him, terrified, then buries her face in the pillow, letting out a small sob.

The mattress sinks beneath his knees as he gets on the bed. She gasps as if she's just taken a drop on a roller coaster, rigid with fear. He holds the gun with his good hand, using it to push her skirt up on her thighs. The bed bounces. He sees the crack of her pale, pretty ass above her panties.

"She told me all about you, though. Said if she was ever in trouble, she could go to you. You owed her. That's the crazy thing about chicks. They're like teenagers their whole lives."

He drops his weight down on top of her, the gun on one side of her head. He feels her tense up, hard as brick. "One thing you should know about me, Beth. I actually prefer blondes. It's something I—"

But she jerks to life, reaching down so quickly, her arm is like a striking snake. She grabs the whiskey bottle from the floor and swings back hard. But he lurches away, and she doesn't even nick him. Instead, she splashes liquid down onto her own face, making herself choke. He almost wants to laugh.

She tries to crawl away, but he grabs the edge of her panties to rip them down. She twists, screaming, and smashes the bottle across his head. This time it shatters. His teeth rattle, and liquor burns his eyes. The gun goes flying as he stumbles off the bed, brushing glass off his skin, touching the scorching spot on his forehead. He's bleeding.

She crouches on all fours to face him, her white teeth bared like a hissing cat. They see the gun at the same time, ten feet away on the floor. She drops what's left of the bottle, and they both dive for the weapon, scrambling across the carpet, grunting and thrashing. He forces all his weight down on top of her as she tries to reach for it. She's a fucking maniac, fighting, screaming like a banshee.

"*Shut the fuck up,*" he growls in her ear. His blood drips onto her hair as he holds her down, his shoulder screeching with pain. "*Shut up or you're not gonna get through this alive, Beth—I promise you...*"

He has her neck pinned with his forearm, pressing her face into the dirty carpet, littered with glass. Her arms flail helplessly, the gun just out of her grasp. He feels her heart hammer through her ribs, her lungs gasping for air. But the more she struggles, the more exhausted she gets and the weaker her movements become. Her fingers finally stop clutching and go limp. She seems to shrink to half her size beneath him. He feels the oxygen go out of her, and the will to fight. She's given up. Maybe even unconscious.

Panting, he pushes himself up and crawls above her, reaching for the gun. But the second he lets go, she comes alive beneath him. With a cry of rage, she grabs something from the carpet and swings her arm up at him. It bites into his neck. A sensation he's never felt before rushes through him, a terror that is physical and mental at once. Her arm shudders as she holds something in his throat, twisting. Jagged, sharp, like a bear trap. He gets onto his knees, trying to find out what it is.

She scrambles out from under him, across the carpet, and grabs the gun, crawling backward until her spine hits the bed. She trains the gun on him, both hands trembling. He can't seem to get to her. He struggles to his feet, staggering back and forth as if he's drunk. He tries to grab what's in his neck, but when he touches it, agony shrieks through his body. It's smooth. Round. And he can't pull it out. *What is it?* He twists and catches his reflection in the dingy mirror. Sees the broken bottle in his neck, the mouth spurting blood like a garden hose, dripping warm onto his chest.

He tries to scream, but only feels cool air rush through his throat, garbled and wet. He tumbles backward, as if pushed by a strong wind, his back hitting the dresser as he slides down, his legs straight out in front of him. He tastes the blood filling his mouth, warm and salty as soup. He tries to grab the bottle again, but his hands are on puppet strings, missing their mark.

The world becomes a hazy blur. Through the mist, he sees her get up, stumble around, drift out of sight. He hears water running. Sees her moving quickly back and forth in the room. His keys clatter as she scoops them off the dresser. A strip of light blinds him as she opens the door and peers out. For a moment she's a silhouette in front of a movie screen. Then the door slams closed. He's alone. He tries to grab the bottle again, but his arm is too heavy, only his fingers twitch, distant and useless.

76

GOODE

Friday Night

Goode is about to pound on the door with the side of his fist when he thinks better of it and uses the doorbell instead. A pleasant chime rings through the night.

"Coming," says a weak voice.

He has his beat-up brown leather briefcase with him, a prop that somehow makes him feel like a door-to-door salesman. A moment later Beth Montgomery answers the door. His first instinct is shock. Her hair is wet from the shower, and she wears an old gray cardigan, holding herself as if she's chilly, even on the warm night. She wears no makeup and looks drained, but what surprises him most is a large patch of white gauze taped to her cheek. Her eye and forehead are bruised, her bottom lip raw and swollen. She told him she'd been injured when he called, but he didn't know how serious.

"Jeezus. You okay?" Out of instinct, he goes to reach for her, but she leans back.

"I'll be fine."

"You sure?"

"It's not as bad as it looks, Detective. Please come in." She holds the door for him, and they head into the living room. "Can I get you anything? I was just having some wine."

"Brought my own, thanks." He sets his briefcase on the coffee table and pulls out a convenience-store bag with two bottles of Gatorade. "Want some?"

She motions with her glass, giving a sorry laugh. "I think I need something stronger than that tonight."

"Can't say as I blame you."

She takes a seat on the couch, curling her knees. He twists open his bottle and lifts it in a silent toast. She returns the gesture and takes a sip, wincing as she swallows.

He reaches in the briefcase again, pulling out a sheaf of papers.

"I'm serving this now, just as a matter of courtesy." He sets the search warrant on the table between them. He told her to be expecting it, but she still seems uneasy. Who wouldn't be? Knowing the cops are going to search your house in a murder investigation is tantamount to hearing that a Category 5 hurricane is on its way to your neighborhood. "You talked to him yet, by any chance?"

"No, but he tried calling." She digs in the pocket of her cardigan for her cell, hits the speaker, and plays back the message. Montgomery's tinny voice sounds helpless and panicked.

"Beth—God, Beth it's me...Shit. I'm at the police station. They brought me in about Cassie. Beth—I swear, this is all bullshit. Goode's a fucking liar! Call my father. Tell him what happened. Tell him to get Alistair to come see me. Hurry, Beth! This is insane!"

The room goes silent again. Beth puts the phone down.

Goode remembers the blustery mouthpiece from the country club. "Did you call the lawyer?"

She shakes her head. "I don't want anything more to do with this. He can rot in jail for the rest of his life for all I care." A furrow works across her brow, and her voice drops to a harsh whisper. "Do you really think he—he did something to her?"

"It's almost impossible to prove until we find the body. But we don't need one to prove a crime has been committed. There's no question he had motive. And circumstantial evidence all points to him. The prints on the handle were partials, but they were his. Blood type in the trunk matched the blood on the knife, both a match to your friend. We're still waiting on DNA, but B-positive's pretty rare. When you got that much evidence, you bring someone in. We can hold him for a couple days. At least until we sift through that dumpster."

She shivers at the mention of it. In the low light, Goode thinks her wine looks like blood roiling in the glass. "Has he—has he confessed to anything?"

"Not yet. What you heard is more or less his story right now. But we've been trying to piece it together. You mentioned Ms. Ogilvy called you around seven thirty. Do you remember him leaving the house after that?"

"No. But I went to bed early. I was tired."

"He must've gone down to meet her. Taken the knife. She would've trusted him. He could've brought her anywhere. My guess is she was blackmailing him."

"I'd believe that," she concedes.

"At the very least, she was a threat. She could've told you what happened between them. And he obviously didn't want that. He had to stop her—however he could."

"My God," she says, barely breathing. "You live with someone for so long. You trust them. You think you know them and then..." She shrugs but doesn't finish.

Goode thinks about that a moment; he's heard it so many times, it's like a line every actor in a casting call is forced to read out loud. *To be or not to be...You think you know someone...* In the end, he's pretty sure nobody knows anything about anyone else. They barely know the truth about themselves. After a while, he settles on his old standby.

"People change," he says.

She gives a soft, sad laugh. "They certainly do."

He senses she hasn't much energy left, so he closes his briefcase, motioning to the warrant. "They'll be here early tomorrow morning. You can stay if you want. But I wouldn't recommend it."

"I'd rather not," she says. "I think I'll get out of town for a few days. Visit family."

"That's probably the best thing to do."

They move into the kitchen, and Goode notices the wooden knife block on the counter. He pulls out one of the blades, inspecting the handle. The brand name's the same as the one from the alley. He motions to the single empty slot. "You found the one that's missing?"

She shakes her head. Goode slides the knife back into the block; they can tag it during the search.

"I still don't get it," she says. "Why would he leave the knife so close? He must've known you'd find it and trace it to him."

"Maybe he just panicked. Sometimes that happens to people. They do something stupid and they can't take it back. The guilt gets to them, so they start making mistakes. On some level, they want to get caught. Even unconsciously. Happens all the time."

She shudders, still holding the sweater around herself, shaking her head in disbelief.

"We finally reached her parents, by the way," he says, going to the door. "They should be in tomorrow to answer a few questions. Maybe they've heard from her."

"Could be, but I doubt it. Cassie hasn't talked to them for years."

"We'll see what they have to say anyway." He puts his hand on the knob, motioning to her bandage. "You sure you're gonna be okay? I can get you to a hospital. Maybe somebody should have a look."

"I'll be fine," she says.

"Has he ever hit you before?"

"Jay? No. Never. He's pushed me around a little, but nothing like this." She touches her bruised cheek. "I had no idea he was capable of any of this."

"You can still press charges, you know. It's not too late. Wives do it all the time, for a lot less."

"I know. But it hardly seems important after—after everything. I just want him out of my life."

Goode thinks about that and nods. "You let me know if you change your mind. In the meantime, you put some ice on that."

"I will."

He steps out into the night. Heads down the driveway to his Chevy and climbs in behind the wheel. Her silhouette is in the kitchen window. She waves to him, and then the light flicks off.

77

BETH

Friday Night

After the sound of Goode's engine fades, the house seems so quiet, as if even the memories are gone, borrowed and pointless as all her memories seemed to be. It's a museum now, a place of past glories. She's always been just a visitor here. She finishes her wine, noticing the unopened bottle of Gatorade the detective must've left behind. It makes her smile. She wonders what he'll think of her after all this is over.

You can still press charges, you know... Wives do it all the time, for a lot less.

Of course he believed Jay had hit her; Jay had a history of violence. What a shocking revelation that had been—the horrible scandal from college. She always knew her husband had dark secrets, maybe not as many as herself, but some, and this one fit into her plan so well, it was more than a coincidence. It felt like fate.

Just like it had been fate when she found that cash. Needing a way out, needing money so badly, and then there it was, in a red duffel bag.

She and Cassie had been playing cards on the coffee table in the living room. Jay was on the couch with his Xbox, trying to concentrate. It was as if they were all a bunch of college kids skipping class. Cass was barely dressed, as usual, showing off her legs, her ass, as if her body were something separate from her that she could offer men, a gift she could bestow, without being guilty of doing anything wrong. None of that had changed in all these years. Nothing could change Cassie Ogilvy. She was a force of nature.

The timer had gone off—*That'll be the dryer*—and she got up to get the laundry before everything wrinkled. Such a dutiful wife, such a good friend.

"No cheating," she'd said to Cassie. Ironic, really.

She could hear them talking down there—Cassie flirting. *You're pretty good at that. You play with yourself every day?*

The extra room was a mess, of course, but then Cass had always been such a slob. Beth had expected that ever since she invited her to stay Tuesday night.

"Please don't tell him about anything, Cass. About me. He wouldn't understand. Princeton boy and all."

"You can trust me," she'd said, the sound of pool balls clanking in the background, the smell of beer in the air. *You can trust me, Beth. You know that.*

She took her time folding Cassie's T-shirts, piling them on the bed, reveling in the simple task that brought her back to their room in college. She used to do Cassie's laundry back then, too, just to keep the dorm neat. It was more than nostalgia; it was pure pleasure, the actual feeling of being young again. But as she went to grab the laundry basket and leave the room, her foot knocked something under the bed. She rolled her eyes; if Cassie left something behind, it would take forever to track her down and mail it to her. She should check, to be sure. She was just trying to be helpful.

Wasn't she?

But there was a note playing low in the background, a building minor chord Beth couldn't ignore. Something was wrong with Cassie's story. She could feel it. She bent down and saw Cassie's red duffel bag tucked under the bed. The bag was quite large and could never have slipped under accidentally. Cassie didn't hide things. Everything about her was so open and unguarded. That's one of the things Beth loved about her. People only hid things that jeopardized them, and Cassie was fearless. So unlike Beth.

The bag was heavy and it took some effort to pull it out. She hesitated before unzipping it.

The Xbox in the living room, like a small distant war.

I said your six, your six! Behind you!

She spread the zipper apart, lurching back when she saw a gun. She began to tremble, afraid to even touch the bag again in case it went off.

Then she noticed rumpled rolls of green and white beneath the weapon, each one wrapped in elastic. Jesus. This thing was crammed full of cash. She sat back on her haunches, shocked. She couldn't even move.

She just—stopped.

Everything stopped.

Ah, too bad. You died. Can I buy you a beer? Cheer you up?

Still working on this one...Help yourself though.

Her hand was shaking as she reached into the bag, sliding her fingers down one side, avoiding the gun like a live grenade. Nothing but rolls of cash, bulging the seams of the duffel, right down to the bottom.

Did Cassie rob a bank?

A flash of anger when she remembered her old friend saying she was so broke she couldn't even afford a hotel room. And Beth had believed her!

The staring eyes, the pretty boxes on the shelves, the people in the audience, the smell of the ocean, Jay, Cassie, a thousand lies.

She heard the crash of glass from the kitchen and flinched. Cassie was always so careless. The pounding of footsteps as Jay ran to the rescue.

"Beth, situation here!" he called, his voice tense.

"Be right there!" She zipped up the bag and shoved it back under the bed. Jesus, money was heavy. Like a corpse.

She ran down to the kitchen to help clean up. Her mind began to work of its own accord, putting square pegs in square holes, knocking marbles into place. She cleaned the broken bottle from the kitchen floor—another stroke of luck. Cassie would have to stay out of her way. She sent Cass into the living room, ordering her to keep her injured foot elevated for the rest of the night. As her husband and her oldest friend played video games, got high, and drank beer together, Beth finished the laundry, her thoughts on nothing but that money.

There must've been several hundred thousand dollars in the bag. Maybe more. *Enough.* That's the word that went through Beth's mind—a simple word, two syllables, that meant everything to her. Enough to get away. Enough to start a new life. She could leave Jay, without worrying about the prenup or anything else. The doctor told her some couples split up after a miscarriage; that's enough of a reason. And she'll have enough money to start over somewhere.

But how?

How would she get that cash, get herself free of Jay, and keep everyone off her tail in the process? Cass would never just let her have that money. She'd have to take it herself. She had to think of a way. It was actually invigorating, after years of her tiresome students, to have something so important to focus on: her way out.

So while her husband and best friend entertained themselves with Xbox, thinking she was doing laundry, Beth quietly eased the bag back out from under the bed. She started transferring the bundles of money into Jay's old blue gym bag. The big problem was what to replace it with. She considered Jay's dumbbells, but it had to be something soft and dense, and no amount of clothing would be convincing. It had to be paper, with a layer of cash on top, so Cassie wouldn't notice the switch. She looked around the room for anything that would work. Her gaze fell on the stacks of her old romance novels.

78

GOODE

The Seahorse Motel is a seedy place, with cracking foundations and bleached-out drapes. Half a dozen cruisers clog the parking lot, lights flashing in the night, police tape lining the perimeter, news vans starting to collect. It's the second time this week that the LAPD has been called to this dive, but tonight it's for more than drunk and disorderly.

There's a woman in a housekeeping uniform sitting in the back of an EMT, a silver thermal blanket draped over her shoulders. As a paramedic tends to her, she shivers like she's been locked in a freezer overnight.

Goode approaches the hub of activity—a room on the ground floor—and sees Dawes in the doorway, a mythical goddess guarding a tomb.

"Is it him?"

"Yep," she says. "Looks like somebody got to him before you did. Saved you the hassle."

"You kidding? I was actually looking forward to it."

He steps into the shabby room. Forensics is already there, a few uniforms hanging about, fingerprint powder on the walls and furniture. Everyone steps out of Goode's way as he walks to a bloody corpse in a half-seated position, the torso leaning sideways toward the floor. Goode's knees crack as he crouches to have a better look. Even with the greasy hair dyed black, he recognizes Rick Squires. Dead as they are, the pale blue eyes give him away.

"Guess the maid found him?"

"Yeah. She hadn't been in all week. They had to unlock the door to do a welfare check."

Goode nods, then winces at the broken bottle shoved into the man's neck. Nothing like severing the carotid artery when it comes to blood loss. This guy's throat has been butchered, his chest and mouth coated with what looks like dried rust primer.

"Retaliation for the botched deal at the rental house?" he wonders aloud.

"Doubt it," says Dawes. "We found this." She flips open the lid of a black case with metal rivets, revealing the stash of heroin. A typical dealer would've taken that case. It had to be something else.

"You find the cash?" he asks.

"Not a cent. Not yet, anyway. But he turned up. Maybe the money will, too."

Goode sighs heavily. "Maybe. But in my experience, a million two in unmarked bills hardly ever just turns up."

79

BETH

Friday Night

Beth throws her biggest suitcase on the bed and the mattress bounces, giving her a visceral jolt. She remembers the way the bed sank beneath his knees when he climbed on top of her.

She can't seem to wash off the motel room, with its fetid smells and moldy carpet. Would they suspect her? Were there any clues in the room? She'd bled enough trying to escape. But they hadn't taken her blood at the police station, had they? Or her fingerprints. And she'd never been in trouble with the law, not like her old friend. She has nothing to worry about. She can calm down now. It's all working out. Still, the panic won't entirely leave her, the way it wouldn't those long nights in the pink bedroom in Bryn Mawr.

The folds of his skin, the way they creased around his cuff links and gold watch, and the wiry dark hairs on the back of his hands, like spider's legs, and the eyes staring from the boxes on the shelves, straight ahead, unblinking, unmoving, unable to help, like an audience of corpses, trapped and immobile, the freezing, the blackness, the pressure, the pain.

When she'd jammed the broken bottle into his neck, her savagery surprised her. As she pushed and twisted and the blood started to spurt, she watched her hand, feeling it didn't belong to her, the way it seemed during a performance.

Staircases. Coils. Snakes.

She tended quickly to the cut on her forehead and hurried out of the room. His SUV was parked right out front, and nobody watched as she climbed behind the wheel. She drove into the hills and parked in the overlook by the dog-walking park, tucking the car in the farthest space behind a copse of trees. She held her phone to her ear, covering the gash on her cheek in case anyone saw her as she hurried the short walk home, listening to Jay's message, demanding she call his father, the lawyer, sounding so entitled. She took a shower instead.

As she was bandaging up, Goode phoned with news about the arrest. He seemed most concerned about her. Sweet man. But there was no need for him to worry. She was much stronger than everyone thought. Always had been.

She rushes back and forth between the closet and the dresser, packing what she'll need. A hanger catches on the corner of the duvet, so neatly made this morning, before they went to the police station.

Was that only this morning? The last three days have mushroomed into an alternate universe. Yet as she stares at the bed, she can still see them. Hear them. Smell them.

She hadn't stayed late yesterday; in fact, she left the school early, giving her apologies to the colleague with the birthday, saying an old friend was in town.

She'd been paranoid ever since she switched the money. Her guilt—and her fear of getting caught—had eaten at her all day. She tried to ask Cassie what was really going on in her life when they were alone in her bedroom the night before. It was one of the reasons Beth stayed up so late partying. She didn't want Cass to discover the switch. But she also considered starting a conversation about possibly sharing the money. She even phoned the next day to see if Cassie would tell her the truth. *I know you, Cass. I know you're hiding something.* But her old friend slithered away from every question, the way she always could. *You don't think I'm ashamed enough I can't afford a hotel? That I've got to sponge off you like some charity case? Why do you think the worst of me?*

Beth was so nervous, she decided to go home early, before Jay got back from his meeting, so she could tell Cassie she'd found the cash. Maybe they could make a deal somehow and she could borrow some of it to get away. Then she could pay Cassie back later, when she got on her feet. She just had to get home before Cass discovered the switch. It would be too late then.

It was Cassie's last night, so despite that she was still recovering from a hangover, Beth stopped to pick up wine—not the cheap stuff she and Jay had been drinking for months, but some nice bottles, spending four, almost five times as much as she'd spent on wine in ages. It was a liberating experience, just buying that wine. Like freedom.

It was late afternoon when Beth got home and saw Jay's Mustang in the driveway. Despite Cassie's flirting and skimpy clothes, her "Hound Dog" husband had been shy about being alone in the house with Cass all week, waiting until Beth got home from work before showing up himself. Not that it stopped him from staring at her every chance he got.

But he was here. Maybe he'd even been here when Beth phoned earlier, because Beth suspected Cassie had the call on speaker. Had Jay been listening to their argument? Did he sit right there and not say a thing? She wouldn't put it past him—or Cass.

She got out of the car, unlocked the kitchen door, placed her purse and the liquor bag on the counter. At the sight of the living room, her heart caught in her throat—they'd been robbed! Cassie's old boyfriend? Or someone else after that money?

But then she heard Jay.

He was—there was no other word for it—*grunting*. Then another small, lustful moan joined his. She'd heard that sound before, too.

She felt her pulse pounding, the edges of her vision dimming with rage, fear, anxiety. She didn't know why she had to see it for herself, but she did. The sounds got louder as she moved down the hall, passing the linen closet, which had secrets of its own. She saw their shadows shifting on the floor outside the open bedroom door. She even thought she could smell them.

But she didn't have to lean out of the shadows to actually see them. Because there was a reflection in the glass on one of the wedding pictures in the hall. Ghostly images. The window. The headboard. The muscles of Jay's back as he thrust.

She wanted to scream, to barge in, to kill them both right there. But the shame was just as strong. She'd invited this into her life. She knew what Cassie was like. She always suspected she couldn't trust Jay, either. And here at last, as if she needed it, was the undeniable proof she'd made the biggest mistake of her life by marrying him.

She rushed back down to the kitchen, grabbing her things. As she was leaving the house, her husband started to come—a sound so familiar to her, yet bizarre to hear from a distance, not right next to her head.

She hurried down the driveway and got back into her car. She didn't know where she would go at first. It crossed her mind to just drive and keep driving and never stop.

But she couldn't run. She needed that money. So her survival instinct kicked in, a cold focus that used to get her through difficult times.

Dissociative disorder, or something like that.

So instead, she pulled into the overlook next to the dog-walking park down the block and turned off the car. The park had a view of the city—a beautiful view—and she sat there, with the stereo on, listening to Chopin, until an idea came to her. It was dangerous, even stupid. If it didn't work, she'd probably go to prison. But she had to take that chance.

She didn't know how much time to give them.

Or herself. To make sure she could go through with this.

But as she watched families coming and going and mothers pushing strollers, she was so preoccupied, it didn't even bother her. She wasn't thinking about kids or the miscarriage, didn't feel that tug of longing and regret. Instead, her mind went around and around, as if composing chords in a new piece of music, doubling back when something didn't quite work. It all began falling together so naturally that she felt like young Mozart composing a symphony; this was something more than genius—it was actually *divine*.

By the time she put the car into drive and left the little overlook full of children and parents and dogs, the sky had turned amber in the west, the sun red as a maraschino cherry sinking through a dirty cocktail glass. She went through the motions again, turning off the ignition, taking her bags, getting out of the car. The door was unlocked, and at first she thought she must've been careless earlier. Of course, as it turned out, it had been Cassie. Cass never locked the door on their dorm room either. She trusted everything—and nothing—in equal measure. It was a perfect combination of carelessness and courage. She seemed to dare life to bring her problems, and the world, intimidated by her nerve, brought her only gifts.

The house was dead quiet again. The living room still a mess. But in the bedroom Jay was alone, asleep in a twisted tangle of her pretty sheets, his mouth hanging open. He always passed out after sex, spent and drained, like a common animal.

Beth already suspected Cassie wasn't home. Her friend had the kind of frenetic energy that if she was in the house, you could feel it, even when you couldn't see her or hear her. Maybe she was tanning in the backyard—or passed out, too. She hung up her blazer, jangling the hangers so Jay would wake up. How he bolted upright when he heard her, the blood draining from his face.

"You okay?" The ignorant, stupid faithful wife. Only half an act, really.

In the bathroom, she ran water to cover the sound as she tapped his pills into her palm, chattering away with him all the while. That he could all but get caught in such a terrible betrayal and still try to hide it—she didn't know if it was sickening or admirable.

"Where is she?"

"Uh, I don't know," he said, so innocently. "Isn't she out there?" He was still lying to her about everything. Then she saw the framed photo on the nightstand. The one she tucked away in the drawer so Cassie would never see. The photo that should not be there. That *cannot* be there.

Jesus Christ, Cassie.

She raced to the guest room and immediately saw that Cass had taken all her things. Beth panicked. *Cassie knew.* She'd figured out Beth took the money. Maybe she even fucked Jay to get back at her for it. Terrified, she ran to the linen closet, gasping in relief when she saw the blue gym bag was still there, and it hadn't been touched. But now what?

Now what?

She tried to stay calm, thinking, adjusting the plan in her head. She went to the kitchen, as she had a thousand times, listening to her husband in their bathroom. The door closing. The water rushing in the shower. The whir of the ventilation fan. It was all so familiar. Her life had become one endless piano scale, the same monotonous sounds over and over again, up and down.

As she dropped the white tablets into one of the glasses of wine, stirring with her finger until they dissolved, she knew that whatever came next, she had finally broken the pattern, changed something important in her life. A change that would affect every note from here on out.

80

JAY

Friday Night

Jay sits in a small room with gray walls at the police station. His father and the lawyer sit across from him, their wrinkled, liver-spotted mouths moving constantly. They've been in here for hours. A metal table hurts his knee when he bangs it, and the stench of stale coffee won't go away. It smells like sweat, too. His? Theirs? Some stranger's? The weight of bad luck sinks over him like a heavy blanket, snuffing out the rage that boils under his skin.

Murder? They're crazy. The lawyer is saying something about the fact the police can charge him, even if there's no body, using terms like "corpus delicti" and "burden of proof," bandying about legalese until he sounds like an actor in a boring cop drama. Jay's mind starts to drift.

Beth will probably want a divorce now. She'd never forgive him. She hadn't even returned his call. Did she even care? Why should she? She probably believes he did kill Cassie. Now he wishes he *had* hurt the bitch, really hurt her, the way she deserved to be hurt. If he hadn't been such a coward, none of this would've even happened in the first place.

Alistair is saying something about circumstantial evidence, asking about the blood in the trunk.

"Jason, pay attention. Alistair asked you a question."

Jay starts at his father's cold tone.

"Why was there blood in your trunk?" the lawyer repeats.

"I have no idea."

"Jason, just be honest with us," his father says.

"I *am* being honest! I have no idea what happened to her." He turns to Alistair, his voice weak. "In your legal opinion, do you think this is going to mean a hard *no* from Milla?"

"Who?" the lawyer asks.

"Forget about your stupid movie, Jason! This is serious!"

"You don't think I *know* that?"

The lawyer is getting frustrated, too. "Jason, I've known you all your life. You can be honest with me. Did you, or did you not, hurt this girl? I'll still defend you. It's my job. I just need to know the truth."

"No!" he insists. And then, in a smaller voice, "Not really."

"We've heard *that* one before." His father sighs.

"It's not like that! Not like the other one! I'm serious!"

"Jason, your fingerprints are on that knife. The girl's blood is on the blade."

"I don't know how it got there. I swear I don't!" His head cramps and he has to squint through the pain. *Wait a minute.* The knife. He didn't make his post-run shake this morning because he was too nervous about seeing the police. Yesterday, either, because of the argument with Beth in the kitchen about the Ambien. Did he even see the knife today? He can't remember. He didn't even look for it. Why would he, if he didn't need it?

And then his mind goes down a very dark abyss with craggy walls, narrowing to a chip in the surface of his thoughts. Did he do this—and forget? Did he black out? How much did he have to drink last night? What was in that weed? Why can't he remember? There were dark spots in the night, yes, but there were always dark spots for Jay. He doesn't want anybody to know how many dark spots there are in his life. Sometimes it seems as if he only half exists, that most of the time you could put your hand right through him, the way they say the universe is more space than matter; the way every atom, every person, every rock, is the same way, he's full of dark, empty places, too.

What happened last night? What really happened? He's not sure.

It reminds him so much of college. Someone has tackled him, shoved him into the boards, pinned him to the mat. But this time, he doesn't have the energy to fight back. He sits there, drained, as the men shake their heads, accusing him, mouths slashed in disapproval. They think he did it. Everyone thinks he did it. What if he gets convicted? Spends the rest of his life in jail? It terrifies him. Because for the first time in as long as he can remember, his father can't bail him out. No one can.

81

BETH

Friday Night

Beth goes to the linen closet and grabs the blue gym bag, letting it *thump* to the floor, before dragging it into the kitchen with the rest of her luggage.

She didn't have to let Jay know about the money. Maybe she shouldn't have. But when the cops became involved so quickly, she wanted to be able to control him. It was just an instinct to her. She'd always been good at adapting. Everyone thought Cassie was the creative one, better at improvising jazz riffs onstage, while Beth was chained to her classical sheet music. But now Beth knew she could improvise, too.

Carrying the last suitcase down the hall, she stops when she sees her CD on the coffee table. She hesitates, then puts the disk in its case, shoving it into her bag. She remembers listening to it last night with Jay, the music she'd recorded in a rare state of hopefulness so long ago. The work that went into that album, the determination, the perseverance. The money! To rent the studio, hire the engineer, do the photo shoot for the cover. She'd done it blindly, with so much faith. That was the worst of it, really, the hope and faith she'd had to muster to get it done. At the time, she'd been very proud of herself. Yet all that effort was now nothing but the soundtrack of waiting for her husband to pass out after she drugged him.

Cassie had taken Jay's cell, of course. Always grabbing what she wanted from life, never worrying about the consequences. What a wonderful way that must be to live.

Beth watched her hand pick up the cell. "Hey, Cass...What's going on?" she asked. She wasn't even shaking, which terrified her more than anything. Why was it all so easy for her? She felt no sense of right or wrong at all. She was just waiting for a new door to open in her life, and now it had.

Cassie was yelling on the phone, her voice distorted. "You fucking bitch! Where is it? Where's my cash?" Beth just muted the phone, so Jay couldn't hear, telling him Cass had forgotten something and she was going down to look for it.

When she ducked into the guest room, she took the phone off mute and hissed "Shut up!" so viciously, her own voice shocked her. Cassie must've been surprised, too, because her tirade ceased. Beth heard the distant tap of cheap heels pacing, loud exhalations of cigarette smoke.

"Where are you?" she demanded. Cassie said she was at Footsie's. "Wait for me outside. I'll be there in an hour."

She hung up, her heart hammering in her ears. Why not just accuse Jay of adultery? Threaten Cassie with going to the police? Take the easier, safer route. If they had to, they could split the money. Even three ways, it was still hundreds of thousands of dollars each, enough to start over. She didn't have to do any of this.

And yet she knew she'd been waiting for an opportunity like this all her life. She couldn't pass it up.

She went back to the living room, pretending Cassie was still on the phone. "*Uh-huh...well, I can't find it. Are you sure you left it here?*" She'd always been a good liar, she knew that. But it was thrilling to realize what a great performer she was, too.

They listened to her music that night, Beth making her plans while guilt oozed out of Jay, until the pills finally took effect and he slumped against her.

She went to the kitchen for the wine bottles, emptying one of them and pouring all but half of the other down the drain. It was a shame to let such good wine go to waste, but she didn't have a choice. And she needed to keep a clear head herself. She set the bottles on the coffee table in front of Jay.

She grabbed the blue scarf she'd tried taking back for a refund, finally ripping the price tag off. In the kitchen, she wrapped the scarf around her palm, and pulled the butcher knife from the wooden block, careful not to smudge Jay's prints. It wasn't until then that her hand began to shake. She took three deep breaths to calm herself, to remind herself what was at stake.

Beth wasn't a brilliant composer; she knew that. But she'd studied enough to understand how good compositions unfolded. It was almost as if every hour she'd spent studying music had been rehearsal for this night.

Cassie had been the star of the show, coming back into Beth's life at the perfect time. Beth had worried about that for so many years, not sure how to protect herself—and suddenly there she was.

I'm not getting you at a bad time, am I?

All Beth had to do was make sure Cassie knew the score—the past was the past. Cassie could stay at the house as long as she didn't talk about Beth's childhood or the fact that it had been Beth—not Cassie—who had dropped out of college and vanished after freshman year.

He wouldn't understand. Princeton boy and all.

They never asked at that music school? If you'd actually gradu-
ated?

No, never.

She laughed. *You always did have an honest face.*

And it had served Beth well, her honest face.

With her hair tucked into Jay's baseball cap, she steered the red Mustang toward Footsie's, flashing through the darkness and light, imagining what her new life would be like. For twelve years, Cassie had been the one person left on earth who could bring Beth's whole world crashing down. But now she doesn't have to be afraid anymore.

She remembers waiting in Jay's car outside Footsie's, seeing Cassie hobble along the sidewalk, looking like a hooker in her miniskirt and heels, struggling with the weight of that red duffel bag, her suitcase an afterthought trailing behind her.

Don't do this, Beth thought. *Don't do it.*

There's still time to turn around. Go back to a regular life.

Then the door opened, and Cassie clutched at the leather upholstery, pulling the bucket seat forward, trying to shove her bags into the backseat of the car, "fuck this," "fuck that" the entire time.

Put some music on. Get drunk. Get high. Don't do this!

But it was already too late. Beth knew that. And her old friend was about to realize that, too. Cass flopped into the passenger seat and yanked the door closed with a slam.

"You got my fucking money, Beth?"

"I've got it," she said in a low voice.

"Good. Cause you have no idea how fucked we are if someone finds us. You don't want to mess with these guys, Beth. Where is it?"

But Beth didn't say anything. She just pulled into traffic.

Cassie lit a cigarette with trembling hands, sucking her cheeks hollow, jittery with nerves.

They drove for several blocks without talking. The sidewalks got quieter. The night darker. It was strange, the silence. There had always been music between them. It's what brought them together in the first place.

She saw the alley and pulled into it, finding a quiet spot that would work. The smell of garbage, filthy and rotting, seemed appropriate. She knew this place well. When they first moved into the house in the hills, they used to have friends over for barbecues and she'd stop here for Kobe burgers or steaks. That was a long time ago, though.

Already another life.

Beth stopped the car. Turned off the engine. They sat in the near silence of each other's breathing. Beth closed her eyes for a moment, remembering how it had felt falling asleep in their beds in the dorm room.

"I don't know what the *fuck* you're up to," Cassie began through clenched teeth. "But you're putting both of us in a lot of danger. You have no idea what—"

But Beth broke in. "I saw you today."

"Excuse me?" Cassie snapped, glaring at her.

"I saw you guys together," Beth said. "I saw you fucking Jay."

Cass froze then. Even her trembling stopped. Her endless supply of energy and nerves just halted. Beth was calling the shots now. And in that moment, that silence, the entire sordid fight played out between them. The accusations. The forgiveness. And the final act.

I think she wanted what I had. She loved the idea of a real family...

As Beth lifted the tangle of silk from her purse, Cassie looked down. Her eyes rounded with terror when she saw the silver gleam of the blade.

82

Southampton, Twelve Years Ago

It rose like a Roman villa between the hedgerows, a secret castle on the shores of a pounding sea. Cassie was talking, nattering away. She could be so hyper, swinging her hands, laughing.

They sat in the back of a long black car. When Cass said they were getting picked up from the Jitney stop, Beth assumed a mother in a minivan, a dad in his Jeep; but there was a vintage Bentley waiting for them at the bus stop in Southampton and a chauffeur who actually opened the back door for them. It was all a joke, Beth thought. A setup. This must be a beloved uncle or a family friend and they were teasing her. It was just like Cass to do something like this and watch until Beth figured it out, and then laugh and laugh. She was always teasing, playing games. Life wasn't enough for her. The normal unfolding of things bored her. She needed more.

But there were no tip-offs that this was one of her jokes. No watchful gleam in her eye, no curl at the edge of her lips. She was just talking, waving her hands, smoking, laughing, telling stories about the great clubs in the Hamptons, and I can't wait for you to meet so-and-so, and you should see this, and my parents will love you, and the beach is so packed down there, and, and, and. Story after story.

Beth did what she always does. She nodded and smiled and said things now and again because it's what Cassie needed. Beth knew how to play her part. She's known how to act in every situation

311

since she was a little girl, always so well behaved. The good girl. And so with Cassie, her best friend, she knew how to behave, too. Cassie couldn't play against a blank wall. She needed an audience. That had been Beth's role all year.

The Bentley pulled around a fountain half hidden in a silvery cloud of water, a pool off to one side, the ocean in the background. A woman with wavy hair stepped out of the entrance to the grand white mansion on the beach.

"Darling!" It was Cassie's mother, hurrying to hug and greet them. Beth had met Alice Ogilvy once before, in the city at Christmas. She was a pleasant, gracious woman. But that was five months ago, a lifetime for young girls living together in the same room.

They were sisters now.

From the moment Beth stepped out of the car until the moment she left, the summer swirled like a dream around her. Private clubs, beaches, bonfires. Handsome cousins stopping by to play tennis and flirt. Margaretta waiting on them hand and foot by the pool.

Every morning Beth practiced piano in the sunny conservatory, with Cassie's mother listening and encouraging her. "You're brilliant, Beth! Brava! Bravissimo!" She'd applaud as if in a private box at Lincoln Center. Then they'd go to the kitchen to gossip and chat. Beth was always an early riser. Mrs. Ogilvy was, too, so this was their private time. Cassie would stumble down the stairs shortly after noon, hungover and grumpy, lighting a cigarette before Margaretta even poured her coffee. It irritated her mother so much.

I wish you wouldn't smoke in the house, Cassie.

Or, *I wish you wouldn't drink so much.*

Or, *I wish you wouldn't sleep so late.*

I wish, I wish, I wish.

Didn't she know, *wishing* it could never make Cassie stop, because that was why she did it in the first place, to bother her mother? If Cassie could just be a little more agreeable, maybe everyone would get along better.

"Why do you always try to bug them?" Beth pleaded with her friend.

"You don't know them," Cassie grumbled. "This is an act."

Beth had tried to forget Cassie's stories about being locked in her bedroom when she "acted up." The confession that first night in college about why she hated closed doors. It seemed impossible to believe these kind, generous, wealthy people could be so cruel. Yet Beth saw for herself the holes in the frame of the door on the big yellow bedroom. They were filled with putty, sanded and carefully whitewashed, but the imprint of the old locks was still visible beneath the fresh paint. Cassie didn't lock that door all summer.

One day, while Beth was in the conservatory, she had overheard a conversation, the acoustics in the big house carrying every word. Mrs. Ogilvy was planning a nice shopping day for "us girls."

"She's not your charity case, Mother," Cassie had snapped. "Stop treating her like one."

Charity case? She wasn't a charity case, was she? Mrs. Ogilvy had been so kind that Beth just couldn't help herself. She'd held secrets all her life, and now she'd finally found a safe place to share them. It was simply like water flowing downriver when a dam broke.

"Oh, how you got through it, I don't know," Cassie's mother would say to her, with the vague admiration you save for people who survive a natural disaster or a terminal disease. "You're so brave and strong. You know what you are? You're a lotus flower. That's exactly what you are."

A lotus flower.

83

BETH

Friday Night

Beth can still feel the way the knife went into her friend's flesh. She wasn't expecting how loud the scream would be or how much blood would come so quickly. Everything moved so fast, a blur of crimson and fire, reality smearing and tearing. Cassie struggling in the trunk, her dark curls wrapped in Beth's fist. The frantic sprint to throw the knife in the bin, charcoal fluid on the blaze, flesh melting from bone. The sound the Mustang made, peeling out into the night. She knew it was happening—she wasn't insane—but it was like sitting in a crowded theater watching the climax of an action movie; it was terrifying, but it didn't feel real.

The social workers had talked to her about the condition when she was a girl. Dissociative disorder, they called it, or some nonsense like that. It happened to many children who were abused and traumatized. A form of PTSD, it was a defense mechanism to help protect the victim from unbearable memories.

Beth could always do what she needed to survive.

At home, she threw her blood-spattered clothes into the washing machine, took a hot shower, scrubbing hard. She crawled into bed to forget, but there was no mistaking the smell on the sheets.

Cassie's green eyes.

Her ragged, wonderful voice.

The sound of Jay's grunts.

Her blood. So much blood.

Bang, bang, bang, bang!

It was Goode's pounding on the door that woke her up later that night.

Bang, bang, bang!

It amazed her she could've fallen asleep at all.

Beth stands at the kitchen sink and pulls the photograph out of the frame. For the first time in years, she sees the image without her reflection on the glare of glass. She touches the photo, her own face, those of Cassie's parents. She remembers those long summer days, the heady scent of the ocean, the swimming pool, lemon oil on antiques. It wasn't just the smell of a domestic world; it was the smell of happiness itself. She learned so much about what she wanted from life that summer; she wished it would never end.

But as August drew to a close and the sun started to set earlier, she finally told her friend she wouldn't be going back to school. Cassie's parents disapproved. They'd pay her tuition if she couldn't get another scholarship. But she refused. She'd taken everything she wanted from them already.

She throws the frame in the garbage bin beneath the sink. She lights a match and brings it to the sharp edge of the photograph; the glossy paper curls and turns dark like a leaf in the fall, starting to burn. She can't risk Goode seeing the photo again during the police search. She doesn't want him to recognize Cassie's parents and make a connection. It was a mistake to leave it out when he was here last night, but she didn't think he would ever meet them. She thought Cassie's parents didn't care enough about their daughter to come all the way to L.A. to find out what happened to her, so she didn't think to hide it.

It was no use trying to hide the photo from Cassie, either. Her old friend had found it snooping around and set it out for Beth to see. Was it a threat of some kind? Or just to show Cassie had learned her secret? Not that it mattered anymore.

She lets the photograph drop into the sink, watching it burn.

She remembers the last afternoon at the summer house. How she lingered alone in the big yellow bedroom, drawing out each moment, touching the old stuffed animals on the shelves, savoring the view of the ocean. These were more than memories for her. They were formative events.

"Beth?" It was Cassie's mother standing in the doorway, her hands hidden behind her back. "I have something for you," she said, smiling. She led Beth to sit on the edge of the bed. "I want you to have these," she said, handing her the Tiffany box.

Curious, Beth hesitated before opening the case, surprised to find the precious double strand of pearls inside, ones she'd seen Cassie's mother wear many times that summer.

"I can't accept these," she said, trying to pass them back. But Mrs. Ogilvy stopped her.

"Please. I insist. They were my mother's. She handed them down to me. I would give them to Cassie, but she wouldn't appreciate them. Besides, she wouldn't get caught dead in pearls!"

"True," Beth conceded with a laugh.

"Don't worry. I've already talked to Cassie about it. She wants you to have them, too."

Tears warmed Beth's eyes. She hugged the woman around the neck. "Thank you. They're beautiful! I'll cherish them!" *Always.*

Beth wore those pearls for the first time posing for that photograph. As she watches it burn, the blue sky turns to graphite and the figures fade like ghosts. She turns on the tap and watches the black petals swirl down the drain.

84

GOODE

Saturday Morning

In the squad room, they're waiting at his desk, looking stricken, speaking quietly with Dawes. When she sees him, her eyes light up in a *Thank God* kind of way. She wears her dress uniform, and so does Goode, freshly pressed, badges gleaming. Butler's funeral is this afternoon, and they're going together.

"Go easy on them," she whispers, meeting him halfway across the room, before leading him back to the desk. "Mr. and Mrs. Ogilvy, this is Detective Francis Goode. The one who's working on your daughter's case."

"Thank you so much for coming." They shake hands and introduce themselves. *Tom and Alice Ogilvy.*

But his mind is already racing. He recognizes these people. *From where?*

The squad room suddenly seems too loud, voices raised, phones ringing. These gentle people look bombarded by the din. He tells them they can go somewhere quieter to talk. He picks up his files, including a thin one marked MONTGOMERY, BETH.

He doesn't try to engage the couple as they walk, clinging to each other. He takes them to an open interview room with gray walls and a box of Kleenex on the table. As they sit down, it's suddenly too quiet and Goode thinks this isn't the place to talk with them either. The slight echo seems to magnify their grief.

He tells them they have a suspect in custody and that there is evidence linking him to the disappearance of their daughter.

"Do you think she's dead?" the woman asks. "Do you think this man killed her?"

"I'm afraid we're investigating that possibility, yes. Can you tell me the last time you saw your daughter?"

"Not for a long time." The woman's voice is clogged with emotion. She crumples a tissue in her hands, pulling, squeezing, shredding. "Not for years."

"How many years?"

Her cheeks color with shame, and she looks at her husband. "At least...six? Seven?"

"We had to cut her off," the man says. "She was always coming to us for money. And all she ever did was spend it on drugs. Once the money stopped—so did the calls."

"But we cut her off emotionally, too," the woman says. "That was a mistake. But it's not our fault. Cassie was gifted, yes. But she was also—she was *difficult*."

"Difficult? Impossible, you mean. She was uncontrollable." Goode notices they're already talking about their daughter in the past tense, as if they were prepared for some tragedy all along.

"Do you think," the woman begins, "she might've...hurt herself?"

"I'm sorry?"

"She tried to hurt herself when she was a teenager."

"She tried to commit suicide?"

She nods. "When she was sixteen. I always thought it was *our* fault. She was so hard to control when she was young. We used to have to—" She hesitates, glancing at her husband. "We used to have to lock her in her bedroom so she wouldn't sneak out. Or destroy something in the house."

"Or hurt one of us!"

"She seemed capable of anything when she was in one of her moods. It got to the point that we just couldn't deal with her anymore. That's why we had to put locks on her doors. We had to take her to see people, too. Doctors. Psychiatrists. There were so many specialists after that. So many pills."

"But it was pointless," grumbles Ogilvy. "Nothing ever worked."

"No...nothing." The woman seems lost in her thoughts, before looking up at Goode. "Do you have children, Detective?"

"I don't, ma'am. Never been blessed."

The man gives a sardonic laugh.

"It can be very difficult. I suppose the worst thing that can happen is losing a child. We thought we lost her, all those years ago. When she did it, I mean. She didn't even close the bathroom door. It was wide open. Like a sign. Some kind of revenge against us for locking her in her room. That's what I always—"

"Stop it," the man says. And she does. They sit in silent defeat for a moment.

"It was the drugs," the woman finally concludes. "If she just hadn't gotten involved in all those drugs, I think everything would've been fine. There are a lot of drugs on the road for musicians. We lost her after all that."

"We lost her years before then. You know that better than anyone."

"I suppose..."

Goode watches as they seem to run out of steam. It's clear they've had this argument before and that their barrage of ammunition against each other is well matched—and useless. He privately notes that child abuse comes in many forms—and in every tax bracket. But he won't take them to task on it. Not today.

"It's a tragedy," he says, sounding compassionate. "Drugs ruin so many lives. We see it all the time."

The mother nods, soothed despite herself. The tissue in her hand is shredded; Goode lifts the Kleenex box and holds it out for her.

And then he remembers.

When he grabbed the tissue box for Beth Montgomery from the nightstand in her bedroom. They're a dozen years older than the photo he saw, but this is the couple standing with her outside that big white mansion on the ocean. He remembers the happiness oozing off them. The man's mustache is silver now, the woman's hair gray, but it's definitely them.

Goode flips open the file marked MONTGOMERY, BETH and finds the printout with her driver's license photo, her employment history, her spotless record, and slides it to them.

"Do you know this woman?"

"My goodness, that's Beth!" Mrs. Ogilvy exclaims. She looks at her husband, and he gives the first twitch of a genuine smile. "She was a friend of my—of Cassie's. Years ago. She was such a sweet girl."

"This woman's husband"—he points to Jay's file—"is a suspect in your daughter's disappearance. There's evidence that he's the one who may have hurt her."

Their faces, already etched with grief, take on new shadows as they try to understand. Goode explains as much as he can without breaking their hearts. Cassie had come to stay with her old roommate. There had been a brief affair with the husband. Montgomery more than likely wanted to cover it up so that his wife would never know.

"Poor Beth," the woman says. "This will be so hard on her. As if she hasn't had enough to deal with in her young life. The things that girl had to go through."

"Oh, Alice, none of that matters at this point."

Goode turns to him. "Actually, sir, I'm trying to get as much information as possible. Anything might help."

The woman continues, grateful for something else to think about. "Beth came to stay with us the summer they finished freshman year. We would sit and talk for hours in the morning—before Cassie woke up. My own daughter didn't really care to talk. She wasn't needy and emotional like that. And she slept in until all hours of the day. Beth was an early riser, like me."

Goode nods, encouraging her, taking notes, asking himself questions. Why did the mild-mannered music teacher have a photo of these people in her bedroom, apparently posing as her parents? He's never suspected her of any wrongdoing, but now the case has taken a new turn; a garden walkway is suddenly an overgrown path.

The woman continues, smiling to herself. "She was such a wonderful pianist. But so shy and insecure. She had terrible stage fright. Used to shake and get nauseous just practicing at the house! I told her, *Beth, you've got to expect some problems that way. Growing up in foster care presents a lot of challenges.* She was a strong girl, going through all of that."

"Foster care?" Goode asks. Things still aren't fitting together for him.

"Yes. Her mother died when she was just a little girl. Of an overdose. Heroin or something. She never even met her father, poor dear. They had to put her up for adoption. Imagine going through all that when you're only four or five years old? She was such a sweet thing, they had no trouble finding a couple willing to adopt her. The Crawfords. They were quite wealthy. Lived outside of Philadelphia, in one of those pretty villages along the Main Line. Bryn Mawr, I think. The man was a doctor. The woman a piano teacher. She encouraged Beth's talent."

Goode is no longer jotting, just listening.

"The doctor, well...unfortunately, he had his way with her," the woman continues. "Beth was twelve or thirteen when it was finally discovered that he'd been diddling her since she was at least six!"

Diddling. Had his way with. How easily people disregard the unthinkable by using harmless words. He shudders at the thought of the girl in the photograph, the elegant woman on the CD case, the smiles, the lies, covering the truth, so twisted and hateful and sad.

The woman continues, her voice taking on a gossipy note. "Beth told me the doctor would bring her these expensive collectible dolls when he came to visit her in the bedroom at night. Could you imagine? Beth said she never even took a single one out of the box." She shivers at the memory. "It was quite a scandal, I'm sure. He went to jail, apparently, for almost ten years. Beth was taken away and put in different foster homes after that. But Beth said Mrs. Crawford continued to pay for her music lessons for years. Easing her guilt, I suppose."

"So she had no other relatives?"

"No one." The woman shakes her head. "No relatives or guardians. Just shuffled around for years, poor thing. She told me Mrs. Crawford had been the only mother she'd ever really known."

No one?

Goode looks down at the photograph in the driver's license. The demure makeup. The pretty face.

I'll probably get out of the way for a few days. Visit family.

He remembers Dawes saying she had to do more digging on Beth Montgomery, but then they both got sidetracked by the date-rape charge. He flips back through the woman's thin file, sees that her early record is sealed by the Children's Aid Society of Philadelphia. For more information, there's contact information for a law firm.

Goode sits back, stunned. He doesn't want to believe he's been duped by Beth Montgomery. It irritates him to no end. Though he reminds himself that the easiest games to lose were always the ones you didn't know you were playing.

"It's a miracle she came through it all so well," Mrs. Ogilvy says. "She was a lotus flower—that's what I always told her. Do you know about lotus flowers, Detective?"

"I'm afraid I don't, no."

"They grow underwater at first. They can survive anything. They grow in mud and filth, fighting among fish and weeds and whatever garbage is under the surface. But when they emerge, they're beautiful and perfect and strong. That's what she was. A lotus blossom. My favorite flower."

85

BETH

Saturday Morning

She's behind the wheel of her car, speeding down a highway. She sees the flashing lights of cruisers in her rearview, sirens screaming. She swerves through traffic, yanking the wheel back and forth. Then she hears a low laugh. She checks the mirror and sees Goode grinning at her from the backseat.

"Damn electrolytes," he says. "You can never get enough."

Beth wakes up with a start, gasping.

For a moment she has no idea where she is. It was the same when she was young. Waking up in different foster homes or group houses. Even though there were no bars on the windows, it was like a new jail cell every morning. She had different inmates all needing to be avoided, different wardens all needing to be appeased, different rules all needing to be followed.

But then she sees the grimy touch-button phone on the nightstand. The dog-eared flyers for local tourist sites: the Hoover Dam. Lake Tahoe. A bus schedule into Las Vegas. She exhales in relief. She's safe.

She gets up and grabs the red duffel bag, throwing it on the bed. She unzips it and pulls out the Glock pistol, detaches the empty magazine with ease. The YouTube instructions she'd looked up the other night were surprisingly simple to follow for someone who'd never handled a gun before. She'd taken the bullets out before putting the gun back in Cassie's duffel bag. There was no way she was going to let her friend have a loaded gun, especially not after she stole that money from her. She snaps the magazine back into the handle with a satisfying whack of the heel of her hand and sets the gun aside.

She empties the rest of the red duffel bag onto the bed. A small library of romance novels tumbles out. Beth doesn't need the books anymore, so she's leaving them behind for the housekeeper, stacking them in neat piles of mauve and pink in front of the window. She smiles as she drops a hundred-dollar bill on the books as a tip.

She steps out of the motel room with the luggage, the door locking behind her. She surveys the sun rising slowly through an amber sky, the peacefulness of the mountains sweeping around her like crumpled gold leaf.

The black SUV is parked in a spot out front, the back door lifted open, a cooler sitting on the ground. She knew the police could trace her car, so she didn't bother to take it. It was probably in a valet parking garage somewhere close to the Ivy, where Jay had left it before his arrest. It would be days before anyone thought anything unusual about it. By then she'd be long gone.

She lifts the cooler into the SUV and opens the lid to check supplies: water, snacks, fruit, all sitting in a mound of ice. She grabs a bottle of Gatorade for the drive. She adjusts the luggage in back, then covers the red duffel and blue gym bag with a blanket. She slams the cargo door, making sure it's locked. She thought that money would make her happier than it does. But it's not happiness she feels. It's something else. That threatening minor chord that has played under her life for as long as she can remember is silent. The fear is gone. She feels free.

She knows it isn't over yet. People will come looking for that money. Goode will be after her, too, when they figure out Jay has been framed. She wonders how much his father will pay to keep him out of trouble this time, or if Jay will really go to prison. She wonders, but she doesn't care. She also doesn't care about the other men who might be looking for the money. The suppliers and drug dealers. They didn't find the cash while it was sitting in her guest room all week long, and it would be a hell of a lot harder to find it now. But even if they did pick up her trail, Beth has been hiding all her life. She's an expert at it. She can do it again.

She twists off the bottle cap and takes a long cold swallow of the Gatorade. Jay was right about the drink. Last night, during the long drive through the desert, she finished the bottle Goode left at the house—and immediately wanted another one.

She wonders if the detective has talked to Cassie's parents by now. She feels a brief flicker of guilt that her story would come out. That all of them would discover the truth about her and who she really is. She wishes she could be there to explain everything to them. Would they understand the world she built for herself wasn't big enough for her anymore? The way the world had never been big enough for Cassie?

She remembers standing on the lawn that last day of summer, the violent Atlantic pounding like buffalo stampeding against the shore.

"We loved having you, Beth."

"Thank you, Mrs. Ogilvy. I loved being here."

"When are you going to start calling me Alice?"

"Try never," Cass said with a laugh.

Cassie's father stepped forward, a rare show of emotion in his eyes. "You have to come again next summer, young lady."

"I'd love to, sir. I will."

But as she looked up at the white mansion and around the grounds, she wanted to come back; but she knew she never would. She was moving on, reinventing herself once more.

"I want a picture of you girls!" Mrs. Ogilvy exclaimed.

"Me too," said Beth, taking out the cheap disposable camera she'd bought in the village. Shutters clicked in the sunlight as the girls posed for pictures.

"Can I have one with your parents, Cass?" Beth asked her.

"What for?"

325

"I wish you wouldn't be so rude," scolded her mother.

"I just want one," Beth said. She handed Cass the flimsy camera, nothing but plastic and cardboard to capture this moment. Then the threesome gathered together, smiling. Beth didn't quite know how important this photograph would become, but with her best friend watching and her arms around these two people, it was the happiest moment of her life.

"I should get going," she said finally, making it her decision.

The driver held the door, and Beth climbed into the backseat. Cassie handed her the old knapsack.

"Thanks again for everything, Cass. I owe you. Big-time."

"Don't worry," she said with a grin. "I'll collect—someday."

As the car pulled down the long drive and she forced herself not to watch the house grow smaller in the distance, Beth leaned back in the plush seat, touching the pearls around her throat.

It's so early, the motel parking lot is quiet.

The VACANCY sign glows blue-white in the light of the rising sun. Barely a single car passes on the highway. Beth walks to the front of the SUV and climbs in behind the wheel, doing up her seat belt. The sound of the buckle is like that of a cocking gun. She watches the front door of the motel for a few moments, then glances in the rearview mirror to check the bruise on her cheek. The bandage is off, the swelling already going down, the cut itself sealing closed. She won't mind the scar.

She twists the mirror away. The pearl necklace is looped around it, swinging gently. It was Mrs. Ogilvy who explained to Beth how pearls were made that summer. A single grain of sand irritating an oyster, year after year after year, caused it to protect itself, eventually creating a perfect opalescent sphere. Pearls, she said, were nothing more than nature's lovely mistakes threaded together on a string. Something that never should have existed. Like a lotus flower. Beth was just another one of nature's many mistakes, too, an improbable thing that had somehow survived.

The door to the motel office swings open, and a figure steps into the sunlight. She has wild dark hair and wears denim shorts, a baggy T-shirt, black boots. She looks so different than she did outside Footsie's, in her miniskirt and high heels.

Help me fake your death and we're in for everything. Fifty-fifty. I'll meet you in the desert when it's all over.

Cassie gets into the passenger seat and shuts the door. "We got the deposit back," she says. Beth takes the money from Cassie's hand, glancing down. Her friend's palm is still wrapped in gauze from the gash Beth made the other night, the shadow of blood seeping through.

"You okay?" she asks, motioning to the bandage.

Cassie wiggles her fingers. "I'll live."

"Hold it above your heart," says Beth, starting the ignition. "And don't forget your seat belt."

Cassie rolls her eyes, but buckles up just the same. "Where to?"

"Good question. Do you care?"

"Not really."

"Me neither." Beth smiles and puts the car into gear. Cassie cranks up the stereo, a favorite song they haven't heard in years, and they roar onto the wide, empty highway together.

ACKNOWLEDGMENTS

It takes a village to publish a book and a writer is only one part of the process. This was never more apparent to me than it was working on *Framed*.

I owe so much to my incredible agent, Helen Heller. This book simply wouldn't exist without her hard work, her confidence, and her brilliant notes. Not only did she come up with the title, but so much of the fun of this story would be lost without her insight and advice.

Many thanks to my amazing editor Millicent Bennett at Grand Central Publishing, too. From our first phone call, to sweating every detail during editing, I'm so grateful she never settled, always pushing this book—and me—to be better.

Thanks also to Penina Sacks Lopez for her careful copyediting; Carmel Shaka, for all her support and help with the manuscript; Meriam Metoui, for her early assistance; designer Brian Lemus and illustrator Daniel Wu for the brilliant cover; and to Tareth Mitch, Erica Scavelli, and GCP in New York.

Huge thanks to Jennifer Doyle at Headline Books in London who supported *Framed* from the beginning; even long distance, it meant so much.

For all their hard work on different phases of this book, I'm so grateful to Sarah and Charles Heller at the Helen Heller Literary Agency in Toronto, to Jennifer Shepherd of Shepherd Management Group, to everyone at the Marsh Agency in London, and to Debbie Deuble Hill and Maggie Pfeffer at APA in Los Angeles.

Huge thanks and much love to my wonderful family, especially to my mother, Nancy, and my brother, Gary, who've always been there for me, no matter what. To Allan and Erlene McInnis, who have encouraged and supported my writing for more than twenty-five years. And to Linda, Michael, and Marla Cranston, who have inspired me all my life—but now more than ever.

Many thanks to Tina Marie Landes, Cindy Clark, Jennifer Hartman, Marcee Corn, Bibiana Krall, Theresa Snyder, Sue Lloyd, Teresa Stone, Annelisa Christensen, Helen Tansey, Joanne Pagliocca, Kerensa Jennings, Wendy E. Slater, Kathleen Harryman, Sam Lee, B. Adrian White, and Tracey Lowther—my first editor and BFF.

To my dear cousin Todd Cranston, who passed away while I was editing this book, we love you and miss you every day.

And to my husband, Mark, much love and endless gratitude for being tough when you had to, for always making me laugh, and for never letting me give up.

Photo © Helen Tansey

ABOUT THE AUTHOR

S. L. McInnis has a degree in broadcasting and has worked in public radio and television. Like the main character in the book, she studied music for years. She lives in Toronto. *Framed* is her suspense debut.